T0354701

# ROSE'S ROMANCE

# THIRD TIME CHARM

## LES SONKSEN

Order this book online at www.trafford.com
or email orders@trafford.com

Most Trafford titles are also available at major online book retailers.

© Copyright 2024 Les Sonksen.
All rights reserved. No part of this publication may be reproduced,
stored in a retrieval system, or transmitted, in any form or by
any means, electronic, mechanical, photocopying, recording, or
otherwise, without the written prior permission of the author.

Print information available on the last page.

ISBN: 978-1-6987-1745-6 (sc)
ISBN: 978-1-6987-1746-3 (e)

Library of Congress Control Number: 2024916867

Because of the dynamic nature of the Internet, any web addresses or links contained in
this book may have changed since publication and may no longer be valid. The views
expressed in this work are solely those of the author and do not necessarily reflect the
views of the publisher, and the publisher hereby disclaims any responsibility for them.

Any people depicted in stock imagery provided by Getty Images are models, and such
images are being used for illustrative purposes only.
Certain stock imagery © Getty Images.

*Trafford rev.  08/12/2024*

www.trafford.com
North America & international
toll-free: 844-688-6899 (USA & Canada)
fax: 812 355 4082

# ACKNOWLEDGMENTS

THE BASES FOR THIS book in producing a romantic novel starts with experiences shared with the lives of some individuals while serving in the United States Navy. There were small parts of subject matter that prompted the general outline of the story. Then imagination took over for the balance of the story of Rose and Marvin.

My gratitude and special thanks to my wife, Beverly Sonksen, for her help in the first reading draft of the story. Her background in English helped immensely. More than a special thanks goes to Carol Darcy who scrutinized each page carefully. Her suggestions and advise were invaluable. Legal help was needed and appreciated from Linda McMillan, a very competent lawyer, for several chapters.

Many thanks to the Marketing Team at Trafford Publishing. Working with their staff was beneficial to help tell the story and then placed in publication.

# CHAPTER 1

"WHAT A BEAUTIFUL PEACEFUL DAY! Why couldn't my life be just that peaceful," whispered Rose McDowell out loud as she emerged from the shop door of Carol's Curls and Crewcuts. She meandered slowly to the edge of the  sidewalk.  Looking at the azure blue sky with myriads of fluffy clouds, Rose absorbed the sights and sounds that were all about.  She relished this daily ritual during her lunch break.

As Rose walked slowly towards Joe's Bar and Grill for a light lunch, the conversation with her parents at breakfast three days before kept running through her mind.

Her father's ultimatum: "Well daughter, since you have graduated from high school and have a full time job now, you will need to be on your own.  You will need to find your own place to live.  You need to start some day to be independent. No better time than the present."

Her mother's rebuttal: "But Donovan, Rose just turned 18. She isn't old enough to live alone.  Besides, she isn't making enough salary to pay all the expenses of living in an apartment. She has no car to drive to work, either."

Her father's response: "I was on my own when I turned 18. Rose can use the bus. She will just need to manage her money wisely. Best lesson in growing up is to become independent. Daughter, you have two weeks to move out."

As Rose slowly walked towards the Bar and Grill, she welcomed the warm sunshine on her face and body. It was similar to a gentle massage, caressing her skin and relaxing her shoulder muscles. Being a beautician was what she loved doing daily but being on her feet all morning was most tiring. And now, including her father's stern order to move out added to the drain on her emotions.

Hearing the cries of seagulls above, Rose raised her eyes to see a dozen or so flying in circles. She noticed a couple of pigeons and a line of sparrows sitting on the overhead wires enjoying ringside seats and apparently watching the crazy antics of the gulls. Rose was amused and smiled. She had not been able to find much to smile about for sometime because of all her dad's harsh words. The information gained from telephone calls to rental ads proved that monthly payments were beyond her income.

"Jean, put in an order for today's special but hold the onions. I see Rose coming in for lunch," said Joe.

"What if she doesn't want the daily special," replied Jean, one of the waitresses at Joe's Bar and Grill.

"When hasn't she ordered the special plate. Poor kid, she isn't earning much money yet at the beauty shop," said Joe.

Joe Reilly, looked at his wife, June, who owned and operated the lounge and grill together. They both felt badly for Rose. They wished they could help her more somehow. They both knew something was troubling Rose in addition to financial problems. Being childless, they both had developed parental feelings for her.

"Why isn't she coming in? What is she looking at while standing on the steps?" asked June.

"Yeah, she is staring intensely at something. I'll go find out," replied Joe. He walked to the entrance and opened the door. "Hi, Rose! What are you watching?"

"Oh, hello, Joe. There's a bad accident near the intersection."

Joe's Bar and Grill was in the middle of the block with a drug store, a men's clothing store, a boutique shop, and a furniture store between the lounge and the intersection where the two cars tried to occupy the exact space at the same time. The sounds of the collision had already drawn a few curious seekers. He placed a hand on her shoulder with a fatherly touch.

"Doesn't appear that anyone is injured. Better call the police though. After you Rose," as Joe held open the door.

A chorus of "Hello, Rose" greeted her from Jean and June and some regular customers who knew Rose, all waiting for their food order from Pete, the chef.

"June, would you please call the police about the accident," added Joe.

"Here's your order, Jean" as Pete placed the plates of food on the serving self. "Oh, Hi there Rose, your order will be right out," he said as he poked his head out of the serving window and gave her a big smile.

Pete was everyone's friend. Besides being an excellent chef, his witty personality kept the staff in a jolly frame of mind. The customers were always impressed with the quality of the food preparations and marveled at the plate presentations he created. Rose smiled back indicating she saw and heard him.

Rose sat down at one of the empty tables. She glanced about noticing the other customers busily eating and carrying on what appeared to be jovial conversations.

As Rose began to reflect on her life while waiting for her food, she could not fully understand all that had been happening in just the past weeks. First, there was that heated argument with her father. With her mother, Maureen, in tears, her dad had given her the ultimatum that having graduated from high school, she needed to be on her own. She had a job and was earning her own keep. She would just need to find an apartment. Despite her mother's pleading that Rose wasn't old enough to be on her own and not earning sufficient income, her father's authoritative words ruled the roost. He insisted becoming independent would be the best for her. Perhaps his thinking was based on his joining the Marine Corp at 18 and served 20 years or because he had become efficient in giving out orders as a Staff Sergeant. She really didn't know. Who really knew her dad's thinking process? It certainly didn't make sense to her. She thought regretfully of her brother, Matthew, who was 15 years old. What was in store for him?

Secondly, she had taken an on-the-job training course her junior and senior years of high school and had been working part time for nearly two years at Carol's Curls and Crewcuts. She was pleased she had chosen this line of work. She was earning an income and saving a few dollars, but not enough to support herself with all the expenses of rent, food, and clothing. Buying a car was only a dream. She just didn't know what she would do. She had taken off one day from work to attend her own high school graduation. Her boss, Carol Delany, had insisted she attend. She had dismissed her dad's poor excuse for not attending. She had even missed the Junior-Senior Prom Dance. After being on her feet most of the day at the beauty shop, she was just too tired to attend the gala event. Besides, she didn't have an escort. No one had asked her for a date. She considered herself popular enough. Everyone seemed to like her and were friendly towards her. Her closest girlfriends, Sally and Jackie, had shared with her that classmates envied her. That really surprised her. Sally thought it was due to the modeling job the high school counselor had helped her acquire during her junior year. Jackie had confided with her that her exceptional beauty and ideal figure helped in being selected for modeling. Carol had helped her with the best hair styling for a red head and also make-up for her complexion. She was most grateful for this help that enabled her to be exceptionally groomed most of the time. The job was short-lived because of her father. He had made her quit modeling. He positively was not having a daughter prancing in front of cameras in a bikini bathing suit and photographers goggling at her. He made the point clearly that modeling lingerie would be embarrassing for the family and damaging to her reputation.

She had turned down countless dates from the sailors who came into the shop for crewcuts or hair styling. There were some she would desired to have dated but her father's tirades stopped her. He had drilled into her thinking of warnings so many times that sailors only wanted to date her for only one purpose and there was no reason to risk the possibility of a date rape and getting pregnant. She had had several discussions with her mother covering the dating situation in detail but her mother agreed with her dad. She loved her parents despite her father's stern methods and demands. She did not wish to disobey them. Both kept telling her not to be in a hurry to date and get married. The right person would come along and she would know when that happened; however, she really didn't know or have the slightest inkling what that emotional feeling would be like. Her mother had shared how she met her dad when she was Rose's age. Why wouldn't her mother go to bat for her? She realized that there was much more she would need to learn about love, dating, and finding the right man but she did know that she wanted marriage and children. The way her life was progressing so far, that wasn't likely to happen. Visions came of being an old maid—perhaps that might even be an excellent choice.

One of the customers accidentally dropped his knife next to her table and the noise brought her out of her reverie. She glanced about the room again. The convenience of the Grill being two doors from the hair salon made sitting at Joe's Bar and Grill on her lunch breaks always enjoyable. This had become her favorite place to relax. The place was always busy. The patronage of the naval personnel and local business men and women kept the place humming from 6 a.m. to midnight. Located only 6 blocks from the Main Gate of the Norfolk Naval Station encouraged much walk-in traffic.  She appreciated how Joe ran a tight ship—allowing no problems.  Looking at Joe who was six foot plus and around 210 pounds, a former boxer, and a karate black belt expert—no one misbehaved a second time after a stern warning.  Everyone respected Joe. The ambience was so pleasant. The walls were covered with pictures and other naval memorabilia given by Navy personnel and gave the place an interesting nautical atmosphere.

"Here's your lunch, Rose," June said, as she noticed Rose being deep in thought as she approached. "What would you desire for a beverage?" she added.

"I'll have a glass of milk, June," replied Rose. "Does this burger ever smell heavenly! I'm famished.  Did not have time to eat any breakfast at home."

June sighed for she knew Rose had undoubtedly skipped breakfast again.

"You appeared to be miles away in thought, Rose, when I brought your lunch.  Is there anything more that Joe or I can do to help? You know we think the world of you! You are such a beautiful, thoughtful, and sensible young lady."

"I hate to pour out my problems to you.  You and Joe have been so good to me all these months while working at Carol's salon, feeding me when I had no money, driving me home when I didn't have bus fare. How can I ever repay your generosity?"

"Rose, Joe and I have never been able to have children.  You are like the daughter we wish we could have.  If you need help, just ask." They would need to wait for Rose to share her apparent problems. Little did June realized how quickly that would happen.

"June, I do have a big, no, huge problem facing me. My dad has indicated that having graduated from high school and working full time, I need to move out of my home and find an apartment. He claims this will help me become independent sooner. I don't understand why he is doing this, really. It's mean of him! I'm not earning that type of income yet that will enable me to support myself. I'm at wits end. I don't know what I should do. I'm in such a nervous state that my work is being affected."

"Joe, please come here a minute, can you? Rose has a problem that we may help solve." After Joe sat down, June continued. "Rose's dad has informed her she needs to move out and find an apartment. Why can't she use our spare bedroom upstairs? She will have her own bathroom. The living room is available to entertain any guy she may be dating. She can have meals with us that we don't eat here. We open at six every morning so she can ride to work with us and have breakfast here which she seems to be skipping too much of the time. If you don't object, Rose, you can even help take orders, serve food, and clear tables when we are really busy until you need to leave for work. You would be on the payroll so to speak and no charge for your meals. Would this be of help to you, Rose?"

With tears running down her cheeks, Rose was able to choke out, "Oh Joe, June, I love you both so much! How can I be so blessed to have two such wonderful friends. Yes, I would love to live with you and pay room and board. I will be thrilled to help with the house cleaning, doing the laundry, or whatever needs to be done and I would enjoy helping here in the lounge, too. Thank you both. You have solved that huge worry I had. Again, I love you both!"

"We are the lucky ones, Rose," replied Joe, "You can be the

child we never were able to have. This will work great for us all. My dear lovely wife, you came up with the ideal solution for Rose. Hey, we better get to work and give Rose time to eat. Should we heat it again for you?"

"The food is fine. I'm so hungry. Being somewhat cold will not matter. But thanks again for being the wonderful couple you are and for helping with my dilemma."

"Oh, by the way, since tomorrow is Sunday and we aren't working the shift, why don't we come to your house and help move whatever you wish to pack and bring to your new home? Is that O.K. with you?" asked Joe.

"Yes, tomorrow will be great. I don't have much to pack, mostly clothes and a few personal items. I will have every-thing ready when ever you arrive. Again, how can I ever thank you. My mother will be unhappy, but my dad will have his wish in getting rid of me. My brother will not appreciate my leaving, either. I've been helping him with his homework for some time."

Rose stood up and gave Joe a hug. As they embraced, June placed her hands on both their backs and made a group hug. Customers watching the tender scene were touched even though they didn't know the reasons.

And so Rose began this first new part of her life's adven-tures by first experiencing the problems related to being independent.

# CHAPTER 2

Joe and June arrived at the McDowell home on Sunday afternoon. They had already met Rose's parents, Donovan and Maureen, who frequented the lounge on several occasions. Upon ringing the doorbell, Matthew, Rose's 15 year old brother, answered the door.

"We're here to help Rose move to her new apartment," replied Joe.

Matthew stood and stared at the Reilys momentarily for he had no idea what they were talking about. Just then Maureen came to the door. "Please come in, Joe, June. It is certainly kind of you to help Rose move. I guess we should have done that, but Donovan left to do a number of errands and I don't know when he'll return."

"Oh, that is quite all right. We are so pleased to help your lovely daughter. And we had the day free to help," replied Joe.

"Where is Rose going?" Matthew imploringly asked his mother. "No one told me she was leaving."

"I'll tell you later, Matthew, as Maureen embarrassingly

looked at Matthew, knowing he would be very unhappy with-out his sister. The two were lovingly bonded as siblings. It brought tears to her eyes which she tried to hide by turning her face away.

Rose came down the staircase with a suitcase in each hand. "I have a box of personal items. Matthew, would you please go to my room and bring the box down?"

As Matthew passed her on the steps, Rose continued, "Thank you, dear brother."

"Here, give me those suitcases. I'll place them in the car," offered Joe, as he met Rose and relieved her of the cases. He carried them to the car and placed both in the trunk. Rose, Maureen, and June stood in the doorway and watched.

"June, I wish you to know that this move was not my idea. I don't want Rose to leave home now. She is too young to be on her own. But her dad insisted that she find her own apart-ment," as Maureen's words were spoken haltingly.

June placed her arms around Maureen. "There, there, Maureen, you don't need to say another word. Rose told us about her need to find a place to live. We understand."

When Joe returned to the house, Maureen said, "Please come to the kitchen and have some coffee and newly baked cinnamon rolls. You aren't in any big hurry to leave, are you?"

"Put the box by the door, Matthew," ordered Rose, as she saw Matthew coming down the steps. She waited until he placed the box, then with an arm around his shoulder, walked with him to the kitchen.

"Why are you leaving me?" implored Matthew. "When did you decide to move away? I never heard any reason why you need to leave."

Mother will tell you later. I hope you will understand. I love you dear brother.

But I have a job now and need to be on my own. I guess we all need to make our way in this world. You will need to do the same thing when you graduate from high school. Just do the very best work possible and make good grades. Sorry I won't be able to help you with your homework anymore. I guess you need to become as independent as dad wants me to be, if that makes any sense to you."

Rose and Matthew joined the others in the kitchen. Rose poured a glass of milk for Matthew and for herself and also selected a roll from the plate.

Maureen broke the silence and asked, "Where will you be living, Rose?"

"I'll be at 1245 West Albany Street." Picking up a pad on the table, "Here, I'll write it down. Telephone number is 441-2552. Of course, you can always reach me at the salon as you have before," added Rose.

She looked at Joe and June with a hidden glance but she did not add that the address and phone were that of the Reilys and she would be living with them. Rose didn't know why she omitted that information. It just seemed inappropriate to reveal the location at the moment.

"How is your income, Rose," ventured Maureen. "Will you be earning enough to take care of your expenses? This is my biggest concern for you, sweetheart!"

"Oh, do not worry, Mother, I have enough of my savings from the past two years to get me started. Now that I will be working full-time, my earnings and tips will be greater than when working part-time. Please do not fret about me, Mother. I'll be just fine." Rose looked at both Joe and June with a big smile, knowing that she had the support of two very good friends.

The silence was becoming overbearing as they finished their refreshments so Joe stood up and said, "If you're ready, Rose, we can leave now. Hate to rush away, Maureen. I need to return home and catch up on the bookkeeping that piles up from the week's receipts. Thank goodness we have Sundays to attend church, rest, and catch up with these never ending odds and ends of office work. I believe June has some 'honey-does' for me, also," said Joe. As June stood up, Joe placed his arm around her waist.

Thanking Maureen for the hospitality, Joe picked up the box of Rose's personal effects and walked to the car. Rose hugged her mother and then her brother.

As Rose stepped into the car, she offered, "We'll be in touch, Mother. Meet me at Joe's place some time for lunch. Why don't you start coming to Carol's salon. I can trim your hair while we chat. If you, little brother, aren't too particular, I can style your hair, also," she said, giving him a big sisterly grin.

As Joe backed out of the driveway, Rose had a difficult time keeping the tears from rolling down her cheeks.

Little did Rose know what fate awaited her. There would come a time when she would not be permitted to go home to see her family and friends.

# CHAPTER 3

THE ARRANGEMENTS WITH ROSE living at the Reilys became
as normal as it could ever be. Rose pitched in and helped June
with the usual domestic chores. The furnishings in her room
were most accommodating. Having access to the bathroom
without having to share with a brother was sheer delight. She
never realized how pleasant just that one thing in life could
affect her happiness. That was the biggest bone of conten-
tion with her brother when both were preparing for school.
Joe and June showered her with their love and concern. They
informed her there was no need to pay any room and board.
Rose objected strongly on this matter, but eventually gave way
to Joe's reasoning—she helped unselfishly in their home and
at the Bar and Grill.

Joe even paid for Rose to take driving lessons so she could
eventually acquire and drive her own car. That was something her dad would never consider doing for her. She was
delighted that Joe had confidence in her.

Joe encouraged many of the sailors and officers who frequented the lounge to consider getting haircuts and styling at Carol's salon. He would suggest that they make an appointment or wait and ask for the beautiful red headed woman called Rose. It wasn't long before Rose continually filled her daily appointment book with customers and the walk-ins. She was pleased with the steady income and the many tips given by everyone. They would thank her for excellent and pleasing work

AND SO THE NEXT MONTH rolled by for Rose pleasantly and with ease. The worries she had before melted away like the last snow in springtime. She was developing a healthy bond with Carol and the other two beauticians. All were much older than Rose, but that seemed to have no barrier for congenial relationships.

At her new home, it was never drab by any means because of Joe's constant line of chatter, his dry sense of humor, and his upbeat personality. June and Rose were kept in stitches from his crazy antics and humorous stories.

With the driving lessons completed, Joe allowed Rose to drive his car with his close supervision until she became confident behind the wheel. She really surprised her dad and mother when she visited them late one evening. Her dad really came unglued when he realized she was driving.

"You mean to tell me that Joe lets you drive his car in this crazy traffic in Norfolk! He must be nuts to allow you to do that!" exclaimed Donovan.

With her dad becoming so irate, Rose grabbed her purse and immediately left without saying another word. She couldn't talk any way, the sobs were sticking in her throat when she saw tears on her mother's cheeks. That is what she expected from her father—more of his belittling. She just wasn't going to allow him to spoil the happiness she was experiencing. While driving back home, Rose shook off her

Dad's remarks.   She was glad  that she wasn't living at home
and  certainly wouldn't let his bitterness affect her confidence.


ONE SUNDAY MORNING WHILE eating breakfast, Joe asked,
"Why doesn't a beautiful lady like yourself ever have a date?
Men must be crazy or dumb for not asking you out to eat  or to
a movie or a dance or a sporting event.  I don't understand!"

   "Joe, I know it may sound strange to you.  The truth of the
matter is, I have been asked many times for dates by the sailors
and other businessmen but I have refused everyone--politely,
of course.  I always seem to find an excuse that they accept.
The problem goes back to my folks, I guess.  Every since I  was
14 years old, both my folks have told me about the dangers of
being date raped and possibility of getting pregnant. They told
me that I should keep my purity, my innocence, as my mother
puts it, until I get married.  Would you believe that I have
never had a date?   My dad especially  has told me countless
times never to date any Navy men.  He claims they have only
one thing in mind and that's getting me into bed.  He states
that Navy men have more than one woman in every port with
whom they can have sex.  I don't know if that is true or not.
Seems like it places every sailor in a bad category.  There must
be some great guys in the total bunch.  I really don't know
how to choose someone I could accept as a date.  Dad and
Mother have me scared spitless.  It's just not only with service-
men, either."

   "Rose, Rose, I can't believe that your dad has fed you that
ridiculous crap.  The  story that Navy men have women in
every port is way over blown.  Well, of course, there are a few
bad apples in the barrel  and they give everyone a terrible reputation.  Your dad should realize that any branch of service
has a few rotten apples.  Tell your dad the Marines have their
share, too!  Please rid yourself of that silly idea, NOW!  I know
it is easier said than done, but believe me, Rose, you need to

change your thinking process. You will never meet any man with that attitude.

"Yes, that same thought has occurred to me, too," replied Rose, hesitantly.

"Now you may accuse me of playing cupid, but I know of a young man for you to meet. He has been coming into the lounge for sometime now. I think he would be someone you would really desire to date and with whom to become acquainted. His name is Marvin Brown and, yes, he is a sailor in the United State Navy. He comes from Denver, Colorado. Forget what your dad and mom have told you about Navy men. I even met his parents when they where here to see him not long ago. He brought them to the lounge for dinner one day and introduced them to June and me. They seemed like the finest people you would every want to meet. Marvin's dad is a lawyer. His mother is a high school counselor. Marvin has a sister, Sally, who is around 16, if I remember correctly. However, she wasn't here because of school. I wish to introduce you two. Do you desire to meet him? I believe that June would agree with me that you would enjoy knowing Marvin. He is a handsome lad, and every bit a gentleman when ever I see him, and he is certainly a credit to the U.S. Navy. I have no idea how long he'll be in Norfolk. Navy men get shipped out very suddenly."

Rose looked at Joe, then at June, and back to Joe again. She was processing mentally all that Joe had just said. She trusted Joe and June. What he had shared made more sense than what her father had ever said.

"Joe, thank you again for your interest and trust you have in me. I need to start dating sometime. Your description about Marvin is most intriguing. Yes, I desire to meet this Navy man. I hate to think what my dad would say if he knew about this; however, you have convinced me that dad is wrong."

"Getting you two together may be a small logistical problem. If he comes in during the evening on liberty, you are here. If he comes in during the day, you're working and probably can't leave the salon with a book full of appointments. He is stationed on a destroyer, the DD789. I could call him and have a message left for him. Tell you what would be better. We'll invite him for dinner on a Sunday when he doesn't have duty. Would that be agreeable with you?"

"Rose, that would be a non-threatening arrangement for you to meet if Marvin accepts Joe's invitation. We have both met and talked with Marvin several times. I can't find any reason why you would not be interested in meeting him," as June reached over and pinched Rose's cheek with a motherly tweak.

"Have another flash of an idea!" Joe bursts out. "If Marvin comes into the lounge, I'll suggest that he needs a trim and to make an appointment with you. You can cut his hair and start a conversation. Then should he accept a dinner reservation to eat here, he will really be surprised when he meets you at the door. How is that for being perhaps a bit devious?"

"Only a person like you, Joe, would put together a scenario like that. You are the greatest! I can understand why June loves you so dearly. You both are making me happier by the day and I'm moving out of the slump I was in for so long. I owe it to you two beautiful people! Again I appreciate your interest in helping me to start dating. This has been a great problem for me for some time. I have even had thoughts of just becoming an old unmarried woman," added Rose.

Joe's ruse did work. Marvin and his buddies arrived for a beer or two the following day. He told Marvin that he was trying to help a budding beautician in the salon next door. She is the best in the state! He and June use her services regularly. If he needed a trim, make an appointment with Rose. Do this as a favor for him and quickly, the salon's closing time was fast approaching.

Marvin used the phone in the lounge to make an appointment. When Marvin told Rose his name, she gave him the haircut appointment for 4:30 the next day. Rose's hand was shaking as she wrote the information in her appointment book. Just his voice alone had piqued her interest in forming a mental picture of his physical features. She was nervous and could not wait to meet Marvin. All the descriptions from Joe and June flooded her thinking. Rose was surprised at her emotional reactions. This was a new and different experience.

Joe knew that Rose would come to the lounge when finished with work for the day. He tried to keep Marvin busy until she arrived, but Marvin's buddy urged him to go to the music concert. Since they had already left when Rose walked in, he wasn't able to extend the dinner invitation.

THE TIME DURING THE NEXT DAY seem to drag for Rose. Anxious to meet and to cut Marvin's hair, she had to work to control her emotions. This was so different for her. She had never experienced any mental or physical feelings like this before and was at a loss as to why this was happening to her.

The appointment time came and she wondered if he might cancel it. That often happened to her in the past with customers whose plans suddenly changed. But at 4:25 p.m., a sailor, dressed in whites, came into the salon. Rose watched him enter and felt her heart jump several beats as she tried to finish with Mrs. Cummings, one of her regular customers. She noticed Marvin approaching the receptionist, Sissy Baldridge, who pointed her out and told Marvin that the last chair was hers. Marvin glanced in her direction. Her heart fluttered as their eyes met and she saw his winsome smile before he sat in a chair and picked up a magazine. Her hands were shaking and it was all she could do to steady them in giving Mrs. Cummings the final combing.

Mrs. Cummings thanked Rose, gave her a generous tip, and went to the receptionist to pay for the service. Marvin, seeing that he was next, laid the magazine aside, and approached the chair.

Rose was thinking about what to say when Marvin looked directly into her eyes, and with the same winsome smile, said, "Joe tells me you are one of the best hair stylists in Virginia. I guess we both know Joe by now, but if I tame down his exaggerations, he claims you are skilled at your job. I only need a trim today." And with that he sat down.

Rose felt herself blush. Why? She really didn't know but she was glad that standing behind him prevented Marvin from seeing her face. She took the plain colored apron from the peg on the wall thinking he wouldn't appreciate the colorful floral colored apron used for the ladies. She placed the apron on Marvin's lap with both arms stretching around his shoulders. In leaning forward, her breasts accidentally brushed firmly against his arm. The touch startled her and she quickly backed away. Rose softly said, "Sorry." She brought the two ends together behind his neck. Her fingers touched the nape of his neck while clipping the fastener to the ends of the apron and a tingle trickled up her arms and spread out across the rest of her body. She had never had that kind of sensation before having placed the apron on countless other men. Why does my body respond in this manner with Marvin? Rose's mind went into super gear with the thought that she had to say something and fast. He might just think she was some kind of a klutz.

Picking up the comb and scissors, Rose began to make the trim around his left ear and blurted out, "Are you stationed aboard a ship at the Naval Station? Just what do you do?" It sounded a little lame, she though, but the words were spoken, nevertheless.

"Yes, I'm billeted aboard a destroyer as a storekeeper. Are you familiar with that rate in the Navy?" Not hearing an answer, Marvin continued. "I maintain the computer records of everything aboard the ship, what was on the ship to start with and what is brought on new, even down to a paper clip. There records are kept so when anything is required such as clothing, foodstuff or hundreds of other items, I record the information.  When supplies become low for anything used anywhere on the ship, a requisition is processed to order the same or a similar product if the original items are not available.  Supplies seem to come in daily when in port and are recorded on the computer records before being distributed where needed. This procedure is repeated again and again. Some days become monotonous but there is always the challenge to maintain accuracy."

"What a huge responsibility.  Wow, I can see your problems if you fail to order all the food, for example, that is needed for the sailors' meals.  And to keep on hand enough fresh fruits, meats, and vegetables to feed an entire crew must be a daily chore," replied Rose.  She hoped she didn't make a faux pas with that quick deduction.

"You're right on!  Gosh, you made an accurate assessment of the problems I have in supplying our ship.  The biggest problem is when we are out to sea for any length of time and deplete some critical things, especially food items.  But the crew realizes that we can't pull into a supermarket in the middle of the ocean and make purchases.  The cooks improvises in making meals with what's in the store room.  Canned goods prevents our starving when out at sea, believe me.  Of course, the Navy has special cargo ships to meet the fleet with food and other supplies if we are gone from port for any length of time."

"How long have you been doing this type of work on your ship?" asked Rose.

"About a year on this destroyer.   But my days are numbered.  Discharge day is this coming November 15.  Consider me a short timer now," replied Marvin.

"You evidently did not plan to make the Navy a career,

then?" asked Rose, as she moved in front of him and looked at his head for evenness of the trim being given.

He looked at her facial features before replying. "No, my plans are to enroll in college and earn a degree in computer accounting systems. The Navy has provided me with excellent experience in this field of work. Why did you become a beautician rather than one of many other areas of work that women with your skill and training might select?" asked Marvin.

Rose moved back of Marvin again and did more trimming. "I did consider secretarial work and nursing, but decided to be a beautician," replied Rose. "My high school counselor helped me considerably in making a choice. I'm glad I did because the work is always challenging, not that the other jobs  might be as rewarding."

"I also get to meet many guys like this sailor," thought Rose. When will I gain enough confidence in myself to accept a date if asked?"

As Rose was touching Marvin's hair in running the comb down through it and clipping the ends that came between the teeth, she felt a strange but wonderful feeling that she had never experienced before.  She had heard of women drawing their fingers sensually through a man's hair.  Now she had some idea of that sensation. She enjoyed the resonating sound of his voce as he was speaking.  Joe was right about his being tall and handsome.  She kept glancing at his facial profile and elated with the effect that it had with her senses.

She was wondering if he would accept the dinner invitation that Joe would extend.  A little voice was saying that she hoped he would.  She really did want to have the opportunity to know this man much better.  She just wished he wasn't in the Navy. All the horrible warnings her Dad had stated about sailors flooded her brain. But the words Joe had offered counteracted her Dad's. She had a flash of a thought of inviting Marvin to eat at Joe's lounge but quickly realized that would not be proper.  She couldn't possibly be that bold.

After completing the trim, Rose gave Marvin a mirror to have him check the finished work. She held another mirror behind his head. As Marvin moved his head from left to right and viewed the trim, he said, "Rose, you do excellent work. Far better than the last trim I received."

After Rose had removed the apron, Marvin stood up, turned, and met the gaze of Rose's eyes. "Joe did not tell me that you were a beautiful beautician. I will need to tell him he left out some important information when he recommended you. I have enjoyed our brief conversation."

Reaching into the pocket of his jumper for his paper bills, he peeled off a five dollar bill. "Here's something extra for you. Thank you for your efficiency, also. I need to meet someone in 15 minutes. How much is the trim?"

"Thank you for the compliments and your generous tip. I also enjoyed our brief time together. The trim is $7.50 and you pay Sissy at the receptionist's desk. Tell Joe that I appreciate his sending you. I'll tell him also for I eat many of my meals at his place," replied Rose.

As Marvin left to pay Sissy, Rose wondered who he was going to meet. Her mind flooded with questions. "Was it a girl friend? Does Joe know him well enough? Is he going steady? Maybe ready to become engaged? Would he be only meeting another Navy buddy? Will he accept the dinner invitation? Will I see him again?"

She watched as Marvin pocketed his change, turned, gazed at her briefly, and gave her a winsome smile that had to be part of his personality. She really did enjoy meeting Marvin, even if briefly. Rose smiled back and raised her right hand weakly as a good bye gesture. Marvin responded with the same motion, turned, and left the salon.

Again the question invaded her mind, "Will I ever see him again?"

# CHAPTER 4

Marvin left the salon and hurried next door to Joe's Bar and Grill. He planned to meet his ship buddy, Chris, where by previous arrangement, they planned to eat, go to the MacArthur Center Shopping Mall to poke about the shops, and then to the Virginia Beach Amphitheater. Randy Travis was booked for the show and Marvin enjoyed the type of music Randy sang.

Upon entering the lounge, Marvin went directly to Joe and admonished him saying, "Why did you hold back on the information about Rose. She's beyond beautiful. Look at this trim she gave me? At least you were right about Rose being an excellent stylists. It is the best that I have ever received. Other than that, I don't know about you, Joe, you can certainly be sneaky."

"I just wanted you to find out for yourself that Rose is a lovely person. I don't know how well you got to know her in so brief a time. Perhaps you should meet her again. But, how can you accuse me of being sneaky? I'm hurt!" as Joe bent over and put his hands over his heart.

"O.K. Joe, you're off the hook. Thanks for sending me to meet Rose. We did have a brief but enjoyable conversation. She is certainly good in maintaining a pleasant chat with customers. She had me talking about myself almost the whole time. I only had the chance to ask her one question about why she desired to become a beautician. I would certainly like to know her better, even the opportunity to ask her for a date. However, she must be already spoken for or going steady or even married. A beautiful women like Rose, well, some lucky guy must have her corralled. I noticed that she wore no wedding ring. But then, most beauticians remove all their hand jewelry because of the chemicals and hair solutions they use."

"Marvin, I know for a fact, one hundred per cent certain, that Rose is not married. Neither is she dating anyone. That should open the door for you if you are interested. And it seems you are! By the way, what are you doing this coming Sunday noon? Do you have the duty aboard your ship? If not, June and I extend an invitation for dinner. We both wish to know you better. No greater place than a relaxing conversation while breaking bread. We haven't much time to visit when busy here in the lounge."

That bit of information about Rose caught Marvin's attention. She seemed to be a gracious lady and so beautiful. Perhaps he should go back and ask her for a date to the concert. But that wouldn't be fair to Chris having no date. Besides, she didn't seem to be the kind of woman to be escorted by two strangers. We've made arrangements for only two concert tickets already. She wouldn't accept a date anyway.

"You seem to have thoughts of a lovely beautician on your mind! I repeat, are you free for dinner, Marvin?" Joe asked, somewhat amused at Marvin's inattention.

"I'm sorry, Joe. Yes, Sunday would be great. I don't have

duty. I accept with pleasure your invitation for dinner. You met my folks, and I sorely miss seeing them. Knowing you and June has certainly filled that empty spot in my heart. Thank you for your friendship. But I'll be home soon. I can hardly wait for that discharge. My sister is so happy that I'll be home by Thanksgiving. Oh, can I bring a bottle of wine? Red? White?"

"June, can you spare a minute?"

June moved from the couple from whom she had just taken an order. She sat down with Marvin and Joe.

"Marvin can join us for dinner on Sunday," said Joe. "He wishes to bring some wine. Do you know what you might be serving?"

"I'm pleased you can join us for dinner, Marvin. We will have more time to talk rather than a 'Hi' or 'So Long' here at the lounge. I thought we would have shrimp. You must enjoy them, you have ordered shrimp on several occasions. White wine would be fine, although it's not necessary going to that expense."

June watched Marvin sipping his coke. She was so anxious for the day to be perfect. She had a difficult time to keep the surprise when he would meet Rose at their house for dinner. Plans could go wrong; however, she and Joe would do all they could to bring the two young persons together.

Just at that moment, Rose entered the lounge. She was distracted immediately by the waitress, Naomi, who had just taken an order from a couple close to the door.

Naomi, seeing Rose, gave her a hug. Rose's back was toward Joe, June, and Marvin.

As they released the embrace, Chris came through the door. Naomi greeted him by name and asked if he desired a table.

"No, I'm joining Marvin for dinner and then we're attending a concert," shared Chris as he pointed to the table.

Rose whipped around where Chris was pointing and noticed Marvin talking with Joe and June. The thought flashed through her brain that they may be asking him for dinner. "I wonder if he will or can?" She felt rather giddy. "Why does this particular sailor affect my composure so much? Should I turn around and leave? Should I tell Naomi what I want for dinner? Should I....Should I....Why is my mind in such a turmoil!"

Without realizing it, Rose found her feet moving in the direction of the foursome, for Chris had already moved to the table and sat down. All three men stood up as Rose approached. The gesture touched her. To her memory, this was the first time that men stood up in respect for her. She met the gaze of Marvin, something she didn't do when styling his hair. She felt even more giddy. She just hoped her own composure wasn't giving her away.

"Rose, you met Marvin while doing your marvelous magic with your comb and scissors. This is Chris Woodward. He is on the same ship as Marvin. Do you wish to join these two of Uncle Sam's finest, or would you prefer to eat with us? June and I are taking a breather and to eat a bit. We had a very busy day! We have been on our feet since noon. Not complaining, of course. Naomi just came to work and she and Jean can handle the crowd."

"Thank you for the opportunity to meet and to eat with Uncle Sam's finest," said Rose, "but I really have something important to ask you. I need your help and opinion. May I bend your ear while we have dinner?"

"Well, you two swabbies lost out now! I'm eating dinner with these two remarkable women. Eat your hearts out!" said Joe as he slapped each of the two sailors on their backs, then offered his arms to June and Rose. They hooked their hands on his arms.

The three moved to the booth that was near the kitchen door. It was the area used by all the employees of the lounge when taking a coffee break, sipping a coke during their shift, or eating their meals. It was pressed into use when the remaining tables and booths were all occupied. Jean approached them and received their orders.

"Now, what is fretting that beautiful red head of yours, Rose? It sounded rather imminent. I was certain you wanted to eat with Marvin and Chris. You could start getting acquainted with Marvin! It's my hunch that he desires to know you. But you know June and I are here to assist you anytime. Oh, by the way, Marvin will be coming for dinner on Sunday."

When Rose heard the words "coming for dinner" she glanced to where Marvin was sitting. He and Chris were laughing at the moment. Once again, she recalled the sensations that invaded her as she ran her hand down his head giving the trim and touching the nape of his neck. "Are these normal feelings? How could that affect me with such pleasure? I've never experience that before. And he didn't meet another woman as I imagined he would! But why should that be a concern to me?" Just as quickly she brought her attention back to Joe.

"Joe, I have been accumulating considerable money from work. It's in a box in my dresser drawer. Would you tell me where you do your banking and help me acquire a checking and savings account? I'm afraid to admit I know very little about finances. Also would you help me shop for a car? You two are so good to me not charging rent, that I may have enough money to buy some wheels. What do you think?"

"Rose, I would be more than happy to assist you in what ever you desire doing. Can you plan your appointments to spring some time during the day to do both these errands?"

"I have four appointments in the morning for next Monday so the afternoon is better. I won't book any from noon to three. Would that be sufficient time to accomplish the two chores?"

"Yes, it would, Rose," replied Joe.

Again, Rose glanced over at Marvin. She smiled to herself as she visualized being kissed by him. She had never had that opportunity. How pleasant would that be? She could feel herself beginning to blush and suddenly wondered from where those thoughts were surfacing. She quickly turned her attention to the food being placed before her. Picking up her fork and taking a bit of food, her eyes roved again to see the sailor named Marvin Brown. "Would he ask for a date? Why must he be a sailor? No, I must not think like that. What my Dad said needs to be forgotten. That really doesn't matter now. Joe's advice is so positive. I need to change my negative thoughts to positive ones. For some reason I feel attracted to him and wish to know more about this sailor."

Joe noticed the direction Rose was gazing and smiling to himself, he thought, "This could be the beginning of a romantic adventure for these great kids! I might just earn my cupid wings after all!"

June also noticed Rose's interest in watching Marvin. She envisioned the two becoming more than good friends. There was even a flash of a thought of their getting married one day and have as pleasant a marriage as Joe and she.

As the three shared a pleasant conversation while eating, Rose would repeatedly and unconsciously glance at Marvin. She couldn't wait until Sunday. Her married girlfriend had told her once that marriage was the most fantastic adventure in her life. Rose thought, "I need that type of adventure in my life. I wonder if this sailor might become part of that experience?"

Rose could not know then that the months to come would be full of heartbreaks.

# CHAPTER 5

Rose, june, and joe had returned from attending Sunday morning church. As the three were walking up the steps to the house, Rose inquired, "What time did you ask Marvin to arrive for dinner?"

"It was sort of open ended, Rose; we did not give a specific time. But I would guess Marvin will be here around noon. Why do you ask? Does meeting him making you nervous?"

"Oh, quit trying to put crazy ideas or thoughts in her head. Of course, she will enjoy his company; matter of fact, we all will. Marvin is one super guy!"

Rose helped June set the table and prepare the lettuce salad. In the kitchen working together, Rose confided with June, " I'm very jittery despite Joe trying his best to quiet down my nerves. What if Marvin asks me to go on a date? Should I accept right away or refuse with the idea of playing hard to date? This was an idea one of my girl friends offered me. She said that women should play it cool in accepting a first request for a date. I am confused with what I think is right and what I have been given as advice, if it can be called that."

June, who was rinsing the shrimp in water, wiped her hands on a towel. She placed her  hands on Rose's shoulders.

"My dear lovely Rose, you are really nervous about meeting Marvin, aren't you?  Not having dated before, I can only surmise what you might be thinking.  I hope that you will overcome your nervousness when Marvin arrives. I know it is easier said than done but there is nothing to be afraid of today so clear you mind of any fear. Sometime after we finished  dinner and cleared the table, Joe and I will  go to our office and finish some much needed bookkeeping. We are really behind on this work.  Whether you will be alone with Marvin in the living room, the den, or out on the patio,  just relax and let Marvin carry the conversation. We know him rather well from our seeing him at the lounge for the last year. We have met his parents and they are super folks! Marvin  is a true gentleman but that doesn't mean he's a prude. Don't be afraid! Just relax! Forget what your dad told you.  Find out if you two have any feeling for  each other and  just enjoy the  friendship. You will surprise yourself for thinking about what you dad has been telling you because nothing will take place except that which will be good and wholesome. I'll stake my reputation on that, Rose."

Rose placed her arms around June.  A couple tears rolled down her cheeks and soaked into June's blouse.

Realizing this, she backed away and said, "I'm sorry, June for wetting your blouse. What would I do without your love and support and words of advice to help me over come the butterflies. I know my own mother would hesitate to tell me these things you shared and I really don't why. I will take your advice. I'll try to rid the fears that my dad and mother have instilled in me.  As you both have said, Marvin is an upright man and sailor and I will learn to become  more confident  in  my own  mind  and thoughts. You don't  know  this,  but when

I gave him a trim and ran my fingers along his head and nape of his neck, I experienced feelings within me that I have never realized before. This didn't happen when cutting other men's hair. Do you suppose that has some meaning, some feelings about the beginning of my relationship with Marvin?"

June placed her arms around Rose in a motherly hug. "I think that you can move on from those feelings you experienced at the salon, Rose. On the other hand, this may be the beginning of a great relationship between you two. I do not claim to be a matchmaker, but knowing you both, I believe you are suited for each other. I really do! Give yourself some time and enjoy getting to know one another. But hey, we need to finish our dinner preparations. Marvin will be here soon. Please put the wine glasses from the china cabinet at each place and fill the water glasses with ice tea. Marvin is bringing a bottle of wine. I'll mix a seasoning packet with the shrimp and place them on the burner. When the doorbell rings, you answer it. Boy, will Marvin be surprised to see you. You're the last person he expects to see! Isn't this fun?"

Rose looked at June with a wry smile that implied she and Joe were a couple of real jokesters, but loving ones! She placed the wine glasses at each setting and was pouring the last glass with ice tea, when the door bell rang. Rose almost poured some tea on the table cloth when her hand jerked but just caught herself in time. Why so jumpy she thought? Setting the pitcher down, she went to the door and opened it quickly.

"I didn't know you were invited for dinner! Not that you shouldn't be! What a surprise to see you again, so soon," blurted Marvin.

"I live here with the Reillys."

"You live here! Joe didn't tell me this when I was invited for dinner! I feel like I have been had, but, I'm not complaining, I want you to know. May I come in or will you and I be eating on these door steps?"

"I'm sorry. Where are my manners? Please come in. May

I take your hat? I thought you might be dressed in civilian clothes."

"Well, Joe's request was to wear my Navy uniform. I'm not real certain why, but wanted to comply with his wishes."

"I would have no idea why Joe asked you to wear your uniform." Rose, backing up and surveying Marvin from head to toe, replied, "You are a very handsome sailor in your dressed whites. I agree with Joe that you are a fine example of Uncle Sam's finest."

"Thank you, Rose. Yes, that's what we wear this time of the year. May I compliment you on your lovely attire. That is one smart outfit! I've only seen you in that beautician's smock that you wore at your salon and at Joe's place. You are, indeed, an attractive person and I must admit, I love red-headed women with green eyes. What a lovely combination.! May I say again, how really sharp is that skirt and jacket you're wearing. Wow!"

Knowing Marvin would be present for dinner, Rose had especially dressed in her better clothes. She had picked out a rust colored blouse, a tapestry and patchwork jacket with short sleeves, and a tiered broomstick skirt. Her mother usually purchased plain pastel colors. But now that she was earning her own income, her selection of a wardrobe took on different colors and styles that complimented her red hair and complexion.

"Thought I heard the door bell ring. Welcome!" greeted Joe as he and June came into the foyer and saw the two young folks still by the door. As a matter of fact, Rose still had her hand on the door latch as if she were ready to make a hasty exit. "Join us in the living room. I believe that dinner is ready to be served. Did you have any trouble finding this place? First time you have ventured so far into any neighborhood in Norfolk, right?"

"Yes, Joe, when you gave me your address, I had no idea where to start if trying to use the bus. I could have done some asking. I took the easy way out and ordered a cab. You do not live too far from your lounge, I gather. But I have another bone to pick with you, Joe. Why didn't you tell me that Rose lives with you? I am sure you have your reasons. In a way I feel like I have been 'set up.' But as I told Rose, I'm not putting in a chit to the complaint department."

"We just thought we would surprise you. Yes, Rose lives with us because her dad informed her she had to become independent and find her own place to live. At the time she could not afford to pay rent. She is like a daughter to us and we both love having her live here. I'm hungry; is dinner ready, June?" asked Joe.

Here is the bottle of wine, June," said Marvin. He handed the container to June and she and Joe disappeared to the dining room.

"Would you desire sitting down until it's time to eat?" asked Rose, as she tried to overcome her shyness. "I have my driving license now. Joe paid the cost of driving training lessons and he permits me to drive his car on occasions. He is helping me to buy a car on Monday. If you have no objection, I'll use Joe's car to drive you back to your ship if he doesn't object."

"Rose, thank you. I appreciate that arrangement. Do I need to take out a special life insurance policy when riding with a newly trained driver?" Marvin jokingly added.

Rose, quickly realizing that Marvin had a sense of humor and was attempting to have fun with her, decided she would go along with that same line. "Yes, you must produce your own liability policy. I do that with all passengers. Navy personnel are no exception."

As she said it, she gave Marvin a big friendly grin and became lost looking into his light blue eyes. With blondish-like hair, six feet in height, a handsome face, and a winsome smile returning to her, Rose was simply entrenched by the sailor before her.

Shaking her head so slightly to break her staring, she said, "Why don't we go to the dining room. You can sit at the table already, and I'll help June with the food."

"Aye, Aye, Madam. You give the orders today and this sailor will obey them to the letter. No semaphore signals are needed for me! I am right behind you!"

Grinning at Marvin, Rose called for Joe who hurriedly came into the dining room. She pointed out his place. June came into the dining room with two dishes of food. Rose went to the kitchen and returned with the salad and the ice tea pitcher which June had refilled. After all the food was served, the ladies joined the men.

" Marvin, how much longer do you have in the Navy? What are your plans when you get discharged?" asked Joe. He thought he would have Marvin talk about himself for the benefit of Rose, who might be reluctant to do so on her own. He still was trying to unite these two persons and hoping for greater things to happen.

They were good questions. Marvin related his plans for the future. Rose was spellbound by the depth of information and wisdom this 20 year-old sailor was revealing. She took particular note when he expressed that one day he would desire to marry a very sensible and intelligent woman and have children, hoping that the person with whom he fell in love was able to have children. When he said this, he was looking at Rose. She just happened to be looking back at him with a fork of food going into her mouth. Rose blushed and quickly brought her fork down to her plate, looking at her food.

Again, her mind was in a turmoil. "Why am I blushing at his plans for the future? The Reilly's intentions for this romantic adventure is certainly overwhelming for me! I wish I had more experience already and a lot more self confidence with this dating of guys."

# CHAPTER 6

DINNER WAS FINISHED AND the two men went to the living room. The ladies started to clear the table. Marvin returned to the dining room and asked, "Can I be of help?"

"No, you're free of K. P. duty today, Marvin," replied Rose. She gently grasped his arm and ushered him back to the living room and to a chair. She admonished Joe to be a better host and returned to help June.

As Rose returned to the doorway, she heard Joe say, "Goodness gracious, isn't she getting bossy these days!"

Rose stopped,  looked back at the men and appeared as though hurt to the quick, retorted, " I heard that snide remark!"

"Only teasing you, Sweetheart, just go chase yourself back into the dining room to help June.  I'll entertain your salty sailor!"

Rose, shaking her head  at Joe's remark, returned  to the kitchen and  asked, "June, do you think Joe would object to

my driving Marvin back to his ship later, at least to the gate if
I can't drive on the base?"

"I can see no objection, Rose, dearest, but I will ask him if
it's O.K."

"Sometime I would certainly enjoy seeing a Navy ship, but
I read in the  newspaper that the base is undergoing tight security and that might not be possible."

"Why don't you ask Marvin. You certainly have nothing to
loose by asking."

"Did I hear someone talking about seeing my ship?" asked
Marvin, poking  his head into the kitchen door.

"Yes, you did!  My goodness, you must have super hearing
ability, Marvin.  Would it be possible to visit your ship some
day?  I have always been curious about those Navy ships since
I was a little girl. I've  been on the base a couple times with my
dad  after he was discharged from the Marines. He hates all
Navy people and the Naval base is not his favorite place.  He
hates buying groceries at the commissary whenever Mother
wants to shop.  He never allowed me to go  because he doesn't
want the sailors ogling me.  My dad makes me so angry!"

"You get angry?  That surprises me!  But you are really in
luck. We will be having a special family and visitor's day two
weeks from today.  I will order  passes for all of you.  You will
need to go through some security screening before the passes
are issued.  Then you need to go through all the metal detector
equipment both at the gate and when coming aboard the ship.
Also there will be a limit as to the number of people that can
be aboard at one time.  It is easier to   track all visitors when
we limit the number.  Just can't have people spread  over the
ship anymore without a guide and close supervision."

Hearing the conversation in the kitchen and not wanting
to be left out, Joe joined them.

"Don't worry about the dishes, Rose, you  and  Marvin
spend some  time  together.

I'm looking right at the person who WILL help, won't you

Joe," commanded June in a joyful voice and continued, "Rose wishes to drive Marvin back to his ship or at least to the gate. I know we haven't a base pass sticker that is current. Is that O.K., Joe?"

"Fine with me," replied Joe. "Rose has become an excellent driver but then look who gave her more lessons in driving all over Norfolk after her training classes," said Joe as he put his fingers to his chest as though pulling out suspenders. "Here are the keys, Rose."

"Thank you, Joe, June. You are both so thoughtful. I love you so much. Marvin, I'm going to change into something more relaxing," said Rose.

With out a word, she quickly went to her room and changed to an embroidered Capri set. It was one of the pieces she had modeled and was able to buy at a good discount. She liked the floral embroidery, the ric rac trim in front of the top and on the hem of the pants. The light green color matched her green eyes. She returned to find Marvin providing Joe with more details for the passes needed for visitor's day.

MARVIN AND ROSE LEFT THE house and went to the car parked under a car port. Rose was surprised and pleased when Marvin opened the driver's door and helped her move behind the steering wheel. "You will need to help me with the best way to drive to the gate," implored Rose. "I have driven many places while learning to drive with Joe, but I always kept my eyes on the traffic rather than street signs. My dad or mother always drove when we were going downtown. I haven't paid much attention to street names, unfortunately."

"Hey, I don't know how to get from point A to point B either. Why don't you drive to Joe's Bar and Grill first. You certainly know those streets. Then I'll recognize how to get to the base from there. You may have to drive back home by the same route. Is that O.K. with you? Do you have a map of Norfolk that could help us, also."

Marvin looked in the glove compartment and Rose pulled out some papers from under her car seat, but no maps were found.

"I like your idea. Let's go to Joe's place. They are open to-day. The relief chef, Sam, is in charge on Sundays. I know him; he worked during the week when Pete went on vacation. We could get a soft drink and visit some more. There are more questions I wish to ask you about what you were telling us at dinner. I certainly admire you for the detailed plans you have for your future. I rarely think about what I will be doing tomorrow, let alone a week from now and certainly not years in the future like you."

"There's more I desire to know about you as well, Rose. There was no opportunity to hear much about you. I guess I did monopolize the conversation at dinner. I'm sorry. But Joe kept asking me questions and thought it was only polite to answer them."

Little did both realize that was the plan Joe had in mind.

They arrived at the lounge and Rose parked the car in the space reserved for Joe by the kitchen's back door entrance. They knocked on the door which was promptly opened by Sam. Rose introduced Marvin to Sam and after shaking hands, they made their way to the main restaurant area and sat at the booth near the kitchen entrance.

Naomi saw them coming through the door and waved a "hello."

"What brings you out on a Sunday? I don't believe I have ever seen you here other than on week days. With that hand-some sailor beside you, just what is happening here, Rose?" Naomi asked with a hint of curiosity.

"June and Joe invited Marvin to their home for dinner this noon. I'm taking Marvin back to his ship except neither of us knew the way directly from Joe's house. He took a taxi from the base to the Reillys. We drove here first and Marvin knows the way to the Naval station. A map would certainly be help-ful," replied Rose.

"There is one under the counter. Let me fetch it for you." Naomi returned with the map. "You can study the streets and mark out a more direct route from the base to Joe's house. It will save you a few miles. If you just had dinner, do you want a soft drink or something more to eat?" asked Naomi.

"I would like a coke," replied Rose.

"Make that two," said Marvin.

Rose spread the map on the table. Marvin came around and sat beside her. They traced back the road which they had just driven to Joe's lounge. Marvin marked the streets to the station. "Now lets go from the base using the main thor-oughfares to Joe's house."

Without much difficulty, they were able to find a direct route. "That should help you get back home, Rose. If you get your own car before visitor's day, you will be able to drive to the base unless you ride with the Reillys."

"Now if I may be so bold, what are your plans for the fu-ture? What do you think you will be doing in five years, let's say?" Marvin asked. He stood up and sat down opposite Rose again.

Rose looked at Marvin for what seemed like minutes. She had no immediate answer for him. She really had never thought that far ahead. Her mind was churning. "Today to five years from now? I'd be 23 years old then, wouldn't I? What would a 23-year old single woman like myself be do-ing? He wants an answer, doesn't he?" She picked up her coke and took several sips.

"I would like to own and manage my own beauty salon. I thoroughly enjoy the work I'm doing. I'm earning an excellent income for an eighteen year-old already. I'm learning some great people skills in meeting and talking to so many different customers. They have all been really super! That includes you too, Marvin," as she showed him her best smile.

"Rose, I said it before and I'll say it again, you are indeed a very beautiful lady. With your outstanding beauty and figure, if I may be so bold to add, you should become a model."

"This may be a surprise to you, I was a model for six months when I was a junior in high school. I worked for Dolow's Department Store at the MacArthur Center. Dolow's is one of the largest department stores. The earnings were large in comparison to my beautician work at the time. But my dad forced me to quit modeling. I enjoyed the experience and learned the many types of clothes and fashions that are suitable for a red head like myself. There are certain colors that clash with women who have hair like mine."

"I was also working at Carol's Curls and Crewcuts part time during my junior and senior year in high school. This was an On-The-Job Training Class in learning to become a beautician. Carol has been so generous and has helped my modeling with makeup techniques and different hair stylings. She has already put me in charge of the salon when ever she takes a day off or goes out with her boy friends. She gives many of her customers to me when she's gone. The other beautician's have been there much longer, but I'm in charge. So far Sissy, Randy, and "Clips", that's Harry's nickname, have not resented my being the boss, so to speak  But then we each have our own customers so there isn't much occasion to be bossy. I just need to  help clean the place and be on time to open and to lock up at night."

"Rose, you surprise me and yet there is no reason to be so.  You have just told me a whopping amount of information about yourself that I am so pleased to hear.  I have no doubt that you will own a salon one day.  The way you have just shared this information with great determination and enthusiasm  in your voice, leads me to believe that you will succeed."  Reaching  for her hands and holding them gently, Marvin added, "I would thoroughly enjoy  seeing more of you while I'm still stationed here before being discharged and returning to Denver. Would you be of like mind and of equal disposition?"

"Geepers, that sounds so legal like!"

"I'm sorry! That it does! Guess it comes from being around Chris too much. You remember meeting him here. He is our legal beagle on board ship. He plans to become a lawyer when he gets discharged around the same time as I. Then I'll not mince words. Would you go out on a date with me?"

"Marvin. . ."

"Please call me Marv. All my close friends do."

"O. K., Marv, yes, I would. But you need to know and it may be difficult for you to understand this, but I have never been out on a date before with a man. I have gone out with my girl friends a few times to movies, but I have turned down all guys when asked for a date."

"Rose, that is very difficult to believe. You are so beautiful. There must be some logical explanation to that situation. I don't wish to be so personal again but I have a broad shoulder on which to lean and to pour out your problems. But no dating at all? That's difficult to understand. If you wish to tell me Rose, I would desire to know your reasons."

Rose, looking right into Marv's eyes, went into a detailed explanation of how her father and mother had more or less brainwashed her into accepting the belief that she would be raped and perhaps become pregnant if she accepted dates. She mentioned how her dad had warned her never, under any circumstances, to ever date a sailor. During her last two years in high school, she worked hard to be on the honor roll in her studies and that meant much homework because learning did not come easily. She indicated the hours of work at the salon and standing even for a few hours every day just tired her out to the point that she had little energy to go anywhere after arriving home. She related the ugly scene of how her father literally threw her out of the house.

With not enough income to rent an apartment, she accepted the kind offer to live with the Reillys.

As she spoke, she noted how Marv showed real interest in her confession about not dating and signs of real concern for her dilemma. She felt good being able to share this with someone she had just met. She was surprised how comfortable it was being with Marvin, a sailor at that, who seem to really care. Again, flashes of the warnings of her father and then the admonitions that Joe had shared with her about sailors came to the surface and then as rapidly disappeared as she continued to gaze into Marvin's eyes. Here was a person she could learn to trust very quickly and easily. She knew then what June meant when she shared her convictions and that she would stake her life on her conclusions about Marvin.

Taking her hands into his again, Marvin smiled and said, "Rose, that is a tremendous burden for a beautiful lady of your age being forced to endure. You have managed to survive remarkably. I would venture to say that your faith in God and other religious convictions have given you the will to carry through each day. I don't know whether to hate or to like your parents even before meeting them. Do you have other brothers or sisters that have had to go through what you did as a teenager?"

"Marv, your insight is correct. I believe the lessons learned from church school classes and our minister's sermons have been a source of strength and a blessing. For the rest of your question, I have only one brother, Matthew, who is 15; no sisters. Donovan, my dad, met and married my mother, Maureen, when she was my age. Sometime before I was born, my dad joined the Marine Corps. We did some traveling and living on different base housing. Sometimes we came back to Norfolk to live when dad had assignments on aircraft carriers. My brother was born here in Norfolk. Dad developed a hatred for Navy personnel when he had those assignments on carriers. I can hear him now as he yelled and raved about you. Well, I don't mean you, Marv, but all Navy people. I can imagine the unkind words he will use if I should introduce you to him. Mother will be fine, but, wow, my dad will be something else!"

"Rose, we will cross that bridge at a later time. I need to get back to my ship. I do have a watch to fulfill from 2100 to midnight. This has been so pleasant getting to know more about you and your family. You have no idea how much concern I have for you at this point. You have, indeed, had it rough as a teenager. I am looking forward to our first date. How would you enjoy dancing, or perhaps a movie that you haven't seen. Sounds as if you haven't had the opportunity to go anywhere these past four years while in high school, working part-time, and now full time."

"I know I would love to dance! I didn't go to the Junior-Senior proms my last two years. I didn't accept any of the dates from boys in my class for reasons you now know. I could have gone alone and just mingled, but I stayed home and studied. I thought of going to the dance my Senior year, but I was so tired from working at the salon that day, kicking off my shoes and laying on my bed was a better treat."

"Then dancing it will be, my pretty princess! There may be some good places to dance in Norfolk, but we have a groovy band playing at the Enlisted Men's Club on base. I will process your security clearance tomorrow so you can drive on the base, assuming you're able to buy a car this week. There is a dance next Saturday night. I'll use a taxi to your place."

"I do plan buying a car! Joe and I are shopping tomorrow. I'll be able to drive from my place to the base. This map with marked streets is just the ticket! I'm really looking forward to my first date, and with a sailor at that. Who would have thought that would be the case after all my dad has drilled into my head, lo these many years," Rose said as she gazed into the prettiest blue eyes she had ever seen on any man.

# CHAPTER 7

Rose could hardly wait for Monday afternoon to arrive. All morning, while she worked on her customers, she was anxious about getting her own car. When she had last counted her savings, she thought she could become an owner of a set of wheels.

The time finally arrived when Rose and Joe drove to the bank.

"This is Mr. Mitchell, the bank vice president, Rose," said Joe. "We have been friends for a long time. Fred, we have the beginnings of a great business lady, so please treat her as one of your most valuable customer."

"My pleasure to meet you Rose," answered Mr. Mitchell, as he clasped Rose's extended hand. "And what can we do for you today?"

"I wish to start a checking and savings account," replied Rose.

After all the documents were signed, Rose was the proud owner of both.

"HOW MUCH DO YOU WISH to pay for a car?" asked the car salesman.

"I have $6,000 cash to pay down on a car. I can make monthly payments on $4,000 so may I see the experienced cars in the $10,000 bracket," replied Rose.

"Why don't we see what you have in the $8,000 range first," remarked Joe while giving Rose a look that said, 'don't give the man your trump card right off the bat.' "

And so the next hour was spent bargaining for the right car. They looked at different years of make, name brands and models. Finally, they settled on a Buick Century, four-door, with radio, cassette and CD player. These extras were a must for Rose. She had a choice of blue or white color. She selected the white. Joe and Rose went for a test drive. When they returned, Joe checked the tires very carefully and bargained with the dealer to replace the front two which were getting tread worn. Rose signed the transaction with Joe's assistance for $8,575 and wrote her first check for $6,000 on her newly opened checking account. "Difficult to come by and quickly spent" was an expression she had heard once upon a time. This all proved to be so true. She knew monthly payments of $125 would accommodate her budget. The paper work was completed and Rose followed Joe back to the lounge. He arranged for a parking space for her behind the Bar and Grill. The ones behind the salon were already filled.

AS ROSE ENTERED THE SALON, she quickly went to her station for a business man had been waiting for 10 minutes.

"I really do apologize for keeping you waiting. It took a little longer than expected to do some banking and buy a car, a first time experience in doing both, I might add," offered Rose.

"Rose, Carol told me where you were and no apologies are necessary," said Robert. "My business can go on without me since I am the owner and have an outstanding manager. I'm pleased that a young person as yourself is taking business transactions seriously. I congratulate you!"

ROSE FINISHED THE HAIRCUT of her last customer for the day, helped Carol and Sissy do a thorough cleaning of the salon, then went next door to the lounge. She sat in the booth by the kitchen entrance reserved for the help.

Joe saw her and joined her. "Well, how do you feel after spending so much money in one day's time. Did it make you happy, sad, or no reaction?"

Rose grinned at Joe. "Thanks, for your help. You did so much for me today. Had the price reduced a bit and two new tires at that. I know I wouldn't have accomplished all that without your help."

"You are most welcome, Rose. But what I'm more curious about, is what happened between the time you left our house yesterday and when you returned. I did not hear you come in. Guess I was in the office doing book work."

"Yes, you were working, Joe. Marvin is precisely the fine person you have indicated. June's opinion is true, too. We came here to the lounge after dinner and had a long talk before driving him to the main gate of the base. It was so comfortable talking to him. I feel like I have known Marv for a much longer time than the few hours we have been together. I have my first date with him next Saturday. He's obtaining a pass for me in order to drive on the base. We are going to a dance at the Enlisted Men's Club."

"Oh, Rose. I am so pleased for you two. You will not regret getting to know this bright young man who has a great future all planned. I just know that you will be a part of that plan, or my name is not Joseph Ralph Reilly."

Rose looked at Joe, grinned and laughed, "I didn't know your name was Joseph Ralph. All I have ever heard is Joe."

"And you better just continue to call me by that, young lady" as he reached up and placed his fist gently on her cheek.

"We ought to get home; June will have our dinner ready. It has been a really busy day and we both know June will want to see your experienced car driven by an experienced driver who was taught by an even more experienced person. How much more experienced can we be? Eh? But we purchased an excellent car for you!"

They both left the lounge for their respective cars. Rose followed Joe home. As she drove, visions of her dancing with Marvin reeled in her head. Being five foot five inches in height and Marvin, six foot, they certainly couldn't dance check to cheek. Dance? I have never danced before with a guy! Someone is really in for a big surprise and it undoubtedly will be me!

"CHRIS, BEFORE WE CLOSE the office today, be certain you make a note to process a security clearance to drive on the base and near our ship on visitor's day for Joseph R. and June C. Reilly and Rose McDowell. As a matter of fact, please obtain clearance for Rose immediately. We are going to the dance at the EM Club next Saturday when 'The Dynamite Five' band is playing. She hopes to buy a set of wheels today and after I take a taxi out to the Reillys, she'll drive me to the base. How do you like those apples?"

"Sounds to me that matters are really heating up between you two!"

"Well, we're proceeding on a very cool basis now, but I can't guarantee that your predictions may not come true in the future. She is certainly an exceptionally beautiful but innocent lady. But then that is what I really have wanted in finding a mate. But time will tell as we become better acquainted. She doesn't fully realize, but we'll be spending more time together before being discharged."

"I'm happy for you, Marv. I'll process those security clearances first thing tomorrow morning."

'THE PHONE IS FOR YOU ROSE. It's your sailor man sweet-heart calling. Guess we can expect many of these types of calls. Perhaps we will need to install asbestos wires for the telephone to keep the lines from burning up!" kidded Joe as he gave the receiver to Rose with the grin he used in teasing people.

"Hello, Marv," replied Rose. "This is a pleasant surprise. Can't wait to tell you that I bought a white 4-door Century Buick today. Really sharp! Joe helped me with an excellent buy! Now you need to get that security clearance for me and we'll be in shipshape, if I can use that Navy expression!"

"Whoppee do! All that in one breath, too! I am so HAPPY for you! Now for the extra expenses of gas, maintenance, and car insurance.  But I'll buy the gas whenever you are haul-ing my butt about and I won't take 'no' for an answer. Chris is working on the security clearance for all three of you tomor-row so you'll be approved to drive on the base. Be certain  to bring your insurance policy for the guys at the gate will check those before a personal base pass can be issued. Am I making sense to you?"

"Oh Marv, you're making fun of me now, aren't you?  I know that I need car insurance.  I purchased that the same time the car dealer made out the loan papers.  It's all included in my monthly payments.  Didn't want to spend all my ready cash on the car.  And if you want me to haul your butt about, as you so colorfully put it, you will be paying for the gas.  No freebies from this hard working gal."

"I love your forceful ways with me, Princess. What I really called about--can we meet at Joe's tomorrow night for dinner, say at 1800 hours, and then decide what we will do from that point on?"

"Marv, why don't you give me the time in a language  I un-derstand.  Someone told me I need to subtract 1200 from the military time to get civilian time, is that correct? If so, will I be meeting you at 6 p.m.?"

"You're my type of woman! You have the military time down cold! But remember that is only true from 12 noon through 12 midnight.   I shall be looking forward to having dinner with you.   Goodbye, and sleep well, princess!"

"Well, if I'm a princess, then Farewell, Prince of DD789!" Rose jokingly answered back.

As the receiver was slipped into  its cradle, a smile formed on her face as she ran the word ' Princess' through her mind and thought 'is that what he believes I am'?

# CHAPTER 8

'WELL GOOD MORNING MR. Bolsey," said Carol, as she greeted her landlord who was entering the salon. "Didn't think my rent was due quite yet."

"No, that is not the reason for this visit. I want to talk to you about a proposition that may interest you," replied Mr. Bolsey.

"Oh, I love to be propositioned!" blurted out Carol, as Rose, Sissy, and "Clips" looked at her in astonishment, knowing her philanthropy of keeping two boy friends on the string at the same time and knowing that Mr. Bolsey was a widower.

"Can we talk in private somewhere, Carol, it's a rather private matter," said Mr. Bolsey.

"Rose, I noticed you are done with Frank's trim. Would you finish combing out Harriett's hair for me while Mr. Bolsey and I go to Joe's place. Is that O.K. with you, Harriett?" asked Carol, as her client nodded her head in the affirmative.

Carol and Mr. Bolsey walked to the far edge of the street next to the curb. He looked up at the second floor of the building and pointed at a cornerstone containing the year the building was erected--1979. "We bought this building 18 years ago, last week Monday. The Emporium Hair Salon was here at the time, if you recall. You moved in when they left and changed the name. Mrs. Bolsey and I moved into the two bed-room apartment. It has been a good arrangement—managing the building, having you as a renter for the past 6 years, and living in the downtown area. But now that my wife has died, I no longer desire to live here. Plan to move to Richmond and be closer to my children and grandkids.   I wish to sell the building now and desire to offer you the first opportunity to buy, Carol."

"Man a live," exclaimed Carol, "this really comes like a bomb shell! It would obviously help to know a few more facts. Why don't we go to Joe's place for coffee and talk over some financial matters."

"Sounds great to me! I'm anxious to sell and will arrange a tempting offer!  My wife and I have always liked you with your positive attitude and happy-go-lucky manners. You just may wish to make mortgage payments and build some prop-erty equity rather than gather  rental receipts. You can live upstairs. That will save you paying rent."

Taking seats at Joe's, Jean took their orders for coffee. Mr. Bolsey pulled some papers from his jacket pocket.  Taking a pen from his shirt pocket, he began to write down some fig-ures. Carol tried to read them in the up-side down manner as he wrote but the figure amounts were too confusing. Waiting until he was done, she sipped her hot coffee that Jean had set before her.

Mr. Bolsey turned the paper for her. "Carol, I paid $60,000 for the building. It has appreciated some since then. However, for this area of Norfolk, real estate has not moved as fast as others. I will sell it to you for the same price. Told you I'd make a tempting offer. As you can see, I have around $25,000 in equity, but will reduce that to $20,000 and you take over my payments which are about the amount you have been paying for rent. I have checked with the bank that's carrying the note and they have agreed to this transaction. They wanted me to be certain of selecting a reliable person. You may want some time to think this over. I don't need an answer today. Perhaps you desire to see the apartment also as part of your decision."

Carol studied the figures before her. Mr. Bolsey answered questions given him. Buying the building was the furthest thing in her mind in becoming a property owner. She looked up at Mr. Bolsey who was waiting for some type of reaction from her.

"Mr. Bolsey, this is certainly a new type of adventure for me to consider. Yes, I wish to see the apartment. May I see it right now? I'm curious. Living there would indeed save the rent money I'm now paying for my apartment. And yes, I would need a day or two to mull this over."

Mr. Bolsey placed three dollars on the table for the coffee and a tip. They left the lounge and went to the street entrance to the apartment, ascended the stairs, and entered into the living room.

"Your wife really knew how to purchase some beautiful antique furniture to furnish your whole apartment!" exclaimed Carol, as she went through each room and lovingly rubbing her hand over each piece. "You have a fortune in this apartment. And all in such excellent condition."

"Yes, my wife really had an eye for antiques. We've been in dozens of antique stores as we have traveled. We've visited Norfolk's stores many many times. As a matter of fact, dealers would call us when they purchased some exceptional pieces. We have attended many estate sales in the past years. I already have a buyer for all of this furniture. All will be sold before moving to Richmond, except for this Colonial rocking chair," as he pointed it out to Carol. "It is special and will be a reminder of my wife each time I gaze upon that chair. I will visualize her rocking and knitting doilies."

"Thank you, Mr. Bolsey, for showing me your apartment. May I see the kitchen now?"

They moved into the kitchen. Carol noted that it had been modernized completely with handsome oak cupboards. There was an island counter with a counter top stove and a food preparation sink on the end. The main sink looked out to the alley which did not offer that good a view. "Will you be taking all your appliances with you?"

"Maybe, I have already selected an apartment in Richmond which is unfurnished. I can take all my appliances or I would be glad to sell them. I do lean toward buying new ones when I arrive at Richmond. I'll make you an excellent offer if you desire any of them."

"If I did buy your building, I would be interested because all these kitchen appliances are furnished in my apartment. I need to get back to the shop for there's a customer waiting. I wish to think about methods of coming up with $20,000. That's a huge number of green backs placed end to end, Mr. Bolsey."

Carol excused herself and returned to the salon. Mr. Bolsey remained to nostalgically view the antique furniture soon to be removed.

IT WAS 5:30 P.M. and Sissy and "Clips" had finished their last customer. After tidying up their station, they left the salon. Rose was about to do the same when Carol approached her.

"Rose, may I share a few facts with you? The proposition that Mr. Bolsey made was an offer to buy this building for $60,000. He wants $20,000 for his equity and then assume the balance of the loan of around $35,000 with the same monthly payments he made. I only have a little over $10,000 in a money market. I was wondering if you would consider joining me in a partnership to buy the building. Would there be the remotest chance that you have $10,000 laying about gathering dust or mold? The apartment above us has two bedrooms, bath, living room, dining room, and a modern kitchen. If you have no objection, we could be roommates and share the expenses of furnishing and maintaining the apartment. But by the look on your face, this is probably too much for you to digest as I reel off all this information."

"Oh, Carol, it certainly is! I really do not know what to say. This would be heavy finances for me. Well, I did have $10,000 as of yesterday. After I bought the Buick, I only have around $3,500 left. Had to buy insurance and license plates. This would be a great opportunity to become a business partner with you, but I don't know how and where I would come up with that much cash right now. It took me the last two years to salt away what I have or did have. If I lived upstairs, I certainly do not need a car to drive to work, that's for certain. Might be able to sell it again for the needed cash. Oh, golly, I really don't know what to do to help you, Carol. Do you need to give Mr. Bosley an immediate answer?"

Carol looked at Rose and shook her head in a negative motion. This truly was a big decision she had placed on Rose's shoulders. Perhaps she should not have been so forthright in her request. But she saw no other way but just laying out the facts and figures.

"JOE AND JUNE, CAN you imagine Carol asking me to go into partnership with her and buy the building where our shop is located and then move in with her upstairs above the salon to a two bedroom apartment?" stated Rose, as the three were eating dinner that night.

"Rose, what does she expect you to invest in this adventure?" asked Joe.

"She is asking me to come up with $10,000 and then help in the furnishing and daily expenses of maintaining the apartment such as utilities and food."

"I am very certain, that you would not be able to get a loan at the bank. You haven't established any credit rating yet. You have your car payments to make now. We would love to help you but there is no way that we could with running the lounge. We are doing fine but not to the extent that we have a large surplus of cash left over each month."

"Oh, Joe, I didn't imply that you were to help me! I was just giving you the information that Carol gave me. I really want to help her, but I see no way that I can. I think I'll visit my folks tonight. I want mother see my new car. Dad will have a hissy-fit and find all kinds of things wrong with it. But I can take his uncaring attitude now."

Rose finished eating and helped June wash the dishes. She drove to her parents and when driving up the driveway, she found her brother mowing the lawn.

"Hi there little Brother, need some help?'

"Hey Dad and Mom, Rose is driving a new car!" yelled Matthew to his parents who were sitting on the front porch. He ran to his sister who stepped out of the car.

"When did you buy the new Buick, Rose?" as Matthew tried to overcome his excitement.

Rose ruffled his hair, and put her arms around his shoulder as they walked up the sidewalk to the front porch. Rose hugged her Mother as she rose from her chair. Her dad rose from where he was sitting and held his arms out to Rose for a hug also. This was new to Rose for he had never done this before. However, she went into her dad's arms and he embraced her.

As he did, he kissed her on the forehead, and said, "Rose, daughter, you are indeed a beautiful young lady and your mother and I love you very much."

This really surprised Rose. To her recollection, she had never heard her dad express any love or affection towards her before this. Her mind was spinning for she was wondering where this new approach was really coming from or what caused it?

"Dad and Mother, and you, too, Little Brother, I love you

all very much. Not living at home makes me more aware of how much you are missed and how meaningful you are to me during the absence. Dad, you were probably correct in forcing me to become more independent. I have been able to earn some good income at Carol's salon. I have a checking and savings account and bought a car. However, I wish I hadn't in a way. Today Carol asked me to go into business with her and buy the building in which our beauty salon is located with an apartment on the second floor. She has asked me to help in the purchase with $10,000 and to move into the apartment with her. I had that much money before buying the Buick. Now I can't do much to help."

Donovan clasped Rose's hand in his and then his wife's hand in the other and led them from the porch and down the sidewalk toward the Buick. As he walked around the car still holding the ladies' hands, he smiled at Rose.

"Daughter, it appears to be in good condition on the outside. What is the condition of the motor and transmission? Those are the most important parts when buying a used car; sorry, an experienced car, the term used today."

"Joe helped me with the purchase, Dad. He asked all those types of questions of the salesman. We did a test drive. He even negotiated with the dealer for two new front tires at no extra cost. Here are the keys, Dad, let's go for a drive and you can determine for yourself how the motor sounds and how it performs on the road."

The family got in the car and Donovan backed out the driveway and headed for the main boulevard.

"My daughter, I am certainly proud of your achievements so quickly. I'm thinking about how we can help with your share in buying the building."

Rose, sitting in the front seat with her Dad, looked at him in pure astonishment as they drove down the street. Her thoughts were spinning! "Did I hear correctly that he is thinking about how he can help me? I am sure I did! But then......

What can I say? This is so unlike him. I should show my gratitude."

"Dad, your help would be appreciated. After I pay off the car, I will pay off your loan to me. Carol will be most pleased for she is really interested in buying the building. That would make me a property owner at 18 years of age, wouldn't it?"

Rose turned and smiled at her mother who looked perplexed from the nature of the conversation between her husband and daughter, yet pleased beyond words. She was happy, more ecstatic, to witness an apparent improved relationship with his daughter. "Thank God for small favors!" she thought.

# CHAPTER 9

"WELL, HOW WAS YOUR day, Princess? You look a little tired?" asked Marvin, as Rose approached the table where he was sitting. He was waiting for her to get off work. "Have you ever seen this lounge this busy at 5:30? Everyone must be eating their evening meal early!"

Rose looked around the lounge and saw all the booths and tables were full but one.

"No, not this early. Must be some reason that I don't know about," replied Rose. "And yes, I am tired. Had a full schedule of appointments today. Didn't have one break. Even worked right through my lunch hour with walk-in customers. But, I won't complain because I earned good wages today. Couple days like this and I'll have a car payment," added Rose.

"I am pleased for you, Rose. Let's eat!" as he handed her a menu. "The dinner is on me, Rose, so eat heartily. Can't have you start getting skinny for I enjoy seeing you just the way you are now," as he flashed a big smile.

Rose glanced up from the menu in time to see the smile and could not help but produce a big smile in return.

"So you desire me just the way I am. Well, how do you like that! If we are giving out compliments, I don't want you to change either!" They continued to look into each others eyes until Jean approached their table.

"Well, what are you two love birds going to have tonight? The special is a ham dinner with yams, a veggie, rolls and butter and your choice of dessert, including beverages. $7.95. Plus tax, of course."

Marvin looked at Rose and waited for her choice on the menu. Rose didn't seem to be in a hurry to make a selection.

"Why don't you give us a couple of minutes to decide, Jean," stated Marvin. "Well, Princess, here is your personal pass to drive on the base. As I mentioned before, bring your registration and insurance policy to the provost guard at the gate and you will receive a sticker to place on your windshield that gives you permission to drive on the base. Chris did a quick job of providing this for you. Joe and June's passes will be ready before visitor's day should they plan to visit the ship also."

"I'm having the special. What do you desire to eat, Rose?"

"Thank you for obtaining my security clearance so quickly. I'll meet you at the provost guard's office tomorrow evening at **1630**," Rose emphasized, saying the military time for Marvin's benefit. "I think I will have the special also. Sounds good to me and I am hungry due to skipping lunch. Glad I ate a hearty breakfast here at Joe's this morning before going to the salon at 8:30. Actually, you don't have to pay for my dinner, Marv. Joe permits me to eat at no cost since I help almost every morning with the breakfast crowd. He and June have been so helpful. They won't take rent money and I eat here and at their home. They won't permit my buying groceries either. They keep telling me that all the work I do for them is worth even more than the food I eat. I still buy some items though. June knows I do and doesn't say anything to Joe. Sort of sneaky of me, don't you think?"

Jean came to the table and took their orders.

Rose was reading the contents on her personal base pass.

"Here is a pen, Rose. Be certain you sign your legal name on the card as Chris typed your name, 'Rose Maureen McDowell.' Didn't know until he gave me the pass that your middle name is that of your Mother's. What a beautiful name for a gorgeous lady! Saying the name just flows out in a melodic manner, 'Rose Maureen McDowell.' I love to say it! But hey, what would you like to do after we have eaten? What would meet your fancy? There is a good movie at the MacArthur Center. You must know where that is located; it's in the same mall where you did all your modeling. I certainly wish I had been a fly on the wall and watched you do all that modeling. You must have been stunning to watch as you walked back and forth on the walkway with the different clothing outfits."

Rose caught the look on his face as he spoke. As she studied his face and his eyes, she tried to interpret his view and what he might be thinking. But it was more the tone in his voice that revealed to her how this sailor was definitely in a class of his own. His compliments were so genuine and sincere. His voice and his facial expressions gave her feelings that had never been experienced before. This was all so new and different for her. "There is something more that needs to be understood about this sailor if we are going to spend more time together," thought Rose. But as June suggested, "just enjoy each other's friendship. If there is any chemistry that may develop between you two, just let it flow."

"Where is our food?" asked Marvin, looking at his wrist watch.

"I'll check with Pete and bring our orders if ready," answered Rose.

In a moment or two Rose returned with the tray of food.

"What do you wish to drink, Marv?" asked Rose. She listed all the beverages that were served.

"You really know your stuff working here at Joe's," complimented Marvin. "Why don't you bring me a big glass of ice tea. We get some strange looking stuff at our mess hall that is called 'ice tea.' It will be a treat to have the real McCoy for a change."

Rose came back with the beverages. They ate in silence. They simply enjoyed each other's company and gazed at one another as they ate.

ARRIVING AT THE THEATER, Marvin remarked, "You really handled your Buick Century neat-o. You had no trouble finding this place and backed right in that parking spot so quickly. I am really impressed!"

"The truth of the matter is, my dear sailor friend, I studied that map we had last week and learned a bunch of streets to travel to places like this mall, for instance. I studied the roads to drive to the beaches in the area and to some of the wildlife refuges. I love to see wild animals and game birds. I thought that while you are still here before being discharged, you might desire to see some of these places with me. I have never had the opportunity to go before. My dad would not take us to places like these. Claimed it cost too much."

"Rose, you precious princess, I would be more than delighted to go with you! I'll find out when I have the duty aboard ship, what days I can pay to have Chris or someone fulfill my duties, and then we can map out all the days I have free. We can plan some real sightseeing, and better yet, some togetherness to enjoy each other's companionship."

Despite standing in the lobby of the theater and people passing by on all sides, Marvin pulled Rose into his arms and placed his lips on hers. It startled Rose for this was the first time he had kissed her. In fact, it was the first time she had been kissed by a man! In spite of the pleasure Rose was experiencing, she was also self conscious of the display of affection in a public place with people obviously watching them. However, Marvin did prolong the kiss and when he released her, he looked into her eyes.

"If I surprised you, I truly am NOT sorry. It was an urge that came out of nowhere and I followed that urging. Do you realize your lips are soft like velvet feels to the touch? I hope you don't object to more of the same. We better purchase our tickets and take our seats. I believe the movie we want to see has already started. Perhaps I can steal a kiss during the movie?"

THE MOVIE ENDED.   Marvin and Rose left the theater and returned to Joe's lounge and ordered a hamburger, fries, and an ice tea.

Rose broke the silence and said, "Marv, the kiss you gave me, despite being in a public place, was the first kiss I have ever had from a guy. As short as it was, I enjoyed it very much. You must be an experienced kisser or doesn't the reputation of a sailor apply to you?"

"Well, Rose, I dated girls throughout high school and some after I graduated and before joining the Navy. I kissed some of them. Some were more bold and kissed me first and I responded. I found out that women's responses to kissing really do vary. However, I don't consider myself an authority on the subject. If you enjoyed my kisses, I shall plant a few more on you and let you decide what you like or don't like! Is that O.K. with you, princess?"

"Well, I think so. You have an advantage over me. I have nothing to compare and really do not desire to go find out, however. But some of my girl friends told me that kissing a lot caused their boyfriends to become aroused and ended up having sex. Two of my best friends ended up pregnant. One had her baby and the other chose an abortion. It was really tragic for both. In a way I was very glad my folks encouraged me not to date. I really don't know if I would have had the confidence and the courage to say NO!"

"Rose, if you don't already know by this short time we have been together, I have the highest respect for you. You are one gorgeous woman. You really are not self conscious of that fact. Looking into those beautiful green eyes, I perceive such a depth of inner beauty as well. You may not realize that either, Rose, but believe me when I say these things. I am not a selfish person and would not force myself on you, or any other woman for that matter, so you do not have any cause to fear me. I know what your folks have been telling you for years. When you get to any point in our physical contact that causes you to feel uncomfortable or even confused, just let me know. I realize that I am the first guy you have dated. I will respect and honor your innocence and naiveness. I'm here as your knight in shining armor ready to defend and help you as I feel myself going from liking you to caring for the wonderful woman you are. I am really grateful to Joe and June for our introduction. And I hope the feeling is mutual."

"Marv, I really do appreciate what you have just said. I do feel very safe and I am gaining confidence when I'm with you. I've never had this experience before. There is so much that I have never learned or been told by my mother. All the stuff that my girlfriends have told me has been really confusing. What one said would be contradicted by another. They all thought they were helping me. Would you help me to gain more confidence and self-esteem? I feel I am lacking in both departments. You truly are my knight in shining armor! Never thought of it in those romantic terms."

"Rose, that's a tall order, but I'm here for you!"

"Thank you for taking me to the movies. I enjoyed holding hands and the few times you nuzzled my neck and those warm kisses. You gave me goose-bumps! You gave me feelings within me that I have never experienced before. June says it's

a matter of chemistry between persons. I'm beginning to real-
izo what she meant by that word."

"Rose, I really enjoy the time spent with you. It is a wonderful sensation, too! But will you take me back to the base? I
have a late watch duty to perform for another sailor. We swap
duties to help each other. He wanted the night off to visit
friends and doesn't need to report until 0800 tomorrow. He
will stand my watch so we can do that sightseeing you desire.
When I see you next time, I'll have all the days marked on a
calendar when I can leave the ship. I'll meet you at 1700 tomorrow at the main gate. Let me also fill you car with gas on
the way to the base. I told you I would pay to haul my butt
about, didn't I?"

Rose smiled her approval and they left the lounge. As they
walked to the car holding hands, Rose was filled with a sense
of well being and a new happiness that she had never experienced before.

After Marvin bought gas for her car, she dropped him off
at the gate. Rose drove home. Her mind began to flood with
thoughts of all kinds. "Can I be falling for this sailor? Will I
regret doing so? I really do need a knight in shining armor!
What will Dad say about dating a sailor? Will Dad help me
buy the salon? Why would he do that? Dad said he loved me!
He hugged and kissed me! Marvin said he is moving from liking to caring for me! I'm beginning to have real feelings for
him! His kisses give me great sensations! Should I really get
involved with this sailor? But why not? He's a great guy!"

When Rose drove into the driveway, she suddenly became
scared. She had driven home while her mind was totally occupied as if she had been driving on auto-pilot. "Too scary
she thought. I need to get control of myself. I could have had
a serious accident!"

# CHAPTER 10

"HERE IS YOUR PASS to get on the base. Wet this glue and fasten the pass in the lower right hand corner of your windshield. The guards at the gate will check this pass each time you enter and leave the base. Your car has been inspected and passes the safety qualifications for the base. We welcome you to visit when ever you can," stated the security officer in a very serious and professional manner.

"Thank you," replied Rose. "I plan to drive my sailor friend directly to his ship and especially to the dance at the EM Club. He was to meet me here by now. Something must have prevented his coming."

But as Rose was leaving the building, she saw Marvin trotting up the sidewalk waving his arms to make certain she saw him. She stood and grinned as he came running to her.

"Sorry I'm late, princess, but could not leave my office right away. Then the darn lock on my locker wouldn't open and had to fuss with that a bit. Need to buy a new one even though I only have a short time left before my discharge. If I can't get the key to open it again, I'll need to saw the dumb lock off."

"You are forgiven, my salty sailor! The unexpected does happen to us all. But I would say that the timing was perfect. I really didn't need you present to have the car inspected and a pass issued. But here, you can fasten this pass on the wind shield for me. Would you then take me to the commissary to buy some grocery items to help June with her household budget since they won't take rent money? Would appreciate it very much."

GOING DOWN THE AISLES of the commissary, Rose picked up an assorted list of grocery items that she knew June could use. They were amused when passing two older ladies when one said to the other, "Isn't that a handsome couple. Oh, to be that young again!"

They checked out at the cashier's station and placed the sacks of groceries in the trunk of the car.

"Would you desire to have dinner at the Enlisted Men's Club? You will also see where the dance will be held this coming Saturday. Are you hungry?" asked Marvin.

"Hungry as a goat eating tin cans," replied Rose. "Sorry, that's an expression my dad has used many time while growing up. Again, I only squeezed in a sandwich and an apple for lunch. We have really been busy with most of the fleet being anchored at Norfolk. I wish to see where you enlisted men hang out and probably drive the women crazy with all your salty sea stories." Rose gave Marvin a toothy grin as she continued, "'I'm really anxious for the dance we're attending! It will be the first for me!"

As Rose ate her dinner, she glanced about the place with the busy activities of dozens of sailors eating dinner—some alone, some with a woman, some in bunches of three to five sailors to a table—but her eyes came back repeatedly to look at Marvin who was looking right back at her. She was thinking of what her father and mother had said about never dating a sailor. Here she was in the midst of many. How could my parents be so wrong? What will be my dad's reaction when I introduce Marvin to him? I may as well introduce him to my folks as soon as possible. Yes, ASAP!

"'HAVE YOU EVER SEEN SUCH a busy day?" asked Carol, as she dropped down in a chair at 6 p.m. the next day. Rose, Sissy and Harry voiced a huge sigh of relief in chorus fashion as they, too, sat down in their customers' chairs.

"When that fleet is in, we certainly receive a large share of the officers and sailors for trims and hair styling," added Rose, "but it won't be for long. Marvin informed me that some of the Atlantic fleet will be going out to sea for some war maneuvers. So don't complain! Pickings may get rather slim!"

Everyone jumped out of their seats after the short rest and began to clean around their station. Sissy and Harry finished first, said their good byes, and left. Rose was bending down cleaning some hair that fell on the shelves below her counter.

The door opened and a person came into the salon. Without looking who it was, Carol called out, "Sorry, we're closed for the day!"

"Can't a man obtain a trim from his own daughter despite your closing time?" asked Donovan.

"Oh, I'm sorry, Donovan, I spoke before I looked to see who came in," replied Carol.

Hearing her dad's voice, Rose stood up and quickly turned towards him.

"What are you doing in a beauty salon, dad? Didn't think I would ever see a Marine in a place like this!"

"Well, a man can change his mind, can't he?" replied Donovan. "But I'm here to talk to both of you. Then I need a trim from my daughter. I have some things to say to her that are very heavy on my mind. Can you both sit down for a bit while I talk to you?"

Rose and Carol sat down on the customers' chairs used while waiting for service. "This must be pretty heavy, Donovan, for you to visit the salon to talk to both of us," Carol commented.

"Yes, it is, ladies. Rose's mother and I have discussed a way to help you in buying this building if you wish to accept the help. Rose, you are not aware of the fact that shortly after you were born, we set up a college fund for you. We have been investing consistently now for 18 years. The amount has accumulated interest and with the principal the total is $12,050.65. Since you selected the On-the-Job-Training to become a beautician, you will probably not attend college. Carol, you asked Rose for her contribution of $10,000 as a down payment. I have placed the money in your checking account already, my dear daughter. Also, all your earnings of $750.55 from modeling that were in my saving account. Here are the deposit slips for your records."

Carol and Rose looked at each other in utter disbelief. Both stared at Donovan. Their faces revealed the same expressions. The information was momentarily beyond comprehension.

Rose jumped up and moved quickly to where her dad was standing and threw herself into his arms. With tears streaming down her cheeks, and sobbing, "Oh Daddy, I can't believe you would do this for me! I really don't know what to say except 'thank you, thank you, thank you' from the bottom of my heart and soul! This is the nicest thing you have ever done for me! I am truly appreciative! But won't Matthew need some money to go to college one day? I can't take all the money!"

"No need to fret, daughter, for we have also set up a college fund for your brother when he was born. There will be money for him when he graduates from high school, that is if he'll stay in school. Carol, I need to talk to my daughter alone if you don't mind. A family matter."

"I'm out of here. But thank you, Donovan, for your gracious help. We will probably be able to start some negotiations with

Mr. Bolsey. Rose, why don't you and your dad join me at Joe's lounge when you're through," as she bounded out of the door into the street.

"Rose, we are having some horrible problems with Matthew. He is becoming so belligerent, so sassy, so difficult to manage and getting in serious discipline problems in school. His grades have gone down the tube. Your Mother and I were not aware of the great influence you had over your brother when you were home. We know he misses you. But the friends he is associating with are real losers. Matthew is with them too much of the time. We are at our wits end. We thought about asking you to come back home to live, but then we forgot the idea. You have moved out on your own now. I'm sorry now that I forced you to do so. That was a terrible mistake. I hope and pray you can forgive me. However, you must admit, you would not have had this opportunity. Joining Carol in a partnership to buy this building and business is certainly a great opportunity."

"Oh, daddy, this is terrible news about Matthew. Do you want me to sit down with him and perhaps try to talk some sense into that silly head of his?"

"Rose, we may see some light at the end of the tunnel. Reverend Matterling had a seminar at our church for "Helping Your Children Survive Cliques, Gossip, Boyfriends, and Other Problems during Adolescence." Your mother and I attended three sessions and had Matthew join us for the fourth. We didn't think he would go with us, but Pastor Matterling called and asked him to attend. He does respect the Pastor, thank God. We just need to follow through with the techniques we learned and some of the knowledge of methods of discipline we gained from some youth leaders.

But we learned something that we wish we would have known while you were growing up during your teen years. I want to say now how sorry I am for actually not being the father to you that I now know I could have been. I hope that

makes sense to you. We never let you date because we were
so over protective. We now know that getting validation from
boys would have boosted your self-confidence and confirm
that you are growing up to be a woman. We now realize girls
must gain their own social status and identity and these are
tied to relationships with boys. We learned that many girls
will lie, connive, or sneak behind parent's backs to be with a
boyfriend. To our knowledge, you never did this and we are
very grateful. But Matthew is lying and sneaking out of
the house. We did not allow you to help define the difference
between acceptable dating and flirting with boys and what is
sexual harassment. Your mother and I were in full denial to
your developing sexually and we now fear there is much you
do not know about yourself physically and perhaps you may
now have psychological hang-ups. Your mother admits now
that you two never had any serious mother-daughter talks. I
am having these father-son talks now with Matthew. It's difficult discussing sexual matters but the seminar provided us
valuable help. I never told you how much we love you or how
beautiful you are. We learned that you could become trapped
in an abusive relationship when you lack confidence and self-
assuredness regarding men. Oh, Rose, sweetheart, there is so
much more that I want to share with you, but my heart is getting heavy with grief."

Again Rose went to her father and placed her arms around
his waist and buried her head against his chest and starting
crying. He responded in like manner and softly patted Rose
on her back and drew his other hand down the side of her
face and then under her chin. He softly moved her away from
him and looked into her watery eyes.

"You have every right to cry, sweetheart, for it probably has
been building up for some time."

"Oh daddy, my crying tears are those of happiness for you!
I have always loved you and mother with all my heart. You
raised me the very best you two knew how at the time. I was

disappointed that I couldn't date through high school but I was never angry at either of you because of your discipline. I just hope and pray that you can get Matthew straightened out and perhaps become a Marine. Perhaps the Corps will be able to help him!"

"Thank you daughter, for those words of forgiveness. You have made this old man feel much younger. Why don't we go join Carol at Joe's. She is probably wondering why it's taking us so long."

When Rose and her Dad joined Carol in a booth, Joe was talking with her. Carol was laughing so hard, she had placed her hands on her stomach as if it hurt.

"That must have been a whooper, Joe. Do you mind telling us also?" asked Donovan.

"No, but I have some more good ones for all of you. But first, Naomi, would you bring my friends a glass of wine. You can drink wine can't you, Rose?" asked Joe.

"I will this time; we really do have some fantastic reasons to have a toast," replied Rose.

June came and joined them after serving food to the tables in her charge. Rose and Carol told the Reillys all the information about receiving the money gift, the excellent opportunity of buying the building, furnishing of the apartment, and moving in. This indeed was something to be elated about and toasts were properly made.

Mr. McDowell was observing his daughter during the conversation and was never happier for her than he was right at that moment! He relished the smiles and laughter Rose was exhibiting. Inwardly, he was pleased that she had forgiven him. He wished he had been more of a father and shared his love for her a long time ago.

# CHAPTER 11

Rose did not know whether it was fate, good luck, a providential blessing or all three rolled into one. As the glasses of wine were raised for a toast to the new salon adventure, she saw Marvin strolling into the lounge. He was wearing civilian clothes— light blue slacks and a Ralph Lauren Polo shirt, the first time she had seen him dressed as such. She could see the cute little horse and polo player. How different and how handsome he appeared as he approached their booth.

"Well, what celebration am I missing with all those glasses raised and tinkling. I could hear the sounds as soon as I came into the place," challenged Marvin.

Rose, sitting on the outside edge of the booth, put her glass down, jumped up and stood by his side. She looked admiringly into his face.

"Pull up an extra chair and join us. We will bring you up to speed and perhaps have a second toast. Naomi, bring another bottle of wine and another glass, would you please?" ordered Joe.

"Dad, this is Marvin Brown, a good friend that Joe and June introduced to me. We have only known each other a short time. We have plans to attend a dance in two weeks.

We've seen a movie but mostly we have been meeting here at Joe's to enjoy good conversation and to become    better acquainted."

Marvin stood up and extended his hand to Rose's father who clasped Marvin's  and said, "It is indeed a pleasure to meet you, Marvin. Rose is my pride and joy!  I'm becoming prouder of her every day!  Please take good care of her! "

"Mr. McDowell, you can be very certain that I'll do just that.  I'm most pleased to have met this beautiful and talented daughter of yours," replied Marvin with much pride.

Rose then briefly told Marvin of her father's money gift to help Carol in buying the building, moving into the apartment above the salon, and sharing it with Carol.

"You will need a good lawyer to help you in the transaction with Mr. Bolsey," added Joe. "I'll  contact my lawyer and see if he has the time to help you two ladies as clients."

"You will also need a title company to help in the transfer of ownership," added Donovan.  "I will call Robert Dowdy, a member of our church, who owns the Fidelity Abstract and Title Company. He handled the paper work on our house. I'm positive he'll do the work for you as a favor to me."

"Oh, how wonderful to have such caring friends to offer help.  Rose and I really appreciate your advice and support," gushed Carol.

"Well, I certainly didn't know I would be dating an up and coming entrepreneur.  I'm really impressed but mostly very happy for you two lovely ladies going into a partnership. I'll try to urge more customers to fill your appointment books to the bursting point. You may need  to  push out the wall to the rear and install more stations for beauticians," added Marvin.

"Just a minute, Marv, let's take  this one  step at a  time. No talk about expansion until we achieve ownership and moved into the apartment. Carol and I need to furnish the whole place including the kitchen appliances. But your idea of expansion certainly will be placed on the back burner. We may need to hire you as our company CPA when we start growing," Rose kiddingly replied.

"Rose, sweetheart, to help you out, you may have your own bedroom set if you wish. Your mother, I know, would agree. She might enjoy some other bedroom furniture to create a guest room," added Donovan.

"Mr. Bolsey indicated that we may be able to buy all his kitchen appliances. That alone will help us save money toward the cost of buying and moving any new appliances to the apartment. With these extra amenities going for us and the help from you folks, we will certainly have a house warming party in the near future. Joe, Donovan, please let us know as soon as you have contacted your friends whether they will take us as new clients," stated Carol.

Glasses were once again filled with wine and raised.

"To the success of a new adventure for Rose and Carol! May all their business days be full of happiness and success for these two wonderful business ladies!" said Marvin, with his glass held high.

There was a chorus of 'Hear, hear!' and their glasses began to make the rounds of clinking sounds. It could not have been a happier moment!

"HELLO MR. BOLSEY," said Carol, as she gleefully held the phone receiver to her ear. "We are prepared to 'talk turkey' on buying your building and the appliances in the kitchen apartment. When would be the best day for you to meet next week? We wish to have our lawyer sitting in with us. I'm sure you would have no objection to that arrangement," said Carol, as Rose stood close by with an ear next to the receiver trying to listen, also.

"Oh, you name the day and time, Carol. My schedule is

very flexible. I'm so happy to hear you want to buy the building," replied Mr. Bolsey.

"I'll call you again after speaking to our lawyer for a time that is best on his schedule," remarked Carol.

"Terrific! I will anticipate your call," replied Mr. Bolsey.

It was around mid-morning when Carol answered the telephone that rang a few times while trying to finish a customer. Picking up the receiver and placing it between her ear and shoulder while combing, she said, "Hello, this is Carol's Curls and Crewcuts."

"Carol, this is Joe. I called my lawyer, Ed Beardsley, and he indicated he would be most willing to work with you concerning the legalities of your purchase. Just call and arrange an appointment. 857-6200. He is someone you can trust right from the start. So, did you get the number?"

"Yes, thank you, Joe," replied Carol. "We appreciate your help. We'll call him immediately. Mr. Bolsey can meet with us anytime. Now we need to hear from Donovan and we will start the closing transactions."

It was the noon hour and both Carol and Rose were able to take a break at the same time. Retiring to the small lounge for the employees, Rose said, "I'll call my Dad and find out if he has phoned Mr. Dowdy."

At that same moment, the extension phone next to Rose was ringing. She grabbed for the receiver. "Hello, this is Carol's Salon."

"Hello, Rose, this is your dad. Mr. Dowdy is ready to help you. Give him a call. Here is his number to help you from searching. Fidelity Abstract and Title—857-3991. Do you remember his name, Mr. Robert Dowdy?"

"Thank you Daddy. Joe told us to call the lawyer he recommended. Now all we need is to arrange for five of us to meet together at the same time to work out all the detailed paper work. Thanks again, Father," beamed Rose.

"Rose, I told your mother about your friend, Marvin. She is

delighted that you have met this young man. I enjoyed meeting him. Why don't you bring him to dinner sometime soon
so your Mother can meet him and we'll have an opportunity
to visit some more. Good luck in collecting all five of you together to finalize the building purchase and to get all the legal
particulars squared away. Good bye, daughter, we love you."

"Daddy, I am sure that Marvin would love to meet Mother,
and Matthew also. We will make a date to see you very soon.
Love you, too. Good bye."

A huge fear sprang into her thoughts. "He met Marvin but
still doesn't know he's in the Navy! Wow!"

"DIDN'T THINK THIS MOMENT would be possible so soon,"
remarked Carol. "Gathering together in one week's time in
the lawyer's office seemed like mission impossible. Thank you
for being present to hopefully finalization the purchase of Mr.
Bolsey's building."

Both Mr. Beardsley and Mr. Dowdy thanked Mr. Bolsey
for sending them all the preliminary papers needed for
examination to determine if the title was free of any liens and
a complete list of personal property that he would sell to the
new owners. There were a few questions to be answered and
it seemed no time at all before Carol and Rose wrote checks
for the amount of earnest money Mr. Bolsey deemed sufficient
to sign the contract of purchase of the building and to accept
a promissory note for the personal property to remain in the
apartment. The final amount of the purchase price and sign-
ing of all necessary legal papers would take place one week
later after all documents were prepared. Rose and Carol left
the building hand in hand in a most joyous disposition. It was
the beginning of a new adventure for both.

ONE WEEK LATER, ROSE and Carol had all the legal documents proving full ownership of what they found out to be
the 'Worchester Building." Worchester was the person who

first built the building when the whole block of various stores were being erected. They were proud to own a part of Norfolk History.

That same week Rose and Carol found themselves in a whirlwind. Still, they were trying to maintain services for their many customers. By juggling appointments, they managed free time for shopping trips to the various shopping malls to purchase the furnishings for the apartment. They were like two little kids running loose in a candy store. However, their plans of purchases for basic needs helped them from splurging. After all, neither one had all the cash available for wild spending. The extra cushion of cash that Rose's father had given her was a real blessing.

The Reilly's gave them a complete set of dishes for four and a twelve- piece set of cooking utensils as a house warming gift. Rose's dad had borrowed a pickup and had brought Rose's bed room set plus an easy chair that just happened to be the right color for the décor of the living room. He also helped deliver two pickup loads of boxes that Carol had filled at her apartment.

Rose and Carol had squeezed in several runs to their own living places to bring more personal possessions. Having purchased all the appliances in the kitchen solved that large problem.

Sissy and Harry's wife, Sally, arranged a house warming party for them on Friday evening in their new apartment. The two new owners were elated and grateful for the many gifts of linens, towels, glassware, and kitchen utensils.

By Saturday, both were somewhat exhausted but the new adventure created the added adrenaline to maintain full speed. Even Marvin and Chris helped. These two good friends had shopped at the commissary and purchased several boxes of staples and canned goods which were delivered by taxi cab. The two ladies were most impressed with their thoughtfulness and concern.

Yes, they would be spending their first night in their new apartment for which they had their friends to be thankful.

Rose was tired and not too certain she wanted to go dancing. However, she knew she could not disappoint Marvin. At 6 p.m., Marvin arrived to escort Rose to the dance. Before leaving, however, she gave Marvin the 'cook's tour' of the apartment.

"Rose, you and Carol have done a wonder of wonders in furnishing and completing a livable condition in such a short time. I'm really impressed with your choice of décor without having to repaint all the walls first. Mrs. Bolsey certainly provided you two a great favor without your even knowing about it ahead of time. You have no idea how proud I am of you at this moment!"

With that, he gathered Rose into his arms and lowered his lips on hers. She knew what she had to do. The memory of her last kiss came back with a flash. She felt the warm sensation of the softness of his lips on hers. If she had to find the words to describe the euphoria that she felt cascading throughout her body, she knew she would be speechless. As Marvin increased the intensity of his lips upon hers, he moved his tongue between her lips.

Rose jumped back from Marvin as if an electrical current had shocked her.

"Oh, I am so sorry, Marv, but the touch of your kiss this time was like a shock. It was an involuntary reaction!"

With that, she reached up and placed her arms around Marvin's neck and moved her lips to his. This time Rose was prepared for what might happen to her senses of pleasure.

But it ended when Marvin asked, "Are you ready for an evening of more embraces and kisses as we dance?"

Gazing up into his eyes, Rose smiled and realized this was just the beginning of a night that she would undoubtedly remember for a long time—her first passionate kisses—her first dance—her first real date--ever. "Marv is certainly helping me feel like a woman! And it's about time, too. His love is helping to enrich by life adventure."

# CHAPTER 12

"Well good morning sleepy head. You must have had a great time at the dance! I woke up just in time to hear Marvin saying good night. When you came down the hallway to use the bathroom at 1 a.m., you really spooked my boy friend, Hank. I didn't tell him you were also living here. Should have. He immediately scrambled out of bed, dressed and high tailed out of here. I tried to persuade him to 'cool it' but he wouldn't listen to reason. Rather a private individual," Carol said upon hearing Rose walking into the kitchen.

Rose was looking at Carol who was standing by the kitchen counter with her back to the door Rose had just entered. She couldn't help staring at her roommate. Actually Rose's mouth dropped open and was speechless. She couldn't believe what she was seeing. She was in mild shock.

Carol finally turned to look at Rose and saw the look of disbelief on her face. "Are you shocked to see me standing here in just my bra and panties? Well, get used to it, kiddo, this is me, and this is what I desire when working about the house.

Sometimes I prefer to be in the nude. Obviously, you now know I am not modest. Actually I like myself. I like my body a great deal. I have a philosophy about this. It goes: 'A woman should wear lingerie so sweet and sexy, she will be hard pressed to get dressed.' Hey, go nude or wear only what I'm wearing sometime, Rose; how will you know you won't enjoy the sensations you'll experience?"

Rose turned, left the kitchen without saying a word, and returned to her bedroom. She looked at herself in the dresser mirror for several moments. She had never really given any thought as to how much she really liked herself. There certainly wasn't any hate. Carol said she enjoyed her body.

She removed her blouse and dropped her skirt to the floor and stepped out of it. She skinned her full slip off over her head. Then the bra was unhooked. She placed the four items on her bed. She continued to look at herself in the mirror, turning about to view her body from different angles. Marvin kept saying what a beautiful person she was. Dad and mother were just starting to say the same thing. Her girlfriends said she had a perfect figure. She realized that this was the first time she studied her body from a different frame of mind. She realized she had little confidence in herself and knew that steps were needed to rectify that situation. It really did come down to how well she liked herself, how she saw herself as a woman. "There must be so much that needs to be known about myself," she thought. "And Dad apologized for not permitting socializing with friends, accepting dates with boys, and learning more of the physical emotions that she now experienced with Marvin."

With a feeling of boldness, Rose left her room and walked into the kitchen attired in her bra and panties.

"What do you know about that? The beautiful Rose has unfolded from the bud! Seeing you in those smocks we wear at work, I didn't realize what a fantastic figure you have, Rose. I am jealous—green with envy, actually. But who bought you your bra? For your full figure, it's the wrong kind! Being so well endowed, you need wider straps and cups to prevent spilling out. Rose, we need to go on a shopping spree and have you fitted with some lingerie that will enhance your beauty even more. Let's not book any appointments on Monday from four o'clock on and we will, well, you know the saying, 'shop till we drop'."

"To be very honest, Carol, my mother purchased my clothes for me. I really didn't have much to say and never did argue with her even though there were times when I preferred something else. I was grateful for what new items I did receive. Thank you for wanting to help. There is so much I probably don't know. You are well experienced when it comes to matters of being loved and making love. You do realize the date with Marvin last night would be considered my first real date. It was fabulous! We danced every number the band played. It was such a sensation to be in his arms and having our bodies so close and his kissing me so many times. Now I wish I were taller. It is difficult to dance cheek to cheek when they don't touch due to Marvin's height. But when ever I looked up at his face, he planted kisses on me. It was truly a romantic evening! Carol, may I ask you some personal questions. The answers may help me understand my emotions and sensations whenever we are embracing and kissing so intimately."

"Rose, I will help you all you wish. We'll spend some time later and chat. You may have more questions. As you know, I enjoy being loved and making love. Two of my boyfriends live in Richmond and when they are here in Norfolk on business, our place and my bed becomes a hotel for them. Hope you don't mind now that we are sharing the same apartment. So far, they both have not been in Norfolk at the same time. I'm keeping my fingers crossed though. I imagine living by myself for so long may have spoiled me. We need to come to some understanding in using our apartment to entertain our boyfriends. I'm sure you will have Marvin up here longer than

just a good night kiss as you did this morning. It will be difficult for you to stay in your room indefinitely when you will
need the bathroom. Walking by my bedroom may cause Hank
some problems as it did this morning. I think Eddie could
care less."

"Carol, I have an idea. I thought about it this morning
when using the bathroom. You know I have a huge walk in
closet that Mrs. Bolsey must have had built. Why don't we
install a stool and sink? On the other side of the wall is our
kitchen. All the plumbing is right there. Why don't we ask Mr.
Bolsey about the plumber who did his kitchen remodeling?
A half bath will also help us in the mornings when we both
need the bathroom at the same time."

"Rose, you smarty pants, you! What a brilliant idea! Let's
call him right now. Maybe we can find out and start remodeling immediately. Having your own half bath would really be
super for both of us, if you catch my drift? Eddie and I enjoy
making love while bathing."

Carol saw Rose blushing and realized her words were too
personal.

They were lucky to catch Mr. Bolsey at his nephew's house.
He was leaving for Richmond early on Monday morning.
Obtaining the name of the plumber used, Carol and Rose sur-
veyed the large closet.

After eye-balling it for a couple minutes, Carol asked,
"Don't you think there is room to install a shower in addition to the lavatory and sink? I believe there is enough space.
Certainly can't install a tub. Let us ask the plumber and get
his opinion. Do you like showers, Rose? There will be times,
of course, when you can use the tub when we are here by ourselves. By the way, what's your reaction to walking around in
your next to nothing?"

"It's so-o-o different! Words are difficult to find to explain
the physical sensations I am experiencing. It's different from
when I showered in gym classes. I was always so embar-

rassed in the nude when the other girls were present. They kept staring at me. Perhaps because my breasts were so large compared to theirs. I hated gym for that reason. Thank goodness I wasn't required to take gym my junior and senior year when working for you half days with the On-the-Job-Training Program. But we will keep this to ourselves, won't we? Won't others think we're gay, or lesbians running around in the nude?"

"You could be right, Rose. This is no body's business but ours. We are far from being lesbians, I can assure you. I prefer everything there is about men and men only. I'm fast creating the impression you will go for men also now that you've broken the ice, so to speak, in dating Marvin. Come to think about it, I need to call Eddie and tell him about our new apartment. He doesn't know I have moved, yet. Boy, will he be surprised! You know, Rose, I need to decide which of the two men would be the better to marry. I never have been in a hurry to have children. Trouble is, I care for both guys for different reasons. But my biological clock is ticking away and I really do want a family one day. I envy you in another way , Rose—your youth! Oh to be 18 once again!"

"I need to dress. I permitted Marvin to drive my car back to the base last night or rather this morning. He's arriving in an hour and we're going to my folks for dinner. My dad requested me to bring Marvin home so Mother can meet him. I wonder what he will say when he finds out that Marv is a United States Navy enlisted man? Do you suppose I will start World War III? By the way, Dad has changed so much in the past week or so, maybe he will not invoke the wrath like that of Genghis Khan on his rampages. Just need to wait out the fireworks!"

"You certainly have a way with words! Must be all that education you received. I dropped out of high school during my 9th grade, started doing beautician work, and attending beauty college at nights. It was rough going for me! This is between you and me and the doorknobs -- I left school because I was pregnant. However, I had a miscarriage. May have been a blessing in disguise. I have been extremely careful ever since in my sexual relationships. Word to the wise, Rose, be very careful when you and Marvin..., well, you know, initiate your bed."

"Carol, that's a terrible thing to say! That's not going to happen! Marvin and I have already discussed the matter of having sex. My mother told me to save my innocence until I am married. I made that promise to myself, too. Marvin honors that. He is more religious than I am. He has a morality value system that is super. There are times when I think about being loved by Marvin and wonder what the feelings my body would experience. Would it help me to really feel like a woman? In a way, I envy you because of all the loving you have had and undoubtedly will continue to have. There are times already when I don't desire to practice abstinence. How do you know when you're ready? What does it feels like? My girlfriends said that sex hurts at first. Is that true?"

"Rose, I have a book in my bedroom that I think will help you immensely. I'll try to find it for you to read." Carol went to her bedroom and returned with the book. "It's called 'Women's Responses on Sex' by Laura Heggle. The book was written by a woman for women. She asked over 2,000 ladies over 40 very personal questions. The answers to those questions will help you to know more about yourself through the frank answers given. Since no names were used with the comments, the ladies pulled no punches. They answered from a gut level. I believe this will help you with much information on masturbation, orgasms, intercourse, birth control, and other female sexuality topics. It certainly helped me when I read it. I don't know why I still have the book, but glad I do now for your sake. It may answer your questions. If not, we'll have that heart to heart chat."

"Thank you Carol. Living with you may be just the answer

to a maiden's prayer. There is so much you can tell me, also what books to read that can help me gain the self-confidence that I'm lacking. I sense the problem but don't know what to do to receive answers. I have mixed up feelings."

"Rose, we can be like sisters. I will share what ever I know that may help you. As I said before, I am not modest and will call a spade a spade. Just feel free to ask. I'm of the thought that there are no dumb questions when asked in all sincerity."

"Thanks again, Carol. I'll take you up on that offer. But excuse me, I really do need to change clothes. Are you going to dress or will Marvin see you running about like a jay bird?"

"Perhaps he should see us like we are right now! Not sure if he would be shocked or thrilled? No, I am only kidding. I'll dress, too. But hasn't' this been a fun time, chatting freely, and bonding? I'm looking forward to our business adventure and sharing the apartment. You are a darn right beautiful sister, if I might say so!"

"Carol, the feelings are mutual! You are indeed more than a friend! Yes, you truly are like a sister. Wow, never thought I'd ever have one! This is more than GREAT! IT'S TERRIFIC!" as Rose grabbed Carol's hands and the two began to twirl.

"Rose, before going to dress, how did you acquire what appears to be a lovely suntan? No white marks on your body from straps might indicate sunning in the nude somewhere. Come young lady, what's the explanation?"

"Carol, I've been slipping over to the Golden Tan Salon across from our place. Been doing this a few times during my lunch break. Hope you don't mind?"

"Not at all, Rose. Your tan actually makes you look sexy. Really!"

"Thank you, didn't realize that would be the case."

"Your tan prompts my brains! Our storeroom could be the ideal place to install a tanning bed. Do you think our customers would desire getting a tan?"

"Why don't we conduct a survey?"

"Rose, your suggestions are so right on the mark! We'll ask everyone the next couple weeks."

Rose returned to her bedroom with Carol's book.  As she walked to her room, she scanned the table of contents.  The topics intrigued her.  She knew immediately this was priority reading.  She realized how much information she needed to know.  Much like cramming for important tests when in high school.  But this information was even more important right now than the contents of any high school textbook  she had ever read!

# CHAPTER 13

"Mother, this is Marvin Brown, who has only five months left of his active duty in the Navy. He is a storekeeper aboard a destroyer, the DD 789. We have known each other around a month. Joe and June introduced us to each other," stated Rose, as she became rather breathless trying to say all the information in one breath.

"Mrs. Brown, it is more than a pleasure to meet you," replied Marvin as he warmly clasped Maureen's right hand into his. "Mr. Brown, we have already met but a pleasure seeing you again," as he released Maureen's hand and shook Donovan's. And this must be your brother, Matthew," as he held up his right hand and they gave each other a high five. "Rose, I can see where you acquired all your rare beauty for your mother is as beautiful as you are. I understand that you both are reluctant to having your daughter date a member of any military service, especially a sailor. Am I here on dangerous ground or has a truce been declared for today?" as Marvin produced a huge smile while casting glances at both parents.

"Marvin, I had a long talk with Joe and June. They pointed out how wrong my thinking was about you. I'm not going into details; Rose has undoubtedly told you about her not dating anyone until she met you. Her mother and I have been so wrong in so many ways. Some of this we've shared with Rose already. I read where a wise person once said, 'Your friends are God's way of apologizing for your family.' That is a powerful statement, but there is no denying that friends constitute an important part of a happy and fulfilled life. We have denied Rose of this her entire life. We should have been encouraging her friendships with her friends in school as part of nurturing her development. We didn't let her interact with her friends in any birthday parties, sleepovers, or other events in school. I even made her quit a rewarding modeling job. What I am trying to say, Marvin, is that we are giving our full blessing to you dating our daughter. I only hope that Rose will forgive us for what we have done in the past. We were just too protective of her and realize now that she is the one to suffer from our actions," Donovan said, as a look of great anguish was reflected on his face.

"Mr .and Mrs. McDowell," Marvin said, but stopped when interrupted.

"Please call us Donovan and Maureen, Marvin. Let's be informal in our becoming acquainted with each other," replied Donovan.

"I appreciate the frankness of your comments, Donovan, for I could see on your face the pain you are experiencing. You have reared a daughter that has the characteristics and moral values that I deem outstanding qualities in a woman. It is I that should be honored to be with such great beauty and a personality that I've enjoyed in our short time together. Thank you for your blessing on our friendship. Please do not be so hard on yourselves, Maureen, Donovan. I realize that you were doing what you thought best at the time."

"And Matthew, it's my understanding that you have been

giving your parents some grief in your lack of self discipline. I'm sorry to hear this. I've seen some of my buddies receiving a court martial and booted out of the Navy with dishonorable discharges for not practicing self-discipline. Their actions will affect them the rest of their lives. Matthew, my dad told me something when I was your age that has been a guide in my life. 'The world is full of wonderful people that you want as friends. If you can't find one, consider being one yourself.' I have found this to be so true. Your sister is one of those wonderful persons! She tells me you are a great brother! I'm very proud of you for your affection for her. Continue to be that wonderful person and with self discipline, your life will become a better, successful, and   opportunities will come your way  because of the wonderful friends you'll meet. How about another high five?"

As   Marvin held up his hand waiting for Matthew to hit his, tears began  rolling down Matthew's  cheeks. "Dad and Mom, I am sorry for being such a stupid jerk. I know you have been trying to change my behavior. My counselor at school has been trying to help me for some time now. What Marvin said makes good sense. I want to be like him. I want to work with computers as he does and enlist in the military service when I graduate. I'll really start to study, apply myself, and earn better grades than I have been. The teachers keep telling me I have the ability but I know I'm not doing my best. I want to be the brother that Rose will be real proud of. You too, Mom and Dad."

Rose, with tears rolling down her checks and sobbing, rushed to her brother and gave him a big embrace. "Oh Matthew, I'm so proud of you! I truly love you little brother! Believe me when I say, you have found one true friend in knowing Marvin!"

"The food is on the table," suggested Maureen, "Let's eat while it's hot!"

The dinner proceeded with  great  conversation. Rose

was pleased. The tension she expected to take place never materialized. Everyone share their experiences. Smiles and laughter abounded. Many questions were directed to Marvin on his Navy experiences and future plans on discharge. He kept everyone entertained and enchanted. Rose looked on with much admiration and marveled at Marvin's social qualities with her family.

Dinner being finished, Marvin reached into his pocket and said, "Rose, here is the list of dates when we can schedule sight seeing, swimming at the beach, and shopping. Donovan, Rose desires to show me some of the tourist attractions and the beaches in the Norfolk area. We are looking forward to spending some time together in the next months."

"As I already said, you have our blessings. Have a wonderful time together," added Donovan.

Marvin shook hands with Donovan, gave Maureen a gentle hug, and another high five with Matthew. Saying good bye, Rose and Marvin left the house for the car..

Tossing the keys to Marvin and stepping into the passenger side, Rose said, "Here, you drive. I wish to study the list of dates and start writing down where we can go with the amount of time available to accomplish as much as possible in the time left. This is going to be so much fun!"

CAROL LEFT THE APARTMENT and went to the Bar and Grill. Not seeing anyone she knew, she slid into the booth by the kitchen door reserved for the help. Joe came out of the kitchen very hurriedly and scared Carol.

"Goodness gracious! You gave me a fright! What are you doing here on a Sunday?" asked Carol. "I thought you took Sundays off and let Pete take charge."

"Pete had an emergency call for one of his relatives who was hospitalized. I came in to relieve him a while ago."

"You are a thoughtful person, Joe. By the way, do you know

that Rose took Marvin to meet her Mother this noon?   I wonder how that turned out!"

"Carol, I don't believe there will be any trouble.  I had a lengthy chat with Donovan about Marvin  dating his daughter.  I tried to talk some sense into him about his terrible attitude.  I related that Marvin is not a sex maniac but a down to earth lad with a high set of moral values and a genuine gentleman.  Donovan has also changed his thinking since he took that seminar at their church.  He certainly doesn't have that macho Marine over- bearing attitude anymore.  He told me that he spoke to Rose and regretted the  poor manner in which  he and Maureen reared  Rose during her teenage years.  I am so thankful that Marvin is an understanding person and will help Rose in many ways changing  from a teenage girl to that of a woman.  You can  help now that you are in the same apartment."

"As a matter of fact, I have already started," replied Carol, "We had a long talk today and how wonderful it is  sharing the apartment.  It's like having a younger sister.  Rose considers me  her older sister.  There is much that I can do to help Rose.  She certainly has an innocent approach to many ideas and personal knowledge.  Perhaps June can be part of the plan also.  Those two have a great rapport and trust in each other."

"Carol, you are so right.  I will speak to June about it now that Rose is no longer living with us.  Speaking of those two love birds, look who just walked  in this very moment! Come over and join us, you two.  We are anxious to know what happened at your place, Rose," Joe said excitedly.

"Everything is simple hunky-dory.  The situation couldn't be better  As a matter of fact, Donovan gave us  his  blessing on our dating.  He and his wife were most gracious.  I even tried to help them with Matthew and may have made some inroads on his lack of discipline.  What do you think, Princess?" asked Marvin.

"Carol, Joe, my dad and mom were two different people

when Marvin came into the room. Marv has a fantastic power
that seemed to permeate the place," Rose said, as she slipped
her arm up over his shoulder and gazed into his face. "I simply
stood back in awe and watched the whole scene take place
before my eyes as he spoke to my parents and to Matthew. It
was as if Marv was spinning some magic spell! It is difficult to
tell you what I saw and how I felt but it was a wonderful and
happy occasion. I don't know what you told my Dad, Joe, but
what ever it was, you must have spun some magic yourself."

" Marvin, Carol and I were just talking about your reception and wondering what type of a reaction took place when
Rose introduced you to her mother. Of course, Donovan had
already met you here in this booth. That was a plus from the
start. What I told Donovan about you should have set him
straight as to your personal qualities. But what ever happened, we are both so pleased that you two can see each other
freely and become acquainted romantically. Who knows,
perhaps you will consider inviting us to your wedding one day.
Eh what!"

"Joe, my friend, that may not be too far fetched," replied
Marvin, as he put his arm around Rose's shoulder and pulled
her to him and planted a soft lingering kiss on her lips.

"Hey you two. Would you name the first kid after me?"
teased Carol.

Breaking the kiss, Rose replied, "Stop it you two! You're
making me blush! But I'll get even with you yet. Just you wait!
But we came here to see you, Joe, before going to the base
to see a movie. I want a coke. Do you want a coke, Marv?
We can give our orders to Joe since he is the chef, apparently.
What happened to Pete? Doesn't he work Sundays? Where is
June today? Don't you have a few 'honey-does' on your list at
home?"

"Man alive, you're full of questions, Rose. Are you writing
a book? Pete had an emergency so I'm his relief. June is at
home doing the bookkeeping. You both want a coke, right?

I'll go fix them. You two should order some passion fruit if we had it. What movie are you going to see?" asked Joe.

"Julia Roberts in 'The Run Away Bride,'" replied Rose.

"Oh ho, going to pick up some pointers for the future, perhaps?" teased Joe.

"Oh, Joe, give me a break! You have picked on me enough already. Go chase yourself into the kitchen and get our cokes, would you please? We don't want to be late for the movie," pleaded Rose.

"Rose, you know, I love you like a daughter. Just trying to get under your skin as a friend so one day when a stranger tries the same, you'll know how to cope with the situation. Your order will be here in a jiffy!" replied Joe.

Carol left the lounge to return to the apartment. She wanted to give the two their space to be alone.

Rose and Marvin studied the schedule of days when he would have liberty. They started to write in the places they wanted to visit. Both were anxious to start traveling about the greater Norfolk area. As Marvin studied the maps, Rose gazed at him. There was so much that she wanted to show Marvin. She knew about many places but never had the opportunity to visit. With her parent's blessings, they were free spending time together with no thoughts regarding sneaking about the countryside.

"Marv, you said something a few minutes ago when Joe was kidding about inviting him to our wedding. You said something to the effect that getting married was a possibility. Did you really mean that or were you going along with Joe's type of humor? I'm confused."

Marv took her hands into his and began to lovingly caress them. He gazed into her eyes and saw the doubt and confusion. "Princess, it appears that you caught me between what is called the proverbial rock and a hard place. I wish you to know that I have been wrestling with my own feelings concerning us. Rose, I have never been in love with anyone before. When does  strong feelings for someone turn into deep affection and unending love?  The type of love for one another that is strong, vibrant, and  everlasting—like what is said in marriage vows—'unto death do us part.' As I told your folks, they reared a daughter with wonderful qualities desirable in a wife.  In the short time we have been together, my liking you is gradually growing beyond those feelings.  You possess such loveable qualities, and your beauty is beyond my wildest expectation.  Never have I met someone like you who has this rare beauty  and  not  aware of what that vision does to me. Probably to other men as well.  I really can't speak for them. But for me, Princess, caring for you has certainly moved to loving you!"

"Oh Marv, your words are causing my heart to beat faster. You are trying to find the words to describe your feeling towards me.  You know you are the first man I have every met and dated.  I care for you far more that I can find words to describe my feelings.  Never being in love before, either, I don't understand  all the parts and pieces of  deep romantic love."

"Princess, our love is growing without a doubt.  How romantic our love becomes will be  tested by our actions and days spent in each other's presence."

"That is very true.  The more that you are loving and trusting me, the more I feel accepted.  And the more I feel accepted, the more open my feelings are with you.  And the more we are open and communicating with each other, the more I desire to be with you.   If we become more intimate, perhaps the more our love will grow.   Does that make sense?  I do know when you embrace me and kiss me passionately,  my whole body feels completely alive, excited, and  tingly.  But I don't know if that is my body and mind saying to me that I love you.  I have nothing to compare, but your kisses causes my whole body to react and seems to release great feelings of love within me. June told me that I may experience what she called 'chemistry.' Do you feel a chemistry between us?"

"My precious Rose, you have described your feelings in a remarkable way. I understand precisely what you are trying to say. Yes, I feel there is a type of chemistry developing between us that is healthy."

"Marv, there's another problem that's bothering me. What happens to us when you discharged and go back to Denver? What happens to our relationship? You know that I just can't leave with you because of my financial interest in the beauty salon with Carol. On the other hand, you may not want me. We are only going steady, I guess. Do you want me in your life? As I tried to express my feelings for you, I don't want to lose you, Marv."

Marvin stood and moved around the table to sit beside Rose. He placed his arm around her shoulder and pulled her close to his chest. He kissed her cheek and placed his face against her temple. "Oh Princess, I do want you in my life. Why don't we continue to work on that chemistry between us. All these activities we have planned will provide the opportunity to spend many precious hours together. We can do this right up to my discharge. Then we'll plan for you to fly to Denver for Thanksgiving and spend a week or whatever length of time you decide to spare from your beauty shop. I know my family will love you to pieces. Mother has asked me twice already to send pictures of you or us. My camera was stolen so I'll buy another so we can photograph the places we are visiting and mail some pictures to her. How does that fit into your feelings and thinking?"

"Oh Marv, that causes my heart to beat faster. With you wanting me to meet your family, I feel your protection and a feeling of security. With my body just beginning to have delicious feelings and you wanting me, my senses are all alert and energized."

Rose turned in Marv's arms to face him, placed her arms around his neck, closed her eyes, and opened her mouth to invite his kisses.

Marvin did not disappoint her. They held the passionate kiss until Joo approached their booth.

Joe jokingly said, "Hey you two, this is a respectable establishment. With the rising heat from this area of the room, folks may start to complain. May just need to start charging you rent for use of the booth.   But weren't you two going to the movies?"

"Joe, Rose and I had some important concerns that we needed to discuss and come to some conclusions. It had to do with our relationship and the short time left before my discharge."

"Yes, I can imagine that could  cause complications. But knowing you two wonderful kids, you have answers. Right?"

Rose responded, "Yes we do,  Joe. Have I really  thanked you with all  my heart and soul for introducing this handsome and wonderful sailor to me?"

Joe sat down opposite the couple.  Reaching for Rose's hand and with a fatherly caress, said, "Rose, my affection and love for you is like an adopted daughter.  My concerns for you would be meeting the right guy that may lead to a life time commitment. By knowing you both separately, there was this gut feeling that you two could be great for each other."

"If gratitude is being bandied about, then my appreciation goes to you, Joe, for your winsome and clever methods to introduce this beautiful woman."

Joe arose from the booth. "You two can stay here and talk as long as you like. We are not that busy tonight for some reason. As I said before, you two have  problems you wish to iron out. Communication is a fantastic tool. June and I have never been angry toward one  another  in  our  21 years of marriage. We communicate on every level—our lives, our business, our love making, our spiritual needs, our financial needs, our emotional needs—you name it.  May I suggest that you two agree right from the beginning to communicate all aspects of your lives. Permit me to order something to eat and to refresh your drinks."

Rose and Marvin continued to do just what their mutual friend suggested. They continued a vibrant and meaningful conversation until closing time.

Rose drove Marvin to his ship. On parting, he gave Rose a longing hug and kiss.

As he walked to his ship and as Rose returned home, both came to the same conclusion that their parting kiss took upon itself an intense communication and deeper intimacy than ever before. Chemistry was, indeed, kicking in.

# CHAPTER 14

MARVIN HAD TWO MONTHS of service before being discharged. They both were aware of the fact that their time had
to be used wisely. There was so much that the two wanted to
accomplish. Rose realized she had to sacrifice some of her
time at the salon. This became easier than she thought when
Carol, Sissy, and "Clips" cooperated beyond Rose's expectation
by taking some of her customers. After all, she could not completely refuse her customers service, for when one left to go
to another salon, the chances of returning again became nil.
Besides, she needed some income.

Marvin was able to free more time than he realized he
would have available. He had temporarily forgotten about
all the leave time that had been accumulating. Arrangements
with his ship's Executive Officer permitted him to take some of
that leave time that had accrued. If he did not take the leave
time before discharge, the time could be lost.

Using the schedule of days Marvin would be free from duties on his ship and Rose juggling customers on her appoint-

ment book to free the same days, they found that two days a week and every other week end could be used for the activities planned. Both were ecstatic over the prospects of spending their time together..

THEIR FIRST ADVENTURE was a day at Virginia Beach. Both had donned their bathing suits under jeans and t-shirts when dressing for the day. Carol helped Rose prepare a picnic basket of food including a bottle of wine. She also rolled two towels in a blanket and squeezed it between the handles.

Placing the basket in the trunk, Rose drove to the base. With the issued pass, she drove to the parking area on the pier near the mooring of DD 789. A toot on the horn and Marvin soon came running to the car. Jumping quickly in the front seat, Marvin moved over and gave Rose a lingering kiss. Some catcalls from sailors walking by caused them to stop. Both looked to see who broke their warm reception.

"Well, are you ready to walk the surf and ride in on some breakers, Princess?" asked Marvin. "And by the way, in looking up Virginia Beach on the website, we have over 20 miles of unbroken sand and surf at our disposal. That is one big beach!"

"And we can also visit the Virginia Marine Science Museum that is nearby also," chimed in Rose. "That visit and lolling on the beach will fill the day easily. And there is a lunch basket in the trunk that Carol helped me prepare. Marv, you have heard it said that 'today is the first day of your life.' With you beside me, our growing love for one another, my folks giving us their blessing to spend time together, Carol and the gang helping to take my appointments, I've never felt happier. Truly this is the first day of my life."

"Rose, you gorgeous creature, you are becoming a romantic. But what are we doing sitting here in the parking lot on the Naval Base when what we want to do are miles away," challenged Marvin. "Get this baby in gear, sweetheart, and lets get the rubber meeting the road!"

With Marvin as co-pilot, maps in hand, and a GPS instrument checked out from his ship, he was able to direct the 25 miles to a parking lot at one of big hotels that lined the beachfront.

"Shall we get a room in the hotel and just forget the beach, Princess?" Marvin jokingly stated.

"WHAT? Did I hear you correctly?" Looking at the grin on Marvin's face, she knew immediately he was teasing her. "What would have been your come back had I said, 'Yes, Sailor Boy, let's go"?"

"Without a doubt, Princess, I would have had to take full responsibility to maintain your innocence as we have previously discussed. Let's move. Pop the trunk on your key clicker and I'll grab the picnic basket. Glad this is a weekday. The crowd must be huge on weekends. I see a spot where we might have more privacy."

Arriving at the area desired, Marvin spread the blanket. Both stripped off their t-shirts and crawled out of their jeans. Each was aware of exposing so much of their body in each other's presence for the first time. Both eye-balled each other for a moment.

"Rose, darling, you have a magnificent figure! You are absolutely stunning! That bikini does you justice! I see why they hired you as a model. Are you fully aware of your natural beauty? In the brief time we've spent together, you nonchalant approach about yourself is so evident. You do love everything about yourself, don't you?"

"Marvin, please. I know I lack self confidence but I'm beginning to like myself. Carol and I had a long chat about this. I should be more proud of myself but you're causing me embarrassment."

Rose quickly sat down on the blanket, grabbed the corners, and pulled them up around her shoulders.

Quickly sitting down beside her, Marvin placed his arms around her and pulled her close. "Oh, Rose, Sweetheart, I'm sorry. I never intended to cause you embarrassment. That's the last thing I'd ever want to do to you. I know you are not obsessed about your beauty. Your sheltered teenage years have not given you the constant reassurance needed. Your folks admitted they failed to keep validating your femininity through high school years. Now that we are dating, I sense you are simultaneously confused from decisions and responsibilities placed on your shoulders at the salon, desirous to be a women as opposed to a teenager, having feelings of sexuality from our embracing and passionate kissing, anxious to please me —Princess, please don't be so hard on yourself."

Dropping the blanket, Rose placed her arms around Marvin's neck. "You are so perceptive, Marv. Your description of me is on the mark. It's like you're in my head. I'm pleased you are so patient with my total situation. Our God has given you the gift of endearment with which you are surrounding me. Thank you!"

Breaking into a big smile, Rose jumped up, pushed Marvin down on his back, and ran toward the surf, yelling, "Last one in is a rubber duck!"

Thinking that Marvin was running behind her, Rose ran even faster and dove into the breaker wave coming into shore.

However, Marvin sat up again, and remained on the blanket. He watched with absolute astonishment and delight the antics that Rose just displayed. His smile was one of amusement as he shook his head in disbelief of the transformation that just took place— from huddling under the blanket to throwing herself into the water in jubilation. Wow!

When Rose gained her stability in the water, she stood up and searched for Marvin thinking he was beside her. When she did not find him, a moment of panic went through her until she saw him still sitting on the blanket. He was waving at her.  Walking out of the surf, she ran back to the blanket, pushed Marvin on his back, and sat on his chest.

"There, you stinker, that's a dirty trick.  I'll fill you full of salt water and sand.  You made a fool out of me! For that you get to spread sun tan lotion all over my body.  My skin burns easily."

"If that's my sentence, then my punishment will be delightful!"

Assuming the sun tan lotion was in the basket, Marvin lifted the lid and pulled out the bottle.  Rose laid on her stomach with her arms stretched out waiting for Marvin's application.

Marvin began to spread the lotion to her back. "Princess, do you realize when in the water your flesh-colored bikini causes you to appear as if skinny dipping?"

"What in the world is skinny dipping?"

"Going swimming in the nude!"

Rose glanced up at his face. "You're joking with me, aren't you?  Guess not! I didn't want to buy this suit in the first place. I picked out a full one-piece suit that would cover more of me. This suit creates feelings that too much of my body is exposed. But shopping with Carol and not being bashful in the least, she told me I should show my figure to the world or at least you would be pleased."

"Tell Carol she is absolutely right on her observation if you bought the suit for my eyes. Bikinis certainly do not leave much to the imagination.  Princess, I'm enjoying my punishment!"

For the next few minutes, each took turns applying the lotion to each other's exposed skin. Both felt the closeness through this intimate act.  No words were spoken but the gazes into each other's eyes spoke volumes. There were times when their faces pulled together like magnets and tender kisses were shared.

"There is still one part of me you need to apply lotion." Rose sat up with her back to Marvin.  Grabbing a towel, she held it

ROSE'S ROMANCE: THIRD TIME CHARM 103

in front of her. "O.K. Marv, pull my top down and apply the lotion to my breasts."

"You're not serious, Princess?"

"Yes I am! My boobs can sunburn, too. In reading my books Carol loaned me, there is a chapter on "Touching is Sex, Too." This is a book on a nationwide study on female sexuality. Many women state that most men are inconsiderate regarding the basic needs involving touching and closeness as a means of communing with his significant other. Remember what Joe told us yesterday? Communications? In reading the many comments by women, I realize my senses have been asleep for a long time. I'm realizing that I'm finally waking up. The sensations are exhilarating. You know that I really dig our kissing, hugging, looking at me in a special way, expressing our feelings, but I want to experience you caressing me. So please start now before I lose my nerve!"

Marvin loaded his hands with lotion. As he reached under the towel and began to caressingly spread the oil, Rose leaned against Marvin's chest and involuntarily drew in her breath and began to moan from the heightened sensitivity being created.

"Rose, your whole body is shaking. Should I continue?"

"Oh yes, the sensations are greater than I ever imagined! You make my whole body feel alive, so sensuous, so energizing, I feel a sweaty hotness and it's not from the sun, either. Oh, Marv, your touch, how exhilarating! Oh how sensual! Oh, Marv, you better stop! Please pull my top back up so I can lower this towel! "

"You wanted to cover yourself because of your modesty?"

"No, silly, because of the 'Thong Law.' "

"The 'Thong Law'? What's that?"

Rose proceeded to tell Marvin what Carol had related to her. She and Eddie were on this same beach a month ago. They both stripped their suits and rubbed each other with sun tan lotion. As they were basking in the sun, two men approached and issued them a citation for indecent exposure. They were told that the beach was public, not private or a nudist section. It was illegal for women to swim or sunbathe topless. The law also says men and women can not expose their bottoms with less than a full opaque covering. It did not make sense to them.  So the local folks call this the 'Thong Law.'

"Wow, one does learn something new every day. That law takes the prize! Oh well!

Princess, do you wish to know that ever since we became acquainted, I had this fantasy of gently caressing your whole body?  What you allowed me to do  to have that fantasy become a reality  is beyond my wildest imagination.  You become even more precious in my sight!"

"My sweet sailor, it was my pleasure to fulfill your fantasy. Because  of  our  long talk yesterday and your feelings and confidence placed in me, I  decided for us both  to experience what ever sensations would happen.  I'm still trying to come back to normal.  What an exhilarating sensation! Wow!  I sense your enjoyment, too. "

"Your boldness did surprise me!  But then I'm learning fast what makes you tick!"

"You realize that most  women wish to go topless when sunbathing.  They do not desire  the white stripes on their bodies from straps, bra tops, and string ties"

"Rose, I noticed you do not have any of these stripes. Yet you have some what of a tan. You certainly do not have white skin. How do you account for this?"

"I cheat."

"You cheat? That's ridiculous.  How can you cheat?"

"I haven't told anyone except Carol; I have been going to the Golden Tan Salon that's opposite our shop on Mulberry Street during  some of my lunch breaks.  Going  out the back door of our salon,  I walk cross the alley, and enter Milly's place.  I strip, rub down with a special lotion, crawl in the tanning bed for 10 minutes at a time, and Presto! Instant tan! No white stripes! Been doing that for several weeks now."

"Sweetheart, you continue to amaze me. Your tan causes you to look sexy!"

"Hum-m. Carol said the same thing. We have been considering installing a tanning bed, also. Our problem is rearranging our shop to accommodate this additional service for our customers."

With each fully oiled, they basked in the sun rolling occasionally from their backs to their stomach. They held hands with eyes fixed on each other. No words were spoken but the connection of their clasped hands formed a bridge for unspoken thoughts to cross.

"I'm getting hungry," as Rose popped up in a sitting position and reached for the basket.

"Let's try some of that fried chicken whose aromas have been tantalizing my taste buds while allowing Old Sol to shine upon us."

"Here, you can uncork the wine. Carol made the sandwiches but I did not see what filling she used."

Marvin took a bite, "Oh, one of my old time favorites-- peanut butter and grape jelly!"

"My favorite, too! Isn't that marvelous to know we have similar tastes?"

Rose placed the chicken, sandwiches, potato chips, and peanut butter cookies on the blanket, closed the lid to form a table, and moved the glasses on top. Marvin filled them with the wine.

"Here's a toast for the fantastic times we'll be able to share. May we both continue in our growing love and gain personal confidence with one another in the days ahead!"

Pressing glasses together, Rose added, "Marv, so many times I respond like a school girl. Thank you for helping me to experience the woman I desire to become for you and my folks. Speaking of folks, have you heard from either of yours?

You haven't talked about them lately. Hopefully, one day the pleasure will be mine in our meeting. Bottoms up!"

"Down the hatch!"

Gazing into each other's eyes, they slowly sipped the wine in confirming the toast to the fullest.

Marvin lowered his glass. "My mother and sister are fine. However, mother's letters indicate my dad is having some mild heart problems. He has high blood pressure. Our doctor keeps monitoring his progress. I sense her concern and plan to call her tomorrow."

The picnic food being consumed, both dressed again in their jeans and t-shirts. Rose placed everything back in the basket and picked it up. Marvin grabbed the blanket, shook off the sand, and folded it. Each having a hand free to clasp, the happy couple made their way to the car, weaving in and around other people using the beach. Arriving at the car, depositing the basket in the trunk, they drove to the Museum.

After paying the admission cost, they became overwhelmed with the enormity of the facility. Watching the sharks in the 300,000 gallon salt water tank was frightening for Rose. Moving to another 800,000 gallon aquarium, they were enthralled with the antics of the harbor seals, dolphins, and river otters. Both were glad that shortening their sunbathing afforded more time to view all the exhibits. They ended their excursion with an exciting film about sea life shown in the huge 3-D I-Max Theater.

While driving home, Marvin shared his heartfelt thanks for Rose's desires to enjoy what Norfolk had to offer. Anticipation increased as they discussed the next outing by more sunbathing on the beach, then taking in the sights and sounds of the Back Bay National Wildlife Refuge.

Both were as excited as a child receiving that first bright and shiny bicycle!

# CHAPTER 15

"THANK YOU GUYS, FOR taking my customers yesterday. I really appreciate the sincere gesture in helping me. Marvin would want to thank you, too. We had a marvelous time. I don't know how it could have been any better," Rose said during an unusual time when none had a customer.

As the employees looked upon Rose, her demeanor spoke louder than her words. The pleasant expression on her face was apparent.

"What exactly did you do that made the day so exciting? Did Marvin ask to marry you and give you an engagement ring? Give girl, we all want to know!" demanded Carol.

"Did you set a wedding date?" asked Sissy.

"Oh you characters! Get real, will you? Nothing like that happened. Although that would be different! No, we just did fun things together. We spent a half day sunbathing, I jumped into a breaker wave once, but Marv didn't desire to swim.

Claims he has spent more time on water than he wishes

to think about. We just talked and shared some very close moments together. We had a delicious picnic lunch and a meaningful toast with wine. We spent several hours at the Sea Animal Museum which was scary, educational, and entertaining. If you have not seen the place, you should go. It's awesome!"

"How long does Marvin have left to spend time with you?" asked Sissy.

"Not long enough. He receives his discharge on November 12. He plans to go home and enroll for the second semester of college. I plan to fly to Denver for a week over Thanksgiving to meet his family. I'm quite anxious to know whether they consider me worthy of their son. Would you all consider working my regular customers into your schedule? I hate to ask this of you. However, you know I'll do the same for you when you desire some time off," answered Rose.

"We will do all we can for you, Rose. We are pleased as punch for your romantic moments with Marvin. We trust that your friendship buds and blossoms into great fruition. And that there's no fruit basket upset," replied Carol, teasingly..

"You make them sound like a couple of fruit cakes," Clips jokingly added.

Customers arrived for Rose, Carol, and Clips about the same time and the friendly conversation ended.


LUNCH BREAK CAME FOR ROSE. She debated whether to obtain a quick tanning session or go to the apartment to prepare a light lunch. The plumbers had obtained the key from Carol earlier that morning. She was anxious to see how the work progressed on her bathroom. Curiosity received the upper hand and she went to their apartment. She walked immediately to her bedroom to play the part of sidewalk superintendent. Perhaps she thought, "bathroom superintendent."

"You should be able to use your bathroom this e[...]ng, Rose," replied Kenneth, who was the boss of the compa[...]

"Of course, you or Carol will need to do some of the p[...]ing. We can do this for you today if so desired," said Sam, [...] plumber's apprentice..

"No, Carol and I would enjoy doing the painting and t[...] trim. The conveniences of having my own bathroom will b[...] pure heaven," answered Rose.

"Your sketches could be followed to the letter. As you indicated, the water pipes and drain were inside the adjoining wall. The wiring for the light in the closet was diverted easily for the light over the lavatory and for your outlet. We really appreciate this form of help. Our job could be done efficiently and thereby save you two expenses," said Kenneth.

Rose prepared her lunch. She turned on the radio for classic music. As she ate her sandwich and sipped on a glass of coke, her thoughts reminisced to the experiences on the beach when Marvin touched, caressed, and excited her body. The yearning, the tremendous excitement of touching her breasts caused her whole body to feel wide awake, super-stimulated. These reactions surprised and pleased her simultaneously. She remembered one woman describing these feelings as 'Wow! My whole body becomes soft and fluid, and completely in harmony with the universe.' She didn't think there was much improvement on that statement. At least she learned more about her own body and Marvin learned more about her.

One of the workman let out a curse that broke her reverie. She jumped off the kitchen stool, put her glass in the sink, and hurried to the bathroom.

"Sorry, lady, please excused my language. I severely pinched my finger in tightening a pipe joint," Kenneth remarked apologetically, while sitting on his haunches and holding his injured finger with a pained expression on his face.

"T_ terrible. Do you need any first aid? We have some in th_ her bathroom," replied Rose.

"_, I am waiting for the pain to stop. The skin isn't bro-ke_hank goodness," answered Kenneth, as his face retained a_lmacing appearance.

"I need to return to work so Carol can take her lunch _eak. She will be here shortly. She will be pleased that the _athroom will be finished by this evening. Carol is a real _rooper, but I feel as if I'm imposing on her space when using our shared bathroom. Her cabinet is full of her own posses-sions. I feel like I'm spying on Carol when moving her items to fi_ mine," related Rose.

"By tomorrow morning you should have your own things in your cabinet above the sink," chimed Sam, not wanting to be left out of the conversation.

He viewed Rose admiringly. "What a beautiful lady" raced through his thoughts. Not having a girl friend, he wondered if Rose was available. She appeared to be his age, too. He would ask Kenneth when Rose left.

"Good bye, guys," said Rose, as she left.

She noticed Sam viewing her from head to toe several times in an admiring manner. Interesting! "Wonder why I never noticed men looking at me in that manner before now? Have they always been doing that? Is it due to being naive? Good grief, get control of yourself!" Rose reflected.

Just as she was starting down the stairs, she over heard Sam say, " Kenneth, that is the most gorgeous woman I have seen in a long time. I wonder if she is engaged or going steady? I have always loved red headed women. Do you suppose she would go on a date if I asked her?"

"There is only one way to find out, Sam; just ask her," re-plied Ken.

"Aw, I wouldn't have a chance with a classy model-like woman like Rose," Sam doubtingly answered.

Rose continued down the stairs with an amusing smile on

her face.  He was an attractive red- headed lad. "Suppose he is Irish like me?"  she wondered.

"HELLO MOTHER, THIS IS  Marvin.  Your letters about Dad's heart problems sounds alarming.  What is the doctor's prognosis?"

Through sobs, his mother tried to tell him that the medication was not helping his dad to respond  as desired.  He was in the hospital as they spoke receiving close attention by the doctors.

"Do you want me to fly home to be with you and Sally until he gets better?  I do have some earned leave time left.  I was taking some to spend with Rose before being discharged.  But it would be more important to use my leave by your side."

"No, Marvin, my crying may be causing you to sense the situation is worse than the problems your dad is experiencing. We know you will be home the first part of November.  That is not very long now.  We are so pleased that Rose will be here for Thanksgiving.  We are so anxious to meet the young lady."

"I can't wait for you to hug Rose.  She is precious.  Please call if Dad becomes worse, even the slightest amount.  Good bye, Mother.  Give my love to Dad and Sally.

KENNETH AND SAM ENTERED the hair salon at closing time.  Sam looked at Rose admiringly as Kenneth approached Carol.

"All finished, Carol.  Here is the key and the billing for materials and labor.  Didn't think we could get all the work done in a day but everything worked out smoothly with out any problems," said Ken.

"You're good," replied Carol.  "We really appreciate your efficiency.  Rose will certainly be ecstatic using her own bathroom facilities."

Speaking almost in a whisper, Ken asked, "Carol, is Rose available.  Sam has the hots for her.  He admired her at noon and has been talking about her all afternoon. Thought he would drive me nuts with his swooning about her."

Returning the whisper, Carol replied, "Tell Sam that Rose is taken. Hope that doesn't break the kid's heart. Rose is one beautiful young lady.  I can understand how enamored he might be." Returning to a normal voice, asked,  "While you are here, Ken, would you have time to assist us in turning the storeroom into a  tanning salon and shelves for towels, lotions, and other items?"

Carol took Kenneth and Sam into the  storeroom. Indicating the size of a sun tanning bed, Kenneth sketched out a blueprint to accomplish the desired amenities.

While they evaluated  the space available, Rose finished with her  customer.  After thanking Rose and giving her a gratuity, Rose went to the storeroom and slipped into a space between Sam and the wall. Sam was not aware of Rose's presence and in backing up,  stepped on Rose's foot. In an attempt to lift his foot, Sam fell back against Rose, pushing her against the wall and sliding down on a partially empty box.  While ending up sitting on the box, Sam fell on her lap. The extra weight placed on Rose caused her to sink into the box ending in a jack-knife position. Sam scrambled to stand upright again.  Embarrassed with Carol and Ken observing his faux pas, Sam extended his hands to Rose. With clasped hands, he was capable of lifting Rose back to standing position.

"I'm so sorry, Miss Rose. I didn't know you were behind me," Sam said embarrassingly.

"Sam, you indicated you wanted to meet me. We did just that even though  my dignity was tipped slightly," Rose answered with a slight laugh.

The commotion brought Sissy and "Clips" to the door entrance.

"What did we miss?" asked Sissy.

Carol related the incident. Having missed the excitement, both returned to finish their customers.  Rose beckoned Sam to follow her to her chair. Carol and Ken walked to the front door entrance.

"Carol, I'll work up an estimate on the material and labor. We will be able to obtain a tanning bed of excellent quality that meets the required standards at cost for you. That should help you considerably," said Ken. "Sam, meet me at the shop at 8 a.m. We have another big installation for tomorrow."

"Thank you, Ken. We appreciate your help and concern for us," replied Carol.

Rose, wanting to assure Sam that the slight accident in the storeroom was not serious from her standpoint, offered, "Sam, please let me give you a trim on the house and share with you information about Sally Fieldson for you to consider."

Sam, slightly bewildered and embarrassed, sat down. Rose placed the apron on his lap and brought the ends around his neck and fastened them.

As Rose began the trim, she said, "Sam, I am going steady with a sailor at the present time. I overheard you say today that you like red heads. Right? Well, I have a girl friend that graduated with me last year from high school who has red hair like mine, has green eyes, my height, and really beautiful. Just talked to her last week and know she is not seeing anyone. She even asked if I knew someone for her to meet. She may have been making small talk but will take her at her word. This is fortunate that we should meet today. With your permission, I will call Sally and ask her to meet you at Joe's Bar and Grill next door tomorrow evening at 6:30. She is going to nursing school to become an RN. Would you be able to meet her? I'll make the introductions."

"Miss Rose, you would do that for me? We hardly know each other. But I would be so appreciative of your help. Wow! I'll be there in my best bib and tucker!" exclaimed Sam.

"We have the telephone number of your shop. I'll call Sally tonight and find out if this playing cupid for you two will pan out. I'll call you regarding her answer. There, you are finished. Here is a mirror to check my work, Sam. And just call me Rose."

"Thank you, Rose, you are one kind lady, and a lovely one at that. I need to go home. My mother will be wondering why I'm late for supper."

"Thank you for the compliment, Sam. I appreciate all the hard work you did in helping Ken with the bathroom installation. One favor certainly deserves another. If you need another trim, please consider our salon. Usually some men have a hesitancy coming to a ladies' hair salon. We have a large number of the military men coming, however."

"I'll be back. Thanks again. Good bye, Rose," replied Sam as he left the salon.

'WHAT COLOR DO YOU wish to paint your bathroom?" asked Carol

"I love the light blue with the white trim that Mrs. Bolsey used. And there is still some of the paint left in the cans in the storage closet. We only need a small amount where the men made repairs. I'll start right after we eat supper."

As Rose was about to pick up the phone to call Sally, the phone rang. She was hoping it was Marvin. She did not need to wait long.

"Hello, Carol's Hair Salon," said Rose.

"Hello, this is the Mercantile Beauty Supply Company," said Marvin as he tried to disguise his voice.

Rose heard through the sounds that it was Marvin but chose to go along with his charade.

"We have told you at least twice, not to call us any more. We bought your terrible  supplies once, and indicated we would never buy again," replied Rose

She replaced the receiver, knowing that Marvin would immediately dial again.

He did.

"Hello, Carol's Curls and Crewcuts, how may I direct your call?" Rose said in a professional tone.

"Land of living, are you ever becoming more confident and a stinker all rolled up in one, Princess," replied Marvin.

"I knew it was you right along, Marv. It was get even time and you had it coming for the many teasing you give me. The trouble is , you're so much better at this game than I am. But I'll learn. Just you wait!"

"Touché! Remind me not to have you get angry at me with your Irish temper. What is on your plate tonight? There's a good movie on the base."

"I plan to paint my new bathroom or at least touch up the places the workmen messed up from the plumbing and carpentry work. Would you like to help me? When we're through, I'll treat you at Joe's place."

"Sounds like a winner. I'll take a taxi and be there in four shakes of a lamb's tail, or maybe six shakes. I'll bring a bottle of wine to christen your new bathroom. See ya!"

Rose thought that christening a bathroom was a little far fetched but had no plans to spoil the spirit of his Naval traditions. If ships are launched when a bottle of wine is smashed over the bow, surely Marv will come up with a quaint rendition for her bathroom. She wondered what it would be as she headed for the pantry to retrieve the paint, brush, paint stirrer, and paper towels.

"THIS SPACKLE MATERIAL needs to be smoothed before being painted, Rose," commanded Marvin. "Do you have any sandpaper?"

Both returned to the storage closet and found a box of odds and ends that Mr. Bolsey had left for the new owners. Dumping the box on the table, luck was with them in finding one small sheet of sandpaper.

Before returning to the bathroom, Marvin embraced Rose and she  surrendered to his passionate kiss.  Finally breaking the clinch, they returned and Marvin sanded the rough edges.

Opening the can, Rose stirred the paint. Laying some paper towels to catch any drips, she painted the required areas. Between their teamwork, all the surfaces needing attention were sanded and painted. All the material was returned to the pantry.

Once again Rose found herself pulled up close for more of Marvin's tender kissing. She loved painting with the added fringed benefits! On returning to the bathroom, Carol was inspecting the completed work.

"This turned out far better than I'd imagined it would, Rose. Your idea of installing a bathroom in this large closet is really super. How great to have an imaginative roomy," gushed Carol.

"Let's use this wine to make a toast. These paper cups will serve the purpose," said Marvin, as he handed one to each of them..

Opening the bottle, Marvin poured the wine. Marvin picked up his cup.

*"Here's to the new loo, Painted a light blue. May the time spent there, By this lady so fair. Be forever so sweet, With her dainty clean feet. And the rest of her lovely bod. Bottoms up!"*

Carol and Rose could not drink because they started to snicker that turned into loud laughter. Both placed their cups down so they couldn't spill when bursting into knee slapping guffaws.

Marvin watched the two women with his own laughable amusement created by their actions.

"Didn't realized my poetry could have such an effect on you two fair maidens. Glad that I came along to make your day funny and deserving with Brown's humor."

"For a minute or two, I thought you were planning somehow to break the wine bottle in the shower for the christening purposes," Rose managed to reply while recovering from laughter.

"Ladies, wine is too fine to run down the drain. You must tame your brain with the juice of the vine. Now that you two have recovered, let's finish the toast!"

They did, finally!

"HELLO SALLY, THIS IS ROSE."

Rose proceeded to tell Sally about Sam Thomkins and his partiality for red heads.

Rose presented information she knew about Sam and tentative feelings about his character. After all, she had only met him. If interested in meeting Sam, she should meet him at Joe's Bar and Grill tomorrow at 6:30. She and Marvin would be present to make introductions.

"Rose, I think I'll accept your cupid playing scenario. Thank you for doing this. Who knows, two red heads could be fabulous or be formidable! See you tomorrow night."

# CHAPTER 16

"SALLY, MAY I PRESENT Sam Thomkins and my dearest friend, Marvin Brown. Sam and Marv, this is Sally Fieldson, my pal throughout high school. Sometimes we were referred to as the 'Red Twins' or as some of the guys would say, 'The Green Eyed Monsters,'" said Rose proudly.

She was happy about the arrangement, because in the recesses of her heart, believed they could become friends like she and Marvin had become.

For the next hour, the two couples shared in jovial conversation after ordering the special dinner of the day. The topics covered the gamut from the experiences each had gleaned from their work areas of expertise. Interesting episodes ranged from the ridiculous to the sublime.

Sam, who Rose concluded to be shy and reticent from the brief encounter in the salon, proved to be most outgoing. That pleased her immensely. She could surmise that Sally was piqued by his dry sense of humor as he related unusual happenings from job. That he was handsome and had an athletic build--these were pluses. Of course, she was extremely proud of Marvin as he portrayed once again his polished social graces throughout the meal.

Joe and June intermittently approached their table to banter a few words and to offer additional services. Both were pleased for the two young couples who were displaying exceptional camaraderie. Joe couldn't refrain from throwing in teasing remarks that caused both Sally and Rose to blush profusely on two occasions due to the double meaning of his humor.

"Miss Rose—Oh, I'm sorry, you asked me to drop the 'Miss'—thank you, Rose, for bringing this fascinating lady into my dull existence to this point in my life. Since graduating last year, my time has been spent as an apprentice journeyman with Ken's Repair and Supply Company. Ken is a knowledgeable teacher. I'm so fortunate. I plan to have my own company one day. There has been no time to consider asking the few girls I know for a date. The first two asked were going steady. Being told 'no' dampens one's enthusiasm to continue asking. Rose, I appreciate your acute hearing when you overhead my partiality for red-headed women. Drinking in the radiant beauty of Sally, I need to pinch myself to determine if I'm actually here for your introductions and for the enjoyment of this pleasant gathering," said Sam, as he fastened his eyes on Sally the entire time.

He was dazzled by the brilliance of her green eyes as they reflected her inner beauty. He was extra pleased that Rose had removed the shaggy appearance of his hair by her clever ruse to accomplish the trim.

"Sam, you can't have the last word. We women have that prerogative. Rose, if you were secretly playing cupid, then I thank you.. Like Sam, since you and I graduated, my time has been involved acquiring that elusive Registered Nurse's degree. I, too, could not afford the pleasure of dating anyone. Of course, that was easy—no one has asked me," rebutted Sally as she kept her eyes studying Sam's intense survey of her.

"The pleasure of bringing you two together is all mine. Joe and June brought Marvin and me together. We have taken Joe's advice to have constructive communication in our new relationship. We are trying to do just that.  Now, if you two will excuse us, Marv and I will take another booth to plan yet another day at the beach or sightseeing or shopping or all three. You will have the opportunity to become better acquainted," said Rose as she nudged Marvin to stand up.

"Rose, thanks mucho. That word 'acquaintance' could not be better selected," replied Sam as he gazed admiringly at Sally.

Sally glanced briefly at Rose and Marvin as they left, then returned her attention to Sam with a winsome smile that reflected her innermost thoughts, "I'm unquestionably intrigued with this man."

Marvin and Rose moved to a booth near the kitchen entrance for their private moments.

"Princess, you repeatedly amaze me.  How coy and clever to get those two together and provide the opportunity to be alone," complimented Marvin.

Rose glanced at the booth they had left.  Sam and Sally were leaning toward each other with eyes fixed.  "It's all up to you two," she thought.  She turned her attention to Marvin as she felt his caresses on her hands and arms.

Gazing into his eyes, Rose's thoughts congealed into a complex mix of all the sensations she had experienced since meeting Marvin.  She saw her love life to this point as a kaleidoscope of emerging colorful emotions—of her sensual areas awakened by his caresses—of the excitement of his pending love for her—of the momentary flashes of lust from intimate moments—of Marvin's total sex appeal—the man she wants to marry.  How could she be any happier than at this moment?

Marvin could sense that Rose's brain was reeling on some deep thoughts from the appearance on her face and the intense gaze upon him.

"A penny for your thoughts, Sweetheart."

"At this moment, my thoughts are priceless, My Sweet Salty Sailor!"

"I love you, Princess!"

Rose's mental senses rang like a fire alarm triggered by a raging flames. He loves me—moi--Rose, this slow blossoming girl—he loves me—and I love him, too.

"I know now that I love you, too!"

Joe, watching Marvin and Rose from across the room, sensed what was happening to those whose concerns were paramount of his interest for the couple. Picking up two bottles of wine cooler and glasses, he approached their booth.

"I've been watching you two love birds. My intuition tells me we have reached a higher level of romance. Am I off the beaten path or hit the nail on the head? Did I bring this wine for nothing?" asked Joe.

"Your insight is on the mark, Joe. We have arrived at a place in our relationship to declare our love for one another," Marvin announced as he moved to sit beside Rose.

Joe slid in opposite them. "My hat is off to you two. My hunch for introducing you two proves my matching skills are razor shape. Eh what? No really, you kids deserve each other and may your romance grow daily. Your personalities harmonize each other. Just hope nothing happens to hinder your future together. If you need anything, let me know. I'm out of here."

Marvin poured two glasses of wine. They raised their glasses as their gazes drank in the love moving ethereally between them. The moments were profound and meaningful for both. Marvin's thoughts flashed to the desire of making love to this lady that pledged to save her innocence for their wedding night and all the many couplings as the mother of their children.

Rose's thoughts moved from the warnings of her parents never dating a military man to that of meeting and now loving a sailor to whom she could surrender her body and soul. Rose brought the glass to her lips and took a healthy sip before realizing they had yet to make a toast.

"Here's to us and our future," said Marvin.

As Rose brought her glass up to meet Marvin's, her arm hit the bottle of wine and as it fell, the liquid gushed out across the table top and into Marvin's lap, soaking his Navy whites.

"On no," cried Rose. "That's not suppose to happen now! I'm sorry, sweetheart! How clumsy of me!"

Marvin looked down at his dress whites. He looked up at Rose with a surprise look on his face as the coolness of the wine began to penetrate the material to his skin.

"Well, that is a new kind of toast, Princess. Wearing wine rather than drinking the bubbly is so cool. And that's for both meanings of 'cool'."

In frustration, Rose set her glass down without looking. It caught the edge of her hand bag. When releasing the glass, it also fell over and more wine flowed over the edge and saturated Marvin's whites even more.

"Rose, I've heard it said, when it rains, it pours!"

"Good grief, Marv. How can you make jokes at a time like this! You can't go back to your ship like that! I know what to do, we can wash and dry your clothes before driving you back to your ship. Let's leave now and go to my apartment."

"Brilliant suggestion, Princess."

They headed for the door. Marvin stopped Joe who was carrying an order to a table. Joe saw the wine stains. Marvin informed him briefly of the accident and how the booth was also a mess. Joe was not alarmed for he and the help had cleaned messes made accidentally by customers.

They bid each other 'Good night.'

Marvin, feeling some of the excess wine running down his leg into his sock, hurriedly grabbed Rose's arm. She sensed his immediate plight and they hastened out of Joe's place, down the sidewalk, and up the stairs to the apartment.

ROSE DIRECTED MARVIN TO her bedroom. She grabbed one of her robes from the bath room plus a fresh towel and wash cloth and pressed them into his hands. She pointed out the shower right off the bedroom. She instructed him to bring his clothes to the kitchen to be washed and dried.

Of course, Marvin knew where all these pieces and parts of her apartment were located. He had been there before in painting the room. He simply chalked up her bossy directions to anxiety and embarrassment created by the accident. He realized he had to change her mood.

The shower was quickly accomplished. Placing the wine soaked clothes in a bundle, he pulled on the robe, and strolled into the kitchen.

"Princess, here's your cargo to finish and refine. If I didn't know better, you did this on purpose to place me in this compromising position of only a robe, and yours at that. Just confess your dastardly deed, my innocent maiden, " Marvin said teasingly, supporting a big grin.

Seeing Marvin in one of her rayon robes causing the sleeves to come to below his elbows, the hemline coming to the middle of his thigh, and just sufficient material to barely close the two front ends—this was too much. The sight was too comical. Rose broke into a laugh which broke all the built up frustration and anxiety.

When recovering from her laughter and gaining composure, she went to Marvin, held out her arms for his embrace and raised her face to meet his. He tipped her chin with his forefinger.

"You are a remarkable lady, Rose. So wise in unexpected situations, yet so innocent in others."

He cupped her face and stroked his forefinger along the line of her chin. He softly pressed his mouth against her waiting lips. He heard her suck in her breath as he moved his lips to her neck below her left ear. He had discovered this was one of her sensual places.

Rose closed her eyes, her body trembling as he continued his kisses, bringing his mouth closer to hers. He then covered her upturned mouth and moved his lips over hers.

She tasted like wine. How different. He deepened the kiss and Rose responded.

She broke off the kiss and pushed Marvin away. "Don't go away, I'll be back shortly."

"My dear Miss Watson, it is really quite elementary. Where will I be going dressed in my best gown, but no shoes?"

"Did I ever tell you that your humor is one of your greatest assets? Again, don't go wondering down to the street until I return. I don't wish to bail you out of jail!"

"Aye, Aye, Madam Captain of My Heart. I shan't move an iota."

Marvin was curious what this lovely vision of a woman had up her sleeve. He looked at his arms poking out of the short sleeves and chuckled to himself. Looking at his legs and then his feet which were at least a yard or more from the bottom of the robe, Rose's laugher rang again in his ears. The sight he created was just the ticket to pull her through the trying minutes since last sitting in the booth. He heard her coming up the hallway.

"Close your eyes, sweetheart! I have a surprise for you!"

Marvin obeyed her command. She approached Marvin and put her arms around his neck. He instinctively placed his arms around her and felt the touch of silky material.

"You can look now."

Marvin opened his eyes. He realized that she had undressed and put on a robe similar to the one he wore. Pushing her back to view her from head to toe, he looked in her face with a nodding of disbelief.

"Does this mean that robe is the only thing that separates your magnificent nude body?"

"No, silly, I am wearing other clothes," as she untied the robe and let it slide off her arms and shoulders.

"You call that five centimeters of transparent fluff— clothes? What is it?"

"It is called a teddy. Carol helped me make the purchase. She said I should wear this at the first opportunity for you to enjoy. She claims that it would make me look sexy, alluring and would excite and arouse you."

"You can tell Carol that her deductions are correct on all accounts. But Princess, do you realize what this innocent re-vealing of your delightful and comely body does to me ? I am strenuously trying to avoid a bigger problem.

Rose moved to face Marvin. Placing her arms up around his neck, she suddenly felt what was 'the problem' pressing firmly against her body. Marvin's tongue was exploring the inner and outer areas of her lips and hands gently messaging her back and stomach.

Joyous sensations were coursing through her. She tried to process this warm and sensual excitement as she was trying to process thoughts in her mind. The task was being cross-wired. Rose had never seen a man when aroused. Dare she ask to see? What would he say? She had heard that discretion was the better part of valor. What does that really mean in our open communication?

Marvin, being in a state of discomfort, pushed Rose back and away gently and looked at her face. In the embracing, his robe had opened. Rose opened her eyes and gazed at Marvin wondering why he stop kissing her. She then found herself looking down at "the problem" Marvin had indicated.

With a sudden and violent motion, Rose jumped back. "Oh no, Marv. I didn't know! I know me! It would be impossible for us to have any intercourse! Marv, this is so terrible, so awful!"

Rose turned her back to Marvin, fell down on one knee and cradled her head in her arms resting on her other knee. Her sobbing was deep and her body trembled. You don't want me! We need to end our relationship NOW so you can find another woman that can satisfy you!!"

Marvin gently reached down to place his hands below her arms and raised her to a standing position. He placed his hands on her shoulders and his head close to hers.

"Rose, I love you. You know that. Please stop crying if you can. Let's talk about this. There is apparently so much you don't know about yourself. Yes, we would be able to have intercourse when the time comes. You need to believe me."

Marvin reached for her robe, and held it up for her to place her arms in the sleeves. He brought the robe ties around to the front and made a bow. He kissed her forehead. He found a Kleenex in his robe pocket. Rose attempted to dry tears despite more flowing down her cheeks.

The spin cycle of the washer ended and the timer alarm was heard. Marvin emptied the wet clothes into the dryer while Rose set the dial.

He pulled out a chair. "Please sit down, Rose."

He placed a chair before her, sat down and took her hands into his.

"May I share some information for you to consider. Do you now have a gynecologist?"

Rose shook her head negatively without knowing what the word meant.

"Rose, would you please ask Carol or June or call one of your married girlfriends and inquire who they recommend as the doctor they use. Pick what seems to you the best and make an appointment. The doctor will perform a complete physical examination. You will undoubtedly be given a pap smear test and a mammogram. Then ask all the questions on the many areas of information you don't know or sense not having. "

Rose continued to wipe away her tears. She looked intently at Marvin. He was telling her information that she should already know.

"Rose, when we do have sex one day, this will open up a huge amount of health concerns—the gynecologist can give you all the info you need—all the means of birth control if you are not opposed to such. Please do not be embarrassed. The doctors have heard many questions. They will not judge you for not knowing your own body or lack of knowledge. Will you do this for yourself and for me?"

"Marv, why is it you know more than I do and you're a man. Why didn't my mother tell me all this? She has never been to a---what word did you use?"

"A gynecologist. An OBGYN if you want a shorter term. I know about this because my mother told my 16-year old sister and had her visit a gynecologist. You see, Sally's room was opposite mine. Mother would have many chats with her. I couldn't help but overhear the information shared between them. But please do not be so hard on yourself, Princess. You will learn quickly enough, Sweetheart."

The timer announced the drying cycle was over. Rose stood up and retrieved the clothes. She folded each, placed them on the table and then sat on Marvin's lap.

Having recovered from the crying jag, she placed her arm around his neck and kissed his lips lightly. "Marv, forgive me for being so childish a little bit ago. You certainly know when I need help. Why don't I forget about wanting to be a virgin on our wedding night and have sex now. Then we will know whether or not we are capable of making love? Besides, I would like to experience that added sexual pleasure of being a woman that Carol talks about."

"Rose, darling, listen to yourself, will you? You are causing me great physical yearnings with your scantily dressed body on my lap. Nevertheless, I desire to help you keep the promise made to yourself. Besides, if we did make love and you became pregnant, what your father and mother have been telling you all these years would be true, even though you are an adult and our act would be consensual. But your folks may not look at that way. If you did get pregnant, our lives would be greatly changed by the necessity of getting married immediately. Rose, there was never any thought on my part to buy protection for you because of your desire to remain a virgin."

"Oh sweetheart, you are so right. You have the cool head between us. I've read that anticipation is part of romance between people. But you won't stop these close sexual encounters like we had tonight, will you? You may have sensed it, you helped me know more about this new dimension of myself as if I were melting within. The description of my intense feelings becomes so difficult to express to you."

"Yes, and from the arousal for both of us, that chemistry is beginning to cook. We just need to keep away from the boiling stage. Do you agree, Princess?"

"I may not want to at times but will try the very best possible. You are an irresistible sailor and I do want you. You can continue to create that delicious feeling of my being a woman anytime though."

"All in due time, Princess. But we need to get dressed so you can ferry my butt to the boat. I don't wish to report late from liberty. It would be terrible to have bad marks on my service record so close to discharge. Do we get dressed together or shall I use the kitchen and you return to your boudoir?"

"Suit yourself, Handsome!" as Rose started to move toward her bedroom.

""Discretion is the better part of valor, Sweetheart. Knowing our close encounter in the last hour, the decision is more or less obvious. No?"

"Again, I say, suit yourself, Handsome."

"You're teasing me now and I love it. Your boldness at times surprises me. Go get more clothes on that beautiful body of yours. What I have seen tonight is etched indelibly in my mind."

"I'm pleased I can be good for something," as Rose scooted away from a tap that Marvin tried to place on her buttocks.

THE MARINE GUARD AT THE Naval Station gate recognized Rose's car while approaching his post.

"Was wondering if you two would show up again on my watch. You have been regular customers, so to speak, while on duty. Stores, you are one lucky guy to have a beautiful woman bring you to your ship on such a regular basis. There must be more going on than meets the eye?"

"Yes, Corporal, we have found one another and I consider myself fortunate without a doubt. Thanks for asking," replied Marvin.

After driving Marvin to the area designated near his ship, Marvin gave Rose a lingering but passionate good night kiss.

As they broke the embrace, he said, "We became close tonight with a sweet engulfing love for each other. In so many ways, I'm pleased, but being too aroused is painful for me, Sweetheart. I want you to know that. But I'll live. And offering your vision of beauty so eloquently is a dreamer's dream. You provided reality. I love you, Princess.

"That goes both ways, Marv. I love you so much! As Joe said, we need to be open and communicate our thoughts and desires. Thank you, Sweetheart, for providing me all the different possibilities and information tonight. Or was it the dumping of the bottle of wine that started a newness for us both?"

"You don't need to bring that incident back to my memory, Rose. I soaked up enough wine for one sitting."

Marvin kissed Rose again, exited the car, and waved as he walked to his ship.

As Rose drove back home, again her thoughts underwent reminiscing of what had happened. She knew that her awakening process was pronounced and inviting. She was feeling confidence seeping into her being. "How exhilarating! And about time, too! How I enjoy this part of my life adventures by being loved," she thought.

# CHAPTER 17

Rose and carol happppened to in the break room at the same time. Both had finished a customer and were enjoying the opportunity to place their feet on the coffee table for a brief time. Standing for three hours rendered a toll on their physical body.

"I needed this time out," remarked Carol. "I probably should book my appointments further apart. Would give me more breaks. But I enjoy the income so will just hang in there. You are very quiet, Rose; I noticed you didn't eat much breakfast. Want an early lunch?"

"Carol, do you have a gynecologist?" asked Rose.

"Oh no, don't tell me, you are .....?" replied Carol.

Rose interrupted Carol. "No, I'm not pregnant, if that's what you were about to say. However the situation did get a bit tense last night. Glad you were out with Eddie. I wanted to go all the way to see if we are capable of sex. I don't believe I'm physically able to do so. But Marv saved the day, so to speak, and is holding me to that promise of remaining a virgin until our wedding night. In some ways I wish I hadn't told Marv my promise. He assured me that we can make love. Besides, he had no protection for me. He suggested I get a physical examination, a pap smear test, and the works. These are health issues I've never considered before."

"Marvin may have just saved your bacon, kid. Don't tell me you paraded around in that teddy we bought? If you did, you must have put Marvin through the proverbial wringer, the poor guy!"

"Well, you said to wear the flimsy outfit at the first opportunity."

"Remember, Rose, you need to use discretion. There's the right and the wrong time."

"O.K. Carol, I got the picture. But Marv sure likes that teddy!"

Rose then continued to tell Carol the events with the spilling of wine, the comical appearance of Marvin wearing her robe, the washing and drying of his Navy whites, and Marvin's request for getting a doctor's appointment.

"Rose, you are moving very quickly into uncharted waters, so to speak. I am so glad Marvin used common sense. I will call my doctor and ask her to consider you as a patient. Dr. Joyce Brooks is a neat lady. She is so personal. You will enjoy your examination and consultation. I'll call her immediately."


ROSE RETIRED TO THEIR apartment for her lunch break. After preparing a snack, she sat down at the counter. While eating, her thoughts reverted to the previous night. Perhaps my boldness in dress and words were inappropriate. What does Marvin really think of me? He seemed to enjoy my directness. Her musings were interrupted by the telephone.

"Hello, Rose McDowell speaking."

"Rose, this is Dr. Brooks' office. Carol called to make an appointment for you. We have a cancellation this afternoon and can see you at 4:30.  Our office is in the Pendleton Building, 8th and Mason Street.  Can you make that arrangement on such short notice?"

"Thank you for your promptness.  I didn't expect an appointment so quickly.  Yes, I have no customers booked for late afternoon.  I'll see you at 4:30.  Again, thanks."

ROSE IMMEDIATELY DEVELOPED a fulfilling rapport with Dr. Brooks.  After a thorough examination, she welcomed the pouring out of Rose's questions and concerns.  The doctor was slightly astonished by the information Rose requested.  However, this was not unusual a situation for young ladies coming from homes where parents failed to tell  their daughters vital information.

"Rose, you appear to be a specimen of excellent health.  However, we will know more after doing the blood work-up, the results of you pap smear test and x-rays.  Continue to eat a balanced diet and do plan for exercise.  Exercise is critical to acquire quality bone mass as you get older.  For your height, you have a perfect figure, Rose.  Your bust, waist and hip measurements are proportional.  I envy you.  Now comes some very personal questions.  Are you active sexually?"

"No, I have tried to practice abstinence so far."

"Oh dear, when you say 'so far' do you plan to be active with your significant other?"

"My boyfriend, we aren't engaged or anything, is holding me to my promise to remain a virgin until my wedding night.  There are times when I don't wish to wait that long."

"Rose, then we need to go into the birth control methods available for you to consider.  Are you ready for these recommendations?"

"Yes, I am Dr. Brooks."

For the next half hour Rose learned about the different methods of birth controls from which to select the best for her.  All this information amazed Rose  as she realized she had to take responsibility to avoid an unwanted pregnancy. Rose related her painful and dread-filled experiences of her monthly periods viewed as a "curse." Rose was pleased with the advantages of the birth control she selected. When the consultation was complete, Rose left the office with a prescription and a number of brochures that she promised Dr. Brooks would be thoroughly studied and followed to the letter. Rose appreciated the compliments the doctor had shared regarding Marvin's sensitivity and openness to discuss plans for the future, the many facets of their on-going relationship, and his insistence on a complete examination.

ROSE DRUG HERSELF out of bed when the telephone rang.

"Did I wake you, Princess, or have you been 'working the back forty since dawn?" asked Marvin as he sensed a sleepy voice on his end of the receiver. "I have the day off tomorrow and wanted to determine what your plans might entail. Should be a nice day. Can you get away to go to the beach again and take in the Ocean

Breeze Waterpark and the Back Bay National Wild Life Refuge you had planned for our next excursion?"

"Marv, you are one reliable alarm clock! I forgot to set mine. I read until the wee hours this morning from those books that Carol suggested and the brochures that Dr. Brooks furnished. I'm so tired but the information gained made it worthwhile. Clearing my appointments for tomorrow and determining what the others beauticians can cover for me, I really can't wait to share another day with you, Sweetheart. As I close my eyes and think about your caresses in spreading sun tan lotion, shivers go up and down my spine."

"In that event, we can add to the euphoria you experienced. If I am still under sentence from our last tête-à-tête on the beach, perhaps I could work off more punishment hours."

"You're still under sentencing until cleared by the judge— me! I'll see you bright and early tomorrow morning. Hope I can keep awake today for there is an appointment book full of customers.  Another payment on my Buick, though!"

MARVIN ARRIVED EARLY  at the apartment.  With the key that Rose had given him, he entered and climbed the stairs to the living room.

"Hello! Anybody home?" "That is strange," thought Marvin, "almost positive she wanted him there early to go to the beach. Wonder where she is? "

He walked to Rose's bedroom and  discovered the bed was made.  Walking further into the room, he  saw the books and brochures  that she  had  indicated  were being read.  He picked up the one entitled, "Methods of Sexual Awakening." He began to fan the pages. The title of one chapter flashed by. Stopping the fanning, he turned back a few pages and read, "Techniques for Improving Intimacy." Intrigued, he read the first lines—"One of the meaningful longings we can experience when we relate to another person is the need for intimacy.  By intimacy we are speaking of  closeness, compassion,the great effectiveness of a relationship that permits continuous  levels of feeling to be explored and enjoyed."

"So this is the type of reading material Carol is providing my naive Princess," Marvin thought. Fanning back through to the end of the book, Marvin found the drawings of a dozen basic postures when making love.Glancing at them quickly, he replaced the book on the dresser top.  In doing so, he saw a box of condoms.  Surprised at seeing them laying out in the open, he quickly tucked  them in the dresser drawer and then left for  the kitchen telephone to  dial the salon.

"Good morning, Carols Curls and Crewcuts."

"Hi, this is Marvin, is Rose there this time of the morning per chance? We were planning to go to the beach today."

"Yes," replied Carol, "we have a bridal party here that called late last night  and asked if we could arrange  their  locks in better condition for a 10 a.m. wedding.  So we are transforming

women into goddesses. Speaking of Goddesses, yours is right
here!"

Taking the receiver, Rose repeated more or less what Carol
had already described.

She told Marvin to make himself at home. She would be
finished in an hour and would be ready to go to the beach.

Marvin returned to the bedroom, picked up the same book
he had glanced at earlier, returned to the living room and settled into the large lounging chair. He started from the front
and turned the pages looking at all the pictures and reading
the accompanying descriptions. Arriving at the end of the
book and studying some of the illustrations in more detail,
Marvin was amazed at what knowledge he also lacked in understanding even his own sexual energy, the art of loving, the
knowledge of one's attitude toward giving pleasure to oneself
and to a partner, and methods of harmonious relationships.

Glancing at his wristwatch, he realized he had been reading for an hour. He returned the book to Rose's dresser, ventured to the kitchen and opened the refrigerator. Grabbing
a coke, he popped the tab. As he nursed the drink, his brain
kicked into over drive in his comprehension of the information he had just digested. Wow! That author really tells the
situation in clear and colorful details. Perhaps this may be
part of the reason why Rose doesn't desire to wait. She wants
to experience the ecstasy the author described.

"Hi, Sweetheart, sorry to keep you waiting. But we couldn't
refuse the bride and her two attendants who desired a hair
make-over for the wedding. We received the call too late last
night to inform you about the short delay on our day's outing
of fun, food, folly, and finding more pleasure with one another.
Hey, where are you?"

Marvin walked out of the kitchen into the living room.
Rose ran to him and threw her arms around his neck, turned
her face upward, and closed her eyes. Marvin wrapped her
in an embrace, pressing her breasts against his chest, even as

she lifted  herself by winding her arms around his neck. His mouth softened as he covered her lips and caught her bottom lip between his teeth, suckling it for a moment. Rose's murmur of surprise pleased him, and he chuckled, with the sound deep in his throat.

Amazing, both were experiencing what he had just read by the lady author. His teeth released her lip and his lips opened against hers. He tasted the delicious flavor, relishing the soft sounds she made and the tension of her fingers against the back of his head as she pulled herself up to his mouth.

Lovingly he moved on, breaking the kiss and moved to the warmth of her cheek and temple, moving down to her neck. A pattern of kisses marked his way as he moved up and brushed her lashes with the tip of his tongue. He could feel her body shiver and was pleased that he could honor the sensations she was experiencing. His mouth whispered words against her ear, and she was unmoving, breathing in short shallow breaths, as she strained to hear the words spoken.

"If we don't stop now, Princess, we may arrive at your bedroom rather than the beach."

Marvin pressed her close with one arm, the other hand moving to cradle her jaw. Her eyes opened, their green depths shimmering with desire, and she caught a deep shuddering breath. He moved back, watching her, and saw the flush rising from her throat from the passionate forces created between them. He brushed her lips with his.

The fragrance of her body combined with the faint aroma of salon perfumes that permeated her clothes made an unusual combination. This is what the future has in store for us in recalling the lady author's suggestive interpretations-a beautiful beautician with a body that boldly bears the blissful balance of the Inner Man and Inner Woman within her.

"Did you hear what I just said to you, Princess?"

"Something about bedrooms and beaches, I think. All I heard was some 'b's' by my ear. Marv, you cause me to crave more kisses and caresses! How can I resist you? I wish you to know, that you do not need to hold me to my promise."

"Rose, Sweetheart, we've covered this ground before. If we give in and have sex, our whole relationship could be vastly altered. Do we wish to risk that problem? We need to have a deep discussion on how we will feel about each other. Are you worried that the close relationship we now have will change between us if we had premarital sex? What our responses will be will help us decide what will—or won't—happen next. I love you deeply. You know what you can do to me! You undoubtedly felt my throbbing against your body when we embraced. You are one very sensual woman, Rose, and your reading completed this far has awakened the ecstatic experiences you desire."

"Unbelievable, or is it! You have just shared the same ideas and warnings that Dr. Brooks spoke about in my consultation. The warning of having sex before marriage was part of our discussion. She gave me a prescription for birth control which I have already started and a box of condoms for you. Since we have decided to have open communications, you should be informed what is happening."

Marvin watched Rose closely as their eyes met while trying to share considerable personal information. He could not be prouder of her ability to have overcome the shyness and naivety when he first met her.

"Well now that you know the healthcare professional side of my menses and other related female factors, shall we go to the beach for some Vitamin D and a quick visit to the Back Bay National Wildlife? I'll take a change of clothes so we can go to Sandbridge Beach tonight. The Bay View Lounge is known for romantic night life with dancing, a menu of mouth juicy shrimp, and many hors d oeuvres that will knock our socks off. How's that for keeping you waiting?"

"As the flies said when they saw the swatter, 'We're out of here'!" quipped Marvin.

# CHAPTER 18

"Carol's curls and crewcuts, Carol speaking."

" Hi Carol, this is Marvin, is Rose available for a moment?"

"Rose, there is a tall, handsome sailor on the other end of this line. Do you wish to speak now or later or can I flirt with him for the time being?" as she give Rose her impish grin.

"Carol, flirting is one of your specialties. Be my guest!"

"Touché my perky partner. Here, take this receiver before Marvin hangs up  because of our nonsense."

"Princess, can you meet me at the Enlisted Men's Club at 1800 hours?   Need to make some changes to our future plans. The details take too long to explain over the phone.   But how are you enduring the day after that fantastic and exhilarating outing we had yesterday?"

"Oh, a bit tired.  But just thinking about  all the delicious and exciting things we did plus your embraces, my adrenaline is keeping me going.   I'll see you at 1800.  Busy with a customer.  Gotta' go!  Good bye, Sweetheart."

"Hey guys, did you hear the mush that Rose exudes on our

telephone? Don't you think we should put a band on such goings on?" kidded Carol.

"You may as well stop all this falderal; you can't get my goat anymore. You're just jealous of young budding love, aren't you? Of course, I know you all love to tease. If that is the case, then give me your best shot," chided Rose.

"Rose, you know we love you dearly. Remember, you're my new sister! But we would love to know what you did yesterday while we were slaving away with both ours customers. You owe us that much," remarked Carol.

Rose appreciated the very closeness of everyone in the salon-- even with some of the regular customers. So she proceeded to describe in vivid details all the activities she and Marvin experienced at the beach--riding on the gentle white capped breakers, viewing all the birds at the Back Bay National Wildlife, the eating of out-of-this-world food at the Bay View Lounge , and the live dance band playing many of their requested music selections.

"We're so happy for you and Marvin. You two lovebirds certainly stuff the day with exciting events!" complimented Carol.

"THANK YOU FOR MEETING me here, Princess. I only have an hour to be with you. One of the destroyer escorts had pro-pulsion problems and limped back to port from the training maneuvers with the Atlantic fleet. We're attempting to get an-other escort ready with provisions to replace her by midnight. I've been on the computer making transfer notations of our supplies being moved over to her. Hope no destroyer acquires any problems while this ship is put into action. We would be short on provisions before requisitioning more. Then one of the aircraft carriers has a glitch in their computer handling all their supplies and new provisions. They radioed the prob-lem and I've been simulating the same on our computers and trying to find a solution. I'm being flown to the carrier on the mail helicopter that's  leaving early tomorrow morning. Sweetheart, I may be gone for up to three weeks."

"Oh, Marv, there goes many of our excursions we had planned!"

"I know Sweetheart. Just can't be helped. You've heard me say it before—there is the right way, the wrong way, and the Navy Way. This is one of those times."

"And with all the discussions we have had on  enjoying romantic times right away, there won't be any opportunity with you out at sea. When you get back, you'll be getting discharged and going home if you use some of your leave time.  It isn't fair, Sweetheart!"

"Rose, darling, I know you're tremendously disappointed, but that's the way the anchor chain unwraps from the storage bin. When the anchor is in free fall, there's nothing to stop the movement until it hits the ocean bottom.  There is nothing we can do about enjoying each other for the next three weeks. We will need to use our imagination and mentally review all the exciting times we have had to this point.  Let those imaginations move into free fall and nothing can stop our recalling those physical yearnings we both experienced."

"Oh, Marv, you get so philosophical at times, yet practical. You see the glass half full and I see it as half empty."

"We better order something to eat before I need to  return to the destroyer and  continue finding a solution for the computer glitch.  I need to pack my gear, too."

"Marv, would you agree to my plan of approaching Carol and determine if someone else might buy my interest in the building and salon?  This arrangement would free me to move to Denver.  Getting another job as a beautician would be a snap.  We have women and men coming into our salon for interviews on a regular basis.  There would be no problem finding employment.  We can rent an apartment and live together if you have no objection to that arrangement while you get your accounting degree and license.  My income will help you get your education. What? You're looking at me as if I had lost my marbles!"

"Princess, when did you arrive with this tall tale? We have never discussed those alternative possibilities. Wow! When you write a love story, you pull out all the stops! I couldn't do a shack up arrangement with you. I respect your womanhood both morally and spiritually. The second thing that comes to mind is the terrible objection our parents would voice to both of us in no uncertain terms. Do we wish to alienate our dads and mothers? I can hear what my mother would say loud and clear!"

"Marv, I wasn't dead serious. Tried to see what your reactions would be. I surely found out! Yes, my dad would undoubtedly have a hissing-fit to end all fits, I fear. Well, I could rent an apartment. You will undoubtedly live at home while in college. At least we would have a place to rendezvous in private. If you're serious about me, darling, and we get married, I'll let you move in with me then. Would that be satisfactory to all parties involved?"

"From the look on your face and the sound of your voice, there is a note of seriousness, sarcasm, mixed with a tad of humor. You're good! Some of what you say makes good sense. We will run all these parts and pieces up the proverbial flag pole and see how they fly. We will have sufficient time to sleep on the matter and pick up the discussion upon my return."

Paying the bill, they left the club to return to her car. As she unlocked the door, Marvin came up behind and wrapped his arms around her, pulling her close. She shivered in response to the warmth from his body radiating along her spine. He placed his hands over her breast and gave them a caressing squeeze. Her breath caught in her throat as the heightened sensitivity moved in and the sensation was like waves of butterflies filling her stomach. He placed his mouth by her ear and whispered words that made her alert and waiting. She felt warm, good, secure, caring in his arms. How could their love be more exciting!  She was reacting with an unbearably aching and feelings of love.  He gently turned her around to face him.  He claimed her lips and  ended  in a kiss that she knew rivaled all the exciting arousals  created by their embracing.

"That will need to hold you until we meet again in three weeks, Sweetheart.  I love you!"

"And I love you.  But being gone for three weeks?   It's not going to be pretty!  Your loving causes me to lose control of myself!  I feel desires and needs which I can't deny, and might do something which I would never do in an unexcited situation.  You make my whole being acutely sensitized with pleasure.  I love you, Marv!  Have as pleasant a time as possible while out on the ocean blue.  It's going to be a long, long three weeks not being able to see you!"

After another sensuous kiss, he opened the car door for Rose.   She moved behind the steering wheel and opened the window as he closed the door.   Moving his head through the open window, he gave her another warm kiss.

Starting the car and driving away was akin to events happening in slow motion.  She saw him waving in the rear view mirror.  Her thoughts solidified to a reverent  prayer that God would look over him with special care.  She knew the days and nights would seem extremely unending.

Little did she know then how unending that time would become.

# CHAPTER 19

"MARVIN, YOU APPEAR AS if having been pulled through a knot hole backwards," said Chris, as he joined Marvin at his table for the noon mess. "Three weeks was a long time to be away. When did you return from the carrier?"

"We landed at 1100. Terrible bumpy flight. Couldn't sleep a wink with the constant jostling. Droning of the motor on that helicopter didn't help for snoozing either," replied Marvin, holding his head in his hands with elbows on the table and gazing at his food tray. "My stomach hasn't settled down. I feel nauseous."

"Best you don't eat that chow. We don't cherish watching you up-chucking those beans, potatoes, and meat loaf," added Chris.

Suddenly a gust of wind came through the port hole window. To add a homey touch, curtains were installed on both sides of the port holes. The wind lifted the material up and caused the hooks to become unfastened and the nautical printed curtain cascaded down over Marvin's head. Part of it

fell into his food and also tipped over his glass of milk, causing
it to spill over the table edge, soaking his dungarees. Startled,
he jumped up from the bench while pulling at the curtain that
fell on his head. The milk continued to drain off the table onto
his pant's leg and shoe.

"Good grief, of all the bum luck! Just put on these clean
dungarees when we returned," complained Marvin.

The shipmates sitting at the next tables began to laugh
at the comical sight of Marvin draped with a curtain and his
frantic attempt in pulling it off.  His milk-soaked dungarees
added to the humorous situation, also.

Marvin became perturbed and not amused in the least.
But as he heard the laughter, his thoughts flashed back to Joe's
lounge when Rose spilled the wine on him. He could recall
Rose's laughter seeing him in her robe which almost ended in
a serious compromising position. Visions of Rose standing before him in her transparent teddy came spinning in mentally
as well. But his brain responses were short-circuited quickly
when hearing his shipmate's next response.

"Seeing Marvin being saturated by milk is so coincidental
of what happened to me last week Friday night. Except I was
soaked with beer and wine. I  had thoughts of keeping this to
myself but you fellows may wish to hear of a fantastic night
with an absolutely beautiful red headed woman," mused Don
Nelson, one of the crew members on Marvin's ship.

"Where did this take place, Joe's Bar and Grill?" asked
Marvin.

"No, this was at the Anchor's Away Lounge, a good place to
pick up a date for the night, if you know what I mean," replied
Don.

He proceeded to describe the events. He and two others
shipmates, Roger
Miller and Pete Jubic, were tipping a few beers at the
Lounge. Two cute women arrived. Roger and Pete left the
table to intercept them before anyone else did. All must have

been copasetic because they took another table for a while
and then left. Wasn't too long after Robert and Pete left that
one guy and two stunning red-headed women arrived. Those
two looked so much alike, they could have been twins. Seeing
me at the table alone, he asked if they could join me. I told
them, "why not, better than drinking alone." We introduced
ourselves, shook hands and ordered a round of drinks.

"Excuse me, Don," interrupted Marvin, "What were their
names?"

"Marvin, I already had five or six beers and rather wasted.
I couldn't tell you their names even if my life depended upon
it. I don't remember except for the one who was unattached.
Seems like her name was Rose-something, like Rosella or Rosina
or Rosealee. Hey, I wasn't concerned about names! I was trying
to stay sober enough to appreciate all the beauty of the shapely
red head who seemed to be taking a real shine to me."

"Could the name have been just Rose?" asked Marvin.

" Could have been. I really don't remember. Well, after
a couple more beers and wine coolers for the gals, the other
couple asked if I would see that, what ever her name was,
returned home safely. It was rather apparent from their actions they wanted to be alone. Told them I would hire a taxi
to take her home and get myself to the ship. Then Rose or
Rosealee, or whatever her name was, moved over to my side
of the table. We held hands and I tried to make contact with
those beautiful emerald green eyes. She had the most delicious wine tasting kisses. The next event was shocking even
in my condition."

"You don't remember the other man and woman's names?"
asked Marvin.

"No, I don't remember theirs either. Well anyway, her wine
and my beer bottles were suddenly gushing their contents
over the table and pouring into my lap, soaking my whites,
much like the milk that was saturating Marvin's just now.

The cool stuff on my genitals caused me to  become sober somewhat."

"Excuse me again, Don, but don't you remember any  first or  last name?" interrupted Marvin.

"No last names were ever mentioned by anyone that I can recall.  As I already stated, my brain was in a fog to clearly re-member even her first name for certain let alone her friends. I was attempting to  stay sober enough to enjoy all the pul-chritude beside me.  My feeble brain was telling me that this luscious babe wanted to share some closer contact.   I asked the waitress to tell the bar tender to call us a taxi.  While we waited, we hugged and kissed.  She must have enjoyed all this based on the sounds she was making."

As Don continued to describe what else took place, Marvin was mentally debating  whether or not  the three could have been Sam, Sally, and Rose.  Two red heads, both with green eyes sounded like them.   If Don only remembered names. Could they have been in cahoots while he was gone so  Rose could  meet another guy and  have the sex he wouldn't give her?  Would Rose break their trust that had been developed? She wanted  to know  what the ultimate sensations were to become a woman. He recalled her saying that she could easily lose control of her body in feeling the desires and needs which she couldn't deny, and might do something which she would never do in an unexcited situation.  She can't take much alco-hol.  She could have been partially drunk to reduce her inhibi-tions.   This all has to be just a big coincident!  Or is it?

But he tuned in on Don continuing with his story.  "When the taxi arrived, she helped me out of the bar and into the cab. She gave him an address I don't remember and then I passed out or fell asleep or both.  When we arrived at her place, she must have asked the driver to help me up to her apartment.  I evidently was out of circulation for an hour.  When I finally became conscious and opened my eyes, I remembered her saying something like, 'Welcome back into the world! Thought you might be sleeping all night!' I realized then that we were in bed and being caressed. She indicated that she had the pleasure of stripping off my wet clothes and had placed them in the washer and they were now being dried. She felt I should return to the ship in clean clothes. I think I remembered to thank her for the consideration. She kept caressing me so I rolled on my side, returning the favor. Then she rolled me on my back. My eyes were on her beautiful face and my hands caressing her while she was doing the same to me. Then 'Wow!' for she really knew how to make love. In no time she collapsed on top of me and whispered in my ear, 'Oh joy of joys, the pleasures of being a woman!' We just continued to caress each other.She had such lovely soft skin," said Don, with a dreamy look on his face.

"Don, are you sure you don't remember any names or the address of her apartment? Nothing?" asked Marvin.

"No I don't. Why do you keep asking these questions? Is this someone you know ?" asked Don.

Marvin did not return an answer.

Don continued his story. "As we were lying there and embracing, a bell rang somewhere. She stood up and put on her robe. She asked if I could stand on my two feet. I crawled off the bed and sure enough, my drunkenness was ebbing away. She took me by the arm and led me to a bath room. Pushing a towel in my hands, she indicated that I smelled like a brewery. She was right for I did smell rather ripe! I took a shower. While drying off, she came in with all my clothes and shoes. She indicated that she could have driven me to the base but ordered a taxi instead. She didn't want to dress again. After getting dressed, she took my arm and led me down the steps. We sat on the bottom one by the door and hugged and kissed some more. I asked her if I could see her again. She indicated that I would have to consider the evening like two ships that met in the night. She was dating another sailor abroad a ship at the present time and would not be able to see me again.

She thanked me for a fun filled night, but I'm not sure why. She did say not to worry for she was on the pill. Glad she was. To that point, the thought never occurred to me. Still in a stupor, I guess. Sure not going to tie on a drunk like that again. I could get myself and a woman in serious trouble. When we heard the cab honking, we kissed again, and I returned to the ship. What do you guys think of a woman like that? What a real dish? Still seems like a dream! Never thought I would meet a woman like her. Wish she wasn't going steady with someone else," related Don.

Marvin was beside himself with a slow burning rage. The whole story unfolded like the situation he and Rose had except they didn't have the sex. Could she have asked Sam and Sally to take her to this bar so she could meet a sailor to use the 'washer-dryer routine" to get Don in bed? Would Rose be that desperate to have an encounter to experience what she yearned? Apparently she thought she could get away with something of the kind while he was gone? He could hear the guys asking for more juicy details. He had heard enough.

He picked up his tray with the now cold uneaten food, dumped the mess in the garbage can, and returned to his bunk area. Taking off the milk soaked jeans, he stretched out on his bunk and mentally reviewed what Don had described of the tryst with the red-headed, green eyed woman. It had to be Rose. The physical description and her loveable actions sounded just like her. Her reading of the books on postures in making love helped in the one night affair. She knew the situation was accidental in spilling wine on him but she could have used the same method purposely to achieve her own desires with someone else. If I would confront her, she would obviously deny the complete happening. She was not that naïve anymore. Who could collaborate the entire scenario? The bar tender might know? No, he wouldn't have any names. Carol wasn't home or Don would probably have said something. Or was she home? No, he couldn't call Carol if she wasn't there. If he questioned Rose where she was that night, what would be her reaction in his questioning her? Did he really want to confront her? Could he trust her to tell the truth based on what Don had described about her? The whole story made him sick! Wait a minute, I'll try calling Sam.

Going to his office, Marvin dialed the Ken's Repair and Supply Company. Their secretary answered.

"May I please speak to Sam if he's in the shop?"

"Hello Sam, this is Marvin Brown. Just wanted to thank you and Sally for helping entertain Rose last Friday night while I was gone."

"Marvin, Rose did call and asked us to spend the night for some fun. She was bored being home alone. Well, we couldn't comply with the request because Sally joined me in attending my cousin's wedding reception that night. Rose wasn't apparently disappointed. She stated she would ask other friends. Sorry we couldn't help her."

"Thanks anyway, Sam. Gotta go. Sorry to take you away from your work. So long."

Marvin returned to his bunk. He continued to mull over the sordid situation late into the afternoon. So she conned someone else to take her to that bar. Wonder who they were? She has more friends that I certainly don't know who could be accommodating. His mind recalled the whole series of events again and again that Don had related. He was thankful he didn't need to report to work until the next morning. At least he was free to make decisions. He finally concluded that Rose wanted to have sex without his knowledge. Being on the pill certainly helped to embolden her sexual desires. Don stated that she was seeing another sailor. Rose was referring to him. All the circumstantial factors pointed in the direction of her betrayal of their friendship.

Knowing the level of trust was completely gone—realizing that they had no serious commitments—understanding that he would be discharged soon—acquiring an accounting degree took priority in his life—he would write a letter and call off their relationship. He retrieved a stationery box from his personal locker.

> *To Rosina, Rosella, or Roselee or what ever alias you wish to be called:*
>
> This note is to inform you that our relationship is terminated immediately and completely. There will be no need to try to contact me. The level of trust we did have is completely shattered.    You accidentally picked the wrong sailor at the Anchor's Away Bar. He just happened to be billeted on my ship. He has described the whole sordid details of the  tryst at your apartment.   I trust  that you are now  fulfilled with the desire to be a woman.  Being on the pill will surely enable you to continue your sexual exploitations or explorations, which ever you prefer. Had you found a different person, I may never have learned of your unfaithfulness.   The love I had for you has completely and irreversibly ended from Don's description of how you wantonly used him with that "washer-dryer routine." It was my belief that it was accidental. But the same methods can't be coincidental when the same procedure was used on Don  and  he found  himself in your bed.   May your life be as successful as you desire, but without me.
> *Marvin Brown*

Marvin addressed the envelope to the salon.  As many times as he had been to the apartment, he did not know the post office address.   He took the stamped envelope to the mail drop near the bridge of the ship. While returning to his bunk area, a message came over the ship's public address system.

"Now hear this. Storekeeper Second Class Marvin Brown, report to the Commander's Office immediately."

"Wonder why they want me? Probably about the trip to the carrier," thought Marvin as he made his way up the passageway and up the ladders to Commander Perkins's office.

"Storekeeper Second Class Brown reporting as requested, Sir!"

"Please sit down, Marvin. I'm the bearer of bad news. Wish I wasn't. We received a phone call from your family doctor that your father had a fatal heart attack while sitting at his office desk this afternoon some time. I am so sorry to relate this terrible information. You have my sincerest sympathy, Marvin. Your mother and sister must be in shock as you appear to be."

"He was experiencing heart problems for some time," choked Marvin, as he reached for a tissue from the box on the Commander's desk and wiped his eyes. His tears were for his mother and his sister that he knew must be devastated.

Commander Perkins came from behind his desk and placed his hands on Marvin's shoulders. "Marvin, I lost my dad two years ago. I can relate to your pain and loss. We also received a call from the Denver Red Cross office acknowledging the death and a request for my consideration to issue an emergency leave to be with your family. After the calls about your father, I requested your service record and have read it briefly before asking you to report here. In reviewing it, your enlistment is ending and ready for discharge. I wasn't aware of that. Your job proficiency marks are remarkable. We will miss your job performance. I noticed you have considerable leave time accumulated so I have already called the Bureau of Naval Personnel and related this emergency situation. They gave permission to issue an early discharge.   As a matter of fact, we will ask the Personnel Officer to call the airport now and book a flight for early evening.   While you pack, say your good byes if you desire, we'll process your discharge papers.   You'll be home late tonight. You may wish to call your mother and inform her of the time of your arrival."

"Thank you Commander Perkins. Thanks for expediting my discharge. Your concern is sincerely appreciated. Serving the last year of my enlistment under your command has been a pleasure. If the truth were really known, I hate to leave. But my life's goals can be better served by a discharge, going to college, and acquiring a degree in accounting."

"Marvin, I also noticed that you just returned from Temporary Additional Duty to our carrier and found the glitch in their supply department's computers.   We will surely miss your invaluable skills you have given the Navy. We can only be grateful and offer our sincerest thanks for you skills and talent, Marvin.   I wish you God Speed and the very best in your future.   Again, our condolences to you and your family. Take care."

AS THE PLANE WAS flying above the countryside now shrouded in darkness, Marvin watched the lights of towns and cities far below merge from one to another. The lack of clouds must have been a phenomenon.   As he watched, he was overcome with emotions about his father's death.   He would need to give all the support possible to his mother and sister. They had been a close-knit loveable family.   His mind began to reflect back to his boyhood days. There had been so many fun-filled outings with caring, loving, and bonding activities. That all ended when he enlisted.

However, he was thrilled that the experiences lingered in the recesses of his mind.  He would always have those memories of his father.  Now he had to forget the memories shared with Rose.  But her betrayal would facilitate that matter quickly. He drifted away in sleep and was surprised when gently awaken by the stewardess at Denver International Airport.

Home, but not the in the manner originally planned.

# CHAPTER 20

MARVIN WALKED THROUGH THE door from the walkway into the waiting area. He was expecting his Uncle Charles to meet him. He was surprised to see his mother. Both rushed toward each other and embraced.

"Oh son, I'm so thankful that the Navy could send you home on such short notice to attend your father's funeral. What a blessing to have you here to help us with the final funeral arrangements. We have an appointment with the funeral director tomorrow at 10 a.m. You can help your sister, too, for she is really grieving. I couldn't convince her to come with me to meet your flight. I dropped her off at your Uncle Charles and Aunt Deborah's. They have a close relationship and trying to help Sally cope with her grief."

Marvin embraced his mother again. He pulled out a handkerchief for his Mother to dab at the tears. I'm thankful also, Mother. I couldn't believe that permission and the paper work could be completed so quickly. But the Commander told me he had lost his father recently. He knew that having me here with you as soon as possible was very important. My pending discharge also helped to speed up the process. I'm happy to be home permanently. And before you have an opportunity to ask, Rose will not be coming here, period! I'm not going into details, Mother, but suffice to say she acted in a most irresponsible manner that permanently changed our relationship. She is out of my life!"

"Oh sweetheart, I'm so sorry to hear of your break up. But I know you have your reasons and I don't wish to know the causes unless you desire to tell me. Perhaps in the plans for your career as a computer accountant, you can concentrate on your college endeavors now. There will be many opportunities for you to meet other women if that should be your desire. Let's go home, son, and pick up Sally on the way."

THE FUNERAL PLANS WERE completed the following day. The occasion was sad for everyone. However, the minister portrayed Roy Brown in the most positive manner and shared various outstanding contributions that he completed in his legal profession. Many of his colleagues from different law firms and a considerable number of his clients were in attendance. The Brown family was pleased to see the out pouring of love and sympathy.

The attention shown to the Brown family continued for the next week as letters, emails, cards, and telephone calls were acknowledged. The family was overwhelmed with the remembrances, concerns, and condolences. Marvin and Sally helped their Mother with the countless thank you cards that were prepared, stamped, and mailed.

Dishes of various foods and deli-prepared trays were delivered to their home by friends, relatives, and Roy's law associates. Sally and Marvin commented that "Thanksgiving" came a bit early for them. Marvin found some time to complete enrollment at the University of Colorado-Denver. He was looking forward to the beginning of classes after the Christmas break. Looking up his friends and sharing time with them occupied some fun-filled days and helped in the closure of his Father's death. The early snowstorms added another incentive to spend time on the ski slopes with his buddies.

"I THINK YOU HAVE a letter coming from Marvin's ship. There is no return address, however. I assume this from the cancellation by the Naval Station," said Carol, as she handed Rose the letter when she came into the salon.

"That's strange that Marvin would write me. He usually calls. I wondered when I would hear from him. I don't know if he had returned from the aircraft carrier or still at sea. It's been a long three weeks," replied Rose.

Rose eagerly opened the envelope. But as she began to read the contents, the disbelief and horror that her face and composure revealed and moaning a continuous string of "Oh no's!" alerted Carol.

"What is it, sweetheart? Is Marvin hurt or worse yet, dead?" exclaimed Carol.

"Oh no, but it's still terrible! Marvin is accusing me of being unfaithful and having sex with someone from his ship. Where in God's name did he ever arrive at that impossible conclusion? He wants nothing more to do with me! He ended our relationship! Ooh no, this can't be happening!" as Rose threw the letter in the air, plopped down on the nearby chair with her head held between her hands and sobbed uncontrollably.

Carol rushed to Rose's side and sat beside her, placed her arm over her shoulder and began to lovingly massage her back in an attempt to console her. The letter was laying on the floor so Carol bent down to retrieve it.

"Is it O.K. if I read what Marvin is accusing you of doing? We'll storm that ship if necessary and confront Marvin with these accusations."

As Carol continued to administer consoling words while reading the letter, she too was bewildered by Marvin's remarks.

"This is just one big mistake. You need to go to the ship or write a letter immediately. You must settle this problem. I'll go with you for moral support if you wish. If you do not wish to work today, we understand. We'll complete your appointments and call others and change them to another time."

"Thank you, Carol. I know I can't work and do justice to my customers. I'm going to my bedroom and think this through. I really don't know exactly what I wish to do. Your accompanying me to the ship is appreciated. I do want to face Marvin and find out who on his ship I supposedly seduced in my bedroom. I just can't believe he would think that I could perform such a despicable act and betray him. I thought our love for one another was unshakable. We agreed to have open communications!"

"We'll find sometime tomorrow afternoon and drive to the base and attempt to see Marvin. Thank goodness you have the permit to drive on the base."

THE NEXT DAY ROSE and Carol parked on the pier near the ship. The Officer of the Day met them at the gangplank.

"May I be of help, Ladies?" asked the Lieutenant.

"We wish to visit SK2 Marvin Brown," replied Rose.

"I noticed that you parked your car by the pier so you have the necessary credentials to drive on the base. Are you relatives of SK2Brown?"

"No, but we were planning to become engaged soon. I received a letter from him which I need to clarify. May we have permission to go aboard and visit with him?" asked Rose.

"I will call the personnel office and ask to page SK2 Brown to meet you here. You do not have the security clearance to go on the ship," replied the Officer of the Day.

"Yes, I have been cleared about a month ago for ' Family Day Visitation' which was canceled," replied Rose.

"If that's the case, I will call the personnel office immediately and have them run a computer check. There would be no problem going aboard."

Rose walked up the gang plank were she was met by the Personnel Officer.

"You wish to know about SK2 Brown. This is in violation of the Privacy Act, but Marvin Brown is no longer a member of the ship's crew. He was discharged early and returned home. His father died and he went home for the funeral. Sorry to give you this information."

Rose looked back at Carol with a startled expression. Carol didn't hear what was said to Rose. Sensing something was very wrong, she ran up the gang plank to Rose.

She placed her arms around Rose's shoulders. Rose buried her head against Carol's breast and began to sob uncontrollably. She patted Rose's back and attempted to console her.

"This is more than I can endure, Carol. First the incriminating letter, and now he left the ship and went home and I don't know where to contact him. This whole mess is going from bad to worse!" trying to speak between sobs.

Recovering somewhat from her sobbing, Rose asked, "Perhaps we can obtain his parent's address from the ship's personnel office, Lieutenant Sir? May we go to the office and acquire his address?"

"As I mentioned, I have given you more that the Privacy Act permits. We can not give you that type of information. Sorry."

"Thank you, Sir, for what you have shared with us," replied Rose. I'll try to find the information elsewhere."

Carol and Rose returned to their apartment. They drove with silence hanging heavily over both of them. The turn of events had become a manta of deep remorse for both. Tears rolled down Rose's cheeks unchecked and dripped on her blouse.

Carol realized she had to help Rose move out of the doldrums.

"Hey, let's go back to the salon and give it a deep cleaning. The lick and a promise we give our stations daily isn't sufficient."

"O.K. with me Carol.  Probably would help me uncork my thoughts.  I still would desire to clear my name and reputation with Marv.  How could he ever come up with all that preposterous stuff about me?  Hey, perhaps Joe or June would know the Brown's address. They met his parents."

"That's a great idea! Let's first stop at the lounge and talk to Joe."

"JOE, YOU MET MARVIN'S parents.  Do you remember his father's first name?  Do you by any chance have their address in your file?" Rose asked anxiously upon arriving at the restaurant.

"No, I don't remember his first name.   It may have been mentioned but the name is gone from my memory now.  And I know I have no address in my file.  Sorry, Rose.  What seems to be the matter?  You appear to be in a state of great anxiety," replied Joe.

"Marvin has broken our relationship.  Besides, he has been discharged and returned home.  His father died.  And on top of all that, he accuses me of being unfaithful while he was out on that aircraft carrier.   Now I don't know how to reach him. I need to explain my side of the story.  How can I call him or write if I don't know his  parent's name or address?  The ship won't give needed information due to some privacy stuff.  Do you have any idea how to find a telephone number?' pleaded Rose.

"Write a letter, Rose, and the ship will be able to forward the letter to Marvin. That would be the first step in telling him your side of the story.  I don't wish to pry into your personal life, but June and I would desire  knowing what caused his change of heart.  Marvin's actions has me perplexed," offered Joe.

"I'm going to write him immediately!" answered Rose.

"'I'll prepare our supper while you do your correspondence. Then we can tackle the salon and give it a deep cleaning," responded Carol.

ROSE SAT AT HER DESK with pen poised to write. As she contemplated what to say, the right words would not gel in her mind. So she read the note again. The anger, hurt, and devastation created from Marvin's accusations and complete termination of their relationship was too much to endure. She ferociously crushed the piece of paper into a ball and hurled it across the room. How could he sully her reputation by calling her a whore!

Staring at the crumpled ball of paper, Rose tried to quell her anger but her thoughts kept nursing her angst. How could he accuse her of such unfaithfulness? Where was the trust they had developed? Why didn't he come to her and find out the truth? Whatever made him jump to such horrible conclusions from the remarks of his ship mate?

"Rose, Sweethheart, how are you holding up?" asked Carol as she gently massaged Rose's back. This has to be a terrible blow to your pride. I can't even imagine how Marvin could believe that his Navy buddy was describing you. It makes no rhyme or reason. I just hope and pray you two can get this mess cleared up. Sweetheart, I'll have supper ready in 15 minutes."

Rose started to write, "Dear Marv." She hesitated. Should a salutation include "Dear" under these circumstances? Rose balled up the sheet, threw it in the waste paper basket, and grabbed a new sheet. She knew that her words must not cause Marvin to become angrier than the tone of his note had conveyed.

> Marvin: Your note, indeed, was completely impossible for me to comprehend. I can assure

you that the woman your ship mate described
was not me. How could you believe I wouldbe
capable of doing such a despicable thing!. I
love you!.

What happened to that trust and the bonding between us? Whydidn't you come to see me
before jumping to such horribleconclusions?
Let's attempt to resolve this terrible situation.

Please write or call me.

I hope and pray that your ship will forward
this letter. They would not give me your address. An officer did tell me, however, that
your father had died. I am truly sorry to hear
this. Carol and I extend our deepest sympathy
to you, yourMother and sister.          Rose

Rose addressed the envelope in care of the ship and added
"Please forward." She took the letter to the kitchen to have
Carol read  and receive her opinions. Rose tried to eat some
food as Carol read. Rose managed to swallow several bites
between the sobs that would not cease. Carol returned the
letter to Rose indicating that the wording was all right.

"I'm sorry, Carol, I can't eat. Would you please mail this for
me tomorrow? I'm going to my room to rest although  I know
I'll have difficulty getting to sleep."

"Rose, I have some sleeping tablets in my bathroom.  Go
take two on your way to your room.  I would suggest you turn
on your radio to some good music to help break the silence.
Sing or hum the words—anything to help free those negative
thoughts.  Check your TV schedule. Perhaps there's a program you'll enjoy."

"Thanks, Carol. Good suggestions. I'll do just that."

"I'll finish cleaning up the kitchen. If you wish, I'll join you
for a while. Cleaning the salon can wait."

"Thanks again, Carol.  Your friendship and kindness  is

helping me through this nightmare," as she headed for Carol's bathroom.

THANKSGIVING DAY AND CHRISTMAS ADVENT season became difficult times for Rose. Going to work each day became a dreadful chore as she attempted to be pleasant with her customers. Trying to be cheerful in carrying on a conversation was tedious. The unwarranted accusation of the note kept plaguing her thoughts. Rose tried to keep her thoughts from the terrible words of the note by thinking of different subject matters, but her mind would return to them again and again. Her fellow employees tried to cheer Rose and bring her into their conversations. They would succeed for some time, but then Rose would sink back into a zombie-like stupor. Carol and the others knew that Rose was in a world of hurt and realized that only passing time would ease the pain. Rose was also appreciative of the support and concerns from Joe, Jane, and her parents. They were puzzled as to what had happened but did not press Rose for any information. She was just too humiliated by the accusations to share the contents of the note with anyone except Carol. She was anxious for Marvin to answer her note.

WHEN MARVIN SAW THE letter with Rose's return address, he was not about to open it. He had definitely made up his mind to terminate all connections with her. He had plans to go on with his life as he determined would be beneficial for his future. He recalled his dad saying to him once when a senior in high school, "Don't get in a big hurry to settle down with the first woman you meet. There are many fish in the sea." He was convinced that Rose tried to fool him when he was at sea. The accidental spilling of the wine on his ship mate was not a coincidence. It may have been an accident for him but not for his buddy. That was a deliberate act to entice Don to her room. If Don hadn't been so drunk, the betrayal would have been definitely more certain. He wondered if Rose would try to send more mail or if his mail marked "Return to Sender" would indicate to her that the relationship was ended. PERIOD.

"ROSE, THIS DOES NOT LOOK GOOD. Your letter was returned from the ship or did the post office return it," blurted out Carol, as she handed Rose the envelope.

Rose received the envelope and studied the hand-written message, 'RETURN TO SENDER.' "Does this mean that Marvin received the letter and would not accept it and wrote this notation or did the ship return the mail with these words? The hand writing is vaguely familiar. I'm confused. If Marvin refused it, then all is lost if he will not open my mail. If the ship returned it to me directly without forwarding it, then Marvin will never receive any of my mail!"

"Rose, why don't we drive to the ship again and try to find out the answers to your puzzling questions. If they did forward the letter, then Marvin does not desire any mail from you. Why not send the same letter to Marvin in another envelope but do not include your return address as you did on this one? If he doesn't know who the letter is from, he might just open that mail out of curiosity. Rather devious but that might work! We can go to the ship later to find answers."

Rose thought Carol's suggestion was excellent. She addressed a new envelope and placed it on the window ledge for the mailman to pick up. The realization that Marvin might open the letter and read her viewpoints helped to brighten her disposition with a positive approach. She actually smiled as Carol drew her close in a warm embrace with more words of encouragement.

ROSE FOUND HERSELF NEAR the telephone office in downtown Norfolk when running some errands and shopping. Out of curiosity, she entered the lobby and found a bookcase full of telephone books from around the country. Finding the telephone book for Denver, she found a table to make an examination. To her great surprise, she found that there were around 2,300 persons with the last name of 'Brown.' She immediately realized that trying to find one family without the first name would be a complete impossibility. She turned to the yellow pages entitled, 'Attorneys.' She knew that the long distance cost would be prohibitive to telephone all the Browns. Besides, would a law office give out an address to a complete stranger? She may just have to face the realization that trying to tell her side of the story would be futile. She may just need to resign to the fact that, indeed, the relationship had ended. Perhaps she would consider the complete situation as a valuable learning experience. Yes, she would move on with her career as a beautician. Carol and she were doing very well, THANK YOU! With light-hearted steps, Rose left the telephone company and drove back to the salon.

ROSE WATCHED THE NEW YEAR'S EVE episodes on TV while sitting up in bed in her cozy room. She even did some channel surfing to learn how folks were celebrating in different parts of the world. Rose realized that time zone changes caused many countries to celebrate long before others. In the meantime, she had a good book to read during television viewings that weren't interesting.

She had been invited to the party that Carol was hosting in the living room. Her boyfriend, Eddie, and two other couples that were friends of Carol's were having a boisterous time. Rose could hear the periods of laughter. She was tempted to accept the invitation but just knew she would be the odd person in their midst. Beside, they often told some very off-colored jokes that she knew would make her blush profusely.

Rose had written some New Year's resolutions that included events and situations that would be beneficial for her future. She decided that the terrible situation with Marvin had to be resolved somehow. Should that not be possible, then the only choice was chalk the whole relationship to life's experiences. She really did learn a wealth of information that otherwise may not have happened. Those experiences would be beneficial for her future. If push came to shoving, and Marvin would not make any compromise or stubbornly refused any reconciliation, she would go on with her life. She decided if any men asked her for a date she would consider their request. Perhaps she was ready to date others now by having a better understanding of herself. Perhaps Marvin had helped her gain more confidence and certainly more self-esteem than she had previously. Yes, that would be considered part of her life's experiences and of life's continuing adventure! It was time to move on! She put on her shoes, went to the salon to retrieve the letter to Marvin, tore it up with a smile upon her face, returned to her room, and promptly fell asleep without any difficulty.

# CHAPTER 21

"GOOD MORNING EVERYBODY!" EXCLAIMED Rose as she skipped into the salon.

A chorus of "Good Morning, Rose," greeted her in return.

"How great to see you back to your normal self, Rose," Clips replied, more or less as spokesman for all the others.

"May I ask what caused this change of behavior? I'm not complaining, mind you, for we are most pleased to see you in this happy mood," Sissy said, while embracing Rose, and patting her lovingly on the back.

"I appreciate all the help you have given me these past unpleasant days. You are my closest and dearest friends and co-workers. Thank you, thank you! I just decided I would put the whole incident behind me and look upon the entire situation as a learning experience of life's joys and sorrows. Just a part of my life's adventures! I decided if Marvin believes what he heard, that's his problem. I know that I'm innocent of what he claimed I did to betray him. I'm going on with my life; again, thank you helping me mature."

THE NEW YEAR STARTED out with great potential for Rose. Her appointment book was full everyday, week after week. She was able to make double and triple payments on the car. She and Carol did considerable shopping for new clothes and filled their closets with some of the latest fashions. Rose did not splurge but realized she was spending much more than her mother ever could when buying clothing for her.

Rose began to accept dates with sailors, officers, and businessmen that were customers. Knowing them in a small measure beforehand, helped considerably in maintaining friendly conversations and even brought moments of joyous laughter. She was gaining more and more confidence by dating. When a date attempted to make moves of unwanted caresses or fondling, she discovered abilities to stop the undesired attention in a friendly and diplomatic fashion. Rose became proficient in using humor that she added to her "arsenal." After all, these were her customers; she did not wish to have them become angry and go elsewhere for haircuts.

A new customer came into the salon making an appointment to have a trim. Rose over-heard that he had requested her. Rose noticed him speaking in a charming manner with Sissy. She noted that he was handsome. As he looked towards her with a winsome smile, Rose was somewhat surprised to find herself smiling back. When he left the salon, she quickly went to the appointment book to see the name--Sam Damson-- the time--3 p.m. She looked at the clock—one p.m.

Sam was prompt. As he approached Rose's chair, he extended his hand. When Rose extended hers, he lifted it up and lightly kissed the back of her hand. This completely surprised Rose. She had heard about this type of greeting, but this was exciting being the recipient for this type of intimacy.

"Hello Rose, I am Sam Damson," as he sat down. "Our mutual friend, Joe, told me about your skills in providing a trim."

"Thank you Mr. Damson, for----"

"Please call me Sam, Mr. Damson sounds so darn formal."

"Yes it does, but I want you to know I don't start calling complete strangers by their first name until I know them somewhat. With Joe's recommendation, I trust he knows you, and so I'll accept that as an informal introduction."

Rose placed the drop cloth around his neck and when clipping the ends together, the light touch of his skin created a sensation radiating through her body. This surprised her. She recalled having that same reaction the first time she had touched Marvin.

"Oh joy," Rose thought to herself, "here I go again with these mixed signals that my senses create."

Her thoughts were interrupted when Sam spoke. "Joe informed me that you are a very beautiful single person without any commitments. Your only goal is your full dedication to being the best beautician possible. I congratulate you as a young entrepreneur, also. Joe indicated that you helped buy this salon. I'm sincerely impressed. It would be my humble honor to know you better."

"Thank you, Sam. Joe certainly gave you much information about me. Yes, I decided to dedicate myself to help my partner, Carol, in establishing the very best salon in the area."

"Will you take some time out for yourself?" asked Sam. "You have heard the cliché, 'All work and no play makes Jack a dull boy,' which I would hastily change to 'makes Rose a sad lady.' There is certainly nothing dull about you! With your stunning beauty, have you ever considered being a model?"

Rose began the styling cut that Sam had requested. Touching Sam continued to generate the confused feelings spreading through her body. "How is it possible to experience such familiar sensations?" she mentally questioned.

"I did some modeling at the department store downtown when I was a Junior in high school. The salary was good, but the work was too sporadic. They did not need me everyday.

My work as a beautician is more satisfactory and brings customers, thanks to Joe. He has sent many a customer during
the time I've been with this salon, just like he did with you.
This work provides a steady income that modeling would
not provide, at least for the short time I was employed as a
model."

"Rose, you are, indeed, a sharp lady with a good business
head on your shoulders. I thoroughly enjoy and appreciate a
lady of your stature. Would I be too bold to inquire whether
you would be available as my escort to a business dinner this
evening? It is not a formal affair so attire would be a cocktail
type dress. Could I pick you up here at the salon, say 6 p.m.?"

"Sam, I am free tonight and accept your invitation. I do
have a dress in my wardrobe you described. I live right above
our salon in an apartment shared with my co-owner, Carol.
Ring the bell at the door to the right of our front entrance. We
have an intercom buzzer system that opens the door."

Rose had finished the trim and presented a mirror for
Sam to examine her work. He acknowledged his satisfaction. Rose unfastened the clip holding the cloth. Her fingers
touched the nape of his neck. Again, the tingling rushed
through her fingers and arms and beyond.

"Puzzling, indeed! But perhaps a welcome sign!" she
thought.

THE BUSINESS DINNER was a new experience for Rose.
Never had she been at a gathering of this nature. She was
greatly impressed by the stunning and expensive dresses worn
by the women. Sam's compliments about her own dress reas-
sured Rose's taste in her selection. She considered his viewing of her person from head to toe with admiring glances as a
form of compliment, also. Sam proudly introduced Rose to
many couples during the cocktail hour before the dinner. She
tried to be as gracious and pleasant as possible despite never
attending such a formal affair. Sam was greatly impressed

with her ability to begin and carry on conversations with each person introduced. She was 18 going on 19, and most of the ladies were much older and undoubtedly more experienced in social graces. Rose decided that inexperience would not keep her from being a wallflower.

She admired the coiffure of every lady. She wondered who their beauticians or stylists might be to create such beauty and elegance. Her type or class of customers did not request this type of hair-do. But she was thinking how their salon could attract such customers. Whenever the ladies did inquire as to what she did, Rose was not reluctant in the least to inform them she was a beautician.

After the banquet meal, Rose found the speeches intriguing. They spoke on topics that were new and strange to her. Several toasts to three men and one woman who were outstanding in their sales efforts presented the occasion to drink wine. The flash of her spilling wine on Marvin raced through her brain. "Will these thoughts never stop?" she pondered. After the toasts, everyone sat down. A Mrs. Suddot had been sitting next to Rose. They had had no real opportunity to engage in conversation to this point. Rose noticed her dazzling cocktail dress and an upsweep hair-do so expertly styled.

"Where do you two live, my dear? Are you from the Norfolk area? Where does your husband work?" Mrs. Suddot asked and then added, "We have so many guests from other cities at these occasions. I have never seen you two at previous banquets we hold every year to honor our outstanding sales personnel."

"Mrs. Suddot, Sam and I are not married. I'm attending as his escort date for the occasion. My profession is co-owner and stylist of a beauty salon. I met Sam only today when he made an appointment for a trim at the recommendation of a mutual friend. Otherwise, I undoubtedly would never have accepted the invitation. I do not know for whom he works.

However, Mrs. Suddot, this is indeed a most revealing evening of sights and sounds to experience."

"Thank you for the information, Rose. Please tell me where your salon is located. Your services may be just what I need. My stylist is retiring after 25 years."

Rose was pleased that they had printed business cards. What an opportune time! She quickly pulled one from her handbag and presented it to Mrs. Suddot.

"Why don't you call me Grace. Thank you for your card. I will call and make an appointment," she said, giving Rose a pleasant smile.

"Thank you, Grace, we appreciate your consideration of our salon," replied Rose as she scrutinized Grace's present hair style and realized the challenge for her skills.

Following several additional speeches, the banquet was over. Sam retrieved their outer wraps from the cloak room. They arrived at the salon and parked the car.

"Would you care to come up to my apartment? I'll make a pot of coffee. We haven't had an opportunity to share in our own conversation tonight. There is more I wish to know about you, Sam."

"And there's even much more I would desire from you, Rose," as he placed his arm around her waist while walking up the stairs.

Arriving in the living room, and to Rose's surprise, they were met by Carol and Eddie who had been in the kitchen. Rose was certain Carol had tickets to a dinner-theater performance for the evening. But knowing her room mate, she knew why they never left the apartment.

"Carol and Eddie, this is Sam Damson. He asked me as his date escort to an award's banquet this evening. Joe sent Sam to me for a trim. How about that guy! He just never gives up playing cupid, does he?"

Both Carol and Eddie greeted Sam cordially enough. But Rose noticed a hesitancy on Carol's part.

"Rose, can we go to the kitchen for a minute.  Excuse us, guys, we have a bit of business to transact," said Carol.

Arriving in the kitchen and closing the door, Carol looked at Rose with a warning type facial expression.    This really puzzled Rose.

"Rose, I believe that Sam Damson may be married and has one boy and his wife or significant other is pregnant.  A lady by the name of Deidre came into the shop last week for a hair cut. When she left the salon, she was met by a man and a little boy out front.  I saw them through the window.  I'm almost positive the guy looked just like Sam.  I could be mistaken, but thought you should know."

"Boy, can I pick the losers.  Bet Joe didn't know Sam as well as he thought.  Let's confront Sam and test him.  Will he lie or confess to his actions?"

Both returned to the living room where Sam was telling Eddie an off-colored joke.  They arrived when the punch line of the story was given.  Both guys were laughing joyfully.

"Sam, when is your wife due to have her baby?" asked Rose. She decided to be direct.

"What are you talking about, Rose?" replied Sam, showing surprise.

"Where are your wife and your little boy?   Does she know that you escorted me to a banquet that should have been rightfully her prerogative to attend?"

" I'm not married!," Sam insisted.

"Then is Deidre your live-in significant other and pregnant with your child?  Tell me the truth!  Are you denying everything mentioned?" retorted Rose with a determined tone in her voice.

"I don't need this third degree from you or anyone else. You're certainly not the sweet innocent woman I thought you'd be!" Sam headed for the stairs and taking two steps at a time, bounded out into the street.

"Thanks, Carol.  That was too close for comfort!  You were

correct with your observation of Sam. By not admitting anything, besides not being married, he admitted everything by implication. I must admit, though, Sam provided me a fabulous time at that banquet. He introduced me to several couples. I saw many out-of-this world cocktail dresses. And Carol, the superb hair-does were absolutely divine. I even gave our business card to a Grace Suddot who may call for an appointment. There's the possibility that she can refer her friends who desire some of the latest hair styles."

"We can easily handle that type of service," replied Carol.

"Let's go to the Grill to see Joe. My treat!" said Rose.

JOE WAS APPALLED WHEN informed about Sam Damson's actions.

"I was so certain of the guy. I visited with him during the entire time he was eating his breakfast and again at lunch. He said he wasn't married. I'm sorry, Rose, in sending him for a trim so he could meet you. I didn't know he wanted to start a romance by dating you. I didn't know what his intentions were. They certainly weren't honorable. We probably don't want to know his motives," Joe responded.

"Joe, don't be so hard on your self. It's O.K. I'll just chalk this up as another one of life's adventures! Seem to be racking up a few lately! Sam did provide me an opportunity to mix with some of the more wealthy and successful sales personnel from throughout the state. I really did benefit from what happened during the entire evening's activities. So not all was lost, so to speak," Rose shared.

LIFE RETURNED TO SOME NORMALCY FOR Rose amidst her friends and co-workers. She continued to help Joe at the lounge when needed. The salon was turning over a reasonable profit. Rose was able to pay the balance of her car payments. New furniture was ordered to replace the old in the apartment.

Grace Suddot made an appointment with Rose.  Her styling expertise gave Grace much satisfaction and, consequently, recommended other ladies in her circle of friends to use the salon.

After considerable brainstorming  many names, they all agreed upon changing the signage to 'Trendsetter's Hair Salon.' Carol and Rose had their new business name registered as a member of the Norfolk Chamber of Commerce.  Not only as new members, but also both became active in the program of revitalization for their section of the city.  Both ladies spent many hours visiting all the businesses in the area urging others to join in the renewal program. Their efforts created a desire for businesses to be attractive and thereby draw more business for everyone.

Their enthusiasm became contagious.  New landscaping was completed; brick buildings were power cleaned; wooden structures were painted; new signage replaced deteriorated ones; and the city repaired curbs, gutters, and resurfaced some streets.

When the program was completed, Carol and Rose were included at the honor's banquet given by the Chamber.  The trophy they earned held a special place in the new 'Trendsetter's Hair Salon.'

THE BROWN FAMILY endured the end of the year's Holiday Season.  The death of Roy Brown shortly before Thanksgiving had a direct affect on the family by dampening their spirits. However, the family had developed a resiliency because of other set backs and deaths in the family. A strong faith in God provided them the needed incentive and courage to face each day.  Their relatives, friends, and Rev. Ranson—all provided unending emotional support.  Marvin's early discharge and presence provided physical and psychological assistance for his mother  and especially for Sally.  Marvin's long chats with his sister helped her immeasurably in coping with the loss of her dad through the grieving days.

Marvin was anticipating Rose to send a second letter after returning the first. When no mail was forwarded by his ship, he determined that Rose understood the message clearly when he purposely added "Return To Sender" in his handwriting. He didn't know for certain if Rose would recognize it. There hadn't been much correspondence between them prior to their separation. Actually, he had a tinge of guilt and doubt in his termination of their relationship. But he wasn't permitting himself to be persuaded otherwise. In weighing all the facts and information again, his decision was final. He would put the romance behind him and move on.

Starting classes for his computer accounting degree at the University became the priority goal. He was satisfied with settling down to the daily routine of attending classes, completing a plethora of homework, performing chores for his mother, and skiing occasionally with his sister and friends on the many ski runs in the area.

Actually life couldn't be any better.

THE WINTER SNOW storms and cold weather gradually melted to the return of springtime in Norfolk. Once again Rose availed herself of the many opportune moments walking around the block during her lunch period before stopping at Joe's for a light meal. While walking rapidly and swinging her arms for the full exercise benefits, her thoughts would move backwards to the introduction of Marvin by Joe and June at about the same time one year ago. Occasionally, a twinge of pain would overcome her inner feelings. She had heard that the loss of a first love could be devastating. But she was determined not to be overwhelmed by remorse in thinking about the past. She would move on with her head held high!

Actually, Rose added variety to the leisure time afforded her by simply arranging her appointments for additional freedom.

She followed the suggestions of Dr. Brooks for a program of exercises. She joined the Slim and Trim Salon for a constructive, rigorous, and invigorating physical fitness regimen with Guy Mattoon, a personal trainer. Carol complimented Rose frequently on the apparent tone her body was undergoing. She would tease Rose during the times when both were cleaning the apartment or preparing theirs meals when completely in the nude. Carol's teasing continued by acquiring the applications forms for Rose to enter the "Miss Muscle Contest."

"HELLO, I'M JOE," as he extended his hand. "New to the community or just visiting?  Nevertheless, welcome to our Grill. Enjoy your meal?"

"Hi, Joe, yes, compliments to your chef. I'm here on business from Richmond. I'm Steven Harks. I own and manage Harks' Import and Export Company. We buy and sell products covering 15 countries plus the U.S."

"Sounds awesome!  Must involve much travel for you, Steven?"

"Please call me Steve. I have five associates who also travel for the business. That's my problem. We operate out of my home in Richmond. I'm absent more than I'm there. We need to employ a hostess with collateral duties to maintain the house. Perchance you know of a woman that would enjoy the challenge?" asked Steven.

"Steve, I think I do. But the last person introduced to her turned out to be a gigolo and a certified sleaze ball. Can her parents and I be present for any interview?" asked Joe.

"Joe, I can vouch that the relationship with our hostess is honorable and strictly plutonic in nature. By all means, anyone can be present," replied Steven.

"Next door is 'Trendsetter's Hair Salon.' Rose McDowell is one of several beauticians, one exceptional young lady. However, she recently became co-owner of the building and of the salon. She's a loyal person and therefore may not be in a position to consider your offer. She is single and no romantic commitments," said Joe.

"She sounds intriguing. I would appreciate presenting the details and responsibilities. The monetary benefits are substantial plus other perks," replied Steve.

"Steve, I'll call Rose immediately and determine if she can meet you here. Then call her parents, also," answered Joe.

"Joe, those arrangements are satisfactory. Thank you for your assistance," said Steven.

Joe was harboring some doubt, even reservations as he glanced at Steven while moving to the telephone. But he couldn't put his finger on the reason for his thoughts. He would listen carefully to all the details. He would scrutinize the sincerity of Mr. Harks most judiciously. He would not allow Rose to be hoodwinked or taken advantage of if in his power.

"Steve, we're lucky. Rose had a cancellation of an appointment and can be here shortly. The McDowells will arrive in 10 minutes. In the meantime, have another cup of coffee. Would you relate what you and the associates perform in daily travels?" asked Joe.

Joe was intrigued with Steven's narrative.

"ROSE, THIS IS Mr. Steven Harks, entrepreneur of Harks' Import and Export Company, with business connections in 15 countries. He has a position as hostess in the company you may desire considering. I informed Mr. Harks of your financial investment in your business. You simply could not walk away from your obligations," Joe shared.

Rose extended her hand with an air of confidence, combined with a gracious smile and looked Mr. Harks squarely in his eyes.

Rose grasped Harks' hand firmly. "Indeed a pleasure to meet you, Mr. Harks. I'm truly interested in listening to your employment offer that Joe briefly described," Rose said.

Rose's parents came into the Grill at that moment and proceeded to wind their way among the tables to where they observed Rose greeting a gentleman.

"And these are my parents, Donovan and Maureen McDowell," Rose added.

"Thank you, each of you, in arranging your time to be present.  My deepest pleasure meeting you.  Please sit down, would you?   I will share the particulars of the work opportunities and other responsibilities involved with the position," replied Steven.

For the next fifteen minutes, Mr. Harks shared the duties for the hostess.  He described the 2,300 square foot house located in a prominent residential area of Richmond.  The place housed the business as well as motel-like features for himself and five associates.  The hostess would have full responsibility to maintain the home.  A part-time housekeeper, Tina Weston, was employed to keep the house clean and help in the  preparation of meals.  He was in the  process of interviewing and employing a maintenance man, Juan Espinoza, for house and lawn care.

He described his associates-- Pedro Gonzales from Columbia, South America.  Rueben Augustino, a banker from Sicily.  Arthur Turner, a jeweler from San Francisco.   Jack Alterson, an insurance broker from Richmond.  Damien Rosterer, an import/export broker living in  Norfolk.  All would be staying at the house briefly when delivering and picking up inventory.  A large safe would be maintained to store the entire inventory.   Only the hostess would be given the safe's combination.  When associates were present, the hostess had the responsibility to prepare and serve meals.  The hostess would be given a substantial allowance to buy needed foodstuff, other household items needs,  and landscaping materials  for the maintenance man.

On a personal level, the starting salary would be $40,000 with increments at periodic times based on job performance.

The hostess would be provided with a new Mercedes- Benz for meeting and delivering associates to the airport, for attending business meetings, for pleasure activities, for visiting family, and for any other discretionary choices.

"That basically is the description of the business, the responsibilities of the hostess, and perks of employment. Are there any questions?" asked Steven.

Rose, the Reillys, and McDowells glanced at one another for several moments. Their minds reeled with the startling information. Rose gathered her composure when realizing her mouth hung open when attempting to comprehend what she heard.

"Joe asked, "How long have you been in business and how long do you anticipate staying in business? Rose would certainly not consider what might be called temporary employment."

"We have been in business for two years. We grossed about two million in sale, yearly. Our products are in constant demand. We do not anticipate closing our door," replied Steven.

"My partner and I have recently purchased the building which houses our business. We're obligated for a $50,000 loan debt. We each contributed $10,000 to purchase the seller's equity. I would not be in a position to leave my partner after assuming this obligation. We are both paying off our loan to the bank," said Rose.

"Rose, I extend my fullest heartfelt appreciation for your loyalty to your partner and to your business obligations. You are to be highly commended. These are sterling qualities we desire for the employment of a hostess. However, if you are serious in taking upon yourself the position as our hostess, I am in the position to write a check immediately for $50,000 to purchase the note from the bank and a check for $10,000 to reimburse your equity contribution," replied Steven.

Once again, all parties concerned stared at each other in

astonishment of the financial offer being made in order to free Rose of her obligations. This time Rose kept her mouth closed; she only smiled slightly as she viewed the reactions of the others.

"Mr. Harks, I would desire," said Rose, being interrupted by Steven.

"Please call me Steve," replied Steven.

"All right, Steve," continued Rose, "I would desire Carol DeLany, my partner, to be involved in this decision. I'll call her immediately and determine if she is available," said Rose.

Rather than calling her, Rose immediately stood up and left quickly for the salon. On arriving, Carol evidently was finished with her customer for she was thanking Carol and presenting her a gratuity.

Moving to Carol's side, Rose whispered, "Would you take a check for $50,000 to pay off the loan for the building?"

"What are talking about, Rose? Have you lost your cotton pickin' mind?" shouted Carol, as Clips, Sissy, and their customers peered questioningly at the two women.

"Not really, Carol. Please come to the Grill and meet the man who made that offer."

"Lead me to that source of wealth, my surprising roommate!"

Rose immediately related to Carol a brief synopsis of Mr. Harks' proposal should she accept his position as a hostess for his Import and Export Market.

Arriving breathlessly from the hasty walk, Rose proudly said, "Steve, this is Carol DeLany, my partner and co-owner of our building housing the salon and apartment."

"You are ready to pay off the bank loan in order for Rose to consider working for you?" asked Carol.

"Yes, I am," replied Steven

"You-u are able to wr-wr-write a check now for $50,000? S-s-sorry, silly question on my part. Obviously, you c-c-can or you wo-wo-wouldn't have said this," Carol stammered, being overwhelmed by the offer.

"Steve, may we have a family pow-wow to weigh the invitation and offer for Rose?" asked Donovan.

"By all means. I'll take my cup of coffee to another table," replied Steven.

Rose presented Carol more information than she had had time to relate coming from the salon. Joe and Donovan discussed and questioned the large salary, the offer of a new car, and other perks. June and Maureen were more concerned with Rose being over 100 miles away, living on her own, and dubious of Rose's capabilities of performing all the duties outlined by Mr. Harks.

"My dear friends, aren't you leaving out an important person? Shouldn't Rose be the one voicing answers to your concerns? She may validate your answers and decision, but Rose is capable of deciding her own future. Rose, you know me! Go for IT!" exclaimed Carol.

"We would miss you, sweetheart, but a two hour drive or so to visit you or vice versa would be feasible," added Donovan as he looked at Joe and June, and undoubtedly spoke for them also when reading their facial expressions.

"This type of work and the salary offered doesn't happen every day," said Rose, "however, I could benefit from the experiences the position offers. Missing you all-- Dad, Mom, Matthew, and you dear friends and Carol, my partner, will be most difficult, but the travel time is reasonable for visits. I will inform Steve that the position will be accepted on the condition of helping Carol's financial debt. Hope all of you are O.K. with that decision?" related Rose, hesitating briefly for any response, then walking to Steven's table to inform him of acceptance.

Steven immediately wrote checks in the agreed amounts to Carol and to Rose. He gave Rose the address and directions to find the house in Richmond. He indicated that a new Mercedes would be delivered, hopefully, within 24 hours. He kindly requested that Rose arrive within 36 hours. He wished to be present on her arrival and roll out the welcome mat. Unfortunately, he had a business trip. Rose's first duty involved driving him to the airport. Goodbyes were offered to all parties present. Everyone watched in astonishment as Steven left the Grill and disappeared down the street.

"Rose, I have heard the admonition, that when one door closes, another door opens. May this be a door of great opportunities and possibilities in your life's adventure," Joe said, as he embraced her with moistened eyes.

June wrapped her arms around both Joe and Rose. The McDowells were in line, awaiting their turn to embrace their daughter.

"Rose, I have Mrs. Snyder waiting for me. I'll see you shortly. We have some planning in dissolving our partnership," returned Carol as she departed with tears trickling down her cheeks.

AGREEABLE TO MR. HARKS' arrangements, the new car Rose would use was delivered early the next morning. Her happy, yet bewildering thoughts about the new adventure showered like fireworks when driving and fulfilling some of the business needs that she and Carol had discussed until midnight. She deposited her check. Arrangement were finalized for having her checking account transferred to the same bank branch in Richmond.

Matthew's disappointment in learning of his sister leaving Norfolk quickly changed when Rose gave him her Buick. Rose gave the title to her Dad for safekeeping until Matthew could acquire a driver's license. Matthew's jubilation caused Rose to be lifted in the air with joy by an over-whelmed brother. She never saw him so happy or realized his strength by practically crushing her against his chest!

Packing her clothes became a problem because of all the

purchases from the proceeding months.  How many suitcases should be filled?  How much room in the car?  What can be boxed for storage?  Decision time became a big problem!

Packing the suitcases and several boxes of personal items in the new car was not as serious a problem after all.  Driving to say good bye to her family was a problem.  But the family understood and cheerfully waved as Rose drove away.

Saying good bye to Carol, Sissy, and Clips became a tearful farewell.

Simultaneously, Carol was gushing tears, thanking Rose for facilitating the paid-off loan, and expressing words of endear-ment for sharing of times together.  Rose understood; she embraced her tightly, and shared tears as well.  She hugged both Sissy and Clips.

TWO AND ONE HALF HOURS  later, Rose found the house at 1813 Maplewood Drive.  Parking, she viewed the colonial styled house that would become her responsibility to main-tain in an efficient and warming manner for all the people entering its doors.   Rose surveyed the beautiful manicured lawn, trees, shrubbery and flower gardens.  While mentally photographing the sights of the house and grounds, Rose real-ized she had been caressing the steering wheel of her new car.  How delightful a perk! And handled like a dream, too.

Totally, Rose felt like a small child in Fairyland, with the magical dust showering over everything and creating a new world and life.

Stepping out of the car, Rose walked up the flower-lined walk with thoughts concerning this new adventure.  She rang the doorbell--the start of another new adventure.

# CHAPTER 22

"WELCOME TO YOUR NEW home, Rose," greeted Steven, as he offered his hand and helped her over the threshold. "How did you enjoy driving your new car?"

"Thank you, Steve. The Mercedes drives like a dream—like a precision jeweled watch. It's absolutely divine! Thank you again. I am grateful that you considered me worthy as your hostess. Actually, everything happening is beyond my reasonable expectations."

"Rose, speaking of precision watches, you must possess intuitive perception." Picking up a carefully wrapped package from the table by the door, "Here is a welcome gift."

Rose opened the package. Her eyes widened and mouth dropped open in astonishment. Rose removed her wrist watch and replaced it with the new gift. The wrist watch contained dozens of small diamonds arranged in rows around the band. She raised her arm and waved it about to increase the sparkling effects.

"Mr. Harks, I mean, Steve, this is the most gracious gift ever received. 'Thank you' seems so insufficient, but I know none other except a sincere 'Thank You.' "

"Rose, you're welcome. We believe a beautiful lady like yourself needs special gifts occasionally. May I offer you the proverbial 'cook's tour' of your new home? Your promptness of your arrival is appreciated. I need to board a 3 p.m. flight today for a business meeting in Los Angles. This will provide you the opportunity to learn from me the quickest route to the airport. You can expect frequent airport trips in the coming months."

The next hour involved entering each room while Steven began to outline additional responsibilities. They arrived at a room with a locked door. Giving a key to Rose, they entered where a large safe was located holding the company's inventory. The safe's combination was given to her. Steven taught Rose the technique of operating the dial. She was admonished to memorize the combination and never record the numbers.

Rose viewed the inventory. Steven identified the contents of the many packages. He pulled out several felt-lined drawers. Three contained hundreds of precious gems. Rose was astounded by the quantity in addition to the brilliancy of the shiny stones. Other trays contained rare stamps and coins that were briefly inspected. Another tray contained small bars of precious metals.

"Rose, you will meet Art Turner, our gem expert. You have the opportunity to learn the gradation scale. This will enable you to sort and grade shipments for him. Of course, he will validate your work. What's your reaction to this part of your duties?"

"Not in a hundred years would I ever realize viewing magnificent un-mounted gemstones especially in this quantity and undoubtedly great value, let alone the sorting and grading. Those little bars appear to be gold and silver, aren't they? And this must be the tweezers-like tool for picking up the stones and this a magnifier to examine them?"

"Rose, your observations are right on the mark! But now practice time! Close the door and open it again. Remember, when I leave, this is your 'baby' to open and have inventory available for our associates," as Steven patted the safe.

Rose opened the safe on the first try. Steven was more than impressed. Rose repeated the process twice more successfully.

"That's awesome, Rose! I misdial too many times." Looking at his wrist watch, he added, "Tina and Juan should be waiting in the kitchen. I asked both to be here by now. These employees are your valuable helpers. I know you desire to extend a welcome and to become acquainted."

The two employees were sitting by the counter nursing a coke. Steven introduced Rose. Tina's sparkling smile revealed the personality traits Rose would learn to appreciate. Juan, a wannabe comedian, graciously held Rose's hand longer than regular handshakes normally last. Flashing an affectionate grin, he looked directly in Rose's eyes. He shared an observation that despite his being 50 years old, Rose was older than his own daughter, Juanita. Getting down on one knee, he inquired if he and his wife, Carmella, could adopt her as their second daughter. They had always wished for a lovely red-haired green-eyed child.

Joining with the apparent humor Juan started, Rose decided to "pull out all stops." Grasping his hand, she brought Juan to standing position, threw her arms around him, and in a fake sobbing voice, cried, "Oh father, where have you been all my life! I want to be your daughter in the worse way! I'm so glad we found each other at last!"

Rose's actions created hilarious laughter. Actually, the response created an immediate 'ice breaker' effect. Steven's knew immediately that Rose would become the ideal hostess.

" Rose, you have a great sense of humor. I applaud you! But, I need to change out my suitcase, gather some paper work, and pack some inventory. You three may continue your silly antics; as a matter of fact, I encourage it.  You will create a valuable team for our company.  Rose, we need to leave at 1 p.m. for the airport," Steven said.

For the next hour, Rose, Tina, and Juan shared information about themselves, their families, their hobbies, their likes and dislikes, and the potential benefits from working for Mr. Harks.  Rose noticed several guarded comments by both Tina and Juan regarding working for Mr. Harks but dismissed their words.  She really didn't know why.  Inasmuch, that they were all new employees, both Tina and Juan realized that Rose's responsibilities as hostess placed her in the position as 'their boss.'  However, with the jovial nature Rose displayed and personal information shared, both concluded immediately they could easily give her their fullest cooperation and loyalty.

Opening the refrigerator door, Rose said, "Two carton of coke,  and some bottled water just doesn't cut it, folks."  She opened three cupboard doors.  "Unless  we  plan to starve to death, a visit to the grocery store is  absolutely  necessary.  I'll buy groceries when returning from the airport.  In the meantime, grab another coke if you wish.  Juan, please give us a tour of the grounds.  I love the outdoors!  I'll tell Steve where to find us."

STEVEN DIRECTED ROSE BY the quickest route to the airport.  Setting the GPS instrument on the dash, Rose realized that the duty of transporting the associates would be a snap.  Stopping at the departure area, Steven retrieved his luggage.

"Steve, we need to stock the kitchen with several items.  Do I pay for purchases from my own income?  We didn't cover the procedure on this point."

"Oh Rose, I'm so sorry.  Forgive me.  I forgot that important part."  Steve pulled out his billfold.  "Here, use this cash for now.  We shall have credit cards issued in your name when I return.  Tina and Juan can take meals with you on days when they're working.  Of course, we cover the needs for any of the associates. They will usually notify you of their schedule in advance when staying at the house. You can plan accordingly. They may call for transportation or they might use a taxi. If you leave the house, be certain to take a cell phone with you. It is necessary always to stay in touch. Good bye, Rose. You are indeed an adoring hostess. I'm so pleased you accepted the position. I'll call you later."

Rose left the airport and reversed directions. She had noticed a grocery store on the way. In the past, she and Carol had a prepared grocery list. This shopping would be strictly different—necessities plus considerable impulse buying! Unfolding the money given her, she cradled five one-hundred dollar bills in her palm. Well, another first time adventure!


THE FIRST ASSOCIATE THAT WEEK NEEDING transportation was the gemologist. Rose realized meeting him at the airport could prove a problem. Neither knew the other. Rose decided to prepare a sign she could display where luggage was retrieved. At first she felt foolish with a sign saying, "Mr. Turner" held head high. She caught the gaze and puzzled looks from dozens of people. Suddenly, Rose realized any man could claim to be "Mr. Turner." That could be a dilemma! Quickly, grabbing a pen from her handbag, she reversed the sign and wrote, "Import-Export Co." Displaying the new wording, the time was relatively short before a well-groomed, gray-haired gentleman approached Rose.

"I am Arthur Turner. Are you the new hostess Steven indicated he would employ?"

"Yes, I am Rose McDowell. It is a pleasure to meet you, Mr. Turner. May I help you with your luggage?"

"I have only this carry-on suitcase because I always travel light."

Arriving at the house, Rose assisted Arthur to one of the guest rooms. She asked about his favorite food dishes. He shared the information. However, more important than eating was his desire to grade the new shipment of gems in his suitcase.

"Mr. Turner, Steven has shown all the gems for my benefit presently in the safe. He indicated that you might help me learn the procedures in grading the many types of gems. I wish you to know, the prospects of knowing this information are both exciting and intriguing."

The next two days Rose was instructed with all the ramifications in grading the many different types of gems. She found the task more than exhilarating. This new found area of responsibilities was more than a challenge. Arthur's thoughts about Rose changed dramatically when she grasped his instructions quickly and accurately. The meals prepared for him pleased his palate. He deemed them right next to gourmet level.

Often he would savor the youth and beauty Rose displayed. His wife had died before they had children. He never remarried. How meaningful his life might have been to have had a daughter similar to the qualities of Rose. Now he could only visualize mental pictures. Rose fulfilled those pictures.

"Rose, when is your birthday? I wish to mount your birthstone as a gift."

"It's past, March 1st."

"In that case, you may look forward to a belated birthday gift then, on my next trip here. Rose, you are a remarkable young lady. I've met many ladies your age in my lifetime. I don't remember when I so thoroughly enjoyed working with and knowing someone of your stature. Your parents are to be commended for rearing a gifted and gracious daughter. On another note, I have an 8 a.m. flight tomorrow. We need to leave by 6 a.m. Will that be a problem, Rose?"

"None whatsoever. That is part and parcel of my hostess' duties. Our supper is prepared, Mr. Turner, if you're ready. Would you open the bottle of wine of your choice for our meal? I enjoy your company because too many meals are eaten alone."

DURING THE NEXT WEEK Rose developed a close relationship and warm rapport with Tina and Juan. With Tina, they found their three-year age difference helpful by placing their interests along the same subject matters—clothes, men and occasionally, the other three 'M's'—music, movies, and muscle toning exercises. Both looked forward to the twice weekly exercises conducted with directions from an exercise video. They exchanged favorite musical CD's and DVD's. Occasionally, they attended a nearby movie matinee after Tina finished her cleaning duties.

There were many days when Juan worked on the grounds. The comedy act on the first day introduction proved beneficial for the continuation of many friendly and meaningful conversations. Rose discovered Juan truly had a "green thumb." His flower garden furnished an endless supply of cut flowers to grace the various rooms.

Rose learned the information from their comedy act was false. Actually his wife's name was Marie and had four children—Sammy, 12; Bonita, 10; Daniel, 7; and Margarit, 3. With some coaxing on Rose's part, Juan's family accompanied him occasionally. Rose and Marie played games with the children in the spacious backyard and provided swimming lessons in the ample size pool.

Rose surprised Marie and her rambunctious children when she rented a costume portraying Snow White. The kids were delighted imitating the antics of their favorite dwarf. Juan informed Rose that his children "had a blast!" Her refreshments wooed the "Dwarfs" even more. Rose was pleased when they clambered for more fun with their "Aunt Rose." Consequently, she planned more adventures for the kids during their summer vacation. The love given and received by

Juan's children convinced Rose that one day in the future her own children would be equally loved.

ROSE WAS SURPRISED when the door bell rang and then heard the door open. A voice called out "anyone home?" She hadn't realized the possibility that Steven furnished keys to his associates.

Quickly leaving the kitchen, Rose answered, "There's someone home. It's Rose McDowell. And you are...?"

"Rueben Augustino, from Sicily, Miss Rose. I'm the company's banker."

Rose extended her hand expecting to shake his; however, she was surprised when Rueben placed his hands on her shoulders, kissed her right cheek, and then the left.

"Your sudden presence caught me off guard, Mr. Augustino. Mr. Harks indicated the associates would give some notification of their travel schedule. I could have met you at the airport."

"Forgive me, Miss Rose. I tried to reach Steven when arriving at the airport but there was no answer to the telephone numbers provided. I didn't know he had hired a new hostess. You are, indeed, a lovely vision. My compliments to Steven's selection. And call me Rueben."

"Well, thank you, Rueben, for the kind words. How long is your stay? And what are your preferences of food dishes. We aim to please!"

Reuben's two day visit provided Rose with memorable experiences. The wisdom gleaned from years of banking plus vivid descriptions of his native country and world travels, held Rose spellbound. She enjoyed his company in the kitchen and his help in the preparation of his favorite foods. Rose appreciated learning his delicious cuisine recipes and the use of different spices.

Before leaving for the airport, Rueben asked Rose to open the safe. He needed two packages of C-1014.

When providing a ride for Rueben to the airport, saying good bye was similar to losing a good friend. The bonding was mutual.

ROSE QUICKLY REALIZED that if associates were constantly bringing and taking inventory, that records needed to be maintained. After all, Steven would undoubtedly ask about these transactions while he was absent.

Returning to the grocery store for needed items and those forgotten on the first shopping trip, Rose also purchased an appropriate ledger book.

Rose recorded a detailed listing of everything in the safe. She had no information on items removed by Steven, unfortunately. But Arthur only delivered more gemstones. Reuben brought nothing but asked for two packages of C-1014. For each entry, Rose's information system consisted of:  date of transaction, initials of the associates, and what was brought in or removed. Now, should Steven inquired, she could provide accurate data.

ROSE WAS WATCHING THE EVENING news when the telephone rang.

"Import-Export Company, Rose speaking."

"Hello sweetheart!  Your dad here!  How are you?  How's your new job? We were wondering how busy you might be for us and the Reillys to visit tomorrow?"

"Hello father. I'm doing really great!  Oh yes, please come! I'm dying to show you our home. Tell little brother to bring his swimming suit. For that matter, all of you can go for a dip. I'll prepare a brunch. Can't wait to see everyone."

Rose's family arrived at 9 a.m. After many hugs, Rose led the way on a grand tour. June and Maureen marveled with the interior decorator's choices of décor for each room.

Rose introduced Tina who came early to give the house some final touches. Maureen's doubts were answered whether or not her daughter was capable of maintaining the home. Rose led the party into the kitchen for brunch.

"Rose, such a tasty meal. We're proud of you. I have no doubts about your capabilities," her mother said, with a gracious smile.

"I only ate a sandwich. Can I go swimming right away without waiting?" asked Matthew, anxious to jump in the pool.

"Sure, why not," answered his father, "Please use the bathroom to change."

Tina stood up, "Folks, working with Rose has been an absolute joy. I so appreciate her friendship. She pitches right in helping me with many household chores which are not her responsibility."

With a big smile, Rose replied, "Tina, stop it! You're too kind. Let's go to the patio. Tina, please bring a tray of ice tea."

"Joe, I haven't heard a 'peep' from you. That is so unlike you," chided Rose.

Sitting next to Rose, Joe took her hand in the fatherly manner as in the past, and said, "Rose, what I've seen—an immaculate house, an excellent brunch, the completion of many responsibilities, your obvious confidence—yes, for once I am speechless. Like the others, you amaze me. On the other hand, I shouldn't be amazed though."

Rose hugged Joe. She reminded him of his endless contributions when living in their home.

Rose's cell phone rang. In answering, Steven was calling from the plane while moving to the off-loading ramp. When Rose indicated that her family and Reillys were visiting and Matthew in the pool, he insisted he'd take a taxi. He wished for her to stay with her guests.

Sitting next to the pool, everyone had an enjoyable time sharing in the conversation and bringing one another up-to-date on their individual lives.

June joined Rose in retiring to her bedroom and changed

into swimming suits. They joined Matthew. They started playing a game of water polo.

Steven arrived and joined everyone on the patio. The water polo game was stopped temporarily. June and Rose climbed out and joined the rest.

Placing his arm across Rose's wet shoulders, Steven proudly said, "Thank you for your welcomed visit to our home. I'm pleased to see you once again. Donovan and Maureen, your daughter has surpassed our expectations as our hostess. Her abilities are outstanding! Has she informed you of becoming a neophyte gemologist? We anticipate even more surprises from her!"

Steven and Joe changed into swimming trunks and joined Matthew and the ladies. With two more players, a serious polo game started once again.  Maureen and Tina cheered everyone on and kept score. Steven and Rose won handily over June and Joe. Matthew expertly and proudly refereed the game.

When everyone had changed back into their regular clothes, hugs and kisses abounded. With the promise to hurry back, Steven and Rose waved goodbye as her loved ones drove away.


RETURNING TO THE PATIO, Steven immediately questioned Rose about Arthur's and Reuben's visits. She quickly informed Steven of the exact number of diamonds, rubies, fire opals, pearls, emeralds, and sapphires contained in the shipment. She indicated that most were ready for mounting. For Steven's benefits, she listed the types of cuts Arthur taught her—pear shape, American brilliant, cabochon, baguette, emerald cut, and a single cut.  All the gems were graded and sorted and added to the ones already in the safe. Rose informed him of Arthur's pending return for 205 different gems to supply two large orders he had negotiated.  She shared that the advertisement paid off. He had sold the 1923 San Francisco Peace Dollar for $6,700.

"Rose, as Joe indicated, you are amazing. In a brief time, your learning is incredible. Either you are a quick learner or Arthur is as brilliant a teacher as his gemstones or some of both. What about Auggie, or Reuben?"

"He placed two packages of C-1014 in his briefcase before we left for the airport. He's a fascinating person. He even taught me two of his Italian cuisine dishes as we prepared our meals together."

AS ROSE AND STEVEN CONTINUED THEIR CONVERSATION on the patio, two men approached. Steven jumped up quickly.

"Rose, meet Damien Rosterer from your city and Jack Alterson, here in Richmond. Both are brokers with Jack working in insurance some of the time. How were your business results, you two renegades? Rose, these two aren't married. I'm giving you fair warning! You know, a word to the wise should be sufficient!"

"Steve, you can certainly be insulting at times! Well, we weren't necessarily in a race," replied Damien; "however, we disposed of 10 packages each."

"Excellent work! Can you stay a while or off to the races again?" asked Steven.

"No, we need more inventory, then we'll scoot out of here," replied Jack.

Rose accompanied the three to the safe. Upon opening, each placed 10 packages of C-1014 in their brief cases. Rose mentally registered the numbers for recording later.

"Damien and Jack, please stay for supper. Steaks cooked as you like 'em plus all the trimins', Rosie's gourmet style!" joked Rose.

While the men discussed additional business, Rose busily prepared their meals—steaks grilled as the men indicated, rice pilaf, tossed salad, baby carrots, potato rolls, and pistachio sorbet. The table settings were appropriately placed;

a bouquet of flower graced the table's center.   She served all the food family style except the steaks. These she served individually.

"Supper is served!   Please come to the kitchen first.   I'll serve  your steak and then seat yourself.  The rest of the food is waiting except dessert.  Steven, would you please pour the wine?  Bon Appetite everyone!"  Rose added cheerfully.

During the ensuing conversation while eating, Rose became fond of the two new guests.  Their experiences varied as much as Reuben's for both had traveled extensively.   Rose discovered the men knew little of her recently acquired knowledge as a new gemologist and she added considerably to the camaraderie.  When the meal was over, Rose received "kudos" from all three for her culinary abilities.  She was grateful for their compliments.

"Rose, your graciousness as a hostess is most pleasant.  I look forward to seeing you next week.  Hopefully, I'll need more inventory.  Good bye for now!" Jack said.

"Double those words for me!" added Damien.

"Triple for me as well!  Sorry none of us can stay. Jack will take me to the airport," said Steven.

They picked up their brief cases and filed out the door. Rose waved good bye as the cars pulled away from the curb. " I am pleased, that they are pleased.  This new adventure just keeps getting more exciting!" she thought.

# CHAPTER 23

T HE DAYS WERE GETTING warmer.  Spring was Rose's favorite season.  She was spending considerable  time swimming and sunbathing on sunny days.   However, Juan did instruct her regarding the simple procedure of heating the swimming pool water on cool days with a flip of a switch.

Applying sun tan lotion brought back memories of the beach adventures with Marvin.  "Why must  today's happenings keep triggering  thoughts of the past?  Why is that part of my life so difficult to  forget?"  Rose turned the volume higher on her DVD player in hopes of drowning out the mental  visions flooding her brain.

When Tina and Juan were absent from performing their individual duties, the days seemed longer and even more boring.  Rose wished that Steven and the associates would plan more frequent visits.   She was beginning to relish their company immensely.  Each enabled her to enjoy a variety of experiences.  Basking in the sun, Rose's mind drifted to the places the associates had described.  She tried to transport herself vicariously--she could conjure up mental visions from their vivid stories.

On yet another boring day, she decided to brave the unknown streets of Richmond to find the library.   She prided herself in finding the place quickly after asking for directions. Rose found many pamphlets and maps about the city layout. Having a library card issued, she checked out two books about Richmond.  Finding a place to read, she found—where to dine, what to see and do, historical attractions, museums, gardens, and best of the listings—SHOPPING MALLS!   She would try to entice Tina to accompany her on these new adventures. Going alone was just a mite intimidating.

Doing some sight seeing and braving all the traffic while driving down Franklin Street, Rose spotted the Lemaire, a highly recommended hotel dining room from her book explorations.  Finding a spot to park, Rose discovered the Lemaire to be named for Thomas Jefferson's own maitre d'.  The luncheon buffet was a delightful treat.  It added a highlight to a day starting out to be boring.  Studying a map while eating dessert, she saw that the Edgar Allan Poe Museum was a short distance of 16 blocks from the spot she was sitting.

Arriving at the Museum, Rose found many of  Poe's artifacts and publications which especially  intrigued her.  Her thoughts reverted back to her high school literature class when reading "The Raven."   Impressed by the sights and entrenched by the remarks of the guide, Rose was startled when her cell phone rang.  She blushed when the touring party shot glances at her.

Quickly finding a place with some privacy, Rose activated the call button.

"Hi, this is Steve.  Plan to be at the Richmond airport in two hours.  How about a ride, my vision of beauty hostess?"

"Hello  Steve, yes, I'll be at the incoming gate platform. You'll never guess where I'm standing this moment—the

Edgar Allen Poe Museum in downtown Richmond. I proudly braved the busy traffic by myself and ate lunch at the Lemaire."

"Rose, you found one of the finest dining places. I would enjoy having you accompany me there another time. Your beauty would add ambience to the place."

"Oh Steve, stop it! Good grief, you're causing me to blush. Good bye! The traffic is horrendous today. I'll leave immediately. See you soon!"

UPON ARRIVING HOME, Rose attempted to open the door. Somehow, the tumbler was stuck. Steven moved his arms around Rose to turn the key, bringing his face close to hers. The immediate nearness startled Rose. She slightly cringed and turned her face toward Steven's. Their faces were close. Steven brushed her lips with a kiss.

"That's a reward for braving that traffic driving to the airport and back just for me."

"Well, thank you. I think!"

Steven turned the key with some difficulty. Entering the foyer, he gently placed his arms around Rose. The hug lasted several moments.

"Rose, I've heard the saying, 'absence makes the heart grow fonder.' I've certainly missed you. Seeing you again creates a happiness that surprises even myself. I told Joe that my relationship with you would be strictly platonic. Everything about you makes that statement difficult to follow. "

"Steve, there have been several boring days with an empty house. You and the other fellows 'make my day' as well. Joe and June indicated their success in life was dependent on open communications. To say I don't miss you would be a lie. Thank you for sharing this openness of your feelings for me. I wouldn't be standing before you today had my last fiancée continued with the openness we had agreed upon. He jumped to terrible conclusions about me without knowing the truth."

"Well, his loss is certainly my gain. Rose, my plans are being changed to be home more frequently.    I did not realize how rich my days become when we're engaging in conversation and eating those delicious meals you prepare."

The two did find considerable delight conversing by the hour.  Steven was impressed with Rose's ability to talk about many different subjects. Actually Rose surprised herself!  She quickly realized more time was needed reading newspapers, listening to programs on T.V. and radio, and doing more library research.  Confidence was indeed a friendly ally.  Back in the recesses of her thoughts, she wanted Steven to be pleased with her station as hostess, perhaps more than pleased!

"Rose, after lunch, I need to drive to New York with a large shipment.   May we trade cars?  I've too many miles on the Porsche.   It may be gratifying for you to drive a 'man's car' for a change!  O.K. with you?"

"Steve, that's no problem.  You'll enjoy the Mercedes, I'm certain.   It would tickle me pink to see New York City sometime.  Do you realize that moving to Richmond is the farthest I've traveled?  Steve, you've met my family and dearest friends. Would you share information about yours?    I would love to know 'what makes you tick' so to speak."

"Rose, there's not much goodness compared to yours.  My mother died from an embolism when I was twenty years old. My dad slid off 'the deep end' and became an alcoholic.  Where he's living or what he's doing is anyone's guess.  He could even be dead.  My sister, Margo, is a year older.  The last address for her five years ago was Paris.  There are no others.  My father was an only child.  Grandparents on both sides are deceased. I'm not proud of my family history, Rose."

The sharing of Steven's family touched Rose.  Her empathy became so strong, that her heart ached.  She felt his pain from the sadness registered on his face.  Involuntarily, Rose approached Steven and placing her arms around him, hugged him firmly, with her head against his chest.  Steven responded by hugging Rose, with his head resting on top of hers. Rocking so gently, they maintained the warm embrace for some lingering moments.

"Rose, the whole day would be so enjoyable embracing you, drawing strength from your nearness, delighting in your hair's aroma, and savoring your beauty, but that darn clock is ticking. I must deliver that shipment by tomorrow or there is real hell to pay. Some of the customers play rough when deliveries are delayed. I'll help you fix a bite and then be gone," at the same time releasing her and placing a light kiss on her lips.

Rose and Steven prepared a light lunch. While lunching, Steven reminded Rose to begin using her cell phone for all calls. When the phone was activated indoors, she was to move to the swimming pool area to talk. All calls from him or any of the associates would always be on the cell phone. He regretted the inconvenience that she would encounter. If anyone used the regular phone, answer it, also.

Rose did question the new procedure. Steven informed her that the reception was 100% certain outdoors. Indoors, there could be skipped signals and parts of a conversation could be lost. There were other reasons which would be explained later. He had wanted to say that the phone system might be compromised but that could be frightening for Rose. Presently, he had to leave immediately.

Desiring to be a faithful team player for the company, Rose stopped her questioning. She would be certain the cell phone batteries were always charged.

Rose stood on the front steps and waved good bye as Steven drove away. She remained standing for a few moments, searching her thoughts. "Do the moments in his arms reflect a serious desire for more intimate relationships? Are my feelings morphing to a different level for Steven beyond his being my employer?" She must face these forces developing between her heart and head.

Once again, the cell phone fastened to the hem of her skirt was vibrating and brought the revelries to the reality of her job responsibility. She immediately followed the walk around the house to the swimming pool area.

"ROSE, YOU HIT THE JACKPOT, so to speak. This is Rueben. Arthur and I arrived at almost the same time but on different flights. We're both starved. We both have considerable paper work to complete. We'll do that while we eat in the airport restaurant so no need for you to make a meal for us. I need to complete some banking transactions, also. We'll need to hit the bank branch on the way home. Can you plan to be here, say, in one hour?"

"Rueben, I'm delighted to hear your voice. Steven just left for New York City with my new car. He indicated it was imperative to complete a delivery by tomorrow. I have his car so your taxi shall await you in one hour."

SITTING IN THE LIVING ROOM, Rose was once again transported mentally to the places both men were describing since entertaining them the last time. She silently envied their exciting lives. But for some evasive reason, Rose sensed that both were 'living on the edge' in a manner of speaking. She just could not identify precisely why these thoughts were nagging her.

"Rose, remember my last visit, I indicated your birthstone ring would be delivered? Here's that late birthday gift," said Arthur.

Rose received the small velvet covered box. She noticed that her hands were slightly shaking from the nervousness of the moment. Opening the cover, the most magnificent aquamarine stone glistened in a silver mounting resting on a small plastic flower, the appearance of a jonquil. "A diamond studded wristwatch and now this meaningful ring," thought Rose. "How lucky can one Irish gal become?" she thought.

"Arthur, how absolutely divine!   Knowing the cuts of stones you taught me, this is an exquisite piece of craftsmanship. Thank you, thank you! This gift will be cherished, believe me!"

"Arthur, I'm obviously envious giving  Rose that fancy ring. However, if there is any consolation, Rose, Steven left instructions for  considerable funds to be placed in both your personal and household banking accounts. That's the reason for stopping at the bank on our return.  Here are the deposit slips for your checkbook records.  My suggestion for you, Rose,  is developing an investment program.  Your checking account will grow with automatic electronic salary transfers and your needs may not warrant keeping so large a balance," said Rueben.

"Yes, Rueben, please set up an  investment program.  You two have become such dear friends during the short time of our acquaintance. You bring excitement! The days are so dull when I'm home alone.  There was a time when I longed for quietness-- no distractions.  Now I desire company every day. Of course that's not possible, I realize.  But now you know that your company is always welcomed!"

"Rose we realize your love of preparing cuisine dishes for us.   However, we would be  delighted to entertain you for a change.    Reservations have been made for three at 'The Tobacco Company.'  The name sounds strange but  they have excellent food with fantastic dance music. This might  be your debut for 'Dancing with the Stars,' with two older 'stars,' that is,  should you have no objection to a varied evening," Reuben humorously said.

"Oh, yes, I love to dance!  And I bet you both can really cut a rug!" replied Rose.

Rose was beyond delight while dining with her two new friends. The preparation of well-plated dishes with succulent food pleased Rose's taste buds.    Both men practically alternated dances resulting in Rose dancing all evening. They were superb dancers and Rose, indeed, considered the evening her debut with 'stars' who literally swept her off her feet.

The associates stayed for two days. Rose had the opportunity to prepare meals that pleased both. Again, Rueben helped Rose in the kitchen teaching her additional Italian dishes. She was grateful to add to her culinary arts.

Rose was disappointed when both indicated their flight reservations. Arthur left with 205 assorted gems to fulfill the orders acquired. Both requested two packages of C-1014. Good byes were made and the house sounds were once again those of Rose's own makings.

PLANNING MORE TIME AT HOME, Steven did live up to his word. He arrived shortly after the two associates had left by taxi. Parking Rose's car in the garage, he entered the kitchen from the garage. Steven viewed the table. The left-over food and dirty dishes indicated a recent meal or a lazy hostess. He selected the first choice.

"Has the newly hired hostess left us in the lurch or are we playing 'hide and seek'. If so, here I come, ready or not!" Steven called out.

Rose was in her bedroom changing into her grungy clothes with plans to change the kitchen back to order. When she heard Steven's voice, she was thrilled! But she noticed her heart began to beat faster. "Why is his presence affecting my feelings in this manner? Am I reacting irrationally? Do I desire his attention and kisses to fulfill some need or inner satisfaction?" she mentally argued.

"Hi, I'm changing my clothes. Be there in a minute!" Rose called out, as she ran a brush through her hair and freshened her lipstick.

Steven did not wait for Rose. Instead, he approached her bedroom door. When almost there, he asked, "Your door is open. May I come in or wait out here?"

"Yes, Steve, come in, please! You've never seen my room

since I moved in. Tell me if you appreciate my efforts in deco-
rating with several accessories. The furniture is adorable that
your interior decorators selected. I couldn't have done any
better."

Steven stood in the doorway surveying the room. Rose
was sitting on the vanity bench and gazing at his refection in
the mirror.

"Well?"

"Rose, how simply adorable—and so homey! You've done
one heck of a job! This room-- it's you-- your personality is
reflected throughout. Oh, here's a special gift from the Big
Apple!"

"Steve, there's no need to shower me with presents! It's not
that I don't appreciate the attention, but that's not my speed,
not who I am. Your gift of this stunning wristwatch has fulfilled my needs for sometime."

Pulling a chair closer to Rose, Steven sat beside her. Rose
pivoted on the vanity bench to face him. Grasping both of
Rose's hands in his, he gently pulled her towards him as he
leaned forward and kissed her with a light lingering kiss.

"Rose, you indicated that communication is important.
You're aware that my work involves traveling to many places.
I have had the opportunity to know many women I have dated.
None have ever caused me to experience the inner feelings
that actually started from the first day I laid eyes on you in
Joe's Grill. I've tried to resist these feelings for you. I've argued with myself about getting serious in a relationship because of my line of work. This mental argument was especially
on my mind during the trip to and from New York City. We've
only known each other for a brief period now. But Rose, there
is a total quality of wholesomeness I perceive about you never
seen in any other woman I know. I'm not saying there's no
one else out there, but you, Rose, have a special beautiful innocence that is so refreshing to experience. I could compare
you to a wonderful magnet that attracts me with a desire to be

drawn close.   Putting the complete picture before you,   I'm falling in love with you. There, I've expressed myself, Rose, and I mean every word," as he leaned forward and warmly kissed her again.

When Steven released his kiss, he moved back slightly and fixed his eyes upon hers. Each peered into the other's eyes as if trying to penetrate the depths of their inner souls. Rose's thoughts flooded her capacity to think rationally. Steven, rising to his feet and still holding her hands, gently coaxed Rose to her feet. Cradling her face with his right hand, he gentle lifted her mouth to his. He kissed her bottom lip. Then he claimed both lips with more passion than  before.  Releasing her hand, he moved his to the small of her back and gradually pressed their bodies tightly together.

Rose knew what could happen from past experiences with Marvin. But now a different man, Steven, her boss, expressed his love to her.  His kisses were creating that sort of fainting type feeling—a tingling warmth.  She felt a light awakening moving, stealing throughout her body from his kiss and from their clinging bodies. "Does this heightened sensitivity mean that I love him or is it just a physical state of wanting? Yes, I do care for him. There may even be some love mixed in all that caring. Why do I have this hesitancy, this little voice that says to be cautious?"

Bringing her hands up between their bodies, Rose's applied pressure against his chest as a gesture to separate.  Steven broke off the kiss and stepped back.  Again, their eyes locked visually.

"Steve, your expression of love and your kisses are so sudden. There was a feeling of desire and need which I won't deny. I certainly do not wish to analyze the heck out of what just happened.  But Steve, please provide some time, some space for me to pull my thoughts together.  Caring for you and your home is an obligation, part of the work as a hostess.  I do not deny that there is a love for you as an expression of the fantastic advantages you've placed on my position as hostess.  My exceptional salary--the car--this wristwatch--and now a gift from the Big Apple.  It's all so overwhelming, Steve!  Do I open you gift now or can I wait until later?"

"Rose, perhaps my feelings for and the longing to have you as a part of my life is sudden for you.  But as I already expressed, you are an exceptional woman with qualities that radiate wholesome beauty similar to the sparkles of your wristwatch.  I wish you to know that I don't relish losing you."

"Steve, there are no plans of my leaving tomorrow! Joyfulness—fulfillment— these are words I use to describe the inner feelings I have when I'm with another person.  With your being home more frequently-- this warmth, this love, this contentment, this togetherness--I know will cause me to move from caring to loving you."

"Rose, you are, indeed, one of a kind.  If I become too impatient, just  haul  off and whack me.  Not too hard now!  I do bruise easily!  But if you desire as I do, to grow our love for one another, please open the gift now.  I know you will be pleasantly surprised!"

Rose slid the ribbon off the edge of the small box.  With hands shaking, she pulled the lid off.  Separating the tissue paper, she drew out a grayish colored box. Before she could open it, however, Steven gently removed the box from her fingers.  He turned slightly so she could not see him opening the cover and removing the contents.

"Rose, darling," as Steven lowered himself on one knee, "please accept this engagement ring as a token of my expressed love to you.  With your acceptance, I wish to place it on your finger now." Lifting her hand, he hesitated for her reaction, then caressingly slipped the ring onto her finger.  Gazing into her face, "May our love grow deeper day by day!"

"Steve, oh yes, I will accept your diamond ring and pledge my growing love for you.  You certainly are serious.  I never expected a commitment of this nature at this time.  You are literally sweeping me off my feet! I feel that when loving and wanting someone close by, you just can't touch enough. Steve, may I touch you now?"

Standing, Steven took Rose into his arms. Rose moved her arms around his neck. Gazing again at each other, they gently nuzzled noses. Then she offered Steven her opened lips. He once again claimed them. His tongue gently massaged the edges of hers. Then both shared an intensity as their kisses quickened and a sense of urgency became almost unbearable. Both realized the union was the beginning of an affection, an intimacy of being loved and wanted. Rose could feel her senses poised, alive, and glowing. She was surprised, yet pleased, by her arousal.

The two spent many hours the next two days before Steven had to leave for another business commitment. They planned their future. Rose was asked to set a wedding date when she felt ready for total commitment. They spent time in each others arms--kissing, nuzzling, caressing. Both agreed that moderate arousal was lovely and intoxicating in so many ways. Rose shared the self promise that she had desired to remain pure and innocent until her wedding night. Steven's desire to fulfill her wish was met with caring and tenderness. Rose felt even more affection and sense of security for her husband-to-be. She was overpowered by emotions of ecstasy. Mentally, she thought of a late fall wedding, but now, perhaps the date should be much sooner. Her anxiousness was kicking in to be his wife much sooner!!

"Steve, while on your business trip, I plan to go home and visit my parents. They will certainly be surprised! You indicated for me to select our wedding day. Would the end of July be O.K with you? When home, I can determine open dates on our church calendar and on reception hall rentals."

"Rose, Sweetheart, I'll leave all that planning to you. As you now know, I have no family. We might invite all the associates and any guests they desire to accompany them. So the number of folks you desire at our wedding would be your family and friends. While you are planning between now and then, Sweetheart, select a month wedding trip to any places in the world you wish to visit, tour, or see the attractions."

"Oh, Steve, darling, what a fantastic trip that will be! That is almost beyond my wildest dreams, yet I know you're dead serious. Oh, that will be fun, fun and more fun! I'll make a list of the places I wish to visit! You certainly would desire to confirm my choices?"

"Rose, when you decide where to go, and how long to stay, the list will be given to the travel agency we use. They will complete all the details for us. We can hash this some more on our way to the airport. We need to leave in one hour, Sweetheart. Give your parents and the Reillys my best wishes. I'll be in my office working on my itinerary for the next month, new information for you, and complete some phone calls by the pool."

"I'll pack my suitcase, also, and leave for Norfolk directly from the airport. Better call my parents, too."

"MOTHER, WOULD YOU DESIRE TO PLAN a wedding for this coming July?" asked Rose, after a warm hug, and then lifting her left hand for her mother's view.

Grasping Rose's hand and hugging her, exclaimed, "Oh, Rose, you and Steven are engaged? What a surprise! Let me sit down! You're giving me heart palpitations! Tell me more! Oh, will your dad be overwhelmed!"

"Yes, Mother, I'm sure Dad will. Steven's expression of love and his desire for commitment with an engagement ring was sudden for me, also. But I care for Steve, deeply. Our time spent together is helping us to know, to appreciate, and to love each other.

"Rose, what do you really know about Steven?"

"Mother, I'm discovering more every day. I realize you're concerned. But, our love increases daily."

Rose's dad, indeed, was greatly surprised and slightly perplexed when informed about the short engagement and wedding. The Reillys were more than pleased. Carol and the rest
of the beauticians were completely bowled over about Rose's
impending wedding. Phone calls to several close girl friends
offered her congratulations. All were happy to learn the wedding would be at the McDowell's church on July 25th. Carol,
Sissy, and June were over-joyed to be asked as the bride's ma-
tron of honor and bridesmaids. In two days, Rose and her
mother had more than completed tentative wedding arrangements. The Reillys offered their Grill for the reception and
the food. Joe and June invited the future wedding party for a
celebratory dinner before Rose left.

Sleeping once again in her previous apartment bedroom
was nostalgic. Rose and Carol enjoyed their intimate chats
once again until midnight.

Rose stopped at the Grill the next morning before returning to Richmond. "Joe, June, you dear friends, you keep giving from your hearts. How can I repay you for your unending
kindness?"

"Well, for starters, you can name your son Joe, and your
daughter after June," Joe said in jest.

"I so love you both," and with hugs for each, Rose returned
to her home away from home.


SPRING MERGED INTO SUMMER. Rose continued her wel-
coming position as hostess. The associates arrived and left
periodically. Each visit brought additional enrichment for
her. Rose maintained her inventory records. Relying on the
accurate data, Rose was enabled to provide exact information
for Steven. He was always more than pleased. Rose enjoyed
his thankful type hugs and kisses even more. Rose and Tina
were kept busy fulfilling the many domestic chores generated
by the numerous associates' visits. Both Tina and Juan were
concerned for Rose with the sudden engagement and pending

wedding. There were so many details they wished they could share with her. However, Tina found time to accompany Rose for several trips to the various malls to begin shopping for the wedding..

Juan and his family continued their visitations to the delight of their children. Rose's completed swimming lessons for the children increased their fun times in the pool. Steven's business arrangements were curtailed to provide quality time with Rose. She was more than pleased! Their love grew, some days by leaps and bounds!

"Steve, I've given my all--my heart, my soul, and my thoughts-- in our precious time together these past weeks. You have shared also. How I've thoroughly welcomed these private moments. Yet, Sweetheart, there's this small nagging feeling, that something more needs revealing. Should I experience this confusion?"

"Rose, there's more. But in due time. Once again, we need to burn a trail to the airport. My itinerary you have covers this trip should you need to reach me."

"Steve, you guys have been selling considerable C-1014. There's only 9 packages left."

"Oh, yes, there will be a large delivery tomorrow. Father Pedro Gonzales will be in charge. He's the last associate for you to meet," said Steven as he got into his car, rolled down the window, and blew a kiss to Rose.

As Steven drove away, Rose mused again on the pleasure in meeting and becoming friends with all the associates. Each had enriched her life as they continued narrating interesting adventures. And now a priest? Interesting! I wonder what fascinating stories he has to share from his travels.

# CHAPTER 24

Rose heard a car horn. Hurrying to a window, she noticed a bakery truck backing up to the garage door. The painted sign on the side --"Tallman's Bakery"—was confusing. Why are bakery products being delivered? None were ordered unless Steve did and failed to inform her.

A man dressed in priest's clothing exited from the passenger car side. Rose then realized this was the person in charge of delivering more C-1014 to which Steven made reference. Moving to the door in the kitchen leading to the garage, Rose pressed the garage door opener. As the door opened, Rose moved quickly to the priest who was waiting for the door to fully open.

"I'm Rose McDowell, Father Gonzales, Steven informed me of your arrival today," as she extended her hand.

Taking her hand, he made a slight bow. "More than pleased to meet you Senorita McDowell. Steven spoke about you as our new hostess; however, I learned that will soon be Senora Harks, si?"

"News travels fast these days!  Yes, we have decided upon a July wedding in Norfolk.  You and your family will be invited, Father."

"You do know I live in a small village near Bogotá, Columbia. My trips to the United States are spotty.  When I do, it's the supervision of deliveries.  Could you  please move your car  to the street, Senorita?  We can back completely into the garage to unload the cargo.  Also cooler working in the shade."

Rose quickly walked to her bedroom and obtained the car keys from her handbag.  Her car was switched for the truck and the garage door closed.

"This is Toby, Senorita, who helps me with these shipments by loaning his truck."

Father Pedro and Toby quickly moved the 60 packages into the house and placed them beside the safe.   Rose's invitation to stay overnight was refused.

"Pleased to have met you, Senorita.  We have more deliveries.  Hope to see you on my next visitation or delivery.  Should we not be present for the wedding, my best of congratulations to you, the future Senora Harks."

"Thank you, very much, Father Gonzales. I wish you could have stayed longer."

JUAN WAS BUSY DIGGING OUT WEEDS in the flower beds bordering the main entrance.  After driving her car back into the garage, Rose strolled to where Juan was kneeling on the ground while weeding.

"Juan, you are one fastidious gardener!  The flower beds are immaculate.   There is another little job to place on your 'to do' list.  When placing the metal tub by the door in the safe room, the men made a long scratch."

"Rose, this weeding can wait.  I'll remove the scratch immediately.   I'm glad to have some left-over paint for that room."

Rose returned to the house.   She obtained her inventory

records and began counting the packages. The entries were entered.    Opening the safe's door, she placed a door-stop against it to prevent the door from swinging shut.    As the packages were neatly stacked in layers, one package slipped out and fell on the point of the door-stop. The puncture was slight, yet large enough for a small amount of the white contents to sift out.    Standing there, contemplating what to do, Juan walked into the room with sandpaper, paint can, and brush.  He viewed the spill.

"Juan, what suggestion do you have to remedy this mess? Steven, undoubtedly, will not be pleased with a broken package."

"Rose, we'll simply tape the tear with masking tape. There's a roll in the kitchen.  Then vacuum the spilled part.  Should Steven notice, inform him the package had a small hole that was taped.  What ever you do, be cool and innocent should he ask.  By the way, you do know what this white powder is called?"

"Yes, Steven informed me the packages contain a special industrial compound used in numerous manufacturing processes."

Juan wasn't surprised by her answer.  He knew Rose was oblivious  of what the contents really were.  He wondered what her reactions might be when the truth was known. And he knew that would be one day soon!

ARRIVING HOME AFTER HIS LAST class, Marvin entered his home just as the phone started ringing.  Dumping his back pack of books, he rushed to pick up the receiver.

"Hello Marvin, this is Chris.  Just blew in to Denver International.  I'm picking up a car rental now and wondered if we could get together.  I have some news that will not necessarily create  happiness for you, I'm sure.  I'm here for a two day seminar conducted by the Colorado Bar Association."

"Chris, what a pleasure hearing your voice.  Hey, we have a

guest room. Why not stay with us for the two nights?  It will give us more time to shoot the breeze."

Marvin gave Chris the directions to find their home.  Upon arrival, Chris was warmly greeted and introduced to Mrs. Brown and Sally.  Grabbing cokes from the refrigerator, the two ex-sailors hastily retired to Marvin's bedroom. They were anxious to share the latest news.

"Marv, first may I extend my sincere sympathy on the death of your dad.   Must have been difficult for everyone to find closure. I'm delighted to meet your mother; she is so gracious. And your sister is absolutely stunning!   Now, before flying here, I first drove to Norfolk to pay a visit to our ship.  Still a few of the old crew left on board.  Also stopped at the Grill to chat with Joe and June. Found some interesting news that will be surprising for you."

Chris proceeded to bring Marvin up to speed on his courses at Harvard University.

He continued to relate his findings about the different shipmates both knew and still remaining.   Bringing  back to Marvin's memory the love tryst that Don Nelson had described shortly before Marv's early discharge, brought him angrily to his feet.

"Take it easy, Marv.  You're the one who jumped to conclusions about Rose and ended your pending engagement."

Chris continued the story.  After Don returned to the ship, he realized that the red-headed gal he picked up at the Anchor Bar and shared her bed, was really special.  He wanted to locate the "wonder" lady.  His shipmates suggested he try the cab company.  Don, despite being drunk, did remember the cab had checker-board painted doors.  He called that particular company and inquired if their records would provide information regarding the address for that night's fare.  When the cab dispatcher was informed why the address was important for Don, the man chose to promote a budding love and provided the street address.  Don located the apartment building.  Her name was Rosalie Reynolds. Don showed me her picture and the similarity was so striking to Rose, they could have been twins. Rosalie's former commitment with her sailor ended in disaster, so now Don and Rosalie are dating hot and heavy.

"Don't you wish now that Don could have remembered her full name? I'm sure your decisions would have been completely different," Chris added.

"Oh, Chris, I acted like a jackass! I made a terrible blunder! What a horrible ordeal Rose must have endured. If I could only retrieve that incriminating letter mailed to her. If I only hadn't gotten so angry and jumped to such horrible conclusions about her. And I didn't even allow Rose the common courtesy of opening her one letter. She undoubtedly had useful information. We did agree to open communications which I violated. Would there be any chance she would forgive me if I pleaded my case?"

"Sorry, Marv, hate to burst your bubble. May I share 'the rest of the story' as Paul Harvey would say?"

Chris shared the information Joe provided when visiting the Grill. Rose did recover from being dumped. She and June bought the building where the beauty shop was housed. The two shared the apartment above their shop. One day a Mr. Steven Harks inquired about someone he could hire as a hostess to maintain his home in Richmond. Joe suggested Rose. This Hark character then wrote a check for $50,000. This paid off the bank note so Carol was debt free. He paid Rose her $10,000 deposit also. All this to spring Rose from any obligations and to encourage her to accept the hostess position.

"Must be some wealthy dude to shell out that kind of dough," Marvin noted.

"The story becomes better or worse, depending on your point of view, Marv. For maintaining his home and for the other business men in the company, Rose is drawing a $40,000 yearly salary. He bought her a Mercedes-Benz to drive. And now the real kicker--he gave her a huge diamond engagement ring. The wedding is scheduled near the end of July."

"Chris, I am totally speechless hearing this information. I know now that I've totally lost Rose. What a terrible, outlandish fool I am! As much as I've tried to erase my memories, the beautiful images of Rose continue to pop into my thoughts."

"Marvin, I know you'll find someway, somehow to forget Rose and continue with your life. Yes, I agree that you could have done things just a little differently when Don told that story about Rosalie. You have definitely lost Rose. With all the beautiful women on campus, can't you find someone that strikes your fancy?"

"Really haven't been looking, Chris. My study load does not provide time to be gallivanting about chasing skirts or slacks, as the case may be."

The remaining time that Chris spent with the Brown family continued with delightful and entertaining conversation. The camaraderie helped Marvin forget the situation about Rose, somewhat. Despite her efforts to resist, Sally realized she was developing a "crush" for the handsome ex-sailor and future lawyer. The situation was obvious to Marvin, but Chris never picked up on the vibes. He did promise that a return visit would be planned later in the winter. Expressing his desire to try the ski slopes, they said their goodbyes. Chris left for the airport but his visit left a bigger problem for Marvin as visions of Rose filled his mind and the realization of the huge mistake he made about the accusations regarding Rose.

"I'M HOME, SWEETHEART! Using the taxi service saved you another trip to the airport. Hello, where are you? It's your Stevey-boy!"

Not hearing a response, Steven checked the garage and found her spot empty. Looking about for a possible written note and finding none, Steven became puzzled over Rose's absence. Going to the room housing the safe, he opened it and checked the new shipment.  A big smile stretched from ear to ear.  Sixty packages at the going price translated into a sizeable profit.

Closing the safe door, Steven retired to the kitchen and poured a glass of wine.  Picking up the National Geographic Magazine, he moved to the living room, and settled down for some relaxation and reading time.  However, fatigue settled in and he soon drifted into a deep sleep.  The magazine slipped from his grasp and slid to the floor.

Parking her car in the garage and entering through the kitchen, Rose noticed the opened wine bottle on the counter.  She knew Steven had to be home, probably in his office.  Pouring a glass for herself, Rose walked into the living room.  Still having her handbag hooked on her arm, she quietly placed it beside a chair.  Seeing Steven fast asleep, Rose moved quietly beside his chair.  Setting her glass on the end table, she moved her face close to his.  She intensely studied his face now containing a vivid five o'clock shadow, the lines in his forehead, the dimple near the end of his jawbone, the lips that formed the welcomed kisses, and the tuft of hairs brushing his forehead.  She had to admit freely that her future husband was truly handsome.  Her eyes moved repeatedly, caressingly over all his facial features.  She was tempted to awaken him with a kiss.

Picking up her glass, Rose curled up in the chair beside him and sipped her wine.  She continued gazing upon his total countenance—her future husband-- the father of their children.  She closed her eyes and her mind wandered among day dreams concerning their future.

Steven began to rustle.  Opening his eyes, Rose came into focus.

"Welcome to our world, sleepy head," cooed Rose.

"There you are!  I came home and couldn't find you so I sat down to read and must have gone out like a light.  It has been a rough two days!  I'm exhausted."

Rose stretched over her chair toward Steven. He leaned towards her. They kissed. "Rita and I visited two different malls shopping for a wedding dress. After a light lunch, we found a theater showing a movie we could appreciate. It was an unusually long show. I was expecting my cell phone to announce your arrival at anytime to pick you up."

"Glad I didn't call to interfere with your shopping plans or pull you out of the movie. Find a gown that fits the occasion?"

Rose continued to share their shopping experiences. Pulling out some pictures from her handbag, she presented five different model-posed wedding dresses for a possible choice.

"See one that grabs your fancy?"

"Rose, with your beauty and figure, any of these five would take my breath away and undoubtedly, everyone attending the wedding."

"Darling, you're no help! But Rita and I favor pose number three."

"That one is, indeed, a magnificent creation! That's the cat's meow! If that's the one you desire, buy it immediately! I can visualize you coming down the aisle wearing it, Sweetheart."

Rose continued to share their shopping experiences between the kissing, watching a romantic movie on T.V., and sipping wine.

"Woe, Sweetheart, midnight already! There's an eight o'clock appointment to meet in the morning. I need to catch some shut-eye. I'm beat. Care to join me?"

"In your dreams, Stevey-boy! Don't you wish!" as both stood and fell into an embrace. The parting good night kiss presented a suffusion of delicious feelings.

# CHAPTER 25

Pedro and estella gonzales were both suddenly awakened by the hunger-pang cries of their baby. Estella rushed to the nursery to pick up Pedro, Jr. Quickly placing a pacifier in his mouth to stop the crying, she carried him to the kitchen. Perhaps her husband could return back to "slumber land." She heard him arriving home late due to a mid night flight from the United States.

After heating a bottle of milk, Estella sat by the window nursing the baby. The sun's rays were beaming over their small village outside of Bogotá. In a few minutes, the rays came streaming through the kitchen windows. She enjoyed the magnificence of the sunrises. The baby's tummy was full. Placing him in the position to pat his back to dispel any air bubbles, she realized he was fast asleep. Gently, she carried her precious baby to the nursery.

Not desiring to return to bed, Estella walked back to the kitchen. Perking a pot of coffee, she once again sat by the window sipping the cup of hot liquid, watching the orange rays magically change to the various shades of yellow.   As she watched, her mind's musings centered on the work in which Pedro was engaged.  She wasn't certain what he did nor why he occasionally flew to the United States.  The trips seem to coincide each time when a Mr. Harks would contact him by telephone or sometimes by telegraph.   She deeply loved Pedro and he provided well for her and the baby. Yet she was confused regarding the reasons he gave involving his work.

Looking at the clock, she decided it was time to prepare breakfast.  Busily removing eggs, bacon,  and tortillas from the refrigerator, the telephone rang.  The unexpected ringing startled her causing the food to  pop out of her hand and fall to the floor. Perturbed with her behavior, she stepped around the mess to pick up the receiver.

"Estella, this is Juanita.  Didn't get you out of bed on this beautiful sunny morning, did I?"

"Buenos dias, Juanita, no, our 'small baby alarm clock' woke us both with his loud crying. I'm starting to make breakfast.  Pedro is still in bed, although I  hear him rustling at the moment."

"Did Pedro arrive late on a flight, say the 12:30 arrival?"

"Yes, he must have been on that late flight. He woke me up at 1:30 getting into bed."

"Well, the strangest incident happened at the airport."

Juanita proceeded to relate that she was at the airport picking up her aunt and was  certain seeing Pedro dressed in priest's clothing.  She was positive that he was walking  down the  corridor,  then  quickly entered into the men's toilet. She  kept watching the exit door, but never saw him leave. The  whole  situation  was  very strange.

"I don't know what to say, Juanita.  Does sound very strange, indeed.   There would be no possible reason why Pedro would be disguised as a priest. He certainly was at the airport, though. Perhaps some one with Pedro's features. Did you see this person from a distance or close by?"

"Yes, it was some distance. I must be mistaken. Sorry, Estella. Viaya con dios."

The ringing of the phone did in fact wake Pedro. He emerged from the hallway into the kitchen in his bath robe. Picking up the coffee pot, he poured a cup and joined his wife. "Who the heck called so early on a Sunday morning?"

Estella retold Juanita Martinez's strange conversation.

"Oh sweetheart, Juanita must need new glasses or something. What a far fetched piece of malarkey!"

Estella accepted the explanation given.

Picking up his cup of coffee, Pedro retired to their bedroom to dress for the day. As he did, he concluded that his actions at the airport needed careful adjustments. Juanita did see him and he saw her. Upon their visual exchange, he had quickly turned his face and ducked into the men's room. Upon removing the priest's clothing for his own street clothes, he peeked along the edge of the door. When Juanita was preoccupied, he slipped quickly among other passengers and left the airport. His betrayal of identity was too close for comfort. Traveling to the States dressed as a priest provided many advantages for his line of work.

Having finished dressing, he returned to the kitchen and warmed up his cup of coffee. Sitting down at the table, he noticed his wife staring at him. A twinge of guilt crossed his thoughts. He hated lying. How could he tell her now that his disguise as a priest was helpful for earning their income. The entire situation was becoming a real dilemma. In many ways, he wished he had never become involved in illegal trafficking. He was placing his family and himself in great danger.

"My dear wife, I sense you are concerned with these trips I make to the United States. Perhaps I need to find employment here at home. This will help to prevent your worrying so much when I am gone so long. This last trip for Mr. Harks was

interesting, though.   I met the lovely young lady he is marrying this coming July.  We are invited but told the Senorita that
might not be possible.  However, if you would enjoy a trip like
that as our vacation, we can certainly make plans to go."

"Yes, Pedro, I would enjoy going. Taking the baby may give
us a few problems.  We have never had a vacation of this kind.
I would like to meet this Mr. Harks and his new wife.   But I
would appreciate your getting a job here at home.  I'm always
upset too much when you are away.  I have this constant fear
that something will prevent you from returning."

"I'll  tell Steven will be there for the wedding and start looking for a new job tomorrow, dear wife."

MOVING INTO THE HALLWAY, Steven called out, "Rose,
please come to the safe!"

Sitting in the living room reading the daily newspaper, Rose
laid the paper aside to join Steven.

"Did you notice this package that has been taped?  Did you
find anymore in similar condition that Father Pedro delivered?
I hate to check each one."

"Steve, that is the only one taped of the 60 new packages
in the shipment." Rose remembered Juan's warning in playing
an innocent role. She wasn't certain why she should, but Juan
was most adamant when speaking about secrecy.

"Thank goodness.  Worried me a bit.  Thank you for your
careful observation when stacking the packages.   Had there
been more taped ones, we might conclude someone was stealing a little from each to make a profit for themselves."

Closing the safe's door, Steven placed his arm around Rose's
waist. They moved to the living room. They embraced.

"Have I told you lately, you're a beautiful woman and I love
you dearly?"

"Yes, you have and I appreciate your loving words. Thanks
for being home more days.  Spending these romantic moments helps my growing love for you, Steve."

The budding love of Rose and Steven moved gradually to a heightened alertness, a euphoria causing both to become closer. Their inner feelings morphed to an exquisite emotional role, a blend of desirability and wholesomeness.

Again the business routine of Steve and his associates continued for the weeks to follow. They frequently showed up unexpectedly much to Rose's chagrin. She preferred their advance notice of arrival. Rose's transporting them to and from the airport was not an imposition. However, each associate brought a variety of exciting stories, so she could tolerate their surprises. The inventory was withdrawn as needed. She had the opportunity to apply her gemologist skills when new shipments arrived.The challenge of grading the various stones' cuts provided her with extraordinary excitement. Rose's position as hostess complimented with the household duties performed by Tina and Juan's maintenance and yard work kept the household humming like a well-tuned fiddle. Everyone was happy and the interchange of their friendships more pleasant than anyone could ever imagine.

"TINA, THE PAPER ON THE cupboard shelves is getting rather tacky. Do you have the time today to help exchange it for new? I'll stand on the counter and hand down all the stuff. We can complete the job rather quickly. Would you be able to accompany me downtown later to make a deposit on the wedding gown and some of the other accessories?" asked Rose.

"Love to, Rose," said Tina, with some hesitancy. She was not in the position to tell Rose that the wedding would never occur.

As Rose was handing all the items on the very top shelf to Tina, Rose spotted an envelope wedged between the board and laminated veneer that covered the shelving. Pulling it out with some difficulty, she opened the envelope. Seeing a CD disc and a note as its contents, she removed them.

"Tina, why would this CD be hidden in our cupboard? The

note states to return to a Mr. Larry Reid, 1430 Catalpa Street. That's the next street over, isn't it? There is a signature of a Sarah Hewitt, also. Suppose it's a borrowed CD that needs returning? But why hidden in the manner I found it? Strange!"

"Rose, your reasoning sounds good to me. I'll return the CD for you on my way home after we finish shopping. I've met Larry Reid once. He's a policeman for the Richmond Police Department."

"Thanks, Tina. He should be pleased to have it returned, finally. Who knows how long it has been hidden."

"Yes, he undoubtedly will be pleased, Rose. However, I would suggest you say nothing to Steven about finding this CD in the kitchen. Mentioning Sarah's name will bring back some bad memories for him as a former employee."

"O.K. Tina, thanks for the tip. Mum's the word!"

Tina knew about Sarah Hewitt. She was Steven's hostess prior to Rose being employed. The last FBI report had indicated her mysterious disappearance.

LARRY REID ANSWERED THE DOORBELL. Before opening the door, he saw a young lady through the security peep hole in the door.

"Sergeant Reid, I'm Tina Weston, the maid for Mr. Steven Harks who lives in the next block. When we were changing shelf paper today, Rose McDowell, the new hostess for Mr. Harks, found this CD addressed to you. The signature is that of Sarah Hewitt. Did the authorities ever find her?" asked Tina.

"Who are you again? Should I know you?" questioned Sergeant Reid.

"No, you don't. But here are my credentials," as Tina held up her billfold for him to read.

"Thank you for your identification. Now I know the reason why you are employed for Steven Harks. The answer t o your question regarding Sarah is 'no.' There have been no new leads according to the latest bulletin published. I'll place this CD in charge of those searching. It may contain some important leads."

"Are you aware that the new hostess, Rose McDowell, is being wooed romantically? A wedding date has been set for July. I helped Rose reserve her wedding gown today. The situation is getting very serious."

"Tina, I don't know all the details. But you can be certain there are others who do. Thanks for bringing the CD. Stop by anytime. Good to meet you."

"STEVE, INDEPENDENCE DAY WILL BE HERE two weeks from today. Would you agree with my plans to have a celebration on the patio and pool area? We can invite all the associates and their wives or significant others except Father Pedro. He indicated to me that he's in the States only when deliveries are required. The rest could draw from the inventory before leaving. "

"Rose, that's one splendid idea! This will create more work for you and Tina, providing she can help. She may have other plans for the holiday. We could celebrate our engagement, also."

"Thank you, Sweetheart! Yes, we could announce our engagement. Not every one knows, except Tina, Juan, my parents, and friends. Even if Tina can't be present, you know my love for preparing meals. Do you wish to call them? If not, I will."

"Rose, Darling, I'll do the inviting immediately. There are some other business items to discuss with each, anyway. I'll be out on the patio making the calls. Let me know when supper is ready if I'm not back in the house before time to eat." Steven embraced Rose. The warmth of their growing love was reflected by the intimacy of their kisses.

As Rose prepared the final touches on their meal, she was pleasantly humming the "Wedding March." Her spirits were at an all time high.  She periodically peeked at Steven through the kitchen window as he made his calls.  Fourth of July would certainly produce a great celebration for everyone!

Perhaps this part of her adventure would be more than she could ever imagine!

# CHAPTER 26

ROSE HAD LESS THAN a week to plan for the Fourth of July celebration. Menus were planned. Groceries, wine, and other items were purchased. Several food dishes were prepped and placed in the freezer. Rose assisted Tina by arranging the guests' rooms for those staying over night. Juan spent several hours of special attention to the patio—sufficient tables and chairs; clean lounge chaises; full propane tanks for the barbeque; clean water for the pool; extra bags of ice in the patio refrigerator; and groomed lawns. Tina and Juan were grateful for Rose's compliments for the dedicated attention to details; however, both had thoughts whether or not their work would have been done all in vain. They had some knowledge of a pending raid on the place. The exact time was not yet determined.

ROSE WAS HOME ALONE preparing hors d'oeuvres for the big celebration two days away, when the sound of the door bell interrupted her work. Wiping her hands on the towel tied around her waist, Rose opened the door.

"Hello" greeted Rose, as she quickly glanced at each man.

"Miss McDowell, I'm Agent Harry Manning and this is Agent Jasper Roderick," as they showed their badges and identification cards, then added, "we are Federal Bureau of Investigation agents. May we come in and visit with you? We know you're home alone."

"Yes, I'm alone. Please come in. Steven is away on business. Tina and Juan did not plan to come to work today. But why is the FBI interested in me?"

"Miss McDowell, please sit down. What we are about to share with you will be difficult to comprehend fully until we present all the facts."

Agent Manning momentarily looked at Agent Roderick, then at Rose, and back to his partner. He was stalling temporarily, deciding where to begin his remarks.

"Miss McDowell, what we are about to say will undoubtedly be a huge shock. We're certain you have purposely been kept ignorant of the real business of the Import-Export Company which Mr. Harks operates. He and those five men called associates are part of a huge drug cartel. They are selling a high grade of cocaine imported illegally, of course, from Columbia, South America. You've met a Pedro Gonzales recently, posing as a priest, who made a large delivery. The packages you have been dispensing from the safe are cocaine. The gemstones being sold are from jewelry store heists and fenced or purchased by Steven Harks. Arthur Turner facilitates the selling of the gems to jewelry outlets plus selling of cocaine to drug dealers. Rueben Augustino is responsible for laundering all the money involved and supplies some drug dealers. Rosterer and Alterson also sell the drugs. All their actions to you belied their real intentions. We're sorry for their actions and words that misled you all these months."

Rose was indeed shocked, appalled, and confused. The

words she heard seemed to be reverberating somewhere in the space around her.

"You mean that I'm engaged to be married to a drug dealer and all the associates I've come to love as friends are too?" Rose blurted out, choking on each word.

"Miss McDowell, the Bureau never desires to be involved in the matters of the heart. We regret your becoming romantically involved with Mr. Harks. The entire process will become extremely painful for you. The reality is this, Miss McDowell, all will be arrested and stand trial including yourself."

"ME ARRESTED! I didn't know C-1014 was an illegal drug!" exclaimed Rose.

"Yes, we are aware of your innocence. We will, of course, help you through this entire ordeal, Miss McDowell. We will need you as an important witness at the trial after their arrest. You can be absolutely assured of our assistance. You were not aware of the fact that your entire house was wired with hidden microphones. This was accomplished by proper legal approval. Every word spoken by everyone has been recorded for sometime. When Mr. Harks became suspicious and asked you to receive and initiate all calls by the swimming pool, we immediately wired that area, also. Your house has been under surveillance 24/7. Everyone has been photographed several times arriving and leaving. Everyone has been followed for some time. Buyers of the cocaine have already been arrested, jailed, and awaiting trial. We have arranged for one of the large buyers to testify at the trial. Mr. Harks' company is part of a huge drug cartel within the United States and other countries. On a humorous note, we all enjoy the pictures of you dancing with the two associates at the Tobacco Nightclub. We know you were not aware of our surveillance for your own protection. We are sharing this information with you because we are asking you to help us capture this part of the drug cartel."

"Why haven't you arrested them by now?" asked Rose.

"Miss McDowell, we were going to make the arrest; then we

heard your celebration plans for the Fourth of July when all or some will attend. We are requesting that you continue with your plans. We prefer to arrest everyone in this house. Do you know who has accepted your invitations?" asked Agent Manning.

"Yes, Steven has notified everyone. So far Rueben Augustino, Arthur Turner, and Damien Rosterer are certain. Jack Alterson is a maybe. Tina is to help me. Juan is coming alone. Their son, Sammy, is very ill and Marie wishes to stay home with him."

"Excellent! With Mr. Augustino involvement, our State Department will begin extradition procedures with the government of Italy; also with Columbia for Pedro Gonzales in Bogotá. If Mr. Alterson isn't present, we know his exact location. Miss McDowell, Juan and Tina, your close friends, will not be attending. They are both under cover FBI agents. We were fortunate that both were employed by Mr. Harks. Of course, their names were fictitious and have already been assigned to another case as I speak. Their reports have been reviewed and clearly indicate your innocence while working for this drug cartel. They actually planted the ' bugs' in all the rooms and by the swimming pool area."

"Tina! Juan! Agents! I can't believe it! They're such ordinary people! I do the payroll! I owe both their wages yet!" exclaimed Rose.

"Miss Mc Dowell, we understand your situation. Both are excellent agents. You can forget that responsibility to pay them. Both are on the FBI payroll. We have retained all the checks you've written for them. You didn't know the checks would be drawn on illegally obtained drug money. Your written pay checks are part of the evidence in this case."

"This information I'm hearing is mind boggling. And you want me to help in the arrest of everyone?" questioned Rose, as she tried to change her mindset about Steven and the associates.

"Yes, Miss McDowell, we are appealing to your civic duty to help us. We realize your involvement with Mr. Harks. We stress again, the importance of removing these individuals from our society. We do not have a search warrant at this time, but can you show us the safe so we can photograph the contents?" requested Agent Manning.

Rose led the way to the room containing the safe. After opening it, Agent Roderick took several pictures.

"Would a ledger containing all the inventory received and removed since working here be of any help?" asked Rose.

"You recorded everything? Does Mr. Harks know you did this?" asked Agent Manning ,surprisingly.

"No, he doesn't. This was strictly my own idea. I keep the ledger in my room. Steven was always asking about each associate's transactions each time he came home. Recording the figures fixed the numbers mentally in order to provide exact answers. I have no more use for the ledger. Do you want it?" Rose asked.

"Thank you, Miss McDowell. This will be important evidence. Now starts your most difficult assignment. Your actions, emotions, and attitude must be absolutely normal. You can not give the situation away. Do you believe you are capable of maintaining your normal routine knowing all the information we have outlined?" asked Agent Manning.

"Won't be easy! I wish I could leave and never come back," Rose responded with fresh tears trickling down her checks.

"Miss McDowell, we know we are asking much of you. Have you heard anyone talking about a Sarah Hewitt?" asked Agent Roderick.

"Why, yes. Tina and I found a CD hidden in our cupboard. Our neighbor, who is a policeman, was to receive it. The signature was that of Sarah Hewitt. Tina delivered it for me," replied Rose, speaking between sobs.

"Miss McDowell, please don't be scared by my next words. Miss Hewitt was the hostess prior to your being employed.

We have not been able to locate her, yet. The recording may contain clues or information concerning her disappearance. There are many reasons for our concern about you," replied Agent Manning.

"Do not mention her name to anyone whatsoever or of finding the CD or of its disposal. Your own life depends on your silence regarding it. Also, don't reveal to anyone that you now know the packages are cocaine and marijuana or that the gemstones were stolen. Do you understand the importance of this request?" asked Agent Roderick.

"Yes, Mr. Roderick, I do now. As I recall, both Juan's and Tina's actions and words indicated the same cautions," replied Rose, as she recalled their past conversations.

"If at anytime you realize there's great danger, even the slightest, go for a walk. In your block has been a type of a utility truck. Perhaps you've noticed these vehicles already during the past months. Approach these FBI agents, disguised as workers, and use the code word, 'Production.' They will whisk you away in a heart beat. These are the agents who have been recording everything spoken in your home and taking photographs," said Agent Manning

"Yes, I saw them on my walks. I didn't realize their real purposes. It does help me to feel a little safer," replied Rose, glancing towards the front windows.

"Miss McDowell, are you positively certain you're capable to continue with our plans for arresting everyone and ending their selling of drugs?" asked Agent Roderick.

Rose began pulling the engagement ring from her finger. "Yes, I believe I can. This ring was probably stolen as was this birthstone. Even this wristwatch," as she started to remove it with a note of disgust in her voice.

"Miss McDowell, we advise you to continue wearing all your jewelry. Removing any of it may lead to questions. You may have difficulty with answers," replied Agent Manning.

"Yes, you make a good point," replied Rose as she slipped

the ring back on her finger and fastened the clasp on the watch.

"We came today for we knew you were home alone. Remember, we hear every word uttered in this place. Should we rush in to make the arrests, don't be overly surprised or alarmed," assured Agent Manning as he answered his cell phone.

"Thank you. Your words have given me some confidence to move through this arrest plan. I've said it before and will repeat the motto of my life—Just another of life's adventures!" replied Rose, with a long sigh.

"Good bye, Miss McDowell, you're a genuine 'trooper' in our books. We need to leave immediately for that call just now indicated Mr. Harks is driving this way. Remember, we will be helping you through this entire situation," replied Agent Manning as the two agents moved through the door.

AFTER THE FBI AGENTS left, Rose returned to close the safe. As she viewed all the packages of drugs and trays of gemstones before closing the door, her thoughts returned again and again to the words of endearment Steven had spoken to her in the past months. "How could he be so sweet and loveable to me? Why did he want to be engaged to be married so quickly? Why have I fallen in love with him? How could he be involved in a terrible situation by selling drugs to kids? And all the Associates and their kindness? Were their intentions just acting? Was all the stories just that? They all sounded so sincere. Have they made me a big fool?"

She viewed the room for the hidden microphones. Going from room to room, her eyes swept the walls, furniture, and curtains for what she remembered the agents called "bugs." She saw nothing that was obvious. She realized all the "bugs" must be well hidden. She tried to understand how Tina and Juan could be FBI people and perform their work in such an ordinary manner. They were here to gather evidence and even to help protect me. Rose retreated to her own bedroom. Throwing herself on the bed, her thoughts filled with the terrible words her parents and the Reillys might say when informed of her arrest with the others. Rose didn't relish the thought of facing any of her family and friends. The embarrassment would be dreadful. Perhaps the FBI agents could inform everyone after the situation ended regarding this terrible mess in which she became involved.

As the many thoughts bombarded her mind, her mood swings changed to a deep feeling of being completely lost, to deep sobs for being dumped by Marvin, to an engagement and marriage that were a sham, and to darn right anger and frustration for being used as a complete naive fool.

But as Rose's thought process was ever changing and draining her emotionally, her body yielded to demands of rest. She drifted into a deep sleep.

# CHAPTER 27

ARRIVING FROM A BUSINESS trip, Steven rushed into the house. "Where's my Sweetheart hiding this time?" called Steven, raising his voice.

Turning to Damien, who had accompanied him from the airport and not receiving any response from Rose, added, "She could be shopping for our celebration."

Going to the kitchen door entrance to the garage, he saw her car. "She must be somewhere about the house," replied Steven.

Remembering that he had found Rose in her room on a previous arrival, Steven moved towards her bedroom. Standing in the doorway, he was touched by the angelic appearance upon Rose's face while in a deep sleep. He quietly stood beside the bed and lovingly viewed her as he listened to her steady breathing pattern. He sat carefully beside her. Gazing upon her lovely form, he realized she was undoubtedly exhausted from the preparations for the Fourth. Unfolding a

light sheet nearby, he gently covered her and returned to the
living room.

"Rose is sleeping," said Steven, as he joined Damien. While
flipping through the mail and opening them to glance at their
contents, added, "She has been preparing for the celebration.
We'll let her sleep. I'll make reservations at the Lemaire for
tonight. Rose has already eaten there. I more or less promised a return visit with her."

"You two go without me. You need to be alone with Rose.
I'll stay here and find a bite to eat. Besides, I need the sleep
and will undoubtedly turn in early," replied Damien.

"Thank you for your understanding our need for privacy.
Besides, the others may arrive this evening. You can be here
for greetings and assigning rooms. I noticed Rose made thorough preparation for their arrival. You know, I'm vague about
the quantity of our inventory. Would you help in recording
the safe's content?" asked Steven.

Moving to the safe, Steven spun the dial. After two tries, he
finally opened the door. Using a clipboard, Damien recorded
the figures. Steven counted the packages of C-1014. To his
surprise, he found 10 packages of M-1242. Pedro had delivered some marijuana without his knowledge. He would not
complain for there was a ready market. Moving to the gems,
Steven discovered the process was difficult if not impossible.
He was not certain of the different cuts of stones within each
grouping. He may need Rose's expertise to accomplish this
part of his inventory.

While Steven was attempting to count the garnets, Rose,
who had awakened and hearing the voices in the room with
the safe, moved to the doorway.

"There's my beautiful sleepy head!" said Steven, as he
brought her into an embrace. Kissing Rose, he realized she
was not responding in the usual manner. Realizing she had
been sleeping soundly, he considered that as the reason for
her lack of spontaneity.

"Hi!  Sorry I didn't hear your arrival.  Thought a nap might help.  It has been an exhausting day," Rose commented, without much enthusiasm in her  tone  voice, already dreading the need of being in Steven's presence and that of Damien.

"Rose, thank you for the extra household work.  Really do appreciate your efforts preparing for the party.  Would you help me with this inventory of the gemstones?  You know these gems by grading within each group.  We have all the packages counted.  Really didn't know what we have by way of inventory," said Steven.

Rose pulled out the trays and counted each grade for  each type of stone.  Damien soon had  listed the contents  of all trays.  Next were 12 bars of precious metal, 15 rare coins, and 21 prized collectible stamps.

"Rose, darling, thank you for assisting with this inventory. I really had no idea what was available.  Your ability in grading was fantastic despite coming from a deep sleep.  You still do not appear fully awake.    I sat beside you for a few minutes and enjoyed watching you deep in the arms of Morpheus," replied Steven, as he embraced Rose and kissed her gently.

"Deep in the arms of who?" asked Rose.

"You know, Morpheus, the god of dreams.  Hey, Sweetheart, being exhausted from doing all the preparation for the Fourth, as a special treat, we'll dine at the Lemaire this evening.  Remember, I mentioned that your loveliness would bring an air of ambience to the place.    We'll leave when you're ready.  Would you please wear that beautiful emerald colored outfit just for me that compliments your exquisite beauty?" asked Steven.

"O.K.  Didn't know that skirt and blouse were your favorites," replied Rose, speaking in a tone of voice that sounded strange even to her own ears.

STEVEN AND ROSE PLACED THEIR orders for their entrée choice.

""Sweetheart, you seem so quiet. You're O.K?" Not ill? How can one person be so lovely and steal my heart before I realized it was missing?"

With a slight smile, Rose peered at Steven's eyes. She studied the gaze upon her from across the table. Her thoughts were confused-- in a state of ambivalence. "The words of the agents whirled through her thinking process. How can Steve sound so sincere? Why did I fall in love with him? The wedding and honeymoon will never happen?" She knew she had to act in a normal manner.

Eating her salad, Rose tried a voice showing a degree of pleasantness. "Thank you, Steve, for eating out, especially at the Lemaire. Silly you! This place doesn't need me for ambience as you once humorously stated. What a superb restaurant! Wish they had dancing though!"

"You should have mentioned dancing, Rose. We could have visited the Tobacco Place instead. We could go there after we eat. Seems you've been there before."

"Yes, Arthur and Rueben entertained me royally one evening. Those two didn't allow me a breather. We practically danced every musical number. I was exhausted but didn't reveal it because both men seemed to enjoy their prowess."

"Yes, Arthur told me about your evening rendezvous. I'm jealous. I haven't had that special treat of cuddling while dancing."

"And you never will," thought Rose. The ardor previously experienced was now badly tarnished. She realized she needed the skill of a professional actress to pull off the FBI's request.

"Thank you for your thorough preparation for tomorrow's celebration. Sorry that Tina quit her job. Her letter today indicated a need to nurse a favorite aunt who's ill. You undoubtedly could have used her help."

Rose smiled. If Steven only knew the truth. She felt a sense of inner power muscling through a bravado that seemed to invade her psyche. She felt its goodness. Perhaps she could accomplish what was asked of her.

"Sweetheart, you appear to be deep in thought. Does your mental images include me?"

"By all means, Stevee-boy!" as Rose threw him flirtatious glances.

"Wow, lets go home immediately to continue on that train of thought. Do we really need to wait until our wedding night to enjoy our deepening love?"

"Just wait and see!" as Rose showed the most sexy smile she could create.

WALKING INTO THE HOUSE, Rose and Steven realized all their guests were present sitting about the living room enjoying a glass of wine. After being greeted with "Hello, you two lovebirds!" Damien presented glasses of wine to the engaged couple.

"Everybody, join in a toast! Rose and Steve, please stand in the middle of the room," ordered Damien.

Surrounding Rose and Steven, everyone touched glasses. A round of verbal toasts were given by each guest. Rose orchestrated each movement. She manufactured a winsome smile, and purposely added graciousness to each "thank you." Rose continued to move among the guests. She found it difficult to exchange pleasantries with each person. She was thankful that Jack had come. All the associates, except Pedro, were present. The FBI agents should be extra pleased.

Approaching Rose, who was speaking with Jack, Steve said, "Rose, please join me in my bedroom. I wish to present you a gift."

Steven and Rose excused themselves. Leaving for the bedroom, their dignity experienced some friendly teasing as they left their guests. Closing the door, Steven gathered Rose into his arms. He tried to kiss her, but Rose made no effort to cooperate in kissing back. Somewhat puzzled, Steven released her, reached into his pocket, and removed a diamond laden necklace.

"This is my wedding gift to wear with your exquisite gown, Sweetheart."

Rose accepted the necklace. She tried to show enthusiasm. "It's very beautiful, Steven." She shifted it several times from one hand to the other. The diamonds sparkled from the light reflecting through the tiny prisms. She admired the skill of the persons who fashioned each facet. She laid it on top of the dresser with the certainty the "baubles" would never encircle her neck.

Slowly pulling Rose's blouse from beneath the skirt band, Steven unfastened the buttons while raining kisses about her face. He embraced her. He claimed her lips with a passionate kiss. Despite the nagging feelings about Steven, Rose was surprised of her slight arousal. Unfortunately, her response encouraged Steven to slide her blouse off her shoulders. It fell to the floor.

"Rose, I need you! I love you! Your beauty overwhelms me! I want you now! I sense you want me, too!"

"But Steve, I do not want to have sex now! You promised me you'd keep my virginity until our wedding!" Rose pleaded, knowing there wouldn't be a wedding.

"Oh Rose, you know I love you and you love me. There's no need to wait to fulfill this love until our wedding! I'll be very gentle. After tonight, you'll wonder why you waited even this long to enjoy our deep and meaningful expression of the bond developing between us."

"But you have no protection for me! I don't want the risk of becoming pregnant!"

"Sweetheart, I do have condoms in my dresser," as he pulled out the drawer and retrieve the package.

Unhooking Rose's bra, he slowly removed it. Pulling the zipper down on her skirt, it fell down around her feet. Rose closed her eyes as she stepped out and kicked it aside. "How much resistance should she now use to stop Steven's obvious desires to make love," she thought.

She considered going quickly to her room, grab her purse containing the key for the room with the safe and lock the door behind her. "Could I do that quickly enough? Wouldn't Steven follow me? If I did this, I could goof up the arrest plans for Mr. Manning," she thought.

Suddenly Rose remembered that the FBI agents were hearing every word. She had to show boldness.

"Stevee-boy, you practically have me undressed! Am I to be your sex goddess all night in YOUR bedroom? You did ask me to be your hostess for ALL the guests in the living room. I'm confused. I'll just dress again and do my job," said Rose, relying on someone hearing her plight, and at the same time picking up her clothes.

As Steven pulled out his shirt tail and begin unbuttoning it, "Wow, I like your choice of words! But no, you don't need to dress again. They are all big boys in the living room and capable of fending for themselves. They know where the food and drinks are kept. You did an excellent job of stocking the larder, Sweetheart. Tonight you're my exceptional sex goddess, using your colorful description!"

Again Steven moved to embrace Rose and placed a series of soft kisses about her face. Moving both hands to cup her breasts, his thumbs caressingly circled her areolas. The touch surprised Rose. At one time she did welcome those caresses but certainly not now, especially by Steven. Dropping her clothes, she brought both arms up between his, then placed them around his neck. She caused Steven to release his hands that were caressing her. She slowly kissed his lips, his nose, his chin, back to his lips. Then Rose brought her hands down and began to slowly finish unbuttoning his shirt while flirtatiously gazing into his eyes. She was thinking hard as to what else might be done to stall for time.

"Sweetheart, I enjoy your taking charge. This will be a night we will never forget!"

"It will be a night neither one of wish to remember either," thought Rose.

First knocking, then shouting through the closed door, "STEVE, THIS IS DAMIEN! JUST RECEIVED A PHONE CALL THAT THE FEDS MIGHT RAID THIS PLACE TONIGHT!

"GOOD GRIEF! Rose, quickly close the safe if open and inform everyone to clear out of here, NOW. Here, use my bath robe! Cram your clothes in this brief case, the keys to your car, and wait for me there!"

Steven started buttoning his shirt. Watching Rose following his orders, his thinking process shifted to high gear. "What basic things are needed? Where do we travel that's safe? Why is this happening to me?" Opening a suitcase, he grabbed a shirt, socks, underwear, and a tie from a dresser drawer and tossed them in the case. He picked up a cell phone and a bank-like container full of hundred dollar bills and threw them on top of the clothes. He snapped the suitcase shut. A chorus of shouts and voices reached his ears. Rose glanced at Steven. His gaze was as if that moment in time was frozen. The door slammed open!

Confronting Steven were Agent Manning and a policeman with drawn revolvers. When Steve saw the handcuffs the officer displayed, he meekly turned and placed his hands behind his back. The cuffs were snapped on and he was lead out of the room.

"Miss McDowell, you obviously look scared. We're sorry you are involved in this raid. But as I mentioned before, we need to place cuffs on you also so Mr. Harks believes you are part of the entire arrest scene. We heard your remarks of being undressed. This prompted our immediate actions. We're sorry that you had to suffer this indignation standing almost nude before us now. I will leave to attend to the other arrests while you dress. I'll be back to snap on the cuffs. Are you O.K.?" asked Agent Manning as he noticed Rose shaking..

"Yes, I knew you would be here. But the slamming of the door and the guns pointing at me was terribly scary," said Rose, with a trembling voice. Suddenly realizing her nudity, she pulled her blouse from the brief case and covered her breasts.

"Sorry, Miss McDowell. We didn't know if Mr. Harks was armed at the moment or not. We prefer to take no chances. I'll be back," said Agent Manning, as he left and closed the door.

Arthur Turner and Rueben Augustino had hurried out of the front door and down the walk but were confronted by Agent Roderick and two policemen and then hand cuffed. Damien Rosterer and Jack Alterson had quickly exited by the back door to the patio. They were met by flashlights shining in their faces, guns pointed at them, and then cuffed. All four were ushered to the kitchen where Steven Harks was already sitting passively.

"Welcome, gentleman! We often 'rain on other people's parties.' I'm the one who called and warned you about the raid. We thought it would stir up some action! Apparently it did! Mr. Harks left Miss McDowell less than dressed. She's dressing now and should be finished shortly. Agent Roderick, would you read everyone their rights when Miss McDowell gets here?" asked Agent Manning, as he left for the bedroom by way of the room containing the safe.

Rose finished dressing and had opened the door. She was waiting for Mr. Manning. When he appeared in the doorway, she turned and placed her hands behind her back as she had seen Steven do. The cuffs were snapped on.

"What will happen to me now, Agent Manning?" asked Rose.

"Miss McDowell, I'll escort you to the kitchen with the other five men. Agent Roderick will read the Miranda Rights. This is a legal formality that must be done on an arrest. In this case, charges will be stated for the possessing, transporting, and selling of illegal drugs, stolen jewelry, and other property We have a search warrant and will remove all the contents of the safe as evidence for the trial. I looked in the room with the safe on my way here and found it open; otherwise, we would have asked you to do so. Everyone being arrested in this house along with the inventory as evidence will make a strong case in court. This is the main reason for making the arrest in the house. Everyone will be placed in jail after we leave here and remain until the trial, including you. We desire the drug cartel to realize that you will be no exception to the arrest. We are subjecting you to inconveniences to save your life. The cartel, we have discovered, has no mercy. Remember our concern for Sarah Hewitt? We fear she could be dead. Bail will be a  huge amount  to prevent any flight; it's unlikely anyone can cover the amount. The FBI will ask for a speedy trial. We will appoint a lawyer for you.  We are asking you to turn state evidence and tell the court how all five men bought and sold cocaine, marijuana, and stolen gemstones. You will be asked to identify each of the men.  As I indicated, we have strong evidence to produce in court to obtain convictions. How long each will remain in jail or some penitentiary will be determined by the court system.  Unfortunately, for your safety from the drug cartel as I have already indicated, you will be convicted also and serve some jail or penitentiary time. We will be instructing the judge or judges involved of your inno-cent relationship with the Import-Export Company.  We will continue to assist you as the situation unfolds. Does this help you for the time being?" asked Agent Manning,

"Yes it does.   I'm really concerned what my parents will think and do when informed of these happenings tonight," said Rose sadly.

"I will do all in our power to have your name omitted from any newspaper, television, and radio publicity that will result from  this arrest.  That  will be  a  start.  We must hasten to the kitchen; we've been gone too long now.   Rose, if there is any consolation, remember, my FBI superiors are very grateful for your gallant efforts in this drug bust," assured Agent Manning.

Rose walked hesitantly to the kitchen. "This really is too much of an adventure, Agent Manning!" declared Rose, releasing a big sigh.

# CHAPTER 28

AGENT HARRY MANNING ARRIVED at the jail the next morning where the members of the Import-Export Company had been booked and incarcerated pending their trial. He asked for Miss Rose McDowell to be brought to an interrogation room.

He first visited the Evidence Room where all the contents of the safe had been logged and stored. Asking for the envelope containing all the personal effects belonging to Rose, Agent Manning removed the wristwatch, engagement ring, and birthstone ring. Each was carefully photographed at various close-up angles. The digital images were e-mailed to the various FBI units in the cities where the jewelry heists happened. He was trying to determine if the items were part of those robberies or may have been purchased legitimately. The outcome would determine whether or not Rose would be allowed to retain them.

Entering the room where Rose was already seated and attempting to use a cheery tone, he asked, "Miss McDowell, how are you managing this adventure in your life, as you philosophically stated to me last night?"

"Agent Manning, you may call me Rose, if you wish. I didn't sleep a wink. Lying awake throughout the night and morning, I tossed and turned with my thoughts rolling around in my head regarding this terrible mess in which I'm involved. Worse yet, what will my parents and close friends think about me being arrested as well. I was allowed to take a long shower this morning. It was a sad attempt to wash away my problems. It didn't help one bit. I didn't eat any breakfast for fear of loosing it."

"Rose, again, you have my deepest sympathies for this confinement now, the trial, and the incarceration you'll need to endure. If there were any means in our power to send you home to your folks, I would in a heart beat. But under the circumstances, that's not possible. Do you fully understand your situation?"

"Yes, I do, Agent Manning, but this does not relieve the anxiety that continues to stir up my thoughts."

"Rose, I wish to help prepare you for the future days. Knowing this may help your anxiety about the unknown."

He shared the information in his attempt to determine the ownership of the jewelry worn and removed when booked. If the jewelry wasn't stolen and it could be determined that none were purchased with drug earned income, they would be hers. Since she only drove the Mercedes, it along with the Porsche, the house, furniture, and appliances would be confiscated and sold at an auction. This was a standard procedure with any drug bust.

"Rose, permission has been granted me to accompany you to the house today after lunch. Please don't be alarmed when you see the four guards that will accompany us. You will be able to box all possessions you desire to keep. These will be placed in storage for you. We have a big surprise! Tina and Juan will be there to help you clean out all the food, Mr. Harks' clothing, and other possessions. In other words, we need the house cleared of all personal effects and cleaned to help the auction proceed in an orderly manner.

"Oh, that's GREAT! To see Tina and Juan once again! How wonderful! And probably for the last time."

"By the way, we found a stunning necklace on the dresser. Is that yours?" asked the Agent.

"The necklace? Oh yes, Steven's gift was to be worn with my wedding gown. He presented the necklace shortly before you arrested everyone," replied Rose, showing no enthusiasm or emotions.

"Rose, again, if we can't determine it's part of any stolen property and purchased by Mr. Harks own money, it's yours and shall be added to the storage items. And now information on the trail and your sentence by the judge."

Agent Manning outlined for Rose's peace of mind what was in store for her during the trial. Mr. Herman Littler would be the prosecuting lawyer. He may arrange a visit before the trial and provide advice for the procedures used to convict the drug dealers. The FBI Administrators had spoken earlier to Judge Harry Madsen who was handling the trial and who would determine the length of incarceration.

"Rose, you will receive a five year sentence with early parole," said Agent Manning.

"FIVE YEARS, THAT'S A LONG TIME FOR WHAT I DID!" Rose shouted uncontrollably at Agent Manning.

"Rose, you didn't permit me to finish. You will only serve six months at the most.

Remember what I've indicated regarding the 'long arm" of the drug cartel people that have not been found and arrested as yet. When they hear about your sentencing, and they will despite our trying to suppress that information, we have found from experience with other incarcerated persons, the cartel tends to move on and forgot those that testify against their drug dealers.  Not always, but past experience helps in our decision-making for you."

"Where will I go for six months?   What will I do with myself?  What happens at the end of the time?  If I'm paroled and go home, can't the bad men still find me?"

"Rose, you certainly have an active imagination.  There is more information I need to share with you.  O.K.?"

With Rose nodding her head, the agent continued.  "The FBI is narrowing down and determining a penitentiary located in a western state.  They wish to move you far from Richmond.  While at the pen, you will undoubtedly be assigned as a beautician and barber for both the men and women residents.  The FBI will place you under the U.S. Government Witness Protection Program.  After the trial, it is highly suggested that your appearance be changed-- a new identity."

"Rose, as a beautician and a beautifully red headed person, can you change the color, say, to black?  Also we suggest using a different hair style.  We will pay for a set of brown contact lenses to change the color of your eyes. You obviously do not wear glasses.  We will buy you two pair that are clear plastic with a light brown tint.  You'll be required to change your name.  You can keep your first name  and  change  your  last name with the same initial.   However, you may select an entirely different name.  After you are paroled, you need to select the city, preferably a large metropolitan area, where you desire to live.  Large cities facilitate getting lost and prevent  the drug cartel from locating your whereabouts.  As a beautician, the FBI will arrange for a beauty shop business, buy you a car, and rent a furnished apartment for one year.  We will transport all your boxed items in storage to your new home.  In one year, undoubtedly, you'll be supporting yourself.   However, I will 'pop in' and determine your progress at various times.  Are there any questions to this point?"

Seeing Rose nod her head negatively, he continued. "Rose, the worse part of the witness protection plan will be complete anonymity. This means you can never travel back to Norfolk or contact your family members, former associates, or friends. As I have stated before, the 'long arm' of the drug cartel will attempt to contact your family, friends, and work associates to determine your address. When no one knows where you are, they can never reveal your address in the city you live. The FBI will write a letter to your parents relative to your gallant contribution as a witness. We will indicate that for your personal security, you are safely living somewhere. I see your tears so you must understand the sadness created by that request."

With tears turning to deep sobs, Rose nodded her head affirmatively. Words stuck in her throat. She wanted to say, "I can't believe I'll never see my family again!" Blowing her nose, drying the tears streaming down her cheeks, and breathing in gasps for air, Rose tried to asked, "May I have until this afternoon to consider a name and a place to live?"

"Certainly, Rose. All these details for your protection need to be placed before my FBI bosses for approval. I'll be back at noon. Before leaving, you will have your street clothes returned for this afternoon rather than wearing the prison garb," replied Agent Manning as he pinched the sleeve of the jumper.

HUGGING TINA, ROSE COULDN'T BE HAPPIER! With tears bubbling down her cheeks, Rose tried to speak, "Tina, my dear dear friend, how wonderful to hug you once again!"

Juan, watching the two women embrace, said, "Rose, we are deeply sorrowful for your innocent involvement in this drug bust. Tina and I wanted to warn you many, many times but didn't dare because of your safety. Had you known the truth, your very life would have been in danger. We were worried the entire time that you would discover the stuff was cocaine and the gemstones were stolen! The FBI is of the opinion that

Sarah Hewitt learned the truth and suffered the consequence. We're fearful she's dead."

"Rose, what Juan so succinctly stated, your life was endangered the entire time. We felt we had enough proof to arrest the drug dealers and extricate you from the house to prevent you from being the next victim. We know you were not aware of the real threat to your job as hostess. Mr. Harks is a vicious individual in our opinion. He certainly is not the loveable guy you became involved with romantically," Agent Manning added.

"Rose, we're thrilled for you that Steven Harks hired both of us as under cover agents. Being with you in the house was always a blessing. We realized we could protect you when necessary. When you were home alone with any of the five dealers, one of us was listening and recording every word. Had you been in any danger, we would have crawled all over this house with drawn weapons," said Tina, as she touched her revolver.

"I didn't realize in the least that my life was in danger. At least that type of danger including my death! It seems impossible that everyone was so phony. Thank you, thank you for what you've done. My feelings for those guys has changed to loathing. I can't wait to testify at the trial," said Rose with determination in her voice.

"Well folks, we must turn to and square away this house for next week's auction. Here's a list of chores made earlier that must be completed today," ordered Agent Manning.

The balance of the afternoon was a busy one. Rose's list indicated the boxing of her possessions, marking each box with code number, "201, For Storage" and stacked in the garage. As she handled some of the items, she wondered when her possessions would again see the light of day. Filling the last box and carrying it to the garage, Rose boxed everything else being donated to charity. Picking up the large trash items, she vacuumed the rug. Reminiscing of the pleasant days spent in her room, she closed the door. " One room finished for ever!" Rose reflected

Rose and Tina continued to assist each other with their itemized lists. At 4 o'clock, the "cleaning crew"' sat down for a breather. Work lists were compared. Left over coke and some food items from emptying the refrigerator were eagerly consumed and enjoyed.

Continuing work another hour and completing the lists of chores, the "crew" conducted a last walk-through of the house, backyard, patio, swimming pool, and front yard. Arriving in front of the garage, high fives were exchanged. Rose brushed her hand along the fender and trunk of the Mercedes.

"Rose, sorry you can't keep that beauty. What a perk for a beautiful perky gal, though," teased Juan as he gave Rose a hug.

"Thanks gang, for your invaluable help! Agents Tina and Juan, I will add your extraordinary service today to your personal records. Say your goodbyes. Rose needs to be returned, unfortunately," said Agent Manning.

The separation was tearful. Rose waved goodbye as Agent Manning drove away from the curb. She kept her eyes on Tina, Juan and the house until they turned the corner. She knew for certain the view would be her last.

THE TRIAL WAS MOVED forward on the court docket.

"Please rise? The Honorable Judge Harry Madsen presiding," ordered the court bailiff.

"Are the prosecuting and defense lawyers ready to select jury members?" asked Judge Madsen.

Both lawyers indicated they were. Three hours were spent in interviewing twenty potential jurists before both lawyers agreed on the twelve persons finally selected. Judge Madsen presented the necessary instruction for the jury to follow. Each was ordered to report for jury duty the next day at 9 a.m.

BRIGHT AND EARLY THE next morning, Rose was given her own clothes. She appreciated the change from the bright orange "uniform" she had been wearing. She was escorted to the court room and seated. This being a new experience, Rose was intrigued with each person who entered the room and found a place to sit. She wondered who they were and why each was present. As the court room began to fill, Rose's feelings of anxiety and apprehension began to "kick in." She was hoping that being a witness and answering questions wouldn't be too unnerving. When Steven was escorted into the room followed by the four associates, Rose realized her level of anxiety moving up a few more notches. As she looked at the back of Steven's head, she experienced flashes of their intimate moments. She really didn't know what questions would be asked of her, but now she had to help convict Steven.

Herman Littler, the prosecuting attorney, made his opening statements followed by Lloyd Martin for the defense.

Rose listened closely as Mr. Littler was speaking. She thought she now understood what would be happening at the trial. She was surprised how little Mr. Martin had to say in defense of Steven Harks and his associates.

When Mr. Martin sat down, Mr. Littler asked for the man who happened to be sitting beside her to take the witness stand. She heard that he was Reggie Mason, a laboratory technician. After being questioned regarding his credentials as an expert on various drugs, he testified that the packages taken from Mr. Harks' safe and now in the Evidence Room were a high grade of cocaine; the marijuana was of pure quality.

Rose watched intensely as the next person was called to the witness stand. To her, he appeared well groomed and wearing expensive clothes. When taking the oath to tell the truth, she noticed a sneer on his face which to her showed he didn't want to be at the trial.

"Please state your name for the record?" asked Mr. Littler.

"Jerome Douglas Cralson."

"Looking at your arrest warrant, Mr. Cralson, when you were arrested on July 3$^{rd}$ of this year, there was found in your possession four plastic sacks of cocaine and one package of marijuana. Did Mr. Steven Harks or one of those four associates seated at that table sell you this cocaine and or marijuana?" asked Mr. Littler.

"My main supplier was Steven Harks. However, Jack Alterson and Damien Rosterer also delivered both as needed when Steven evidently was not in the area," replied Mr. Cralson, in a sneering tone.

"Do you see these three individuals you named in this court room?" asked the prosecuting lawyer.

"Steven Harks is on the far left with Jack Alterson beside him. Damien Rosterer is sitting on the far right," replied Mr. Cralson.

"No more questions, Your Honor," stated Mr. Littler.

"Does the defense wish to question this witness?" asked Judge Madsen.

"No!" answered the defense lawyer; the judge then excused the witness.

"I call Mr. Paul Sibley to the witness stand." After Mr. Sibling took the oath, Mr.

Littler continued, "For the record, state your name and occupation."

"Paul E. Sibley. I'm the head teller of First Bank, Richmond, Virginia."

"Are you familiar with Steven Harks and or Rueben Augustino?"

"Yes, I know both very well. They were frequent customers at our bank for the last two years or so."

"These are copies of the bank records of the Harks Import-Export Company that we secured by a subpoena from your bank. Do you recognize these records of the said company?"

"Yes, I do recognize those records. I assisted with the deposits and withdrawals for both men many times when they did business at our bank. I referred both to the Investment Department also for other financial transactions."

"Do you see either of the men in the court room?" asked Mr. Littler

"Yes, Steven Harks is on the far left of their table and Rueben Augustino is the third person from the right."

"Thank you, Mr. Sibley; no more questions, Your Honor."

"Does the defense wish to cross exam?" asked Judge Madsen.

"No, we don't," replied Mr. Martin in a noticeable low voice.

"You're excused, Mr. Sibley," ordered Judge Madsen.

Rose realized she was sitting on the edge of her chair due to her intense interest in the "drama" she was witnessing. "I wonder when they are calling me?"

When Arthur Turner left Richmond to deliver the 200 plus gemstones, the FBI had him under surveillance to Chicago. There he stopped to make his deliveries to Wholesale Gems, Inc. and to Gemstones, Inc. Several photographs were taken as he entered and exited both businesses. When Arthur left each establishment, the four FBI agents split forces with two approaching the owners of the two businesses. When informed that the deliveries were those of stolen jewelry and gemstones removed from the various mountings, both owners agreed to a plea bargaining and to testifying at the pending trial.

Jeremy Wathson from Wholesale Gems, Inc. and Ricky Monderstand, owner of Gemstones, Inc., were called to the witness stand separately and questioned about the deliveries of gemstones during the last two years. Both in turn testified to questions asked relative to the bills of sale presented as evidence of merchandise purchased from Harks Import-Export Company.

Ricky Monderstand was the second to be questioned. "Do you see the person in the court room who made these many deliveries of gemstones?" asked Mr. Littler.

"Yes, Mr. Arthur Turner is the second person from the right at the table," replied Mr. Monderstand.

"Thank you. No more questions, Your Honor."

The defense lawyer refused the opportunity given for cross examination.

Following was the jeweler, Rob Dingersole, who upon questioning, described the robbery of his store in Chicago on June 17. Some of the unusual cuts of stones stolen had been precisely identified as the gemstones sold to both wholesalers.

Rose's mental thoughts reverted back to the days when she helped Arthur Turner grade the many gemstones. She regretted that he had gotten himself involved in such a messy business. She recalled how fond she had been of his friendship on the many occasions spent with him.

"I call to the witness stand, Miss Rose McDowell," ordered Mr. Littler.

Rose's mind was still occupied with the thoughts of Arthur Turner and didn't hear her name. Suddenly she realized the court room had become deathly quiet. Looking at Judge Madsen, she then heard Mr. Littler say, "Miss Rose McDowell, please take the witness stand." She stood up.

She knew she was blushing when she noticed many others looking in her direction. Her legs felt like rubber pegs as she walked to the witness stand and started to sit down. She suddenly stood back up when asked to take an oath. Immediately before her were Steven and his four associates. Rose, thinking she would be unable to look into their eyes, suddenly realized she could without any difficulty. She actually had deep-seated resentment for each. They were all such phonies. Her thoughts were quickly interrupted when she realized Mr. Littler was speaking to her.

"Please state your name?"

""Rose Maureen McDowell."

"Were you employed as a hostess with the Import-Export Company?"

"Yes, I was."

"What was the nature of your job as a hostess?"

"I managed the home owned by Mr. Steven Harks. With domestic help, I made meals for him and his associates when they stayed for extended visits. I was asked to maintain the inventory of C-1014, M-1242, gemstones, precious metals, rare coins and stamp. Mr. Arthur Turner taught me to be a gemologist and helped him grade many different gemstones he brought to Mr. Harks' house. Also, I assisted all five persons when withdrawing any of the inventory."

"Can you identify Mr. Steven Harks and his associates?"

"Yes, they are the five men seated at that table," said Rose, as she pointed a finger at each individually, saying their name. She realized she was looking at each with much contempt.

"You mentioned C-1014 and M-1242. What were those products?"

"Mr. Harks informed me the packages contained a special industrial compound used in various manufacturing processes."

"At any time, did you become suspicious that the packages were cocaine and marijuana?"

"No, I had no reason to suspect that the packages were illegal drugs. I believe Mr. Harks description of the contents for I thought he was an honorable and trusting person."

"Can you describe this paper containing recorded items listed as Exhibit No. 3?"

"Yes, this is the inventory of everything in the safe which Mr. Harks and Mr. Alterson themselves made prior to the arrest. Mr. Harks requested my assistance in identifying the various grades of the gemstones listed."

"What is the nature of this ledger marked Exhibit No. 4?"

"This is a ledger that I personally maintained and contains the inventory received and checked out to Mr. Harks and the four associates seated at the table, the date of their transaction, and their initials."

"Did any one else know about this ledger?"

"No, maintaining it was strictly my own method to keep accurate tracking of the inventory."

"Can you identify this picture listed as Exhibit No. 5?"

"Yes, this is the bakery truck which delivered 50 packages of C-1014 and 10 of M-1242, which I now know as cocaine and marijuana, by a Pedro Gonzales, dressed as a priest. He informed me that he was from Columbia. The entries are in my ledger. I was informed that the driver was a young man called Toby—no last name."

"Can you identify this picture as Exhibit No. 6?"

"This picture was photographed by Agent Rodrick after I opened the safe and shows the contents within the safe located in Mr. Harks' house, or I suppose, former house."

"No more questions at this time, Your Honor, but do reserve the right to recall the witness."

"Duly noted.   Any cross examination?" asked Judge Madsen.

"Yes, why was a detailed ledger kept without Mr. Harks' knowledge?" asked Lloyd Martin, the lawyer for Mr. Harks and four Associates.

"When Mr. Harks returned from business trips, he inquired about the transaction of the four Associates. Desiring to prove my proficiency as his hostess, I kept a detailed record. I was, therefore, able to provide precise information. This record keeping was done in an innocent manner for I didn't know the Import-Export Company was dealing in illegal drugs the entire time I was employed. For me, secrecy was not an issue," Rose replied, in the best professional voice possible.

"No more questions, Your Honor," replied Mr. Martin, disgustingly.

"Thank you, Miss McDowell. You may be excused," said Judge Madsen.

As Rose left the witness stand, she glanced at Steven. If looks could kill, she knew she would be dead before reaching her seat.   She had never seen him showing  contempt as it was  being directed at her.   Surprisingly, she felt good about her testimony and continued to her chair with an air of much satisfaction.

"Any more witnesses?" asked Judge Madsen.

"Yes, permit Agent Harry Manning, who just arrived, to the witness stand," requested Mr. Littler.

"Agent Manning, approach the witness stand," ordered Judge Madsen.

"Agent Manning, describe these  reports marked as Exhibit No. 7 and 8," requested Mr. Littler.

"Report No. 7 are the arrest warrants of those five men," as Agent Manning pointed at each and stated their names. "Also that of Rose Maureen McDowell.   They were charged with possession, distribution, and the selling of illegal drugs and fencing of gemstones from the robberies of six jewelry stores that were reported to authorities.  All six business owners have been able to positively identify several stones that are in the Evidence Room from digital pictures sent to them and compared to records and pictures sent to our office.   I also witnessed the reading of their Miranda Rights the evening all were arrested."

Looking at Rose momentarily, he continued. "Report No. 8 is a list of the contents removed from the safe by authorized FBI agents with a search warrant issued by Judge Madsen. All the listed items on this report   can be found in the Evidence Room in this building.   Sorry for my lateness, Your Honor, we were attempting to identify  more gemstones that  were stolen from records received  from the various jewelry stores experiencing robberies. We now know that the Import-Export Company owned by Steven Harks purchased the stolen jewelry. His associate, Mr. Arthur Turner, removed  the various settings and sold them again as loose un-mounted gems. The platinum, gold, and silver was  melted down and fashioned into bars for reselling. The stamps and coins have been much easier to identify and eventually will be returned to the rightful owners as we receive their reports."

"Thank you, Agent Manning. No more questions, Your Honor," replied Mr. Littler.

"Any cross examination" asked Judge Madsen.

"None, Your Honor," replied Mr. Martin.

"If no more witnesses from either side, this court is in recess until 9 a.m. tomorrow morning for closing statements and jury deliberation," ordered Judge Madsen.

THE REILYS WERE EATING breakfast. Finished eating, Joe picked up the daily paper. Staring at him was the face of Steven Harks with the caption, "Drug Kingpin Arrested." He quickly scanned through the rest of the story.

"June, this is horrible! Steven all his gang were arrested for selling illegal drugs, stolen gemstones, coins, and stamps. All the names are listed, but Rose's is not mentioned. Perhaps she wasn't involved with this arrest. I'll try calling her. June, do you have her number?" asked Joe.

June retrieved her telephone directory and found the number Rose had provided. The response by the operator indicated the number had been temporarily disconnected or no longer in service. Joe then called Rose's parents. They had had no communications with Rose. Both families were completely puzzled and concerned. Subsequently, they began to hear the story about the arrested drug cartel members on television several times but never a mention of Rose. Everyone was at wit's end and not certain what steps to use to locate her. Even more distressing, why didn't Rose contact them.

THE COURT FOR JUDGE HARRY MADSEN was called to order the following day. With irrefutable evidence provided by the prosecuting attorney, the jury returned a conviction of the five drug dealers of the charges presented. Rueben Augustino was held in jail pending extradition procedures. Steven

Harks, Arthur Turner, and Jack Alterson were sentenced to 30 years in the penitentiary. The FBI would begin extradition procedures against Pedro Gonzales. His court hearing was pending. Rose was sentenced for five years, pursuant to the previous plea bargaining agreement, with parole privileges due to her willingness to provide state's evidence. The judge also gave her consideration due to the total circumstances of her employment as a hostess. Judge Madsen regretted that she had been drawn into the drug cartel's web unknowingly, a lovely innocent woman whose life would be inherently changed. He helped Rose by keeping her name from the press and the media from being present during the trial.

One newspaper reporter, however, attempted an identification from hearsay by using "Roselyn Mae Dowling" in his story. The judge considered this breach of his ruling as no consequence in an attempt to identify Rose.


"ROSE, I'LL BE ESCORTING YOU TO THE selected penitentiary. We'll leave at noon tomorrow. Between now and then, we need to perform the make-over discussed. Have you selected a name and a place to live?" asked Agent Manning.

"Yes, change my identification papers to Gertrude Brown. When paroled, I wish to live in Denver, Colorado. You indicated a large city where I could get lost among the population. There are around 2,300 families with the name of Brown in the Denver area," Rose proudly stated.

"My goodness, you have done your research. Your choice of name does sound like a much older person. That's good. Our main office will be informed of your selections. We will keep you here for safety sake with four FBI agents guarding you around the clock."

In reality, Rose chose the name for two reasons. Gertrude was her great grandmother's name. Since she had to admit she still held a remnant of love for Marvin, and knowing she would never be Mrs. Marvin R. Brown as she once dreamt, she would at least have his last name.　She thought that others might consider this  poor logic; nevertheless, she would stick with that reasoning.

"We've asked Agent Gil Dorsey, who did some hair styling before joining the force,  to help dye your hair, and to give you a new style of your choice.  Here are the contacts and glasses. I'll see you tomorrow.  There are several arrangements to be completed before then."

"What new adventures will be added to my life by Agent Manning's arrangement?" thought Rose AKA Gertrude, as she watched him leave.

# CHAPTER 29

Agent Manning arrived at the Quality Motel near the airport where Agent Johnny Dorsey had spirited Rose AKA Gertrude secretly during the night from the holding jail. He knocked on Room 12 that had been previously reserved for Gertrude. While slipping on her jacket, Gertrude peeked through the security unit in the door. Seeing both of her agent friends, she opened the door. She noticed the other guards in the parking area.

Walking in and seeing Rose transformed from the make-over, Agent Manning realized that had he met her anywhere, he would never have recognized her.

"Gertrude, the make-over is outstanding and should provide a new complete identity. Agent Dorsey, your work is exemplary," said Agent Manning with an element of surprise reflected in his voce.

"Yes, I hardly recognized myself when viewing my own reflection," replied Gertrude.

In addition to the dyed and short hair cut, brown contact

lenses, and tinted glasses, Agent Dorsey had Gertrude wear a two piece black suit, grey colored blouse, knee high hose, a pair of square toe pumps, and a sports bra, that flattened her ample bosom. He had also given her a small paper box containing three each of socks, bras, and panties for her use in prison.

Agent Dorsey quickly checked out  Gertrude and himself from the motel.    Entering an unmarked car with two plain cruisers accompanying them, the three sped to the airport.

After waiting for thirty minutes in a secured room, they boarded Flight 1252 to the city where the selected peniten-tiary was located. The administrators of the U.S. Government Witness Program attempted to use every measure to maintain the highest degree of secrecy  for persons in the witness pro-gram and Agents Manning and Dorsey proved their skills in carrying out the orders.


"WARREN BRANON, I'M AGENT HARRY MANNING  and this is Gertrude  Brown.  Also Agent Johnny Dorsey who assisted me."

"Miss Brown, welcome to your new home, in a manner of speaking.  We are completely aware of the entire situation for your imprisonment.  I have reviewed your file thoroughly and understand fully all the relating circumstances. You are the first woman resident who is a barber and beautician during my watch thus far.  We have always had men. The women will absolutely appreciate your services.  Regretfully, we only have one space left in the women's section.   You will be placed in a compartment with Bertha Gorsey.   Every woman who has been placed with her, has requested a transfer.  She is not the easiest person to know or to like.  She is the oldest resident we have in both age and length of imprisonment.  I had her brought to my office and we had a productive chat.  We came to an understanding relative to her behavior and problems of congeniality with the other women and prison staff.  She is a very negative person.  By appealing to her needs to maintain a clean record when applying for any possible parole in the future, we may have made a break through," related the Warden.

Pushing a button on the side of his desk, a women inmate trustee entered the Warden's office.

"Miss Radley, please take Miss Brown to processing.  They are anticipating her arrival.   Thank you Agents Manning and Dorsey.  We will do what we can to help her," replied the Warden, as he graciously smiled at Gertrude.

"Good bye, Miss Brown.   Until we meet again relative to the plans we have already discussed, I wish you the very best," said Agent Manning as he warmly held her right hand.

"It has been my pleasure to meet you and enjoyed  doing your make-over.  I wish you the very best, also,"  replied Agent Dorsey, as he smiled and gently placed his hand on her forearm.

FOLLOWING THE PROCESSING PROCEDURE, Gertrude was escorted to the room for a prison uniform.  Moving to a changing room, she donned the new attire.   Her suit and blouse were placed in storage pending her release.  Holding her box of extra clothing items, Trustee Radley walked Gertrude to the women's section of the penitentiary.  There she was placed in charge of Sergeant Michael Bidley.

"Miss Brown, I am Mike Bidley.  Warden Branon has briefed me relative to your assignment to share the space with Bertha.  Everyone calls her Big Bertha here.  After you have had an opportunity to visit with her, I'll escort you to the combination Barber/Beauty Shop.  We haven't had a barber for one month now.  I know the men, and especially the women, will appreciate a person with your skills in providing better service than what they have had before.   I believe I could do better than the latest barber by  placing a bowl over the guys' heads and cutting along the edge."

Arriving at the designated compartment, Sgt. Bidley said, "Big Bertha, this is Gertrude Brown, who will share your apartment."

BIG BERTHA SMILED AND gazed at Gertrude for a period of time. Gertrude, holding her box of clothing items, stood and stared back.

Breaking into a friendly grin, Gertrude held out her right hand, and said, "Big Bertha, this is a distinct pleasure meeting you. I assume that the top bunk is mine. You undoubtedly would prefer to be in this compartment by yourself. I'm told that this bunk is the last one in this women's section. As soon as there's an available bunk elsewhere, I'm out of here. You may have your entire space back again. In the meantime, I'll be as quiet as a church mouse at night. I'm a barber slash beautician, and will be in the shop working all day. So in effect, you will still have this compartment to yourself during the day. Of course, I could hang upside down like a bat at night from the ceiling up there," pointing up with a finger and displaying a winsome smile.

"Lordy child, look at you. You are the most pretty young one I've seen here. You have a sense of humor, I do believe. That's good! I think I like you."

"Big Bertha, I know we'll enjoy each others company while I'm confined to this five-star hotel. I'm certain you have gourmet meals and all the perks! Are you ladies permitted to go to the beauty shop?" asked Gertrude, attempting some wry humor.

"Yes, we are, but the women don't want to go much. They need to go by a row of cells with guys to get to the beauty place and they say all kinds of dirty things to us, so we don't go. We calls it the 'Whoope Row.' You're gonna have to go by them too. By the way, why you in this pen?" asked Bertha.

"Well, the guy to whom I was engaged to be married this month was caught doing something illegal. Being an accomplice, I was sentenced to the pen also," replied Rose, in an attempt to be purposely vague about the real reasons.

"That's a bum rap you got. Sorry for you, Gertrude," replied Bertha.

"I understand you are the oldest in age and in terms of imprisonment. When are you eligible for parole?" asked Gertrude.

"I'm in the pen for life for murderin' my husband. Came home from work one day and catch him in bed with a woman. I gives that whore a whipping and chased her out. She is still runnin, I imagine. Well, I strips down to nothing and climbs in bed with him and tells him to start poking me. He couldn't. I wraps my legs round his old skinny butt and pulls his face down between these big girls of mine and smothers that no good bum. He was flaying his arms about like he was doing the breast stroke. Get it? The breast stroke while I smothers him between mine. The big cheat! So don't know when I get a parole," confessed Bertha.

"Gertrude, sorry to interrupt your visit. Are you ready to check out your working area?" asked Mike. "You are scheduled to start in the morning. You will be escorted for several days. Undoubtedly, you will be moved to a trustee status later this week and allowed to go and return without escort."

As they moved down through the various corridors and through two doors, they arrived at the row of cells which Big Bertha referred to as the "Whoopee Row." She understood quickly why. Despite the guard beside her, the men residents really whooped away with whistles, some vulgar terms, and sexual innuendoes. Much to the chagrin of the guard, Gertrude slowed down to almost a stop with hands on hip and stared down several of the more noisy inmates.

Raising her voice, Gertrude said firmly, "Listen up, I'll remember this should you use the barber shop. Could be pay back time!" The volume of noise slightly diminished.

Moving down the corridor, she repeated the admonition

several times. However, the catcalls continued, but Gertrude showed a posture that indicated she was not embarrassed, flustered, nor intimidated. Noticing two residents with their hands through the bars, she approached both, grasped the hands, and said, "I'm Gertrude, should you desire a haircut, the shop will be open in the morning."

Arriving at the shop, the guard opened the door and then gave the key to Gertrude. "I'll be back in one hour to escort you back to your compartment," added Mike.

The shop appeared to be adequate as she stood in the doorway and glanced around. She examined the older style of barber chair which she knew about but obviously never used at Carol's salon. She performed a detailed inventory of the equipment and supplies.

She noted the items low in quantity. The place needed a thorough cleaning. Finding a closet, she found two well-used push brooms, dust pan, furniture polish, and some cleaning rags. Next to the closet was the rest room. Opening the door, she knew from the terrible odors that the place required priority in the total cleaning process.

At the end of the hour, Mike arrived as planned. Walking into the shop, he was greatly impressed with the work Gertrude had accomplished to brighten the place as a result of her sweeping, dusting, and polishing of furniture.

"Miss Brown, you certainly are not afraid of hard work. I have never seen the place in this great a condition, ever. It actually gleams! I'm one of the guards who will be bringing the men residents in groups of five or six who desire your service. Are you ready for the onslaught tomorrow?" asked Mike.

"Ready or not, I'll be here with a smile on my face, and scissors in hand. By the way, what is the procedure for ordering supplies needed, laundering of towels, washing of cleaning rags, and perhaps acquiring some up-to-date reading material. Some of these rag-tag magazines have been here too long," relayed Gertrude showing real concern in the tone of her voice.

"I'll take you to the office where you make these requisitions on the way back to your compartment," replied Mike.

Arriving at her compartment, Big Bertha was sleeping soundly. Gertrude quietly made her bed and placed the box containing her extra clothing items on a wall shelf next to the bed. On the shelf was a Bible. Opening it to the place where there was a marker, she sat down on the only chair in their room. She would have climbed up the ladder to the upper bunk but realized her shaking the bed might wake Bertha. Turning to the open pages, she noticed that "Psalm 23" was underlined. She read the six verses. She recalled hearing them before by the pastor of her church in Norfolk. She read them a second time and then continued reading the following numbered Psalms. She began to sense a feeling of comfort and well being as the words flowed out to her with meaning. She discovered that a previous reader had underlined some favorite parts. As she turned the pages, she found even more underlining. When she arrived at Psalm 140, the words jumped out at her when she read, "Deliver me, O Lord, from evil men, preserve me from violent men." She continued to read more sentences that were speaking loud and clear about her own experiences of the last weeks. Suddenly, visions and thoughts of Steven Harks and the Associates popped into her conscious thinking. She had indeed been delivered from evil men who fooled her with their phony attention and affection. Had she learned that the stuff was cocaine, she might be dead like Sarah if that is what the FBI considered had happened. She continued reading every line of the remaining Psalms. The words of the Lord were speaking to her, loud and clear.

Waking up and seeing Gertrude reading, asked, "What you doin'? Reading the Good Book? That's good. Some other gal left it. I can't read. Wish I could."

"Big Bertha, if you have the desire to learn, I'll help you.

We'll use the Bible as our textbook and start with Psalms 23," confided Gertrude with an authoritative tone to her voice.

"Would you! No one has done that for me before. Thanks, Gertrude," replied Bertha with a tone of thankfulness to her words.

And so Gertrude became a reading teacher. Each evening, Big Bertha diligently applied herself to learning many new words and especially to the correct pronunciation. As she made great strides, along with constant compliments and words of encouragement, Bertha surprised even herself.

Speaking slowly and with determination in pronouncing each word, Bertha ventured," Gertrude, thank—you—for—your—help. I never—went—to—school. Will—you—help—me—to –spell—the---words---now?"

The confidence that Bertha developed from learning to read and by writing short sentences, boosted her self-esteem--actually it blossomed. The belligerent and down right nasty attitude towards everyone in the past was replaced with kindness and a spirit of cooperation. All the women residents were pleased with the dedicated interest that Gertrude exemplified in the personality make-over. There were some women residents who concluded that they could have done the same personality changes had they really taken an interest in Big Bertha like Gertrude.

GERTRUDE HAD WORKED FOR five days manning the Barber/Beautician Shop.

Mike and another guard, Johnny Elson, escorted the male residents to the shop, four or five at a time. She was surprised to find that each had leg irons which caused them to shuffle their feet. When several inmates, wearing leg irons and hand-cuffed to a chain going around their waist, she became apprehensive. She attempted to take all these new experiences in stride without showing noticeable anxiety. Using the people skills developed at Carol's Salon, she asked questions of the men that might elicit responses.

She discovered that the method worked for many. Others simply sat in silence, perhaps due to having a woman barber for the first time. Gertrude realized that her work was similar to a production line. The time spent cutting the hair for each male residents was approximately 10 to 12 minutes. She was seeing around 35 during a 7 hour day. Having acquired magazines relative to the interest of the men, she noticed their waiting became more pleasant.

Practically begging the women residents to consider using her expertise, none desired to venture through "Whoopee Row." Gertrude realized she had to take some action regarding this drastic situation.

GERTRUDE WAS GIVEN TRUSTEE STATUS after the first week. Using the opportunity, she asked for an appointment with the Warden. Arriving at the time requested, Warden Branon graciously welcomed her into his office.

"Gertrude, there are rumors and stories floating about the staff regarding you. All good, I might add. I was about to send for you regarding some information I needed to share."

The Warden proceeded to show her the contents of e-mails received from Agent Manning. The FBI had closed out her personal banking account and it was placed in escrow until time of parole. The wages paid her by the cartel were confiscated, however. Agent Manning had wired by electronic transfer $500 of her own money and it was already placed in a personal account. She would be able to withdraw funds as needed. A request on her part, more money could be sent.

"You must be doing a fantastic job of cutting the male resident's hair." Opening the correct window on his computer, the Warden added, "The men are requesting a transfer of funds from their accounts to yours as a gratuity for your service. Although the amounts from each are for less than a dollar, this is certainly a first during my tour of duty. This certainly indicates the men are appreciative of your abilities. And it's your money to spend as you desire. Then I have a report on your transformation skills with Big Bertha. How kind and thoughtful to share your personal touch in helping her read and write. The guards indicate a remarkable change in her attitude and self-discipline."

"Thank you for the compliments. But the reason for my request to see you relates to all the women residents. None will go to the shop because of the corridor called, 'Whoopee Row." You may have heard about this. The men harass and humiliate the women."

Gertrude continued her request to establish a miniature beauty shop next to her compartment in an area sufficient to accommodate a table and three chairs. Knowing she now had a personal account, an additional request was made concerning the purchase of a hair dryer, and other specific items needed in providing various personal services for the 50 female residents. The sink in her compartment would be nearby for use. There would be a need for a heavy duty electrical cord to power the stationery hair dryer and hand held equipment.

"Should you approve this, Warden Branon, I would be able to cut the men's hair Monday through Friday noon of each week, and for the women, Friday afternoons, Saturdays, and Sundays as needed."

Opening another window on his computer, the Warden added, "Gertrude, there's a budget of $4,200 to use for the Barber Shop. The figures indicate that $1,240.52 has been spent on various purchases to date. If you wish, you may consider using any part of the allocated funds for your Mini-Beauty Shop."

"Warden, your name for the shop is clever!  That's what we'll call the place!  I would appreciate the table and chairs be requisitioned as soon as possible.   I'll ask Mike Bidley if he'll consider buying all the provisions needed from the Oppenhimer Beauty Supplies in the city. He has been so helpful in the shop. With his help, the Mini-Beauty Shop can be up and operating by this week end, perhaps. Thank you for your cooperation, Warden Branon. The women residents should be pleased."

"Gertrude, your vision and initiative are commendable. I'm sure the women will certainly be more than pleased with your efforts. I'll arrange for the delivery of the furniture immediately. Feel free to make an appointment anytime. You are indeed a beautiful young lady. I have a daughter, Millicent, who is two years older than you. Same height and stature. Sorry, I know your age from your records. If I borrowed some of her clothes for you to wear, would you consider being our guest for a weekend or even for holidays down the road? I believe my daughter and you would enjoy each other's company."

"Warden Branon, I would enjoy these extra considerations. But I need to decline the invitations. The other women may not understand. They may consider this an indication of favoritism. I'm still in the process of becoming acquainted with them. With the Mini-Beauty Shop, hopefully, I'll be able to develop a favorable rapport. You know what I mean?"

"Gertrude, again you're wise and considerate. I understand that jealousy might raise its ugly head and make matters worse for you. Again, please visit anytime you need help."

The Mini-Beauty Shop was in full operation within two days. Her first "customer" was Big Bertha. Gertrude was challenged to oblige her by creating corn-row braids. The sign up sheet for services was soon filled for the hours that Gertrude had posted. The female residents were most appreciative for the accommodations that Gertrude had managed to place in operation for their benefit. The rapport that she desired with everyone was achieved and then some. The spin off from this new operation was more noticeable by the guards. They sensed a happier atmosphere that permeated the entire wing of the prison. This made their work more tolerable and enjoyable.

BIG BERTHA INCREASINGLY IMPROVED WITH her vocabulary and spelling under the tutelage of Gertrude. Even Susan Quicken, nicknamed Susie Que, and Mildred Monson, with a moniker of Milly MO, assisted Gertrude, who was now given the nickname of "Gertie."

With determination to speak correctly, Big Bertha cornered Gertie. "I have some bad news you ought to know. I think you are a-virgin. Am I wrong? You will not be for long."

"What are talking about Big Bertha? Yes, I'm still a virgin! But what do you mean 'not for long?' "

Bertha shared in halting words the situation that happened around once a month. There were eight guards appointed to the women's section. These guards were rotated on the duty roster for three daily shifts. When Guards Leonard Lawrence, nicknamed, "Big Dick" and Sam Godsen, nicknamed, "Little Dick" were on the same midnight shift, they covered for each other by forcing their choice of female residents to what the women named the "Dick Room." Susie Que, Milly Mo, Sandie Bay, and Nora Ivy had been their favorites for the past several months. Bertha knew with out a doubt, that Gertie would be added to the list. The women were constantly intimidated with threats by the two men. They were afraid to talk for fear of severe reprisals. It seemed to the female residents that not much could be done to prevent these forced midnight walks.

Upon hearing this calamity of the tryst, actually rape, these two guards were performing and allowed to continue, Gertie knew some action needed prompt attention. She knew immediately, a plan had to be devised to stop this form of abuse and hopefully have the guards arrested on statutory rape charges. She definitely knew she would not be a victim. Of that, she was determined--hell or high water. She was grateful for Bertha's alerting her to this deplorable situation.

Gertie had an idea. Gathering the seven women who the guards had been selecting, she laid out a trap that might be sprung. All agreed that the plan might work if the Warden would agree. Capitalizing on the Warden's word that his door was always open, Gertie made an appointment to convey the plan.

After Gertrude informed the Warden about the rapes, he was totally shocked in realizing this sordid situation was happening. He had only heard rumors, but no actual proof. The Warden learned the 'Dick Room" was labeled Bravo 125. Mildred Monson even had the condoms that were discarded carelessly from past encounters with both guards. These could be used as evidence in determining the guards' DNA.

"Gertrude, this will be stopped! Now! Your trap has merit! I so appreciate your bringing this terrible situation to my attention! I will personally install a hidden mike and transmitter. When I hear your selected code words, 'Gee, you're great!' we'll barge in and catch these two sleazy characters in the act. Sorry for the need to place you in this embarrassing position. But I do admire your spunk and determination to end this terrible situation that has been taking place much too long. We cannot have this situation taking place in this penal institution. Again, I wish someone would have reported this violation the guards have been perpetrating. I'll personally extend apologies to the ladies involved."

The midnight shift arrived when both of the guards were on duty. Without fail, Leonard Lawrence forced Gertrude from her compartment despite Big Bertha's threats. Sam Godson's favorite was Susie Que again. In the trap, all the women who might be selected had agreed to appeal to the guards lustful desires by suggesting that a four-some love making would be a fantasy they would enjoy performing in reality. Both guards succumbed to the sexy enticement staged by Susie and Gertie.

Arriving in the "Dick Room," both women were stripped of their clothing in short order. While being kissed, caressed, fondled, and literally pawed over, both women unbuttoned the men's shirts and removed them, pulled of their T-shirts, then loosen their belts and unzipped their trousers. Gertie, considering the two guards were in a sufficient compromising position, placed her arms around the neck of Leonard and allowed herself to be kissed rather passionately. She knew Susie was performing her share of the sting from the moans Sam was emitting. Breaking the kiss and forcing herself to caress his chest with one hand, while caressing him lower down with the other, she said the code words. In a few seconds, Warden Branon, Administrator Michael Huckaby, and a city policeman with his drawn revolver, practically tore the door from its hinges while coming through. The guards knew they had been caught literally and figuratively with their pants down. They were allowed to redress, then handcuffed, and lead away. Hastily grabbing their clothes, the two women scrambled to the corner of the room, dressed and were then escorted back to their compartments by Warden Branon. The women residents quickly learned that the trap worked without a hitch. Gertrude pointed out each of the women who had been violated in the past. The Warden expressed his deepest apologizes to each and wished that someone had complained much, much sooner. There was great rejoicing that night and not much sleep by anyone.

With notarized affidavits furnished by each of the female residents who had been raped, and the witness by Warden Branon and Administrator Huckaby, both guards, following a hearing and highly publicized trial, were sentenced for statutory rape. The women residents appreciated that the two guard replacements were devoted family men. The fear which the female victims had experienced was now completely eliminated. Many gave the credit to Gertrude. However, she continued to build a better rapport in her unassuming manner. It really was personal—she had her own innocence to preserve. Being raped was not part of her life's adventures!

# CHAPTER 30

THERE SHOULD HAVE BEEN no surprise to Gertrude that the residents of any correctional institution usually develop a sophisticated means to spread news almost the speed of light. In this penitentiary, the system was named the "Grapevine Express."

Before Gertrude arrived at the Barber Shop, the entire male residents must have learned of the sting operation which she was instrumental in pulling off. When the first group of men came into the shop, she could tell by the manner of their visional glances along with facial smirks that she had been involved in ending the sex escapades of two guards and sending them to prison. However, she acted as nonchalant in her daily routine as if nothing had happened. She realized this ploy was not easy to accomplish. Trying to engage the men in normal conversation as before, she came to the conclusion the men just didn't wish to respond. She provided an extra twist in performing a vigorous scalp massages for each. By doing so, there was a tendency for them to at least express thanks for the added treat. This became the "ice breaker" for more conversation

The whole scene in being a barber was rather amusing to her. All of the male residents seemed to fall roughly into three categories. There were some within her age range whose demeanor was of a sisterly nature. The men twice her age and older approached her in conversation and physical presence on a parental level. The third group caused more amusement for Gertrude. These were the men whose viewing of her and words spoken almost in whispers so the other men waiting couldn't hear, could be classified as romantic in nature or paraphrased in words--"I wish you were my girlfriend." She enjoyed their banter of these conversations. However, she guarded her words carefully so no one would misconstrue their meaning to be of a personal nature.

Not knowing who actually transferred money to her account, Gertrude posted a sign on the wall, "To those giving gratuities, Thank you."

Gertrude received permission to purchase from her own personal account a 30-cup coffee maker, several cans of coffee, Styrofoam cups, and sugar/creamer packets. Each morning, she had a fresh pot of coffee ready for the men to enjoy. On many days, another new pot was needed for the afternoon groups. She increased the types of magazines. The librarian of the institution gave her the extra current events magazines and the daily newspapers. She had Mike buy crossword puzzle and Sudoku books. Permission was granted to have a bottled water company deliver a dispenser with a standing order weekly of three bottles of water. The men soon learned through the "Grapevine Express" that the amenities were paid from her personal account. The men realized they were the benefactors of their own gratuities. The men were grateful; not surprising, her personal account increased proportionately.

GERTRUDE RECEIVED A NOTE to report to the Warden's office. Hanging a sign on the door "Temporarily Closed" for the benefit of the guards, she headed for his office. Sitting in the waiting section, Gertrude saw a well-groomed woman. She thought it might be the Warden's wife for she had not met her at this point. She left her chair, extended her hand, and introduced her self. She was wrong.

"I'm Sandra Whittington, a member of the local Gideon Auxiliary. I'm waiting to visit with Warden Branon relative to starting a Bible Study class for the women."

"That is very commendable. In my opinion, the Warden will consider that request with seriousness," replied Gertrude in a caring tone of voice.

At that moment, the Warden entered the waiting room area. Seeing the ladies already in conversation, he invited both to have seats in his office.

"Gertrude, Mrs. Whittington sent a letter earlier this week requesting our consideration of starting a Bible Class for the women. With your relationship and rapport with the women, do you believe they would attend the classes on Sunday and Wednesday evenings, say around 7 o'clock?" asked the Warden.

"Yes, there may be 5 or 6 to start the class. Knowing the women, it will grow. I will certainly be part of your class," replied Gertrude.

"Then, Mrs. Whittington, you may start this coming Sunday evening if you wish. Each time you or other ladies arrive, please come to my office. A trustee will escort you to the women's section. Gertrude is a trustee also, and we'll give her a key to use room number B-125. She will take you to the women's section now. Gertrude can introduce you to the other women and also show you where your classes will be held. Thank you, Gertrude, for your personal help once again."

Susie Que, Gertrude, and Big Bertha extended personal invitations to the women for attending the first class. Bertha was especially excited for this afforded her the extra opportunities to learn more reading skills. Mrs. Whittington was pleased with the many ladies who shared their interest and desire to learn more of their spiritual side of life.

During the course of the class Gertrude caught Susie's glance and her smirk. She knew what her thoughts were regarding the very same room where they had successfully achieved the sting operation.

"JOE, THIS IS DONOVAN. WE RECEIVED a letter today from the Federal Bureau of Investigation. It concerns Rose," trying to speak with a lump in his throat.

Continuing the best he could, Donovan attempted to share with Joe that Rose had testified at the trial of Steven Harks and the associates. For her protection against the revenge of the drug cartel, she has been placed under the U.S. Government Witness Protection Plan. She is all right and living under a different name and in a city that can not be revealed. She can never contact us. We can expect people to try to reach us by mail, telephone, or in person under some pretense to find out where she lives.

"We have lost our beautiful daughter forever, Joe. All we have left are memories. We have placed her picture in a prominent place in our home so we can reflect back on the precious years that God allowed us to share her life each and every day. I now regret terribly not telling her enough how much I loved her. Now it's too late," Donovan said, speaking with much difficulty.

"This is so sad, Donovan. There was this strange feeling stuck in my craw while Harks interviewed Rose. As I think back, he was too smooth an operator. Never being able to see Rose again--that's worse than horrible! I was planning to call you later today. What you mentioned in that letter did happen regarding someone contacting me," replied Joe.

He proceeded to share how a man who gave his name as Roger Furnel with the United Life Insurance Company came into the Grill at noon time. He asked for us. He had a policy with our names on it as beneficiaries for a life insurance policy supposedly taken out when Rose lived with us. We know she was not issued a policy. She would have told us. The policy was cancelled for lack of monthly payment for four months. The company wanted to refund the money she had already paid on the policy. He wanted her address to mail the refund check.

"I told him she never furnished an address and have had no communication since she was involved in a trial in Richmond. Please bring me the address of the FBI tomorrow, Donovan, and I'll inform them of this incident. It's probably a phony name and a fictitious company, but good for the FBI to know. Never thought about trying to obtain more information from him. We can expect more of these character trying to contact us," replied Joe.


THE 'GRAPEVINE EXPRESS' WAS once again sending out its latest news. Word spread quickly that Gertrude would be paroled near the end of the year. The women flooded her with questions relative to her plans. Where would she live?

What would she be doing? What would happen to the Mini-Beauty Shop? Who would cut the hair for the men? Who would spearhead the Bible Study class?

She could only tell everyone that she had no answers. Gertrude had not been contacted by Agent Harry Manning at this point nor had the Warden said anything. She only knew she would be paroled one day in the future. But the questions did prompt her to take some directions and a plan of action to preserve the continuation of the Barber Shop and Mini-Beauty Shop. She realized she couldn't wait or plan for another female inmate being incarcerated as being a beautician.

Arranging an appointment with Warden Branon, she shared a plan to teach two of the women she felt had a possibility for being a Barber and a Beautician. She would instruct them daily in the techniques of performing the various skills necessary until the day she was paroled.  She received the Warden's blessings and permission to  proceed post haste.

Questioning Big Bertha, she halfway asked and with sub-tlety informed her that being a beautician could be a skill to learn.  Any productive progress on her part may help when the time came to apply for a parole.

"You mean, Gertie, that you want me to learn what you know to do the beauty work when you leave?"

"Exactly! Big Bertha, your speaking ability has certainly improved greatly!  I'm so proud of you!  Now, remember, if you goof in doing any cutting hair, you minimize the mistake. Hair does continually grow to cover these boo boos.  Lord only knows how many I've made.  I'll be directing every move. How about it, Big Bertha?"

With a nod of her head indicating "yes," Gertie had one down and one to go!

She strolled  down the corridor to Susie Que's compart-ment.  Approaching her in much the same vein of question-ing and suggesting, Susie stared at Gertrude while mentally weighing the request.

"You wish for me to join you daily at the Barber Shop and while you teach me the skills,  cut the men's hair?  What if I lop off an ear or two?  What happens then?"

Gertrude broke into laughter that caused the women in the nearby compartment to be disturbed.

"Susie, you're a real joker, and you need to be dealt with in a royal manner.  Do you wish to view the box full of bits of ears I have stashed away?  I'll give you the box in order to continue the collection.  Hey, I'm serious!  Would you desire to learn the trade?"

"I have a long time yet in serving my sentence before any possibility of parole.  You seem to enjoy the work.  Hey, why not give it a shot for a month or two if the Grapevine news is true regarding your parole. I'll certainly know by then if I can do the work properly."

"Thank you, Susie. I'll ask the Warden to consider you as a trustee in order to walk to the shop daily. I'm as sure as shootin' that you'll take to the cuttin' as a duck takes to water!"

Gertrude worked daily with her two protégés. Once both moved past the nervous apprehensive phase, confidence kicked in and they made great strides to learn the techniques required. The men were very cooperative and understood why Gertie was teaching a replacement—the "Grapevine Express" thing. The women were a little reticent and apprehensive whether Big Bertha was up to the task. With detailed instruction in doing the shingling, teasing, setting curlers, setting a perm, and different styles of comb outs, Big Bertha again surprised her self (and what the women claimed as "victims") in the ability to accomplish each technique. The women warmed up to the "new" beautician. Gertrude was more than pleased for when she left, both shops would be functioning.

AGAIN THE "GRAPEVINE EXPRESS" was in action. This time it was among the female residents. Gertrude thought the conversation with the Warden was in confidence, but the women barraged her with questions similar in nature--"Why didn't you accept the Warden's invitation to share Thanksgiving with his family?" When her new found friends shot phrases at her such as--Go Girl!--Accept the invitation!--What a great way to spend the day!-- Go for It!--and many similar admonitions, Gertie sent word to the Warden that she had reconsidered his invitation. The women had urged her to do so.

Receiving a package from the Warden containing a blouse, skirt, and jacket, Gertrude credited Millicent for having fashionable taste.

Sharing an enjoyable Thanksgiving Day and the week-end with the Warden's family was just another wonderful adventure to add to her list. She and Millicent bonded quickly. They enjoyed each others friendship and the several hours spent on girl-talk.

ATTEMPING TO BALANCE a practice business assignment for his accounting class, Marvin finally picked up the phone after five rings.

"Hello Marvin, this is Chris. Didn't pull you away from that which you love most, am I?"

"Chris, my dear old Navy buddy, how the heck are you? If you mean my lover being Accounting III, yeah, you pulled me away alright! But glad you did! How's your law degree progressing?"

"Everything is on track! I hope to finish in the top of my class. But the real reason for calling is terrible information about Rose. Call it homesick or what, I drove to Norfolk and visited our old rusty bucket of a ship again and then a long chat with Joe and June.

"Is this really bad, Chris? Maybe I don't wish to know."

"You can't fool me, buddy! Down deep you still have a spark of affection for Rose. Well, she never married that Harks fellow after all. He was actually a drug dealer, making millions from cocaine. Also a fence for buying stolen gems. Rose was asked to testify at the trial. He and all his cronies are serving time in the pen. She is now under the Government Witness program. No one but the FBI knows her whereabouts. Her folks are really broken up and grieving and so are the Reillys."

"Chris, what have I done? Somehow by jilting Rose, I've caused her family terrible grief! Probably for Rose, too. I just know they really hate me! Rose, too! She's out there all alone, who knows where! How I wish a terrible wrong could be made right!"

"Marv, you're a great person! I knew you would care! Having sympathy and empathy are your strongest suits.

You're a religious person, I know. You're a survivor, and perhaps you helped Rose to be a survivor, too."

"Thanks Chris. You've put the situation in perspective, somewhat. I do appreciate this news about Rose but I hate myself for what I've done to her. Call again, will you?" as Marvin had to terminate the call due to a big lump in his throat. It had to dissolve before he would have been able to say more to Chris.

As he continued to gaze at the phone, his thoughts returned to the last meeting with Rose. How he wished those moments could be relived and then continued from that point. But that possibility could never be.

LIFE AT THE PENITENTIARY for Gertrude and her many friends continued day after day in pleasant ways. There seemed to be no major problems surfacing. Her beautician protégés continued to gain skills and became extremely proficient. She could only judge their progress by the compliments received from those on the receiving end. She was pleased for Susie and Bertha becoming proficient so quickly.

The librarian started a General Education Degree class for the female residents. She asked Gertrude to encourage everyone who never graduated from high school to attend the class. To her surprise, those desiring GED's quickly enrolled. Big Bertha was the first to place her name on the enrollment form. Twenty-one more realized the opportunity being offered and Room B-125 was pressed into usage for the class. Another incentive would be a graduation ceremony held for the class with the Superintendent of the Public Schools and the Warden presenting the diplomas.

The Christmas advent season had begun. Gertie decorated both of her shops with festive decorations for the Christmas holidays. The spirit of the season caught on and spread to all the other women. Knowing she had a large amount in her personal account, Gertie asked Mike to purchase a large supply of

Christmas decorations. These were made available for any of
the female residents to use for their own compartments.

Walking daily through "Whoopee Row," Gertie and Susie
Que had developed such a rapport with all the male residents
by cutting their hair at least twice, some three times, that the
usual catcalls and remarks had stopped. Actually, it was
rather pleasant to walk by these compartments. They were
greeted with various types of pleasant salutations. Gertie,
by learning many of the men by their first names was able to
greet them with personal greetings. Susie Que soon picked
up on the same approach. This was most noticeable for the
guards who patrolled the area. They appreciated the change
in attitude the inmates were demonstrating. Both ladies were
amused one day when an apparently a new inmate made a
"wolf whistle" and was immediately squashed by a threat of
"Shut your mouth or we'll shove it full of toilet paper!"

Christmas Day arrived. The Bible Class was given permission to sing religious and secular Christmas songs throughout
the facility. The ladies were pleased with the compliments
received.

Many of the female residents had received gifts from their
families and friends during the preceding days of Christmas.
These were placed under a small tree that Gertie had decorated near the Mini-Beauty Shop. On Christmas morning, the
ladies gathered in groups to open their gifts. Gertie knew that
some did not received gifts. She had Good Old Mike purchase
extra beauty and hair products with her own funds, wrapped
them, and had these under the tree for gifts to those without
any.

And so the week after Christmas, the decorations and
tree were dismantled and stored for perhaps another time.
Everyone was sad the holidays had passed for it had been the
first time the season had been observed so joyously. Rose was
embarrassed with all the 'thanks' received for her leadership.

IT WAS DECEMBER 29 when Gertie received a note to report to the Warden's office just as she was headed for the shop.

"Susie Que, here's the key. You open the shop today. I'll see you later," requested Gertie.

Arriving at the Warden's office, she broke into a big smile as she saw Agent Harry Manning speaking to Warden Branon.

"Gertrude, are you ready to break out of this place with our blessings?" asked the Warden, showing a big smile in return.

"I wondered when the day would arrive! Agent Manning, you are a sight for sore eyes! You are certainly a man of your word. This penitentiary life has been very different. But I'm more than ready to move on with my life's adventures at some other place," replied Gertrude as she held out her hand to him.

"Agent Manning, Gertrude has been a model citizen. You probably have some idea of what this young lady can accomplish when she gathers her courageous will power, and places it in motion. Wow! The influence Gertrude has had on people in this place has been astounding," shared the Warden. "And we will miss you. Thank you for spending Thanksgiving Day with the family. Millicent was also pleased with the Christmas gift you sent, also. We went out of town for Christmas Day to be with my wife's parents or we would have had you at our house again."

"Oh, you didn't know, we have been corresponding. Millicent already sent a Thank You note and regrets about not being able to have me at your home over the holidays," said Gertrude.

Agent Manning knew he had to take charge or the conversation would continue all day. "Gertrude, we have plane tickets to Denver tomorrow at 9 a.m. You can pack, say any good byes, and what every else needs to be accomplished. I've reserved a room near the Denver International Airport. A furnished apartment has been located and a new car is waiting for you. All possessions boxed in Richmond have been placed in your apartment already. You'll be able to drive to your new home tomorrow. We'll check out some potential beauty salons for you, too. How's that for your start of a new adventure?"

"Oh, Agent Manning, all that sounds like something too good to be true!" gushed Gertrude.

"Gertrude, if I don't see you before you leave, God speed to you in the years to come. You have been a blessing to many persons in this place, probably more than you will ever know," said the Warden.

"Thank you, Warden Branon. You have been very kind and helpful. I appreciate everything you've done.    As you know, both women are doing great work. It pleases me no end that they caught on quickly to the skills needed to perform the needed services. May I move half of my personal money account to Susan Quicken and to Bertha Gorsey to use at their own discretion?" asked Gertrude.

"See what I mean, Agent Manning?   What a giving person you are, Gertrude.   Yes, we will make the transfer of funds as you request. I'm already late for a meeting.  If you two wish to stay here for anymore discussion and planning, be my guest. Good bye, Gertrude," as he held out his hand and warmly clasped Gertrude's before departing.

"I'll see you at 7 a.m. tomorrow, Gertrude, in the penitentiary discharge room," ordered Agent Manning. "Using your own words, another part of your new adventure is waiting for you!"

# CHAPTER 31

GERTRUDE WAS IN A state of ambivalence upon returning to her compartment. The obvious well-planned arrangements by Agent Manning kept spinning through her mind. What laid ahead for her was being processed over and over again. There apparently was so much to be accomplished that the actual prospects were overwhelming. Gertrude knew she had to grab a mental handle on the situation. She then remembered one of the songs they sang in the Bible Class—"One day at a time, Lord Jesus, that's all I'm asking of You. Help me this day, show me the way, one day at a time!" Yes, that's what she needed to do. She begin humming the song as she headed for the women's quarters.

Arriving at her compartment, Big Bertha was administering a perm for Lucky Lilly.

"Well, look whose playing hooky from work this morning!" teased Big Bertha, as she applied the last hair roller.

Gertrude examined the completed set of hair rollers for the perm. "Big Bertha, you're doing exceptional work! Actually superb work! You're in complete and full charge  now!  I've been  paroled and leaving tomorrow  for a  new and, hopefully, interesting life!"

Big Bertha immediately embraced Gertrude. Lilly stood up from the chair.  Despite the drape around her neck and body, she placed her arms around both in a group hug.

"You're going to be missed, Gertie!  Something awful! You've done changed many lives, especially mine!  I'm gra-gra-grateful for what you have done for me," gushed Bertha, as tears rolled down her cheeks.

"Thank you, Bertha.  It has certainly been my pleasure to be helpful and assist you becoming a beautician. You've become a dear friend!  I'll always remember you as my roomy.  I need to tell Susie Que now.  See you all later," replied Gertrude as she broke the hug and moved down the corridor.

Reaching the barber shop, Gertrude watched Susie through the small window in the door while she was  performing a hair cut.  Susie, Guard Mike, and the inmate, Jake, receiving a trim, where busily engaged in conversation.   She noted the men waiting were drinking coffee and reading magazines.  She was pleased that the Warden and other staff members allowed her ideas to be implemented.

Suddenly, Mike noticed Gertrude looking through the window.  He immediately left and joined her.

"Susie Que indicated you may have had a visit with the Warden.   Did you per chance  receive your parole as the Grapevine Express has been announcing?"

"Yes, Mike, I leave early tomorrow morning.  Mike, thank you for the shopping you have completed for me so many times or really for the many  others  who  benefited from the purchases. You've been a true friend.  Susie will undoubtedly need your support.  I've transferred half of my personal account to her.  She'll be able to purchase the  extra things for the shop the men are enjoying.   What  a relief for me that Susie has become proficient so quickly."

"Gertrude, you have become a delightful person to know. You're so generous with your many talents! You've had a great influence with the male residents, and probably the female residents, too, that has been really wholesome. Actually, I've been smitten with you myself. You're a gorgeous lady, indeed, Gertrude."

"Thank you, Mike, for the compliments! You have been a great help in what I tried to do. Again, thank you. Perhaps we should join Susie and tell her I'm leaving. It's super that she seems to have everything under control."

BIG BERTHA, WATCHING GERTRUDE leaving, quickly realized she had to take charge of the situation. Thanks to Gertie, she had learned a desired skill that seemed to be welcomed by the other women. She wanted to show her gratitude— why not organize a farewell party. Sharing the party idea with Lucky Lilly, for whom she was doing the final comb out process, and Milly Mo, under the hair dryer, both agreed that the idea was great. Finished with Lilly, Big Bertha began sharing the party idea with other female residents. Some were away to their respective work stations, but without exception, Big Bertha received the "Go Ahead!" from everyone present.

Approaching the two guards on duty, Big Bertha shared the plans for the farewell party at 7 p.m. Could room B-125 be used? The guards were aware of the influence which Gertrude had had upon so many individuals. A required call for permission from the Warden's office was quickly approved.

Big Bertha started recruiting the help to plan the event. Amazingly, everyone was capable of keeping the party a secret. At 7 p.m., Gertrude was asked by Big Bertha, under the disguise of helping her for the last time with more writing skills, to accompany her to room 125. They wouldn't be disturbed there.

Walking into the room, Gertrude was indeed surprised

by the chorus of voices "For she's a jolly great lady, that no-body can deny!" Gertrude was moved and grateful as she was hugged, extended best wishes for life's successes, and given words of appreciation for her leadership. Bertha was pleased that the occasion was successful. The guards present indicated that in their knowledge of the past, never had a pro-found and meaningful farewell party been held for a paroled female resident. Gertrude was flattered and humbled with this information.

GERTRUDE AND AGENT MANNING were on the early flight for Denver International Airport as scheduled. Wearing the same clothes when arriving at the penitentiary, Gertrude had considered the clothes Millicent had given her. They were much more fashionable. But if part of the disguise was to ap-pear old fashioned, dowdy, or even appear as a dowager, then she'd play the part. Agent Manning acknowledged her better judgment, also.

"Gertrude, I have already identified from advertisements, four beauty salons for sale as of yesterday. I haven't seen any of these. As I indicated, we'll stay at a hotel this evening. Your car is to be delivered tomorrow around noon. We'll ob-tain a map and mark the four salons. After we eye ball all four, you may determine which one you desire. Hopefully one will meet your standards. We need to 'strike while the iron's hot' so to speak for the best could be sold right from under us. Here's your new Social Security card and a 30-day temporary driver's license. This is your car insurance policy and an apart-ment lease, both paid for one year; and a bank draft for the balance of your money from the Richmond Bank that we held in escrow. You may open your own bank account. You can obtain a permanent driver's license from the Denver DMV as soon as possible."

After a succulent meal at a nearby airport restaurant and a restful night's sleep, Gertrude was anxiously waiting for the delivery of her new car.   She was more than ready to start salon shopping!

Arriving at the fourth salon and after a walk-through, Gertrude exclaimed with great enthusiasm, "Agent Manning, this is the salon I desire! It has the most modern arrangements of the four!  Can we call the real estate office and determine if it's still available?"

Gertrude was ecstatic when the realtor indicated the salon was still on the market.   Meeting with a title insurance firm mid afternoon and the owner of the salon, Gertrude became the new owner. She was thrilled!  When looking through papers left in the salon's office desk, she found what evidently were the  names, addresses, and phone numbers of a  Babs Brooks and a Laurie Bealer.   Wondering if they were the former beauticians and  still available, she placed the paper in her handbag with plans  to phone them later.

Leaving the title company, Agent Manning asked, "Are you ready to see your apartment?

"Yes, I can't wait to see my new home!" beamed Gertrude.

"Hope you will agree with our selection," said Agent Manning with a hint of doubt in his voice.

Arriving at the apartment complex, the elevator moved  to the fourth floor.

"You're close to the elevator in apartment 402.   Here are the keys.  Welcome to your new home!"

Upon entering, Gertrude saw all her boxed possessions. She simply stood and gazed upon them.  "What a great sight for sore eyes," she thought.   She remembered thinking when she boxed her possessions—"when would they see the light of day again? This is the day—December 30—over one year since Marvin made those horrible accusations—now living in this city where he also lives somewhere—having been in the pen after loving a drug dealer. What's next?"

Watching Gertrude just standing still for a period of time,

Agent Manning asked, "Is there something wrong? Don't you like the location? The apartment? The basic furnishings?"

"Oh No, Agent Manning! I'm sorry! My mind was wondering about somewhere in the past! This is a fantastic place! Your selection is great!"

"Thank goodness, you had me worried just a bit. If you wish to start unpacking, I'll help. I noticed you have the boxes marked with their contents. Brilliant idea! I'll make the distributions. You unpack. Did you notice the restaurant we passed three blocks away? You can eat there until you stock your kitchen."

"Agent Manning, I know it's your line of work, but your personal involvement in my protection is so appreciated. And your assistance in acquiring a beauty salon—the Buick—much like the one I had in Norfolk—this apartment with a view of the park across the street—wow! All so great!"

"Glad to be of service, Gertrude. Why not use my cell phone and call the telephone company to have your apartment and salon phones activated before their closing time. You may wish to call those former beauticians, too. Would be terrific if one or both can work for you. I'll start moving boxes."

Surprisingly, reaching Babs and Laurie on the first try, and both anxious to become employed again, was truly pure luck. Gertrude learned that the salon had been closed for only 15 days. Both beauticians indicated they would call all their former customers and make the announcement of the new opening on January 3. Both indicated they would be ready to help place the salon back in operating condition the day after New Years. Gertrude realized that the salon could be up and running quickly. January 2 would be a busy day in purchasing the supplies needed plus a dozen other required jobs.

"Gertrude, would you please open this small package?"

She didn't recognize it. She had not filled this box. Snapping the tape holding the flaps, she lifted out a cloth bag. Opening the bag, she removed her wrist watch, birth stone ring, and the necklace. She looked at Agent Manning with a look that revealed both shock and puzzlement.

"Gertrude, the engagement ring was part of a jewelry store robbery in Chicago. It has been returned. However, we can find no trace of the other three items to any robbery. Therefore, they are yours to keep or dispose. Note the appraisal sheet in the box. The value of each is listed. The registered gemologist has indicated that he will buy all three for $40,000 should you wish to sell. That's your call."

"Agent Manning, knowing what kind of person Steven is now, I'm not surprised that he gave me an engagement ring that was stolen. He is certainly something else."

Gertrude studied the appraisal sheet. She was shocked that Steven had given her the two gifts of such huge value. The birthstone was a special gift. She mentally debated whether to retain the gift or sell with the other two items. There was no way she would keep all the diamond loaded jewelry. The sale of both would be a grand nest egg to pay for salon expenses in the start up stages. Yep! She was going to sell all three! Each would bring back too many horrible memories if kept! Besides, it just wasn't her "thing" to wear expensive jewelry.

MARVIN AND HIS MOTHER were attending church on a beautiful sunny Sunday morning. During the service, Marvin suddenly noticed a young lady two pews ahead of theirs. From the back she had an uncanny appearance of Rose. She had the red hair and styled in a similar manner as Rose's. He was hoping she would gaze to the right so he'd see her profile. But she kept holding her head forward.

Nudging his mother and speaking in a whisper, "Mother, who is that red-headed lady sitting ahead of us?"

Using the edge of the church bulletin and a pen from her purse, Mrs. Brown wrote,

"Linda Powell, sophomore at the University. Her parents

are beside her. I'll introduce you after the services. Now, listen to the minister."

Marvin could not remove his eyes from Linda. As he continued to view the likeness of Rose from the back, his thoughts began to reminiscence to the last days with her. "Where is she now? Could be anywhere in the U.S. Why was I so stupid to blame her for unfaithfulness? She'll never see her family again because of me. Worse yet, I'll never see her again. How could I have hurt someone so terribly—one for whom I still have precious memories and feelings?"

His mother brought Marvin back to planet earth with a firm poke of her elbow to his rib cage. He glanced at his mother, whose facial frown spoke loud and clear—you're in church—pay attention to the sermon!

The last hymn was sung. For Marvin, this was not soon enough to end the services. He had to meet Linda! His curiosity was at "Code Red." When Linda turned to leave the pew towards the aisle, Marvin had a full frontal view. Certainly not the facial shape as Rose, but—wow—the brilliant emerald green eyes! He knew he was staring but couldn't help himself. Linda was a vision of beauty!

Moving towards the aisle, he turned to determine if his mother was following. He wanted the interception of Linda and her folks to be timed correctly. Luckily they did.

"Linda, this is my son, Marvin, who was staring at the back of your lovely hair-do more than listening to the minister," said Martha, Marvin's mother, in a chiding tone of voice.

"Hello Marvin," as she extended her hand. "I know who you are—now a pleasure to finally meet you. And these are my parents, Robert and Marcella."

Marvin was captivated momentarily by the introduction to Linda and was admiring her radiant smile. His mother made a quizzing glance at him for a moment as to why he hadn't said anything.

Overcoming the moment of hesitancy, Marvin answered,

"Mr. and Mrs. Powell, and Linda, my deepest pleasure to meet you," as he shook hands with Robert, Marcella and then Linda's, holding hers a little longer.

"You do know, son, you could have met Linda some time ago had you come regularly to church with your sister and me," again chided Marvin's mother.

"Yes, mother. You are so right!  I have missed knowing a beautiful lady!" as Marvin kept smiling at Linda.

The church greeting committee provided various beverages and finger food refreshments between  church services.

"Linda, if you'll find a place to sit, I'll pick up  beverages and some snacks," said Marvin.

Filling two glasses with orange juice and placing two brownies on a small plate, Marvin joined Linda at the table she had selected.

"Mother informed me you're a sophomore at the U. What are your major and minor?"

"Same as your dad and my dad-- a law degree. My minors are Spanish and German."

"Phew! That's a heavy schedule, Linda.  I'm in the accounting field—hope to become a CPA one day soon."

"Marvin, my belated sympathies on the death of your dad. You undoubtedly didn't notice my folks and me at the funeral. There were so many in attendance.  Your dad was an outstanding lawyer! Actually he was  my mentor along with my dad.

Marvin didn't notice his Mother and sister approaching their table because of his intense interest in Linda's complimentary remarks concerning his father in addition to being "lost" looking at her sparkling green eyes.

"Son, we're at your mercy!  Sorry, Linda, to break up your friendly chat. Marvin's uncle and aunt have been invited for dinner and I have more preparations to finish. Why don't you plan to join us, Linda?  This will give you two more opportunity to continue your chit-chat."

"Thank you, Martha. I'm pleased to accept your invitation.

I drove my car, too.   I'll take my folks home first and then join you as soon as possible.  Until then!" as she gave Marvin a confiding smile that he learned to cherish and enjoy in the days that followed.

# CHAPTER 32

"DEBBIE'S HAIR SALON" HAD its opening on January 3 as planned. Gertrude decided to keep the signage. Based on Bab's remarks, the salon name had developed the benefits of "Good Will" in the business area. Gertrude could not have been more pleased with the enthusiasm and energetic contributions from Babs and Laurie the day before. The rapport between the three was outstanding in preparing the place for the opening day. Better still, the customers of the two previous beauticians hadn't the opportunity to really find another salon during the short closing time. Both beauticians had many appointments confirmed when customers were called regarding the new opening. Gertrude considered the situation very fortunate to have reopened a salon with a large customer base and two proficient operators.

Gertrude had colorful business cards printed. She found the downtown area full of opportunities to greet people and present each a card. Spending some time on just three days doing this form of advertising was fruitful. Her efforts begin to establish her own customer base.

Babs and Gertrude developed an especially close bonding. She learned from their personal conversation that Babs and Mike DuPont were engaged and planning a marriage for June. Babs was retaining her purity and innocence for their wedding night. Laurie, on the other hand, had a personality similar to her former partner, Carol, inasmuch that she dated several men for the extra close relationships she desired.

"Gertrude, have you ever learned or have the desire to learn to ski or use a snowboard?" asked Babs when they had a break time between customers.

"No, and not really interested in learning how. Why do you ask?" queried Gertrude.

"Well, I dig the sports. But it's not fun going alone. Mike hates skiing. Darn it! I'm trying to introduce him to cross country skiing now. Great exercise! He's been on the trail with me four times already but he doesn't like that sport either."

"Well Babs, I'm sometimes willing to learn if you're ready to teach the skills involved. I might be interested in trying something new and different. You're a good friend and would like to help you out somehow. Do I need to hire a ski instructor?"

"How about both ways! I can teach you. There are some cool good looking hunks as ski instructors at Copper Mountain. With your good looks and winsome smile, Gertrude, you just might land a real bonus!"

"Babs, are you trying to set me up with a ski instructor?"

"Oh, you're good! You catch on really fast! But can't I play cupid? I think you need a man in your life!"

"Babs, I've had two guys in my life so far. Didn't work out with either. I'm in no hurry to tie the knot at the present time. My present goal is establishing a first class salon. But when do you wish to go skiing, next month some time?"

"How about his weekend? I haven't skied for sometime!

I'm anxious to go right away. Is Copper Mountain O.K.? A handsome ski instructor is waiting for you, I know! We can plan our appointments accordingly. If we have a customer that needs services immediately, Laurie could step in for us. We have always helped each other before. Do you have any problems with that 'boss'?"

"No, I don't! Let's go for it, Babs! Can you help me buy the skis and other gear needed this afternoon after we close?"

"Absolutely! I'll drive on Saturday. Can I meet you here at the salon, say, 5:30 a.m.? It's a long drive. Hope the weather cooperates!"

MARVIN AND LINDA MADE arrangements to meet in the Student Union for lunch each day to enjoy each other's company and become better acquainted. However, Marvin discovered that Linda was dedicated to completing her law degree and indicated that their friendship should be strictly platonic. She wasn't ready to be serious with anyone, to become engaged, or to be involved in marriage until established, hopefully, with her father's law firm. If not there, she'd apply to other prestigious law firms. Marvin shared his plans of being entrenched firmly in a CPA firm or even starting his own before settling down with a wife and kids. With this understanding, the friendship continued without any romantic involvement. Both were comfortable with the arrangement.

"Linda, have you learned to ski?" asked Marvin at one of their daily chit chats.

"Love the sport, Marvin! Really haven't taken the time from my studies to whisk down the slopes."

"I've been burning the midnight oil over my books lately. This sedentary life is the pits! Why don't we plan to visit Copper Mountain this coming Saturday?"

"Marvin, fantastic idea! The Copper's slopes are fast! Snow pack is excellent! I heard the report just this morning on the T.V. while eating breakfast."

"I'll stop by your house at 6 a.m. Is that O.K. with you, Linda? Not too early?"

"I'll be ready! Have a class in 10 minutes. Anxious for Saturday! See ya!"

COPPER MOUNTAIN'S SNOW BASE was in ideal condition. The sun was shining brightly. The ski instructor Gertrude selected was a skillful teacher. She surprised her self in learning all the needed basic skill quickly. She had the usual beginner's falling-down syndrome. She knew she'd have some bruises on her bottom to show for her efforts, but that was part of the entire experience. After a dozen trial runs on the beginner's slope, she developed the sense of balance, but more important--confidence.

"Let's go for the big one, Gertrude! See that ski lift? It goes to the immediate level for skiers like you. I'll be right with you the whole way down."

Taking the lift to the starting point, both skied down the run.

"Gertrude, I'm so proud of you in grabbing on to this skiing skill so quickly. Took me much longer than you to master this run. You're a natural!"

"Babs, I never realized how exciting it is to whiz down the slopes! Thank you for asking to learn this sport. Gosh, we completed that run in no time! Let's make good use of our lift tickets and do four more runs! Then my treat at the restaurant. Probably need to rest a spell, anyway, by then."

The restaurant was packed with hungry skiers. They had to wait to find a place to sit. Babs straddled the bench seat while Gertrude proceeded to the cafeteria line. Picking up hamburgers, fries, cookies, and cokes, she joined Babs.

While eating, Gertrude pulled a paper from her backpack. "Babs, you know there is a trade newspaper published for the businesses in a five block area around us. Thought we'd place an ad for our salon. The cost isn't much. Advertising may help bring in a need for our services. Look it over and give me your critique. Handing out business cards has been rather successful, but we need to fill our appointment books. Don't you agree?"

Babs studied the wording and the layout for eye appeal. Hearing considerable laughter at the next table, Gertrude turned and shot a glance at the apparent happy skiers. Her eyes LOCKED on Marvin sitting amidst the people at the noisy table! Seeing him was beyond belief! Suddenly she had difficulty breathing! It was as if the oxygen had been sucked out of the place! What a coincidence! What a small world! She couldn't take her eyes off him! Her heart started beating fast!

Suddenly she noticed the lady to whom he was engaged in conversation. Another red headed women with green eyes! "He's still fulfilling his desire for this type of woman!" she thought.

As her vision included both, her thinking process became erratic and unsettled. "Wonder who she is? Is she his wife? He hates me. I really don't hate him. Should I speak to him? No, I can't do that! I can't believe he's sitting there! Never thought I'd ever see him again! What are the chances of both skiing on the same day? Our last farewell was on the ship dock! His letter said he never wanted to see me again! This is really troubling! I need to get out of here!"

Babs turned to Gertrude to share a suggestion when she noticed her staring at someone at the next table. Glancing in the same direction to determine the reason, she shifted her eyes back to Gertrude.

"What are you watching so intensely, Gertrude? Your facial expression is like you've seen a ghost! You're as white as a sheet! Are you O.K.? Something wrong with the food? asked Babs as she rubbed Gertrude's back.

"Oh, yes! I'm O.K.! I'm all right! Just lost in thought! Watching a couple at that table flooded my brain with memories of a boy friend I had once upon a time. Did you have a suggestion for the ad?"

As Babs was expressing some additional wording, Gertrude glanced quickly at Marvin again. He was looking at her but he was not seeing her—his vision seemed to be going right through her, ending in space behind her. Turning back to Babs, she had to apologize and asked to have the suggestion repeated.

"Woman, you're in a bad bad way! You ask me for help and your brains are wandering around like a whirlwind. Hello! This is earth speaking!" kidded Babs as she shook her head in gesture at Gertrude's inattention.

"I'm sorry. We need to leave, now! If you're through eating, let's make one more run on the slope and then go home. I've had enough for one day."

But it was seeing Marvin that was enough—too much, really.

ARRIVING HOME, Gertrude could not comprehend the occasion of seeing Marvin and on a ski slope at that. That night and Sunday were spent in fitful sleep and agonizing moments as their great times flooded her thinking; but then, the words from the accusation letter came back repeatedly.

Driving to work Monday morning, Gertrude's mind was still in a state of much confusion. She tried mentally to take charge of the situation—starting of a new week with a new salon to operate—working on several appointments to keep busy—finalizing the advertisement—finding ways to forget having seen Marvin on Saturday. That would be a difficult task.

Driving down Broadway Avenue with her mind engaged in deep thought and not concentrating on the traffic lights, Gertrude ran a red light!

"WHAM! CRUNCH! A truck broadsided Gertrude's car on her side! The impact was serious! A broken left arm, and a head concussion leading to unconsciousness! After the ambulance's hasty trip with sirens wailing, Gertrude was admitted to the ER room of General Hospital. Finding her purse in the car, the police had her identification. The folded paper with the advertisement provided the address of her business. Telephoning the salon, Sergeant Taylor informed Babs, who answered the phone, about the accident. He informed her that Miss Brown was unconscious and taken to General Hospital with a broken arm. Her car was being towed to Charlie's Storage Company. The purse would be delivered to the Hospital.

"Laurie, Gertrude was just in a serious car accident! She's unconscious at General Hospital! Has a broke left arm to boot," said Babs with a sobbing voice.

"Oh the poor kid! How tragic! Babs, I can handle the shop alone. Someone needs to be with Gertrude when she regains consciousness. Why don't you leave now?"

Gertrude began to regain some consciousness around three hours after the accident. Babs sat beside her clasping a hand. She watched Gertrude's face as she began to stir slightly.

"Gertrude, can you hear my voice?" asked Babs as she stood up and leaned closer.

"Oh, I hurt! Hurt! Pain! Whose here?" as Gertrude realized hearing a voice in her delirium.

"It's Babs, Gertrude. I'm here beside you! You were in a terrible car accident. You're in the hospital. I'll call the nurses!" as she grabbed for the call signal cord attached to the bed.

"My arm! It's heavy! Can't lift! What-What," as Gertrude's eyes closed and she drifted into semi-consciousness again.

Two nurses arrived. Babs shared what had happened and the words spoken for the nurse's information. They checked her vital signs.

"Her vitals are fine! She needs much more time to rest. She's a healthy young lady and should survive this concussion. Once she's fully conscious, however, we can perform the necessary test to determine if there are any damages. Thanks for being here. Call us should she gain consciousness. We need to notify her family. We do have her purse containing her name, age, and address. Do you have any family information?" asked the nurse.

"I'm sorry I don't. Miss Brown has recently moved to Denver. She bought a beauty salon and I work for her. I know nothing about her family. I'll ask when she gains consciousness."

Babs watched Gertrude move in and out of consciousness for at least another hour. The nurses were notified each time she became somewhat lucid. Babs was becoming gravely concerned. Dr. Brewster stopped on his rounds but Gertrude was not responding at the moment. He would be back.

Gradually Gertrude became fully conscious and retained that state of condition. She looked at Babs with a strange expression which translated to-- where was she, what had happened, and why was her left arm so heavy?

Babs pressed the call button for the nurses. "Gertrude, you were in a terrible accident with your car. You're in the hospital with a broken left arm. You've been unconscious for a long time. We're worried about you hitting your head so hard! Where do you hurt? Please tell the nurses who will be right here!"

Fortunately, the nurses and Dr. Brewster came into the room at the same time. They administered all the necessary tests to determine any head injuries or brain damages. After a thorough examination, the doctor informed Gertrude that she would be back to full health in a short time with more rest. The cast on the arm could be removed in three weeks. The radius bone was cracked rather than broken. Turning to Babs, continued, "As soon as you learn about Gertrude's family, please inform the Administrative Office."

"Gertrude, you're one lucky kid! I'm glad you were in great physical condition! The doctor has determined you'll be discharged in a week. Isn't that great! The hospital and your family need to be informed.   Where can I locate them?"

"Babs, I have no immediate family. They are all gone! I live here in Denver alone. There are many Browns but no relatives whatsoever," Gertrude replied in a soft monotone voice with no feelings.

From the tone of Gertrude's voice and evasive eye contact, Babs became a little suspicious that she was not receiving all the truthful information.   However, there wasn't much that could be done at the moment by doing more questioning. "I must return to the salon, Gertrude.   Laurie is holding down the fort on her own. We'll cover all your appointments too, so don't you fret a single freckle about the shop.  We are both so pleased to have you as a boss, but more so as a friend.  We're both so lucky you came along to save our necks and hired us back again. If there is anything you need, let me know."

"Thanks Babs. Your words  help to  give me some  relief about the salon.   I love you and Laurie like sisters. I'm the lucky person to have you both as employees and friends! To think about it, I'll give you my keys for the apartment so you can  bring me some of the books on the end table that I started reading. I may feel like reading tomorrow. Right now, the medication must be kicking in again. I'm so sleepy!"

"I'll be back in the morning with your books before going to work.  Thanks to you, I have a full day of appointments. Get that rest! Until tomorrow morning!"

BEFORE GOING HOME FROM WORK, Babs found the building and entered Gertrude's apartment. She discovered the books quickly.  She found a book marker projecting out of the top of one book.  Opening it to move the marker to the center, she saw written on the back of the cardboard, the name "Mrs. Marvin R. Brown" three different times.  She studied the names. Picking up the telephone book on the end table, she found the name. She couldn't believe what she found! There were dozens of "Marvin R. Browns" listed.  She then realized there were hundreds of Browns living in the Denver Metro area as well. Studying the book marker, she saw the last of the three names had the middle name written out, then scribbled over with the initial "R" written again. She examined the deleted name. The best she could determine, it was either a "Roy" or a "Ray." She placed the books in her backpack and left.

"GOOD MORNING, SLEEPY HEAD.! How is Mrs. Marvin R. Brown this morning?" asked Babs, with a degree of firmness in her tone of voice.

"What in the world are you talking about, Babs? Where did you come up with that name, for heaven's sake! You know I'm not married! I'm like you, still a virgin!"

"Right here on your book marker, written three times in the same handwriting that appears similar as your writing on the rough draft of the advertisement. Who is Marvin R. Brown? I looked up the name in the telephone book but unfortunately there are dozens with the same name. Which address goes with your name?"

"Oh, Babs, have you lost your mind? I don't know what you're talking about! I never noticed the writing on the back of that marker. News to me! Must have been left in the book by someone else. I purchased the book at a garage sale," replied Gertrude, wishing she didn't need to lie to her good friend.

Babs closely observed Gertrude as she "spun the tale." Again, she was suspicious of her friend's answers. She debated questioning Gertrude some more, but decided she'd first do some of her own detective work.

"O.K. if you say so, Gertrude! I'll stop by again in the morning. Anything else you desire? T-bone steak? Caviar? Squab under glass?" kidded Babs as she did a curtsy bow and left waving good bye.

That evening Babs decided to research the "Mrs. Marvin R. Brown" mystery. Assuming that the initial "R" could be the father's name and the deleted name appeared to be either a "Roy" or "Ray," she bracketed all the Browns starting with those two first names. She knew this would be a chore in calling each for there were many. She would start with the "Ray Browns." Dialing the first name listed, she asked if they had a relative by the name of "Gertrude Brown" adding that she was in the hospital and desperately trying to find any relatives. She then asked if they knew a Marvin R. Brown. She had no success with any Browns with "Ray" as first name. Starting with the first of the names with "Roy," she continued with no success until dialing yet another "Roy Brown, when Marvin answered the phone.

"Mother, there's a Babs Brooks on the telephone inquiring about a Gertrude Brown that was in a bad car wreck and in the hospitable. Do you know anyone by that name? Anyone in our family?"

"Sorry, Miss Brooks, neither my Mother or I know of anyone in our family by that name."

"Do you know of a 'Marvin R. Brown'?" asked Babs.

"Well yes, that's my name. Why are you inquiring about me?" asked Marvin.

"Well, Gertrude Brown has a book with a marker that has your name written three different times upon the back side. One middle name was spelled out that apparently was "Roy" and then deleted. So I've been calling all the "Roy Browns" in the telephone book. Miss Brown indicates the name was written on the marker by someone else who left it in a book she purchased at a book sale. Did you sell or give away any books here in Denver recently?"

"No, I didn't. I haven't the slightest idea how my name is on that book marker. However, there are many Marvin R. Browns in the area. Must be someone else beside me. Sorry, I can't help you. Good luck in your search!"

Babs was disappointed with the answers. She was no further with positive information than when she started. At least she found a Marvin R. Brown. What could be the connection?

What is Gertrude not telling her?   She debated calling the balance of the listings  starting with "Roy." She'd do that tomorrow.  Even the ones that did not answer the telephone on her first try.

"GOOD MORNING, BOSS!   You appear so much more refreshed!  A good night's sleep must have helped you considerably!  With that arm in a cast, you won't be doing much work at the salon when discharged.  But Laurie and I have the situation under control.  We worked all your appointments in with ours.  I've submitted that ad you developed to the agency handling the newspaper.  Then Mike, my fiancé, might be with me when stopping to see you  after work.  I want you to meet him.  I'm running late!  Take care!"

"Thanks again, Babs for taking charge.  You're a jewel!  Have a great day!  Good bye!"

Babs wanted to tell her she talked to a "Marvin R. Brown" at a resident of  a "Roy Brown" but decided she needed additional information.

"GERTRUDE, THIS IS MY fiancé, Mike.  I wanted him to meet the gracious lady who removed me from the unemployment lines."

Picking up Gertrude's hand gently, Mike lightly kissed the back of her hand.  "Gertrude, Babs has been sharing so much about you, I feel as if I already know you."

"How sweet!  Babs, you've got a keeper!  Mike, my pleasure to meet you also.  And it's Babs and Laurie who are keeping me employed.  This thing is keeping me from work for three weeks!" as Gertrude held up the arm with a cast.

"Gertrude, have you given any more thought to the name on that book marker?"

"Babs, drop it already, will you?   It's nothing, I told you!  It has nothing to do with me!  Really!"

Hearing that weak explanation, Babs knew there was more

to the story than being expressed.   She'd call the same "Roy Brown" number again.

"Boss, we stopped to see you on our way to a dinner-theater production.   We saw their ad in that newspaper  in which we'll have our own printed.  Well, we need to go now.  Laurie indicated she'd visit you tomorrow. Anything else you need?"

"You might find the address where my car is stored. I need to call my insurance company to take charge of the wreck.  My poor brand new car!  Wonder if it can be repaired?   Have less than 100 miles on it.  Probably will be charged with the accident because of running a red light.  I'll have to attend a court some where when discharged.   Oh well, enough of my problems! Have a great evening, you two lovebirds!"

As the two left the room, Gertrude was concerned why Babs was so adamant about the name on the book marker. Lying was not her thing! Why had she written Marvin's name on that marker in the first place!   Should have thrown the darn thing in the trash a long time ago! "Oh well," she thought, " with all the Browns living in the Denver area, she'll never find Marvin."

# CHAPTER 33

Babs was determined to find an answer to the " Mrs. Marvin R. Brown" mystery. She was convinced that Gertrude knew more than what had been said to her. Dialing the same number used before for the "Roy Brown" residents, Martha Brown answered the phone.

"Mrs. Brown, this is Babs Brooks. I called yesterday and talked with Marvin. I'm trying to find relatives for Gertrude Brown who is still in the hospital. The marker in her book with "Mrs. Marvin R. Brown" is a puzzle that needs solving, if possible. Is there any information you can provide that may help? Gertrude has indicated that she never married. Has your son ever been married? The doctor at the hospital has asked me to help find her relatives, if any," said Babs.

"Miss Brooks, my son's name is 'Marvin R. Brown,' the 'R' is for his father, 'Roy.' No, my son has never married. However, I will give this more thought regarding our Brown family. There are some papers in my husband's desk that may reveal information. I'll do some research.     Please give me your number and I'll call in the morning," replied Mrs. Brown.

Babs gave the number for the hair salon.

When Marvin arrived home from his afternoon class at the University, his mother informed him about the second telephone call from Babs Brooks.  By then Martha had already examined some of the genealogy that was in her husband's desk. She found that her husband's  brother's name was Marvin Roy Brown and married a Heidi Sterling.  He died from wounds received during World War II. They had a son named Samuel Roy Brown who married  a Marcella Bigleys.  They had a daughter and a son but no names were given.

"Son, your dad chose your name when you were born.  I named your sister.  From the family chart which your dad had in his desk, you were obviously named after his brother, Marvin Roy.  I wasn't aware that your grandparents exchanged the first and middle names for their two sons until today.  I never knew your dad's brother's family.  There is the possibility that the daughter of Samuel Roy Brown's son could be Gertrude. Your dad, unfortunately, did not keep up the family records with names of present day children.   Miss Brooks indicated that Gertrude is around twenty years old, same as your age. Why don't you go to the hospital, visit her, and determine if she is related to your dad's brother.  If she is, I'll go visit her, also. If she is not related, at least we have tried.  Miss Brooks indicated she is in room 302 South at General Hospital," related Martha Brown.

"O.K. Mother, I'll make a visit  after my afternoon class. Would be nice to find a lost cousin, wouldn't it!" replied Marvin.

MARVIN WALKED INTO ROOM 302 very quietly when he saw the lady was sleeping.  She was laying on her side.   Her face was towards him.   Walking up next to the bed for a closer look, Marvin was startled when he noticed the facial shape of

Rose. However, the color of the hair was completely different. He debated waking her so he could ask the questions regarding her family background. He was hesitant to do so realizing the lady's need for rest was important. Seeing a chair by the side of the bed, he decided to sit and wait for her to awaken.

When he stepped back, his body accidentally hit the bedside table causing it to roll against the bed railing producing a loud metallic "clang." The noise woke Gertrude.

She opened her eyes and saw only the legs and waist of a man standing beside the bed.

Rolling over to her back, she looked at the face of the man who was staring at her.

"MARVIN, WHAT ARE YOU DOING HERE? HOW DID YOU FIND ME? HOW DID YOU KNOW I WAS IN THE HOSPITAL?" shouted Gertrude, with a voice trembling from the shock of seeing him.

"Rose, is that you? Your face! Your hair! Your voice! It is you! Oh, princess, what has happened to you? Your arm is in a cast? In a hospital in Denver? Oh, what have I done to you? Oh princess, can you every forgive me for the terrible ordeal which you have undoubtedly suffered since writing that terrible letter full of accusations?" pleaded Marvin, as he leaned over Rose and picked up her right hand.

"Oh Marvin, yes, yes, yes, I do forgive you! Your letter said you didn't want anything to do with me, so I tried to go on with my life. But you were always in my thoughts as much as I tried to forget you!" sobbed Rose, with tears streaming down her cheeks.

Pulling the chair next to the bed, Marvin continued holding her right hand and gently wiped her cheeks with the corner of the bed sheet. Then he lovingly caressed her forehead repeatedly.

"Oh, Rose, Sweetheart, I tried to forget you also, but you were always in my memory--time, and time again. You have no idea how I wished that letter had never been mailed. It was written in anger. And I didn't open the one letter you wrote to me. Had I done so, this past year might have been so much different! Princess, I love you, even more so! Forgiving me has lifted a heavy weight from my mind. You're so precious! Now I know why you are living in Denver, also!  Chris visited our ship in Norfolk and stopped to see the Reillys. Joe told Chris about the letter from the FBI.  Chris called and informed me you were under the Government Witness Program and hiding somewhere after testifying at a trial for drug dealers. You're living here! Oh Rose, thanks to Babs Brooks persistence, she found me by telephoning dozens of Browns. Then my mother sent me to see you, a Gertrude Brown, with the possibility of being a long lost cousin. Rose, my long lost Princess, I found you! I thought I'd lost you for ever!" shared Marvin as he leaned over and gently kissed her lips.

Speaking in broken breaths from attempting to stop crying, "Marv, how absolutely wonderful you want me back in your life!  I tried to keep Babs from searching for you because your letter said you wanted to  permanently end our relationship. Babs has become a dear friend!  She is even more so now! Her persistence really did bring us together! Oh Lord, bless her!"

"Rose, did the FBI require you to change your entire appearance to hide your identity?  Your beautiful red hair is now black! Those lovely green eyes are  brown!  Your name is Gertrude Brown!  Is somebody  trying to find you?" asked Marvin as he again placed kisses about her face, ending with a lingering one on her lips.

"Marv, how I enjoy your kisses!  Never thought I'd have your lips touching mine again!  Sweetheart, there is so much to say. My broken arm is the result of a car accident.  But I guess you know that already. The nurse gave me a shot for the pain shortly before you arrived. I'm getting very very sleepy. I'm—I'm--so," slurred Gertrude, as she drifted into a deep sleep.

Marvin continued to sit by her bed and gazed lovingly upon

her face. His thoughts raced backwards in time to the romantic situations they had shared. The delightful time at the beach came flashing back in vivid details. Visions of her standing in the apartment in only her teddy and bath robe parlayed over the beach fun filled times. Again, he was pleased that fate and her friend, Babs, together, made this blessed union possible. He had to tell his mother.

Releasing Rose's hand carefully, he tiptoed from the room. Moving down the hallway to the bank of telephones, he dialed his home number.

"Mother, you will never guess in a hundred years, who Gertrude Brown is—she is none other than Rose! Can you believe that? Isn't that beyond belief? Can you come to the hospital now? Rose should be awake again soon. The nurse gave her a shot for pain; she fell asleep while we were trying to forgive one another," said Marvin, with great enthusiasm.

"Marvin, my son, what a blessing! I'm so pleased for you! I'll be there as soon as possible. I can hardly wait to meet your Rose!"

Marvin returned to Rose's room. He quietly sat beside her bed again. Gently placing his hand on hers, he gazed upon her lovely features. The black hair styled so differently than she wore previously was observed closely. Her face appeared leaner. Marvin realized she may have lost weight. He wondered what other changes may have taken place? Was this due to his blundering and idiotic actions? Had she lived a stressful life? Had his actions caused her personality to change? Watching her stirring while she was sleeping, he realized what needed to be done in the days ahead. He did not wish to lose Rose ever again! That was certain! Seeing her sleeping so peacefully, his love for her "bubbled" over as his eyes slowly followed the outline of her body covered by the sheet. He would buy an engagement ring tomorrow. He closed his eyes and said a short prayer that she'd accept it. If she agreed, they would plan for a wedding on Valentine's Day. Moving the chair away from the bed, he laid his head upon the mattress with his hand clasping hers.   Closing his eyes, he continued to develop plans to discuss with Rose after her nap; but he, too, soon fell asleep.

Babs and Marvin's mother both arrived at the hospital at the same time.   Riding the elevator to the third floor and not knowing each other, they rode up in silence.   The elevator door opened and both moved in the direction of Room 302. They arrived at the door simultaneously.

"Are you per chance, Babs Brooks?" asked Martha Brown.

"Why yes, and you must be Mrs. Brown coming to see Gertrude?" asked Babs.

Despite never having seen each other before, Babs embraced Martha.   Breaking the hug, both looked in the room at the most tender scene possible—to Babs, Gertrude—to Martha, Rose—sleeping peacefully; to Babs, a strange man with his head resting on the bed—to Martha, her son finding his long lost sweetheart.

Moving her finger to her lips to indicate silence, Martha grasped Babs hand and pulled her away from the door.   "That is my son, Marvin R. Brown, you have been searching for who is now sleeping beside his long lost sweetheart.   I don't know all the parts to their lives, Babs, but after one year, they have found each other once again.  What we are seeing should bring great happiness to my son, Marvin, and your friend, Gertrude. Her real name is Rose Maureen McDowell.   Hopefully, we'll soon learn why her name is now Gertrude  Brown," whispered Martha as they moved to sit down on a sofa in the corridor.

"Mrs.  Brown, My fiancee..." said Babs as she was interrupted.

"Babs, please call me Martha.   I suspect we will become close friends in the days to come."

"Thank you, Martha.  I know we will.   My fiancée and I are getting married soon. I wish to have Gertrude as my maid of honor.   We have become such dear friends in a relatively short time she has lived in Denver. She's like a loving sister to me! You didn't know she is also my employer. Gertrude purchased an on-going beauty salon in the downtown Denver area. Laurie Bealer and I were rehired by her after our former employer closed the salon. We're in charge of the salon while Gertrude is recuperating with the broken arm she suffered from that terrible car accident."

Rose began to slowly awaken. Seeing Marvin asleep and holding her hand, her rustling woke Marvin. He sat up quickly, surprised that he had fallen asleep. Rose realized that Marvin had been beside her bed the entire time. She smiled and moved her right had towards his face. She caressed his cheek and then his lips. Marvin moved to claim her lips in a meaningful kiss. Rose placed her arm around his neck and pulled him more firmly to her.

When releasing the pressure of her arm from his neck, Marvin moved his face beside hers. Whispering in her ear, "Rose, I realize that I have always loved you! I guess it was only denial. Then I was told you were marrying a Steven Harks. This made me suffer greatly, for I knew I would lose you forever. I now believe that God in his infinite wisdom has brought us together again using the hands and minds of others." Sitting down on the chair again, he continued, "Rose, when you are discharged from the hospital, we have serious decisions to discuss. I blew it when closing the door on open communications that we had agreed upon. That will not happen again, Princess!"

Hearing the voices coming from the room, Martha and Babs quickly entered.

"Babs, meet my son, Marvin," as he stood to clasp her hands.

Bending over Rose and kissing her cheek, Martha softly said, "And you are his precious Rose. I'm so happy that you have found each once again. You're so beautiful, Rose!" as

Martha bend over again to kiss her cheek, then cupped her face with her hands and smiled.

"Mother Brown, at last I'm finally meeting you!  Babs and you must have already met.  Thank you, Babs, for being so head strong with that book marker thing.  I'll explain one day why I wanted you to stop your detective work.  Now I am so pleased you kept right on searching!  I adore your spunk!"

"Yes, Babs, if I may call you by that name, also.  Thank you for bringing this 'vision of beauty' back into my life.  I thought I had lost her forever.  But I believe that a providential power used many individuals  that has cause a precious moment to happen in this hospital room tonight.  I'm totally convinced of that!"

"I'm sorry, family.  But it's long past visiting hours.  Please say your good byes, now," ordered the nurse who started taking Gertrude's vital signs.

As the three moved out the door, they turned to smile and in a chorus, said "Good night!  See you tomorrow!"  With a big smile, Marvin blew her a kiss.

After the nurse had finished with her duties, Gertrude's thoughts were whirling through her  thinking process. Visualizing the big smile Marvin gave her in leaving the room, it played in her mind over and over again.  She closed her eyes and begin to pray a prayer of thanks for the renewal of their friendship and the loving desire of Marvin wanting her back in his life.  Whispering an "Amen" at the end of her prayer, she closed her eyes and drifted off to a blissful sleep.

# CHAPTER 34

"GOOD MORNING GERTRUDE, I imagine you're anxious to leave this hospital! You appear so happy! I talked to Babs and I bet it has something to do with a Marvin Brown showing up in this room yesterday?" asked Laurie.

"Laurie, you have no idea how happy I am! Marvin says it was a providential situation. I'm inclined to agree. I really don't know. But Babs practically accomplished the impossible by calling the many Brown families until she found Marvin's dad and mother's telephone number. She was so persistent! I love her! I love her so!" beamed Gertrude.

"We are extremely happy for you, Gertrude! Please don't worry about the salon, though. We have all the bases covered. We have our appointment books filled solid! You may wish to think about hiring another beautician, Gertrude. You know there is space enough to add another. Who ever you hire could use your station until you're able to work again. We could then put in another station. I happen to know of a man, Kenny Sanders, who has completed a cosmetology course and has some experience already. In fact, we've dated," shared Laurie.

"Go for it! Call him and find out if he wishes to work for us! Let me know! I'd like to interview him here in the hospital if necessary. If we are growing our business, we need to add more help!" beamed Gertrude. "And I have a request. Here is the key to my apartment. Would you please pick up a package on my dresser addressed to a Roscoe Chandler. I had it ready to mail but forgot it Monday morning, and then this darn accident. Mail it with Fed-Ex and insure the contents for $40,000. We need the money to up grade the interior of our salon. Perhaps the outside, too. I'll write my home address on a business card."

As Gertrude was writing on her card, Marvin came strolling into the room.

Carrying a large bouquet of roses held in front of him in an attempt to hide his face, he walked directly in front of Gertrude. Moving the flowers aside, he greeted her, "Good morning, Princess!"

"You big tease! How beautiful, Marv! Thank you! Laurie, this is Marvin. Marvin, this is Laurie, the other beautician at our salon. She has been a jewel to keep the shop running while Babs spent so much time with me after the accident," added Gertrude beamingly.

"Laurie, my deepest pleasure to meet you! My thanks on behalf of my sore paw Princess lounging about all day long!" joked Marvin.

"Oh, don't mind him, Laurie. My ex-salty sailor becomes a wannabe comedian now and then. But it's one of the traits I love about him!" said Gertrude.

"Marvin, you have one tremendous gal in that bed who is chomping at the bit to be released to return to work. I'm as pleased as everyone else that you two found each other once more. You must have a lot of catching up to do," said Laurie.

"That we do. Besides having hired skilled beauticians,

Rose, both Babs and Laurie are beautiful women. Wow! Isn't there a law against having three raving beauties in one salon at one and the same time?" quipped Marvin.

Shaking her head in a negative fashion along with a grin, Gertrude looked at Marvin who was still standing beside the bed holding the bouquet of roses. "Laurie, see what I mean? How can a poor sick woman like myself have any chance whatsoever, to compete with a smart aleck whose initials are MRB!"

"Touche, my Princess! You win! Here are red roses for my beautiful Rose!" as he set them upon the small cabinet beside her bed.

"I can't be here too long. Babs has opened the shop early this morning and we both have booked many appointments. Yours too! I'll run that errand for you after work today, Gertrude. Goodbye you two! Have a great day!" wished Laurie, as she rushed out the door.

Gertrude gazed at each opened flower. As she moved her eyes about, she noticed a shiny metal object attached to one bud. She reached to pluck it off. She looked at Marvin with a puzzled look! "You really mean this, Marv! An engagement ring!"

Taking the ring from Rose, he picked up her left hand carefully, and caressingly slipped it on her ring finger. "I mean this with the deepest sincerity that I could ever manage, Princess. I love you with all my heart, soul, mind, and wit! Will you have me as your husband?"

With tear running down her cheeks, she stretched out her good arm toward Marvin. Their tender embrace continued until a nurse came into the room to take Gertrude's vital signs. Breaking the embrace, Marvin moved aside for the nurse.

"I'm sorry! Did I break up an important occasion?" said the nurse as she wrapped a blood pressure cuff around Gertrude's arm.

"Yes, in a big way! I just asked my Princess if she will marry me!" replied Marvin, "but you came in before she answered me."

"Yes, yes, I will, Sweetheart!" chimed Gertrude.

"Well, I'm sorry for the interruption. Congratulations! When is the big day?" asked the nurse as she picked up Gertrude's hand and counted her wrist pulse at the same time observing the diamond ring.

"If my Princess with a cast on her arm has no objection, we'll be married on Valentine's Day!"

"Next month, Marv! I may have this darn cast on yet! But then that may not be too great a problem!"

"No, Sweetheart, it really isn't. If you look more closely at the roses, you may find more to your liking!"

"I'm through here, you two. I'll ask the doctor to check your arm today and determine when the cast can be removed. It was only a cracked bone. I believe you are a healthy woman and healing may take place faster," said the nurse.

Gertrude studied the roses again. She found a small box wedged between three stems near the vase. Pulling it out, she opened the small box to find their wedding bands.

"Oh, Marvin, you are serious! I do want to marry you! This is moving so fast, though! There are wedding plans to organize! "

"I know Sweetheart, but let's omit all the complications. How does this sound? Our minister has us booked for Valentine's Day at 6:30 p.m. Mother and the church ladies will prepare a reception following the wedding at the church. I've called Chris. He can fly here to be my best man. You undoubtedly wish to have Babs and Laurie as your attendants. Perhaps my sister, also. We'll take a honeymoon trip during my spring break. We'll mail announcements the first part of next week. Once upon a time you indicated that if we were married, you would allow me to move in with you. Are you still honoring that choice? If not, I'll rent an apartment. Is there any thing you wish to add, change, or delete? This is up for negotiations under our open communication agreement!"

"Marv! You're good! You need to become a wedding consultant! No, I don't know much more that needs to be considered. Well, yes, I'll need time to purchase a wedding dress. And yes, the invitation is still there for you to move in with me. You'll enjoy the apartment with a beautiful view of the park. Haven't had much time to meet any neighbors, yet. Another benefit, the rent is paid for the next year through the witness program."

Suddenly, Laurie came rushing into the room. "Sorry, guys, I was driving out of the parking lot when I remembered leaving your business card with your apartment address here on the bed," said Laurie as she picked up the card and headed for the door.

"Oh Laurie, before you leave, see my engagement ring? Marv just proposed. We are getting married on Valentine's Day. I wish to have Babs as my maid of honor and you and Marvin's sister, Sally, as my bridesmaids. So reserve the date on your calendar and don't book any appointments for the day, either. Tell Babs, too. I'll call her also," said Gertrude.

"Gertrude, how wonderful! Thank you, I would love to be your bridesmaid. I'm not surprised of your getting married so soon. Marvin found you and doesn't wish to loose you again. Right? How romantic--on Valentine's Day," said Laurie.

"Thank you for your friendship and being a bridesmaid. Your unselfish efforts in keeping the salon in operation. You and Babs are very dear to me. Take the money from petty cash to mail the package," replied Gertrude as Laurie waved while going out the door.

Reaching into her handbag beside the vase of roses, Gertrude retrieved her billfold. Opening it, she removed her driver's license and social security card and gave them to Marvin.

"Why are you giving me these, Rose?"

"Look carefully at the name."

"Says Gertrude Brown on both cards."

"Yes, the same name is on all my papers—insurance policies, car registration, bill of sale for the salon, apartment rental—everything. This is now my official name. Your mother and you are calling me Rose. My two employees only know me as Gertrude. You need to forget the name of Rose because of my identity under the witness program. I hope your mother hasn't told Sally and all her friends. The drug cartel people may still be trying to find me. FBI Agent Manning indicated the cartel has a "long" memory for betrayers. My testimony placed some big named drug dealers in the penitentiary. They are not happy campers! Do you understand my immediate problem?"

"Princess, I do. I definitely do! I'll take care of this problem immediately and inform my family of the importance of your identity. And by the way, what happened to you after I sent that terrible letter of accusations for which I'll eternally regret having done. Why did you select my name?"

"Well, Marv, when you kicked me out of your life, I decided to help Carol develop the best salon in Norfolk. All my efforts were directed to that goal. Then Steven Harks wanted a hostess for his company. It was a challenge in fulfilling all the duties required to maintain his home. And I enjoyed every minute. Of course, I didn't know he and the others were drug dealers at the time. Obviously, I never would have accepted the job. Steven treated me great—new car, large salary, expensive jewelry gifts, a large expense account, and so forth. He asked me to marry him and I accepted. He, like you, honored my wish to remain a virgin until our wedding night. I thought he was a loveable and generous guy with whom to spend my life, but I realized   that his interest was   only a sham when I found out he dealt in drugs and stolen gemstones. I was told he wanted a quick marriage so I couldn't testify against him as his wife. He really did not love me; only wanted me as his sex toy. Then the FBI asked me to help in their arrest in his home and the convictions of all five dealers at a court trial. In order to hide me from the drug cartel, the judge sentenced me for five years. I was paroled after spending almost six months in the penitentiary, Marv.

"Oh, my poor sweetheart! I feel absolutely terrible to have indirectly caused you these horrible experiences! Six months in the pen! That must have been frightful! How did you manage to survive!"

"I just did with God's help! And much determination! The Witness Program helped, too. It started with my new identity immediately after the court trial and before going to the penitentiary. The Warden was super! Actually, all the administrative staff members were kind and helpful. Life was actually an unexpected good experience. I was a beautician for the women and the men's barber. My cell mate was a very large Negro lady and we became the very best of friends. I taught her to read, write, and speak better. Actually all 50 women in our building became good friends. They came to the mini-beauty salon I was permitted to establish near my compartment. I taught my cell mate to be a beautician to replace me and another lady as a barber before I left. I helped to start a Bible Study Group with the assistance of the Gideon Auxiliary and worked with the prison librarian in a GED class. The ladies gave me a fantastic farewell party. When asked to change my name, my reasoning may sound strange or corny to you. Gertrude is my great grandmother's name. Since I still had a spark of love for you despite the terrible things you said in the letter and knowing we would never meet again to become your wife, I would simply use your last name. I also resolved never to get serious with another man. I chose Denver because you lived here and with 2300 or more Browns, I could become lost as far as the cartel is concerned. So that's pretty much what happened in a nutshell."

"Princess, you forgave me when we first met yesterday. I

will always be in your debt. I caused you so much grief and, undoubtedly, a lot of anxiety, I'm sure. Your folks don't know where you are and you can't contact them either, can you? They must really hate me. Yet from what you said, I sense you had some form of an unexpected adventure!"

"It's interesting that you should use that word "adventure," Marv, for that word has always been in my thoughts as to what was happening in my life—starting the day my dad told me to leave home to be on my own—living with Joe and June—falling head over heels in love with a sailor introduced by them—sharing part ownership of a salon with Carol—you, Carol, and Dr. Brooks helping me overcome being so naive—working for Steven Harks—spending six months in the penitentiary--owning and operating my own salon now--and I can add to that adventure by having that same ex-sailor as my future husband and the father of our children. Actually, God has been good to me in my many adventures! Now as to the witness program, it is true, Marv, we can't contact my parents. I really don't know if they hate you or not. But that doesn't affect my deep love for you now despite all what has happened."

"Oh Princess, how I love you, too" as he leaned over and kissed her. "Do you remember once saying that you measured life as a glass half empty and I saw it as half full. I do believe you have changed your viewpoint on life! You now indicate God is on your side—that's your cup running over! Then you indicated helping the Gideon Auxiliary in prison. That's an interesting coincidence. Three weeks ago, my minister mentioned that when I graduated from the University, I would meet the requirements for joining the other men in our church who are in this Gideon ministry. The church guys tell me it's a rewarding couple's ministry."

"Marv, that will be super!   As your wife, I can be an Auxiliary member! I helped Sandra Whittington  start and grow a Bible Study Class.  She helped me  learn important

Bible concepts. By the way, speaking of classes, don't you have any today?"

"Princess, I do. But my place today is beside you, not in class! We have indeed had open communications and there is probably more we need to discuss and agree upon!"

"Well, now that you mentioned it, remember when we were at the beach and you were mean to me? Do you remember when I sentenced you to always love and to caress me? Well, my dear future husband, I'm continuing that same sentence by renewing the provisions thereof starting on our wedding night. Is that crystal clear?" ordered Gertrude, with a tone of voice that was sweet and gentle.

"My Loving Warden, is this a life sentence that I'm facing?"

"My loving future husband, I do believe you understand the situation precisely!"

"Then, I accept all the terms of endearment of your decree, Princess," as he claimed her lips for the first time with a deep and sustained force since their uniting in the hospital.

Breaking the embrace, Marvin sat on the edge of the bed and gazed into Gertrude's eyes. They held that visual embrace for some time. Again, they embraced and kissed. With his mouth close to her ear, he whispered, "my dear dear Princess, my angel who has landed back into my life, how I truly love you!"

"And I love you so much, joy simply fills my whole being!" Gertrude whispered back.

There tender and meaningful embrace was broken when Dr. Coverington, while making his patient visitations, approached the bed and said, "And this must be the young man the nurses have been telling me about who is more than a relative—yes, the future Mr. and Mrs. Marvin Brown."

Marvin, standing up and extending his hand to the doctor, replied, "Thank you, Doctor, yes, we have made plans to be married shortly after your release her. Do you believe she needs to wear the cast through Valentine's Day for that's our wedding day?" questioned Marvin.

Picking up Gertrude's medical chart and studying it for several moments, he replied, "That cast can be removed on February tenth, just in time for the wedding. Come to my office on the tenth and we'll cut it off. Your fiancée was fortunate by not sustaining any permanent damage from the concussion."

"We'll be there, Doctor, and could you include in that appointment the medical needs required for our marriage?" asked Marvin.

"You probably should make an earlier appointment to see me, say the day after you're released from here. Waiting until the tenth is pushing the envelope a tad."

"We'll call your office and make an appointment. Thank you, Doctor. We really appreciate your medical evaluation of Rose. She will undoubtedly tell me that I caused the accident," said Marvin, jokingly.

"Well, hardly. See you kids around the first and the tenth," said Dr. Coverington as he left the room.

"You know, Marv, you indirectly caused the accident. More than you know!" voiced Gertrude.

"Hey, I wasn't serious! Only joking! But you sound serious, Princess!"

"You didn't recognize me in the restaurant last Saturday at Copper Mountain when skiing. I saw you and almost had a heart attack! On the ski range, at that!"

"You were there! Why didn't you make yourself known, Princess?"

"Remember, the words in your letter--'Nothing to do with me'? Besides, you were talking with a lovely red-headed woman that I thought could be your fiancée or your wife!"

"Oh, you mean Linda Powell! She's just a friend of the family. We see each other on the campus at the University. She's studying to be a lawyer. She doesn't desire any romance in her life. And I'm so happy to know you have learned to ski. We'll hit the slope right soon!"

"Yes, I enjoyed learning to ski and I certainly didn't know the information about Linda; however, I still would never identify myself to you under the circumstances. Well, when driving to work on Monday, my thoughts were reflecting back to the sailor I met over a year ago and then by chance to see on the ski slope. I wasn't paying attention to traffic and drove through a red light. That's when I was clobbered. So you see, you were indirectly the cause of the accident, my sweet ex-salty sailor!" said Gertrude reflecting partial humor in the tone of her voice.

"I'll take the full unmitigated reasons for placing you in this hospital. And I am so happy I was the cause! If you weren't here, I wouldn't be here, chances are, and we wouldn't be planning a marriage in a couple weeks! And we have one beautiful Babs Brooks to THANK, also!"

"Marv, Sweetheart, I'll agree with your conclusions to the crossing of the 'T' in 'Thanks'! Now there is one other matter we need to resolve. Will I need to pour wine on your wedding suit in order for you to remove it on our wedding night? And you may be interested to know I haven't worn that teddy since you last saw it!" said Gertrude with a lilt of humor.

"Oh you're so good! You won't let me forget that incident either, will you? Well, I am so pleased you have developed a sense of humor and have the loving desire to forgive me over my hasty and incorrect conclusions about you. I love you dearly for that my Princess! You have no idea how much your forgiveness means regarding that accusation. Your love is precious, Rose!"

"No, no, that's not me anymore. Remember!"

"Oh yes, I'm sorry! I forgot, GERTRUDE! But then you know that well used cliché--'A Rose by any other name, is still a Rose or smells like a Rose, or looks like a Rose, or something like that! Despite  your name change, you'll always be my Rose!" as he embraced her with a kiss.

And so Marvin, at last, joined his innocence Rose, AKA Gertrude, in her ongoing life adventures!

# EPILOGUE

LIFE DURING THE FIRST year for Marvin and Gertrude was filled with great compassion and love. The second chance of being united in a renewing friendship and then a marriage created a union making every day a welcomed blessing. Their decision for open communications on each issue in their daily lives produced a loving bond that was envied by their host of college friends, their church family, and employee/families at the salon.

The apartment complex where the newly wed couple resided went on the market. Seizing the opportunity, the Browns formed a limited corporation and purchased the complex. Proceeds from the sale of Martha's residential home and life insurance settlement from her husband's death nearly paid the asking price. Martha moved into an apartment unit and became the manager, assisted by her son and daughter-in-law.

Romance blossomed for Martha as well. She and Harry Perkins, a widower from the extended church family, began to spend considerable time in each other's company. Marvin and Sally were thrilled with their mother's choice and for her increased happiness.

The FBI sent a second letter to the McDowell's indicating their daughter was well and living a quality life but unable to indicate where she was living. Debbie's Hair Salon became well known for the excellent hair styling performed by Gertrude, Babs, and Laurie. Kenny Sanders was added to the employee list; the salon prospered.

Agent Harry Manning visited Gertrude and was pleased with the success of her business and events in her life. He was pleasantly surprised to find her married. When told the story of their early romance, broken by the drug dealer and penitentiary episodes, and then the unusual method of meeting again in the hospital, Agent Harry wished the newly-weds the heartiest of congratulations. The FBI's monitoring of the activities of the drug cartel showed no apparent interest in an attempt to find Gertrude. She was pleased and greatly relieved!

Chris Woodyard became smitten with Sally during the wedding day of Gertrude and Marvin. They continued their early stages of romance via daily e-mails. Sally began classes at the University of Colorado with a major in law. She desired to follow in her father's footsteps.

The latest news during the end of the first year—Gertrude became pregnant.

The following couple of years were also promising.

Marvin graduated with his Associate of Arts degree in Accounting. He gained experience by employment with a CPA firm. Marvin remodeled an area on the ground floor of the apartment complex and established a satellite office where he completed most of the part-time work for his firm on a daily basis.

When it was learned that Gertrude had the nickname of "Gertie," the moniker was used by everyone. In fact, the signage of the salon was changed to "Gertie's Hair Salon."

Agent Manning made a second visit. After another year of kooping track of the drug cartel and despite many more arrest and convictions, there was no imminent danger for Gertrude. The constant fear nagging Gertrude began to disappear. She was permitted to visit her family and friends in Norfolk. The uniting was touching and Marvin was never blamed for his jilting of Rose AKA Gertrude. Both parents were happily anticipating becoming grandparents.

Martha and Harry Perkins were married and he moved in with his bride. He sold his residential home, and the proceeds paid off the balance of the apartment loan.

Sally continued her law degree. Chris flew to Denver occasionally to see her. He gave her an engagement ring on her birthday. Their marriage would take place the month after he graduated from Harvard University. An offer by the Brown and Powell Law Firm for Chris to join them was accepted. Sally was especially ecstatic! She has chosen which apartment they wish to occupy when married.

Marvin's satellite CPA office flourished. He obtained his Bachelor of Arts college degree. The company for whom he was working was available to purchase and Marvin grasped the opportunity to buy it. With the accompanying customer base, he was enabled to have a continuing thriving business.

"Gertie's Hair Salon continued to prosper. Babs was replaced with another beautician when she took maternity leave.

Chris and Sally exchanged their marriage vows. Chris moved up in partnership in the Brown and Powell Law Firm as did Linda Powell. She was so pleased to be able to work with her father and to use Mr. Brown's office, her mentor. Sally found employment with another law firm.

Agent Manning made a third visit. He was confident that all those associated with the Steven Harks' drug cartel had been arrested and serving time in various penitentiaries. The entire Brown family was greatly relieved.

In case you're wondering, twins were born in September—Marvin R. Brown, Jr., weighing in at 6 pounds 5 ounces and his sister, Rose Maureen Brown, at 6 pounds 3 ounces. Gertrude knew, without a doubt, that their births were the height of all her life's adventures, although she was looking forward to many more.

Printed in the United States
by Baker & Taylor Publisher Services